P9-DMU-605

Callahan's Key

BOOKS BY SPIDER ROBINSON

Telempath
Callahan's Crosstime Saloon
Stardance (with Jeanne Robinson)
Antinomy
The Best of All Possible Worlds
Time Travelers Strictly Cash
Mindkiller
Melancholy Elephants
Night of Power
Callahan's Secret
Callahan and Company (omnibus)
Time Pressure
Callahan's Lady
Copyright Violation
True Minds
Starseed (with Jeanne Robinson)
Kill the Editor
Lady Slings the Booze
The Callahan Touch
Starmind (with Jeanne Robinson)
Off the Wall at Callahan's
Callahan's Legacy
Deathkiller (omnibus)
Lifehouse
The Callahan Chronicals (omnibus)
The Star Dancers (with Jeanne Robinson)
User Friendly
The Free Lunch
Callahan's Key

SPIDER ROBINSON

Callahan's Key

BANTAM BOOKS

New York Toronto London Sydney Auckland

CALLAHAN'S KEY
A Bantam Spectra Book / July 2000

SPECTRA and the portrayal of a boxed "s" are trademarks of Bantam Books, a division of Random House, Inc.

Book design by Carol Malcolm Russo/Signet M Design, Inc.

Library of Congress Cataloging-in-Publication Data

Robinson, Spider.
Callahan's Key / Spider Robinson.
p. cm. — (A Bantam spectra book)
ISBN 0-553-11163-9

1. Callahan, Mike (Fictitious character)—Fiction. 2. Bars (Drinking establishments)—Fiction. I. Title.

PS3568.O3156 C34 2000
813'.54—dc21

99-051311

Published simultaneously in the United States and Canada

Bantam Books are published by Bantam Books, a division of Random House, Inc. Its trademark, consisting of the words "Bantam Books" and the portrayal of a rooster, is Registered in U.S. Patent and Trademark Office and in other countries. Marca Registrada. Bantam Books, 1540 Broadway, New York, New York 10036.

PRINTED IN THE UNITED STATES OF AMERICA

BVG 10 9 8 7 6 5 4 3 2 1

This one is for
Guy Immega

ACKNOWLEDGMENTS

THIS BOOK WOULD NOT have been possible without certain key speculations by cosmologists Alan Guth, Sidney Coleman, and Sir Martin Rees, which I encountered in John Brockman's splendid book THE THIRD CULTURE; my thanks to them for their unwitting assistance.

Possible or not, this book would have been much less *plausible* without the witting assistance of the following friends, colleagues, acquaintances, and kindly strangers: Guy Immega (roboticist), Douglas Beder (physicist), David Sloan (physicist), Jaymie Matthews (astrophysicist), Jef Raskin (interface expert; chief designer for the Macintosh), Douglas Scott (cosmologist), Michael Spencer (blacksmith; philosopher), Bill McCutcheon (astrophysicist), David Measday (astrophysicist), Joseph Green (writer; NASA alumnus), the uncredited creators of the NASA website, Dean Ing (writer; auto designer/builder; military aviation expert); Laurence M. Janifer (writer; polymath), Ben Bova (writer; space travel expert), Douglas Girling (systems analyst; aerospace

expert), Ed Thelen (Internet Nike expert), and Ted Powell (programmer; cyberhistorian; skeptic).

And those are just the people who helped with the *science* component of this story! (Any errors arising from my misunderstanding of what they told me are, of course, all *their* fault, for not explaining it better.)

Other invaluable assistance, advice, inspiration, or permission to quote was provided by Spider John Koerner (musician), Don Ross (musician), the Beatles (the Beatles), David Gerrold (writer; cat servant), Stephen Gaskin (hippie; writer; Head Judge for the first and second annual International Cannabis Cup competitions in Amsterdam), Virginia Heinlein (retired naval officer; biochemist; widow of Robert A. Heinlein), Lord Buckley (saint), Will Soto (tightrope-walking juggler), the Key West Cultural Preservation Society, and just about every Key West local I've ever met. Special thanks must go to the superb Key West writer Laurence Shames, whose contribution to this story (like those of Rees, Guth, and Coleman, above) was crucial, although quite unwitting. And my ongoing gratitude goes to the *alt.callahans* Usenet newsgroup, for keeping me grounded.

All their efforts—and any efforts of my own—would have come to naught without the massive ongoing love and support of my cherished wife Jeanne . . . or the acumen of my agent Eleanor Wood . . . or the sagacity and kindness of my editor Patrick LoBrutto, who found several structural defects and showed me how to fix them. And my friend Ted Powell deserves a second mention here, for his work as volunteer creator and keeper of my website (which can be found at http://psg.com/~ted/spider/).

Another second mention, and credit where it's due: the new name that Doc Webster suggests for gamma-ray bursters, herein, is my own invention . . . but the exquisite topper Mei-Ling comes up with was coined not by me but by Dr. Jaymie Matthews (who also came up with the title for my triweekly Technology column in *The Globe and Mail,* "Past Imperfect, Future Tense").

Finally, my thanks to the late great madman Henry Morrison Flagler, without whom the whole enterprise would not have been necessary—and to you, without whom it would have been pointless.

—Howe Sound, British Columbia
9 June, 1999

Reality is what doesn't go away
when you stop believing in it . . .
—PHILIP K. DICK

If it ain't one thing, it's two things.
—GRANDFATHER STONEBENDER

Callahan's Key

CHAPTER ONE

Cold Reboot

"The future will be better tomorrow."
—J. Danforth Quayle

IT'S ALWAYS COLDEST before the warm.

Oh, it could have been colder that day, I guess—I hear there are places up north where fifty below is considered a balmy day. But it could be a lot hotter than where I am now, if it comes to that. This is just about as warm as I care to be—and the day the whole thing started, I was as cold as I ever hope to get again in my life.

It was only twenty below, that day . . . but for Long Island, that's unusually frosty, even in the dead of winter. Which that winter surely was: dead as folk music. Dead as Mary's Place. Dead as Callahan's Place. Dead as my life, or my hopes for the future. You've read Steinbeck's THE WINTER OF OUR DISCONTENT? Well, 1989 was the winter of our despair . . .

It's the little things you remember. You know how snow gets into your boots and makes you miserable? I had been forced to stagger through a drift of snow so deep it had gotten into my

pants. A set of long underwear makes a wonderful wick. The damp patches from above and below had met at my knees almost at once.

Not that snow of yesterday's blizzard had fallen to a depth of waist height. Long Island isn't Nova Scotia or anything. My long soggies were simply the result of my tax dollars at work.

Just as I'd been in sight of my home—driving with extreme caution, and cursing the damned Town of Smithtown that should have plowed this stretch of Route 25A yesterday, for Chrissake—I had seen the town snowplow, coming toward me from the east. I'd experienced a microsecond of elation before the situation became clear to me, and then I had moaned and banged my forehead against the steering wheel.

Sure enough, the plow sailed by my home at a stately twenty miles an hour, trailing a long line of cars and trucks nearly berserk with rage . . . and utterly buried my driveway with snow, to the aforementioned waist height.

I knew perfectly well that there was nowhere else I could possibly park my car along that stretch of two-lane highway anywhere within even unreasonable walking distance of home in either direction—*except* the one driveway that I knew perfectly well the sonofabitching plow was about to stop and plow out, which it did. The one right next door to mine. The driveway of the Antichrist, where I would not have parked at gunpoint.

Of *course* the traffic stacked up behind that big bastard *surged* forward the instant it fully entered Nyjmnckra Grtozkzhnyi's drive and got out of their way. Of *course* not one of them gave an instant's thought to the fact that the road under their accelerating tires would now no longer be cleared of snow and ice. And there I was, big as life, right in their way, with my forehead on the steering wheel . . .

So by the time I got that snow in my pants, trying to clamber over the new dirty-white ridge that separated my home from civilization, I no longer had to worry about parking the car. Or fixing the damn heater, or putting gas or oil in it, or any such

chores. Just paying for the final tow—and, of course, the rest of the payments to the bank. Needless to say, the only car in the whole pileup that had been totaled was mine; *all* the people who'd caused the accident drove away from the scene. And of course they'd all agreed it had been *my* fault.

On the bright side, I was reasonably unhurt. Indeed, the only wound I had to boast of was an extremely red face. Not from anger, or even from the cold. Those goddam air bags are *not* soft. They never mention that in the ads.

So I was not looking forward to going through my front door. In the first place, I hated having to tell Zoey that we were pedestrians again. A nursing mother does not often receive such news gladly—and especially not when the temperature outside is twenty below and nothing useful lies within walking range. And in the second place—

—in the second place I knew exactly what I was going to see when I walked—okay, hobbled—through that door. And I just didn't know if I could take it one more time.

Is there anything sadder in all the world than a great big comfy superbly appointed tavern . . . so unmistakably empty and abandoned that the cobwebs everywhere have dust on them?

I'd tried to keep up a brave front, and sustained it maybe six months. Then I'd gradually slacked off on the mopping and dusting and vacuuming and polishing. By the end of a year, I wasn't even fixing leaks. What was the point? No way in hell was Mary's Place ever going to reopen. We—I, Jake Stonebender, its proprietor, and all of my highly irregular clientele—had made the single, fatal mistake of pissing off Nyjmnckra Grtozkzhnyi. Our Ukrainian next-door neighbor—and the beloved only aunt of Jorjhk Grtozkzhnyi.

Town Inspector Grtozkzhnyi . . .

Have you ever seen the total stack of paperwork required to legally operate a tavern in the Town of Smithtown in the County of Suffolk in the great State of New York in these United States of America? I don't mean the liquor license: assume you have

that. Let's just say if I'd had that stack of paperwork—all of it six-point type, and consisting mostly of blanks for me to fill in—in the trunk of the car with me that day, I could have just climbed up on top of it and *stepped* over that goddam heap of snow left in my driveway by one of Inspector Grtozkzhnyi's minions. In order to open Mary's Place at all, back in '88—in less than five years, for less than half a million dollars—I had been forced to run it outlaw, counting on its isolation and the fact that I made no effort at all to attract business to protect it from official attention.

But as Bob Dylan forgot to say, "To live outside the law, you must be lucky."

So it killed me, every time I walked through those swinging doors and saw my dream, shrouded in spiderwebs. I always saw it, for a brief instant, as it had briefly been: full of warmth and life and laughter and music and love and magic. It re-broke my heart every time. It had been much more than just my livelihood, *far* more than simply the only thing my wife and I owned besides a Honda presently being dragged away for burial, two noble but battered musical instruments, and a small fortune in baby gear.

It had been the home and the nucleus of an experiment so grand and important and urgent that I know of no parallel in human history, an experiment that, had it succeeded, might conceivably have brought an end to much human misery. And on the very verge of success, at the moment of its greatest triumph, the critical mass it had brought together and fanned to ignition temperature had been smashed, scattered like glowing gravel across the countryside by the most destructive force man has unleashed in the last two millennia: bureaucracy.

So it was with maximum reluctance and a deep sense of failure that I entered my home and former workplace that day. I lurched through the outer door, stopped in the foyer, called, "Hi, Homey, I'm Hun," to Zoey, and stomped my boots together to

knock off a few shards of snow before pushing open the swinging doors to go inside. Unfortunately, someone had entered just before me and done the same thing, leaving a slick I had failed to notice.

Which is why I lost my footing and slipped and fell flat on my ass.

Now I had snow under my *shirt*, that had migrated *up* from my pants. (You see the little things you remember?) I said a few words that could have gotten me ejected from the cheapest brothel in Manila, and sat up. Thank heaven for the thick furry hat that had partially protected my skull when it whanged against the floor. I took it off and felt my head with my hand, was relieved to confirm that I probably wouldn't raise a lump. My ass was a different matter. I got wearily to my feet—

—well, I started to. I got *just* far enough to raise my entire, already inflamed face up in front of those swinging doors before they burst open.

The Big Bang. The slow, slow expansion. The Heat Death. Empty cold eternity. Someone slapping my fucking *face*—

"Jesus Christ, Duck, knock it off! What the hell are *you* doing back?"

"Nap later," the Lucky Duck said. "You're working."

Ernie Shea is known to one and all as the Lucky Duck because around him the laws of probability turn to Silly Putty—which combined with his short stature explains and may even excuse an irascible sourpuss personality reminiscent of Daffy Duck. He is a mutant, the bastard offspring of a pookah and a Fir Darrig, two creatures commonly thought to be mythical (everywhere except Ireland), and strange things *always* happen around him. It's sort of a paranormal power.

I was too groggy to think through the implications of his presence.

"The *hell* I am," I snarled. "I haven't worked in over a year. The goddam bar is as dead as Nutsy's Kells . . . and the Folk

Music Revival developed ice crystals in the brain from the defrosting process, they had to put it back to sleep again. There *is* no work, you dumb pookah!"

"You're working," he repeated. "Nikky's here. Come on."

"Huh?"

I levitated, then looked down and stuck my feet firmly to the floor. This was too weird not to be true. At my gesture, the Lucky Duck went back inside, and I followed him. And there, standing at my bar, impeccably dressed as always and wiping drool from the chin of my baby daughter Erin, was indeed and in fact Nikola Tesla.

Perhaps the name rings a bell? Forgotten Father of the Twentieth Century? Father of alternating current . . . the condenser . . . the transformer . . . the Tesla Coil . . . the very induction motor itself . . . the remote control . . . radio . . . the crucial "AND-gate" logic circuit . . . and all the essential components of the transistor? (Tesla held patents on *all* of these . . . and literally a hundred more.) Friend of Mark Twain and Paderewski, sworn enemy of the evil Edison and treacherous Marconi? Perhaps the single most outrageously shafted and dishonored man in the history of the human race, screwed out of more credit and money than anyone since the guy who invented sex? *That* Nikola Tesla?

Okay, perhaps it seems a little odd that he was going barhopping in the snow at age 133. Especially since he'd died forty-six years earlier, in 1943. But Nikky has more fiber than I do, I guess: he doesn't let a little thing like death slow him down. "Hi, Nikky," I called out. "What's up?"

"Jake!" he cried, in that memorable baritone. "Excuse me, Erin."

"Sure, Uncle Nikky," my fourteen-month-old said, releasing his fingers.

"Thank heaven you are here," Tesla said to me, wiping his fingers off on Erin's barf-scarf and handing her to the Lucky

Duck . . . who reluctantly accepted her and held her at arm's length. "There is little time to lose."

I sighed. Somehow I *knew* what he was about to say. It had been that kind of a day. "Go ahead. Tell me about it."

He took a deep breath himself, and those incredible eyebrows of his drew together. "Jake, Michael and I need you to save the universe."

I slammed my hat to the barroom floor. "God damn it. AGAIN?"

"Jake—" Zoey began, coming out of our living quarters in the back.

"No, I mean it, Zoey. I'm sorry, Nikky, but this is starting to piss me off."

He nodded gravely. "It is exceedingly aggravating."

"Jake, it's not—"

"Zoey, when the hell did I ever sign any recruitment papers? I would have been a conscientious objector for Nam, if I hadn't already been 4-F."

"Jake, it's not as if—"

"Enough is enough, you know? You can go to the well once too often."

"Jake, it's not as if you had—"

"Do I have any training for this shit? Do I have my own tools? All I ever volunteered for in my life was going up on stage to make music, and running a bar, and helping you and Erin conquer the planet, and I've blown two out of three so far."

"Jake, it's not as if you had anything better—"

"No, I'm serious: twice is as much as any man ought to be asked to serve his . . . I'm sorry, love, what did you say?"

"It's not as if you had anything better to . . . oh, never mind, I won't say it."

Well, if she'd decided not to say it, then it was probably something that would have stung like hell to hear, so I stopped trying to guess what it might have been. Besides, by then she was taking my

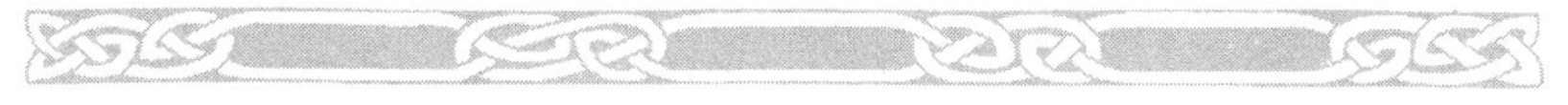

clothes off, which is likely to distract me no matter how busy we are.

"Jesus Christ, Jake," the Lucky Duck snickered, "even considering it's cold outside—"

"Duck," Zoey said, toweling me briskly with a *huge* bath towel, "would you like me to sit on you while Jake makes a snowman out of *yours* so you can compare?"

He shriveled. Making two of us.

"Out of his *what,* Mommy?" Erin asked. Zoey ignored her and kept drying me; I endured it with what dignity I could muster.

"Nikky," I said, "I appreciate the confidence you and Mike are placing in me—I'm really flattered, okay?—but—"

"Are they talking about Daddy's penis? That's silly. It gets *much* bigger than that, I've seen it—"

"—thank you, Erin, but excuse me, okay? Daddy has to tell Uncle Nikky he isn't going to save the universe this time: after that we can discuss my penis." Zoey pulled sweatpants up me to help change the subject. "Nikola, I would like to help you . . . but you have got the wrong man."

He looked somber. "There is no other, Jacob."

I went into my Lord Buckley imitation. " 'What's the matter, Mr. Whale? Ain't you hip to what's goin' *down* in these here parts? Don't you read the *Marine News*?' " He didn't recognize the quote, and I didn't have the heart to sustain it anyway. "Nikky, let me explain it in words of one syllable," I said in my normal voice. "It's all over. The Place is dead. *I got no crew.*"

"They yet live."

"Sure. Scattered all to hell and gone. Shorty and his wives are out west, Doc's retired to Florida, Isham and Tanya went up to Nova Scotia, the rest are scattered all over the Island. I see Long-Drink once a month if I'm lucky, and he's the one I still see the most. Christ knows what the hell ever happened to Fast Eddie. Like John Lennon said, the dream is over."

Zoey had finished dressing me (fuzzy slippers, sweatshirt, bathrobe), and picked that moment to yank the bathrobe belt tight around my middle, hard enough that I made a little *peep* sound. "There," she said contentedly. "Erin, Bless your father."

The Duck had set Erin down on the bar; in a shot she crawled down to the far end, down onto the counter and over to The Machine, studied the combination, and pushed the go button. The conveyor belt hummed into life, and dragged an empty mug to its fate.

Nikky watched this soberly until he was sure Erin did indeed have sufficient coordination to be safe where she was. (She could walk great, at fourteen months, but was far too smart to attempt it on top of the bar.) Then he turned back to me. "How many could you assemble, if you sounded the tocsin¿"

Warm clothes and the prospect of coffee were beginning to mollify me a trifle; my voice came out perhaps two tones lower and ten decibels softer than before. "Aw, hell, Nik. I guess . . . shit, I guess *all* of 'em. Sooner or later. Everybody that's still alive. If I started working the phones right now, I could probably muster fifteen or twenty by this time tomorrow—all the ones that are still close by. But *where¿*"

"Beg pardon¿"

"You can't have a club without a clubhouse. If twenty people all showed up *here*, tomorrow—even if they showed up on foot, in the dead of night, from different directions—fifteen minutes later the town, county, state, and feds would all come in the door right behind 'em, waving warrants to dry the ink. We tried. Several times. Old Nyjmnckra Grtozkzhnyi over yonder never sleeps. That's why everybody's scattered. There's no place to meet.

"For a while a few of us tried taking over some existing bar and turning it *into* our place—and it was a disaster. We even tried declaring ourselves a religious group and renting meditation space, but we kept getting caught drinking and tossed out. A couple of folks even tried it without booze or music, but it didn't work: I knew it wouldn't. And I am never going to be allowed to put alcohol and a large group of people in the same

room again—not in this state. Probably not anywhere: I'm marked lousy with the feds, too. Some sister-in-law of Inspector Grtozkzhnyi has one of those triple-digit GS numbers, wouldn't you know?" I trailed off, distracted by the scent that promises surcease of pain.

By now The Machine had finished producing a mug of God's Blessing: Irish coffee. "Would you come get it, Mommy?" Erin called.

Zoey went and got the cup, and brought it to me. It was snowcapped and warm to the hands, and now that it was closer I could detect that second, subtler scent that promises surcease of care. "Nikky," I said, "I don't have a crew, I don't have a place to put one, and the machine you want was disassembled for parts long ago. You've got more chance of building a new Titan booster. I'm sorry." I closed my eyes and took a long deep pull from my Irish coffee.

"Suppose a suitable place could be arranged?"

Warmth and goodness flowed into me, radiated slowly outward from my esophagus to bring solace to every discontented cell. I was out of the stormy blast, in warm dry clothing, and my two beloveds had put the caffeinated Water of Life into my hand, and there was more. *What* problems? Things slowly began to soften and shift inside me.

All right, I said to the inside of my skull. *I won't be fifty for another eight-point-four-but-who's-counting-years yet. If I can have Irish coffee, and Zoey and Erin, then I guess maybe I* could *get back on the damn horse one more time.*

Time to start negotiating the fee . . .

"Nikky, we're going about this all wrong. We've skipped ahead to question three or four. Question *one* is: *What is the deadline?* You're talking about a major operation—and the last two times we only had a few hours' warning before the roof fell in. Literally. How much time have I got to assemble the string and get 'em plugged in *this* time?"

He frowned—and the sight of Nikola Tesla frowning can be

disheartening, if you haven't got Irish coffee in your hand. Those eyebrows, you know. "I am not sure, Jake. But I do not see how it could be more than . . . say, on the order of ten years."

I did a spit-take, which fortunately fell short of him. It is a terrible thing to do a spit-take with Irish whiskey. Grandfather Stonebender used to say that after you die, Saint Peter will suspend you head-down in a barrel containing all the whiskey you've ever wasted, and if you drown, to hell with you. But I was so relieved at Tesla's words that I almost didn't mind. "Ten *years*? Jesus, for a minute there I thought we had a problem."

Those mighty eyebrows rose again, to the top floor. "You feel that might be adequate?"

"To get the bunch of us telepathic again? Yeah, I think that's probably doable—if you can really deliver a place, and maybe a little expense money. Tell you the truth, that's about the kind of time scale I was thinking in when everything went to shit."

"Really?"

"Hey, I don't want to sound cocky. What the hell do *I* know? This is blue-sky R&D. But we were telepathic three times—twice with help, and the last time by ourselves. You know yourself: once the software runs two or three times, you're practically ready to ship product. I allowed a ten-year fudge factor because . . . well, let's face it, we're a bunch of lazy drunken goof-offs. Hell, I was prepared to let *twenty* years go by without another success before I would have started to worry. But if we're under the gun . . . well, we saved the world twice before, with a hell of a lot less warning. What's the matter?"

Tesla was looking even more grave and somber than usual, if you can imagine that. "Jake, you know that I rarely employ hyperbole."

"Well, hey, Nikky—*you've* never needed to."

"And I never use scientific terminology with imprecision."

"Not that I've ever caught you at. Make your point. I can see it's bad news. *How* bad?"

His brows lowered even further, until he looked like Jehovah

brooding over what He'd done to poor old Job. "I do not wish to dishearten you, now that you are feeling optimistic. But I cannot allow you to accept this responsibility in ignorance of the stakes."

"I *haven't* accepted yet. We're still two steps away, talking about whether I can deliver. After this we discuss what I'm being offered. But by all means, let's be clear on the stakes first. We're talking about the end of the world, right? What could be imprecise about that?" The coffee began to kick into second gear. "Oh, I get you. Right, okay. Doubtless old Mother Gaia will endure, whatever happens: technically we're only talking about the end of the human race or something like that, is that it?"

I had not thought he could look any more uncomfortable, but now he looked like Jehovah the day of the Assumption, trying to explain to the Virgin Mary why He'd never called her since that night. "I am sorry, Jake. The second time you and your friends became telepathic, the stakes were indeed, as you doubtless meant to imply, only the fate of humanity . . . *and* all the other forms of life in this solar system down to the last virus. The third and most recent time, you were fighting to save *both* all terrestrial life *and* all the members of the nonhuman civilization called the Filarii: Mr. Finn's people, and their attendant subspecies."

"And this time?" It wasn't me who said it, it was Erin.

"This time the stakes are so much higher that a ratio cannot be formulated. My first words to you were most carefully chosen, Jake."

I had absorbed enough caffeine now for my short-term memory to be functional. Those words came back—and suddenly I understood him.

"Oh, my stars."

"Precisely," he agreed.

"You need me to save the *universe*."

"In its totality. Every last derivative of the Big Bang. All of creation."

"From *what?*"

"The quest for knowledge," he said sadly.

I couldn't help it. I fell down laughing.

And kept laughing, even though I had just added the precious last mouthful of whiskey to my afterlife hazard. The Lucky Duck roared along with me, and so did Erin, he an octave lower and she two octaves higher. Zoey did not. Neither did Nikky.

But he did wear a small rueful smile. How could he help it, and be an honest man?

You meet people all the time who believe, deep down in their hearts, that "madscientist" is one word, that most scientists are weird warlocks willing to risk all our lives by playing with forces they don't really understand. You want, if you have half a brain, to smack such people. And then you remember Oppie and Teller and the boys sitting around back at Trinity before Zero Hour, taking bets on whether or not they were about to ignite the atmosphere—or Taylor, using a hydrogen bomb to light his cigarette—and you change the subject. But in your heart you know that while individual humans may be fallible or quirky, science itself—the search for truth—is holy.

And now the Father of Twentieth-Century Technology himself, a man who had dedicated his life—both his lives—to the pursuit of knowledge, had told me with a straight face that the team to which he had sworn allegiance was going to destroy not just the solar system, not merely the Lesser Magellanic Cloud or even the whole Local Group, but *everything*. Can there *be* a funnier joke?

Well, yes. To fix the situation, he was depending on a widely dispersed bunch of barflies.

I don't know how long I might have kept on laughing. I was just beginning, in fact, to realize that I might have a small problem in stopping, when the two men with guns came in. That did it. Instinct, you know.

I don't know how it is everywhere else, but in the New York/Long Island area, common disaster generally tends to bring out the best in people—the *first* time.

During the first great East Coast Blackout, for instance—what was it, 1965?—we responded magnificently. People helped one another, sometimes heroically; there are hundreds of stories. Then some of them sat around and thought for a year or so about what chumps they'd been. The *second* time the grid went down, there were still heroes . . . but there were also many incidences of looting, vandalism, rape, and general mischief.

Well, the snow I had so recently trudged through was that of the *second* road-blocking, Island-paralyzing blizzard that winter . . .

It's funny, the little things you notice. The first gun was a Smith & Wesson .44 Magnum hand-cannon. It wasn't even the most powerful handgun in the world back when Dirty Harry made that claim for the .357 Magnum, and there are some today that would give it a permanent case of barrel droop, but I knew it would have no trouble killing a truck. The other gun was a collector's item, a .455 Webley that had probably seen service in the Argonne Forest . . . but threw a bigger slug than the Magnum. It was only after I assessed both weapons that I took in the guys holding them, even though they were much more interesting. Old habits die hard.

The Magnum was being steered by a skinhead. He had covered every other square inch of his body with furred garments like something out of *Road Warrior*, right up to his nose, but apparently just could not bear to cover his shining statement to society. His scalp and ears were reddening as circulation returned to them. Nonetheless, he was bright-eyed. Too bright-eyed for adrenalin, drugs, or madness: it had to be a combination of at least two.

The Webley was held by a sour-faced guy who looked like a Vermont storekeeper, dressed like a Long Island wannabe-survivalist, and had eyes like a serial killer with a toothache.

In this weather, neither of them had been able to locate a ski mask. No professionalism anymore. Maybe they planned to leave no witnesses. Maybe they just didn't plan.

Baldy pulled fur down with his free hand to display a broad

vulpine grin and swastikas tattooed (wrong way round) on each cheek. "Surprise," he cried. "We're collectin' for Good Will!"

"You, Skinny," Rambo said, meaning me, "get the till. Everybody else, turn out your pockets on this table here. *Now*." He gestured with the Webley for effect, and began shaking out a sack.

I sighed and stood up. "Boys," I said, "ordinarily I'd be happy to play with you, but I'm a little busy right now, I have to save the universe. Here's the very best deal I can cut you: you lose the iron, you clear the door within thirty seconds, you can live. You don't even have to apologize, okay?" I spread my hands. "What could be fairer than that?"

Baldy looked to Rambo for guidance. "I think he said 'no,'" Rambo explained. Baldy nodded and shot me twice. In the chest first, and then low in the belly. He started to look away to savor the shock and horror on everybody else's faces, and then did a double take.

I shook my head wearily and walked toward him.

Behind me, Zoey growled once, and subsided.

Baldy's eyes were like golf balls, and his skull had stopped reddening, but his grin got even bigger. Obviously I was wearing some kind of Kevlar vest. Figure out why later. He shot me three times in the face.

Zoey growled again. I stopped a couple of feet from him and folded my arms across my chest. "*Now* you're going to have to apologize," I said.

He looked at the gun, then me, then the gun, then me, then the gun—

Erin piped up from over on the bartop. "Can I have his mittens, Daddy? They look just like woofy dogs."

"Yes, honey," I told her.

That unstuck Baldy from his loop. He yanked his gaze toward Erin—then began quartering that section of the room for whoever had actually spoken.

"You're really stupid," she told him.

He stared at her, slowly worked out that he was in fact being

addressed, and dissed, by an infant. Even with all he had to think about already, this outraged him. Or perhaps he was just panicked, operating on drug logic. In any case, he plumbed new depths of stupidity: he lifted his gun and shot Erin.

She giggled. "That tickles," she informed him.

Nikky, the Duck, and I all leaped at the same instant, and were barely in time. Between us, we were just able to restrain Zoey. My wife is a large lady; it took everything we had, and we might not have managed it if her forebrain had been functioning at the time. She bit me on the ear and drew blood without realizing it. I got hold of her face and held it a couple of inches from mine until her eyes focused and I could see she recognized me, and then I said very urgently, "We *do not* have time to dick around with disposing of bodies just now."

She closed her eyes momentarily—then nodded and slumped. We let her go at once, and I turned back to my guests.

They were backing away, very slowly—but froze once I was looking at them again. Rambo wasn't even bothering to gesture talismanically with his Webley; it hung forgotten at his side. Baldy's scalp was so pale, it seemed to glow, and his swastikas blazed like embarrassment on his white cheeks. He snapped out of his trance, cracked his piece, took a speedloader from some pocket . . . then saw my expression and dropped both on the floor.

"I am very very sorry," he said sincerely.

"So am I," Rambo said, "even though he did it."

"I got excited, you know?" Baldy said. "I thought it was a midget."

"You're an asshole," his partner told him.

"No argument. And I really am very very very sorry."

"Not yet," I told him. "But you will be."

"You're gonna take our souls now, right?"

Beside me, the Lucky Duck emitted that wonderful honking laugh of his. "What do you figure the market value of these two souls might be?"

"Two rubles?" I hazarded.

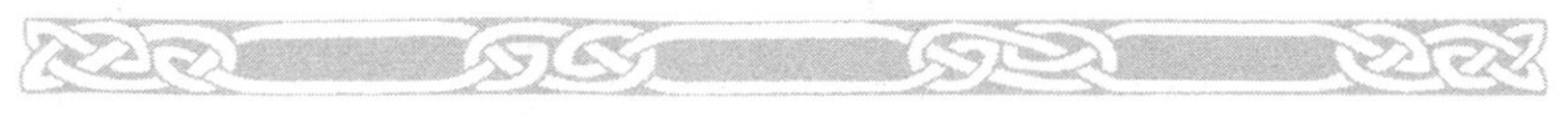

He looked at me. "There's no need to insult them."

I shrugged. "Do I need a reason?" I turned back to the cowering pair. "Your souls I condemn you to keep. But we'll have your clothes."

They gaped.

"All of them."

Both of them, as one, looked to Zoey. Whatever they saw in her eyes made their knees start to tremble. Baldy turned to Rambo. "Shoot me," he begged.

"Me first," Rambo said, and lifted the Webley toward his own head.

Erin got him square in the eye with a jet of high-pressure hot water from the hose in the sink behind the bar. He dropped the gun and started tearing at the fastenings of his coat, crying, "I'msorryI'msorryI'msorry—" After a moment Baldy followed his example.

After a while I moved forward to collect the guns. The pair backed away as I approached, shedding items of clothing as they went.

"Can I look at the guns, Daddy?" Erin asked.

"Sure, honey," I said, and brought them to her, reloading the Magnum for her before setting it down within her reach.

Even half naked in the midst of total confusion and terror, this got to Rambo. "You'd give a loaded gun to an infant?" he asked me.

"Somebody gave one to you," I said. "Keep going."

He glanced at Erin, who was struggling to lift the Webley—fumbled with shirt buttons—said the hell with it and tore the thing open.

It was reasonably safe, would have been even if Erin had been a normal baby. Everyone in the room—except the two stripping penitents, Tesla, and the Lucky Duck—was bulletproof. The rest of us had all long since been impact-shielded by Mickey Finn, that cyborged Filarii warrior I mentioned earlier. I myself had once personally tested the shielding by setting off a nuclear weapon at arm's length, and it worked just fine. (Okay, I'm ex-

aggerating a *little:* it was only a homemade pony-yield nuke, strictly kiloton-range stuff. But I wasn't worried about stray .44 slugs.)

A little while after that, we sent those fellows on their way, traveling considerably lighter than when they'd arrived. When we last saw them, they had *none* of the stuff they'd arrived with—not even Baldy's nipple rings. But since it was twenty below out there, and the sun was setting by now, we didn't send them out totally naked. Each was tastefully attired in a little strip of plastic, locked very tightly around his thumbs behind his back, doing just what it was designed to do: secure a bag of garbage. And, of course, each now wore a label as well: the word "LOOTER" in large capital letters, written across his belly in indelible laundry marker. No idea what ever became of either of them.

"Erin," Tesla said later, as we were all refreshing ourselves after the rude interruption, "I owe you an apology. Intellectually, I am perfectly aware that you are of high normal adult intelligence. After all, I was present on the night of your birth: I myself helped you interface with Solace, with the Internet, so that we could defeat the Lizard's dark side and save humanity. I know Solace accelerated the maturation of your cortex, and I'm aware that you've been raised with the help of an AI kernel she left behind when she died. But I confess that emotionally, I have continued to think of you as merely a very precocious infant—perhaps because your strength and coordination lag somewhat behind your intellect. Yet you acted more quickly and more rightly than any of the rest of us, just now, with that water hose. I thought we had lost the one in the camouflage gear." He bowed and kissed her hand. "I shall not make the same mistake again."

When my kid dimples, she *dimples*. "Thank you, Uncle Nikky. When I'm sixteen, I plan to start having sex—would you like to take a number? I can squeeze you in the single digits if you hurry."

Tesla was a virgin until shortly after he died. But he's made up for it since, and he was always a hard man to faze, and besides I think he was born gallant; he took it without blinking, and did not even glance at Zoey or me. "I would be honored, dear lady. You have my phone number," he said, and bowed again. *Then* he glanced at Zoey and me . . . and returned our grins.

"Okay, that little sideshow just now was fun, but let's get back to business," I said. "Nikky, I was going to ask you to explain exactly how the quest for knowledge is going to doom the universe, next, and then what the hell you expect us to do about it—but we can get to all that crap later. Right now, let's cut to the important part: what's in it for me?"

This time Tesla blinked.

"My standard fee for saving the universe," I said, "is a bar, and enough money and clout to run it."

"Yes, of course, Jake. I told you, all these things will be arranged."

"I want 'em *now*. All of a sudden I've had enough of this dump. Enough of Long Island. Hand me the keys to my new cash register, and we can sit around and spend the next ten years figuring out what to do about Armageddon."

His mustache went back and forth a few times, as if to scrub something off his lower lip. "I, uh, do not exactly have a site for you, yet."

I nodded and held out my hand. "Okay. How about enough money to buy one?"

He looked pained. "Jake, you know I don't use money."

I sighed. "I'm supposed to save the universe on credit. Didn't you bring me *anything* for a down payment?"

"Yes." He gestured. "Mr. Shea. Ernie. I brought him back here from Ireland."

I felt like an idiot. In all the confusion, I had failed to think through the implications. The Lucky Duck was back!

The Duck gave me his most insolent grin. He held up his hairy right hand, its hairy fingers clenched in the makings of a

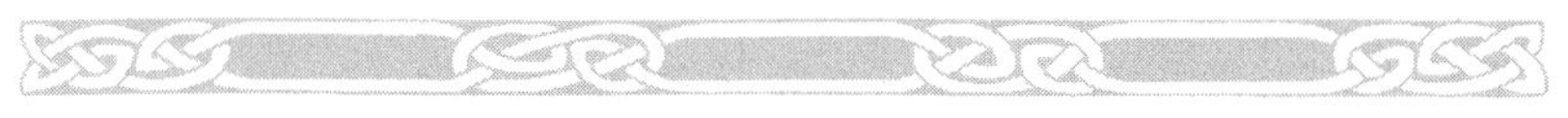

fist. A shiny quarter rested atop them. "Call it," he told me, looking me in the eye, and *snapped* the coin straight up in the air with his thumb without looking at it.

As if I needed the demonstration. "On its edge," I said automatically, kept looking at his mocking grin, and waited for the sound of the coin hitting the floor. After a while I got tired of waiting and looked up. The quarter was neatly wedged into a small crack in the ceiling.

"I win," I said.

He spread his hands and bowed, a rude imitation of Tesla's bow to Erin. "Exactly."

I turned to Nikky. "This is all you bring me, to save the universe with. A half-breed pookah with the luck of the devil."

"Yes, Jake."

I nodded judiciously. "Should be enough. Okay, I guess the first—oh damn, *again?*"

Someone else was coming through the swinging doors, trailing snow.

Like any sensible person, he was swathed in clothing, including a ski mask, only his eyes showing and those in shadow. In stature and stance he rather resembled an orangutan, with slightly overlong arms, reminding me of a guy I knew. He carried a large, very old, very battered suitcase.

"We're closed, friend," I called out.

"And we're busy," the Duck added. "If you want to rob the joint, see the kid with the Magnum over there."

Without setting down his luggage, the newcomer shook off his other glove and reached upward. That's when I recognized him, before he even got the ski mask off: I saw the hand.

I glanced around and saw that everyone else recognized him too; they were all waiting for me. I took a deep breath, nodded a silent three-count, and we all chorused, at the top of our lungs: "EDDIE!"

Fast Eddie Costigan nodded, looking more like an orangutan

than ever now that his face was visible. "Hiyez," he said, and waved.

We swarmed him. Well, all of us except Erin, who had to be content with dialing him up an Irish coffee (she knew his prescription) while the rest of us hugged and pounded and kissed him. He accepted all this stoically.

Fast Eddie is the greatest piano player alive. Of somewhat lesser importance, he is also the oldest member of the original Callahan's Place, save for Mike Callahan himself, and after Callahan's was destroyed by the nuclear weapon I mentioned earlier, he continued to fill the piano chair for *me* during the short happy life of Mary's Place. But I hadn't seen or heard a word of him since the day Inspector Grtozkzhnyi shut us down, almost a year and a half ago.

When the greeting rite was done, I said, "So what've you been up to, Eddie?" and before he could answer, turned to Zoey and mimed the words *four words, tops*. She looked dubious.

He didn't let me down. He brushed past me, heaved his suitcase up onto the bar next to Erin (nodding to her; she grinned back), popped the latches, and flung the lid open. "Got it, Boss," he said.

The suitcase was full of cash. Not neat stacks of wrapped crisp bills. Just a heap of used cash in varying denominations and conditions. It was a big suitcase.

I blinked at the swag, glanced briefly at the Lucky Duck—he was grinning like Daffy—and looked back at the money again. "So you have," I agreed. "How much is that?"

"Enough," he said.

"Well," I said, "I sure wouldn't want to ask a snoopy question or anything, but—"

"Poker," he said.

"Isn't that risky, Uncle Eddie?" Erin piped up, sliding his coffee toward him.

Eddie looked at her, and slowly shook his head no.

"Oh," she said.

He picked up the mug, said, "T'anks," and rubbed her head. Then he took a sip, sighed, and turned back to me. "I know it ain't enough ta bribe Gargle-Name," he began. "He's a hard-on."

I hated to see him wasting words like that. "Of course not," I agreed, "but this *is* Long Island. For half that much cash we could get him *and* his two immediate superiors transferred to Guam, or fired for buggering sheep."

Eddie grinned. "Let's."

I sighed. "This morning I probably would have. I'd still like to. But you came in in the middle, Eddie." I gestured toward Tesla. "Nikky says we're on a mission for Mike again."

Eddie's eyes widened. "No shit."

"Yeah. Don't worry, we got a ten-year jump on it—but I don't think we ought to start with bad karma. Besides, I'm thinking of moving out of Inspector Grtozkzhnyi's jurisdiction, anyway. Things have happened today that make me feel I've finally had enough of Long Island. The whole New York area."

Zoey smiled broadly. Erin looked alert.

"How about you, Eddie? That work for you?"

"Open up someplace else?" Eddie's face is always a collection of wrinkles, but now they all sort of fractalized. "Where?"

I took Zoey's hand. "Any ideas, love?"

"Someplace warm," she said.

"That does sound good," I agreed. "But where do we find a warm place where all the ornery crackpot weirdo rugged individuals we know could unanimously agree to move to? The warm places in this country are all full of people wearing expensive golf shoes. Or worse."

"A challenge," she agreed.

"Nikky? Any idea where Ground Zero is going to be?"

"Not for another few years yet," he said. "But that need not affect your choice of immediate location. The thing is to make a start, reassemble the group."

"Roger that. Okay, anybody—any ideas? We need a place

somewhere that's warm, hasn't got a whole lot of red tape, and will tolerate extreme weirdness. Anyone?"

Silence.

The phone rang.

"You're welcome, Stringbean," the Lucky Duck said.

Erin bent over the Call Identify box. "Daddy, it's Uncle Doc! In Key West—"

Invisible little tongues of fire appeared over every head in the room. As one, we began to grin.

"Thank you, Ernie," I said respectfully. "Put him on the speakerphone, honey."

CHAPTER TWO

Going South

"One word sums up probably the responsibility of any vice president, and that one word is, 'to be prepared.'"
—J. Danforth Quayle, December 6, 1989

"HI, UNCLE DOC!"

"Well, hello, Erin. How are you, dear? Having fun?" Doc Webster has one of those booming voices that sounds like he's on a speakerphone even when he isn't. When he *is* on a speakerphone, he could pass for the Great and Wonderful Oz. He is a large man, built like a very successful walrus, and it gives his voice a certain resonance and authority. And it probably doesn't hurt that he was one of the best doctors on Long Island for over forty years, until his recent retirement.

"Yeah," Erin assured him. "Some stupid men shot me and Daddy just now."

"Really? That must have been exciting for them." Doc is bulletproof, too. He was there that night. "If your parents need any help disposing of the bodies, I still know some people up there. I could—"

"Hi, Doc," I cut in. "Don't sweat it; we let 'em live."

"Really? Hello, Jake."

"They did penance. Let it pass; it's a long story and we have more interesting things to talk about."

"*You* have news, too?"

"Boy, do I ever. But you first: it's your dime. Before you start, though, let me introduce the audience. You're speaking to me, Erin, Zoey, Fast Eddie, the Lucky Duck, and Nikky Tesla."

"Am I really? How wonderful! By God, that's practically a quorum. I wish I was there."

"You are," Zoey pointed out. "Hi, Doc."

"Hello, Zoey—and you too, Eddie—Duck—Nikola." Greetings were called back. "Look, am I interrupting anything?"

"You are completing something, I think," Tesla said. "Pray go on, Sam."

"Well . . . okay—but everybody pour themselves one and find a comfortable chair, okay? I'm going to be talking awhile, and I've been rehearsing this for a long time so I'd appreciate it if none of you would interrupt until I finish my pitch, because it's really important to me to—"

"Doc?"

"—try and . . . dammit, Jake, I asked you not to interrupt. As you pointed out, it's my dime."

"So let me try and save you some of it. You are about to launch into a typically eloquent sales pitch for beautiful Key West, subtropical paradise, delineating its many charms and virtues and ending with a casual mention that you've located a property for sale down there that would make a really terrific bar."

There was a brief silence. Then, in a much softer voice, Doc said, "You must be reading my mail."

"Allow me to briefly summarize the events of the day so far. First I wrecked the car and got snow in my pants. Then Nikky showed up and gave me ten years to reunite the gang, on account of how we have to save the universe. I told him I'd need a new bar, someplace where you don't get snow in your pants, and money. He produced the Lucky Duck. Then Fast Eddie showed up with . . . how much money, Eddie?"

"A shitpot."

"And donated it to the cause. And then you called. You see the way this is shaping up?"

Another long pause.

"The whole, entire universe?" the Doc asked finally.

Nothing gets past him. "Yep."

"*And* you and Erin got shot."

"With a .44 Magnum," Erin agreed. "Looters trying to take advantage of the blizzard." She giggled. "It tickled. And they were so funny. Even before they were naked, I mean."

"It sounds like you've had a full day."

"Well, we're certainly off to an interesting start," I said. "From here it's going to get *busy*, I think."

"Let me get this straight," he said slowly. "You are, really and truly, going to move down here. All of you. And open a bar. And try and reconvene the company. My dearest dreams are coming true."

I glanced around me, took a census of eyes. Zoey's eyes first, then Erin's, then Eddie's, then the Duck's, and finally the wise, sad old eyes of Nikola Tesla. Then for good measure I rechecked Zoey and Erin. There were no dissents. "That's the plan."

"God damn it, Jake," the Doc burst out, "if you had any *idea* how much time I wasted rehearsing my spiel . . . I didn't think I had a chance, I didn't really think any power on earth could ever convince you to leave Long Island, but I felt like I had to—"

"Snow in your underpants and .44 slugs in your face are powerful arguments," I said. "What the hell, Sam. This business has been going south since I opened it. Might as well go all the way."

"You can't get any farther south than this without getting your feet wet," he agreed. "Just give me a minute to shift gears, okay? Christ, I feel like I was braced to lift a half-ton truck and it turned out to be a hologram. Just a second."

We heard him put his hand over the mouthpiece of his phone, and even with that filter, his bellowed "WAA-A-A-A-HOO!" nearly broke my speakerphone.

"There," he said a moment later, "I think I'm back up to speed

now. Boy, I'd forgotten how much fun those bootlegger turns are. Okay, when do you get here and what do you need?"

"I don't know and I don't know," I answered truthfully. "Let me get back to you on both. I haven't really got my mind wrapped around this, yet."

"*You* haven't? I feel like Scrooge on Christmas morning."

"We'll work all that stuff out. I'll let you know when to expect how many of us as soon as I know myself. How's the housing market down there?"

"Pricey."

"Figures."

"Worth every damn penny. But bring a lot of pennies."

I glanced at my venture capitalist. Nikola Tesla frowned. He died owing a fair amount of money to a number of people, back in 1943—but I happen to know he subsequently went to considerable pains to repay all of it. (Without being caught at it, a good trick.) He had committed himself to underwriting this particular Quest, and I was confident that he would come across. Eventually. But I could see from his expression that it might not be Real Soon.

Fast Eddie spoke up. "Dey play poker in Key West?"

There was a pause, and then the Doc's laughter began, and built to the point where it strained the speaker. "Eddie, God damn it," he boomed, "I have missed you."

"Yeah," Eddie agreed.

"Well, get your ass down here. You're right: money won't be a real problem. Plenty of optimists you can bleed, down here. I got a piano for you you're gonna like, too—and nothing you won't."

"Good dere, huh?"

"Worst thing happened to me since I got here is sunburn," the Doc assured him.

"Well, you got what you basked for," I said.

He riposted at once. "Yes, that's the fry in the ointment."

God, it was good to volley with him again. It had been too long. "But I'm sure the women there like to get off on a tan gent."

"Enough to cosine a loan, some of 'em."

Erin applied Daughter Block. "*Daddy* . . . if you and Uncle Doc are going to do that, I want my nap now."

(One of the very few quirks of my daughter's personality that I do not find totally enchanting is her strong dislike of punning. She got some of that from her mother—but Zoey's distaste for puns is probably not much stronger than that of any normal healthy human being. I attribute Erin's abomination of them to the influence of her earliest mentor: Solace, the world's first self-aware silicon intelligence. Nobody hates double-meanings more than a computer, trust me.)

"We don't do it on purpose, honey," I said.

"Same with me and my diaper. *I* learned to stop. You can do that if you have to—I just don't want to smell it."

"Come on, darling, I'll take you in back," Zoey told her, and held out her arms. "You boys wipe yourselves afterward, and wash your hands." Erin crawled to the end of the bar and leaped into her mother's arms.

"Don't go, Erin," Doc said quickly. "You either, Zoey. We'll try to control ourselves. I . . . I guess I just want you all in the room listening while I say this. Since I moved down here I've been a happy old fart. But this . . ." He paused a moment. ". . . this is the happiest day I've had since . . ." Another pause while he thought about it. ". . . well, I guess since that last time we saved the world."

"Same here," I said, and for a second I thought I was somehow hearing my own voice fed back through the speakerphone—then realized everyone else in the room had said the same thing at once. We looked around at each other and grinned. "It's gonna be good to see you again, Doc," I said.

"There's a little less of me to see, actually," he said, sounding smug.

"Really?" The Doc had been trying to lose weight for as long as I'd known him, without notable success.

"Yeah, I seem to have misplaced thirty or forty pounds. I'm on the Half-Chinese Diet."

"What's that?" Zoey asked.

"You can eat anything you want—but you have to use only one chopstick."

I grinned. Erin rolled her eyes. But it wasn't strictly speaking a pun, so she let it pass.

"That's great, Sam," Zoey said. "But seriously, how did you do it?" My beloved is one of the most sensible people I know, with fewer illusions and delusions than most—but she is human, and a product of her culture. Like every other female in America, she suffers from the irrational conviction that she weighs too much.

"Zoey," the Doc said, "I could tell you that a big man burns more energy just walking around in this climate, and that's true. But that's not it. I don't think so, anyway. The best I can say it is, in Key West the air is a meal. It tastes so good you just don't get hungry as often. Being here satisfies the appetite."

"That good, huh?" the Lucky Duck threw in.

"You get peckish, head for your local restaurant . . . and along the way you suck in a few lungfuls of frangipani and jasmine and sea salt . . . you soak up a few eyefuls of bougainvillea and palm fronds and sunset and skimpily dressed college students on bicycles . . . and when you get to the restaurant, you find that one Cuban sandwich does the work of two, and somehow it feels like a piece of Key lime pie would just be gilding the lily. You end up having the walk back home for dessert."

"Sounds rough," I said.

"Well, it's an easy job, but nobody's gotta do it."

"What's the downside?" the Duck asked the Doc.

"The what?"

"Come on."

"Okay, maybe I'm exaggerating a hair. The downside is high prices, mosquitoes like birds with teeth, cockroaches the size of New York rats, and tourists—but they've got that last one almost

under control. Like New Orleans did: herd 'em all into a long narrow pen where they can be milked conveniently, and it's easy to hose away all the vomit in the mornings and so forth. It's called Duval Street. Real humans don't have to go there—but the funny thing is, we do, sometimes. Like going to the zoo. Of course, the animals escape from time to time . . . but when they do they're almost always on bicycles or mopeds, so they're easy to shoot."

"How's de heat?"

Doc knows Eddie, and understood that he wasn't asking about the climate. "Let me put it this way, Ed. The cops here ride around on bicycles in short pants, and most of them won't slug a drunk unless they have to."

"Huh."

"There hasn't been a shot fired since I came here, let alone a GSW. There's only one way on or off the island, so there's no high-speed chases. It'd be a nice peaceful place to practice." There was a slight wistful note in his voice. The Doc had always intended to keep practicing medicine until they planted him . . . and had retired only when, within the same month, he developed a tremor in his right hand and his eyes went bad on him.

"Okay, okay," I said, "this is costing a fortune and we're already sold. We've got a million things to do and a million decisions to make. Go have a Cuban sandwich and we'll get started. I'll get back to you on what we'll need and when as soon as I figure it out. I'm really glad you called."

"Jake, take me off speakerphone for a second," the Doc said. "Good night, everybody. You've all made me very happy."

They all bade him farewell, and I switched off the speaker and picked up the handset. "I'm here, Sam."

"You're healed, Jake."

I thought about it. "Well . . . heal*ing*. I don't know about healed."

"It's finally scabbed over, at least. I could hear it in your voice the minute you picked up the phone. You've got your juice back.

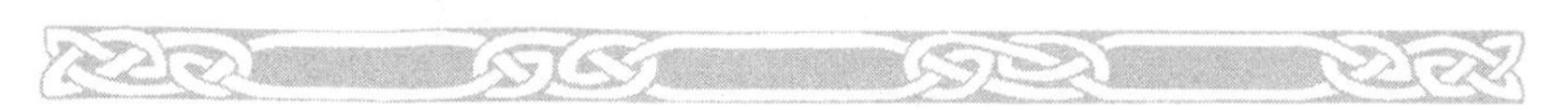

You're ready to take on your Aspect and raise up your Attribute again."

I probed my soul. "You know, I believe you're right."

"I'm so glad," he said. "I was worried for you, Jacob. Very worried." There was the faintest suggestion of a quaver in his voice.

I was moved by it. Also a little scared retroactively, if that makes any sense. I'd known the Doc a long time, and he had seen me through some major traumas without letting his worry show. Had I really been *that* close to the edge?

Yeah, I guessed I had. "So was I, Sam," I said. "I just couldn't seem to do anything about it. But I guess I had a kind of epiphany."

"Isn't that a brand of guitar?" he said quickly, but a trace of the quaver was still there.

"You're lucky Erin didn't hear that." Back when Mary's Place had been operational, we'd had a guy in one night, a heroically drunken Classics professor from Stony Brook. A guitarist friend of mine was performing that night, and the prof squinted blearily at the "Epiphone" label on the head of his guitar, and read it aloud—pronouncing it "epiphany." The resulting laugh had been memorable. The Doc had explained to him that Epiphone was the little-known Goddess of Long-Necked High-Strung Women with Large Navels.

"The success of a pun," he quoted philosophically now, "is in the *oy* of the beholder."

"Yeah, well, Erin may be more success than even you can handle," I said. "Look, I gotta go. As the ratio of a circumference to a diameter once said to the bottom of a boat—"

He beat me to the punchline. "'Keel, I'm pi.' Jake, it's going to be good to see you. Give your ladies a kiss apiece for me."

"I'll try to fit yours into the schedule," I promised, and hung up the phone.

Fast Eddie, practical as always, was behind the bar, playing

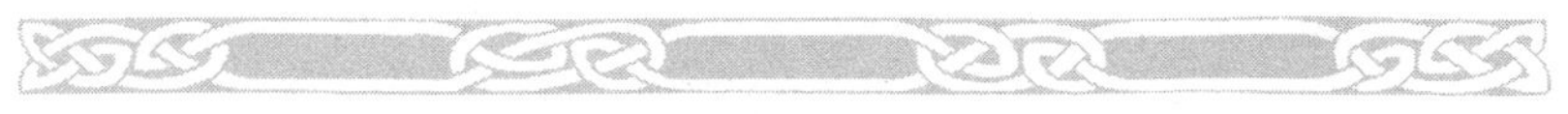

The Machine like a piano, producing coffee for everybody, except Erin who claimed caffeine "corrupted her clock-chip." He did not need to ask our individual prescriptions; as I watched he dialed for a double shot of Irish whiskey in mine, and a single shot for Zoey. Suddenly my vision refocused past him, on The Machine itself. Conceived and built by an eccentric—okay, a monomaniac, who had earned the name The Slave of Coffee—it was a miracle of inspired design, combining state-of-the-art technology, clever engineering, and patient honest craftsmanship. It was superbly functional, visually impressive, sturdy. It weighed something over two hundred pounds, empty . . .

I scroaned. That's a cross between a scream and a groan, similar to greaming. "Oh my God, *what have I done¿*"

My wife was at my side, her hand on my shoulder. "What is it, Jake¿"

"It just hit me." I turned toward her, making groping motions with my hands. "Zoey . . . dear God in Heaven . . . I've committed us to *Moving*!"

"It'll be okay," she said soothingly at once. "We have drugs."

"But, Zoey—you know what Twain said!"

She nodded. "I know. Two moves equals one fire." She looked around the room and shrugged. "This place could use half a fire, right about now."

Fighting for control, I glanced around myself. At first I didn't get what she meant, saw only large heavy awkward objects that would soon have to be moved a thousand miles . . . and then it began to sink in. Dust everywhere that Erin couldn't reach. General small untidinesses. I noticed a chair cobwebbed to its table. A dead light I hadn't gotten around to rewiring. A general air of listlessness and defeat. And much too much space, way too empty.

"Well," I said slowly, "this was a real good place to be, once."

"Got dat right," Eddie said.

"But you're right, love. Not anymore. This is no place to be raised by a kid. Let's get the fuck out of here."

She grinned. "Attaboy."

"Only, *how?*" I greamed. "Jesus, it'd take everybody here just to get The Machine there on a truck—if we *had* a truck—let alone all the rest of the—" Suddenly I remembered. "Oh, Christ, I don't even own a *car* anymore—"

"Jake, calm down," she said, putting her arms around me. "Breathe slowly. Answer this: What are friends for?"

I got a grip. "Oh. Right. To help you move. I forgot." I hugged her back. "Thanks." A thought suddenly struck me, and I pulled away. "But hey—most of our friends are all scattered to the four winds." Thanks to their favorite innkeeper spending the last year or so in a funk . . .

She took me by the ears and kissed me firmly. "Calm down, I said." She turned to the Lucky Duck. "Ernie?"

He just grinned.

The door opened and Long-Drink McGonnigle walked in, stamping snow off his boots and talking as he came.

"Jake, God damn it, I got something to say and I want you to shut the hell up until I finish saying it, okay? This place has turned sour for you, you're no good here anymore, spilled milk is bad for the stomach—Christ, you don't even keep your *driveway* shoveled anymore, I had to park out on the damn road and hike in—and I'm telling you it's time you got your thumb out of your ass and moved on, before you turn into an impacted wisdom tooth of a man—move anywhere, I don't care where, out of state—hell, Florida even—I mean it, I'm serious as a heart attack: serious enough to get on the horn and organize a Moving Party to run you and your family out of town on a rail right away, and if you don't . . . what the hell are you all *laughing* about?"

The only one who wasn't laughing was the Lucky Duck, who smirked at me and said, "You can always leave these little things to me."

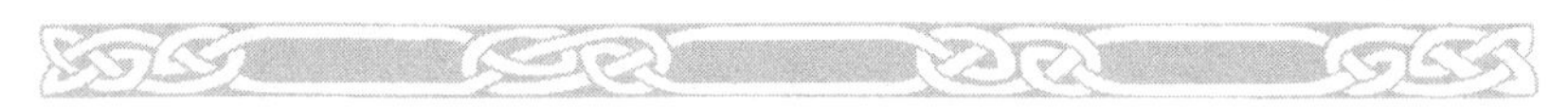

• • •

Eventually we got Long-Drink straightened out. I studied his reaction with some interest. The Drink is one of the least sentimental people I know, at least publicly. Not as sour as the Lucky Duck, mind you—Long-Drink definitely knows how to have fun—but he works pretty hard on being unflappable. Yet I knew this news would affect him emotionally at least as deeply as it had Doc Webster; like him Long-Drink is sort of a founding father, one of the oldest living patrons of the original Callahan's Place, and one of the steadiest customers of Mary's Place until they shut us down. As he began to grasp what we were telling him, and understand that we were really and truly planning to reunite the company, in a Place Without Snow, I watched his face to see whether he would let any of his emotion show.

He closed his eyes briefly, then reopened them. The corners of his mouth turned up. "Well, now," he said. "That doesn't suck much at all, does it?" His eyes were bright. Then he blinked six times fast and they were normal again. And that was it. "Now comes the hard part," he went on.

"You got that right," I said.

He went to his usual spot at the bar, slid into his chair, and rested his elbow on the bar. It was oddly beautiful to watch: as easy, graceful, and inevitable as Paladin dropping slowly into that gunfighter's crouch of his on *Have Gun Will Travel*. McGonnigle is several inches taller than me, or just about anybody, and damn near as skinny—but I'm pretty sure people would have called him Long-Drink if he'd been five feet tall. Eddie took a mug from The Machine and slid it down the bar to him, and he fielded it without looking. "You need a Dortmunder."

A planner, he meant. Like John Dortmunder in Donald Westlake's books: the guy that plans the caper. "Right."

He shrugged and knocked back half his coffee. "Then you want Tanya Latimer."

He was right. Tanya is an ex-cop, smart, tough, and decisive;

she could get a riot marching in step. The reason she's an ex-cop as young as forty is she was blinded in the line of duty, and late-life blindness improved her already impressive organizational skills a great deal. Also her husband Isham, though only twice the size of a normal human being, carries enough muscle for three of them—and I was already dimly sensing that muscle was going to be required here. Finally, for reasons known only to her and to God, Tanya played the tuba: she and Ish had to move at least once a year themselves. "Brilliant, Long-Drink," I told him.

"Redundant," he said.

So I gave Tanya a call, and explained the situation. There was nothing reserved about *her* reaction; her "Y-Y-Y-Y-YES!" could have been clearly heard out in the parking lot . . . and I did *not* have her on speakerphone at the time. Soon I did, though, at her command; Tanya's not a person to waste time. "All right, you beautiful loonies, let's get this damn show on the road! Zoey, you still have the old phone files: give them to the Duck and Fast Eddie and have them start tracking, find every regular you can and tell 'em it's railroadin' time—"

"Why those two?" Zoey asked, already heading for the Rolodex. "I can handle it."

"Don't argue. Because they talk less than you. Or anybody. I want you and Erin to fire up the Mac and do the same thing by E-mail and newsgroup. She knows the system better, but she can't type or mouse as fast as you."

"Yet," Erin qualified.

"That's right, honey. Don't worry about overlapping with the Duck and Eddie: the point is to get as many bodies as possible, fast—besides, anybody who gets the first message won't be home long enough to get the second. McGonnigle, you're a night watchman, you gotta know somebody with a five-ton truck we can rent for a week who won't skin us—"

"Rent, schment," Long-Drink said. "I know where I can get one for free."

"Yeah?" she said suspiciously. "How much will *that* cost?"

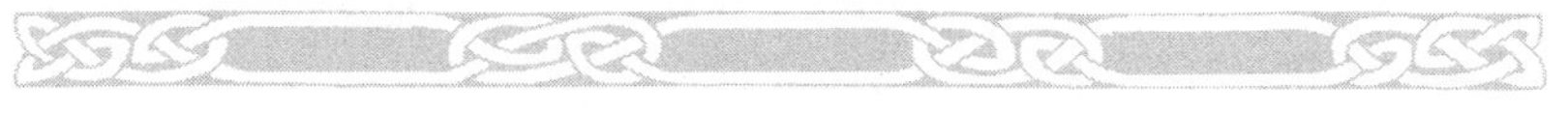

He shrugged at the phone. "Hell, as long as we promise not to bring it back, and not to tell anybody it didn't really have a full load of expensive items aboard when we stole it, and to dump it somewhere in the Keys where it won't be noticed for a week or so, we might even make a few bucks."

"Rent one," she said firmly. "Defrauding an insurance company is lousy karma to begin a move with."

Long-Drink sighed. "When you're right, you're right. Okay, one five-ton, coming up. I can get us a driver, too." He threw me a dark look. "Assuming somebody ever shovels out the goddam driveway around here. What else?"

"Boxes. You're in charge of boxes. Hundreds of boxes, all shapes and sizes, but get as many as possible in the size they ship hardcover books to bookstores in: they have the most useful dimensions."

"No sweat. One of the places I guard is a bookbinder."

"Good. Get them flat rather than assembled if you can; more in one trip that way and they take two seconds to put together. Get some of those tape-guns they use."

"Check."

"What about *me?*" I asked.

"You put everything you and Zoey own in the boxes."

"Oh my God." I was sorry I'd asked. My worst nightmare. Decision-making. *Millions* of little decisions. What to keep. What to dump. How to package it. Hundreds of 3-D jigsaw puzzles, made of precious breakables. Trying to figure out how to intelligently *label* hundreds of jigsaw puzzles . . .

Tanya heard the tremor in my voice. Her rapid-fire delivery didn't slow any, but her voice softened. "Keep it simple, Jake. Don't try to do any sorting: you'll only confuse the shit out of yourself. You already know where everything is right *now* . . . so when Long-Drink brings you the first assembled boxes, you start right there in the bar. Start with the north wall, to the left of the door as you come in. The first thing you see you want to take, you put in the box. You keep doing that until the box is full. You label it 'Bar N-1.' The next box is 'Bar N-2.' And so on for east, south, and west walls. When the walls are bare, do the middle of the room; this time you label the boxes 'Bar-1,' 'Bar-2,' with no letters. When the bar's empty, you go on into the back, and start a stack of boxes with 'Bed N-1,' 'Kitchen N-1,' and 'Bath N-1.' A robot could do it. Then when you get to Key West and you're surrounded by boxes and you want to know where the hell something is, you just have to remember where it used to be."

That sounded sensible. Even better, it sounded doable. But—"Tanya, we're going to need a lot of muscle. More than just your old man, I mean."

"Don't worry," she said. "Jim Omar's back."

For the first time in a while I began to really relax. I'd rather have Jim Omar than a forklift and a chain hoist. The weird thing is, he looks like a normal person: built solid, but not at all "cut" or swollen like a bodybuilder. The muscles don't show . . . until he uses them. Once, years ago, he'd been helping me on another move, and there came a point where four of us were having trouble getting my refrigerator off the back of a pickup. There wasn't enough room in the truckbed and we kept getting in each other's way. Finally Omar got impatient. He told the rest of us to climb out . . . and then I swear he wrapped his arms around that fridge, heaved it up to chest height and held it there, walked to the back of the truck, and jumped off with the damn fridge in his arms. He did not drop or damage it on landing. Then he carried it into the house and set it down where it belonged—and his arms and thighs reverted from Popeye-cartoon monstrosities to normal human size again. Later that day, after the move was done, I saw him eat a pound of chopped meat, raw—then he sat down to the meal I'd laid out for everybody, and ate two shares. He'd been out of the country for about fifteen of the last twenty years, but if he was stateside again, a lot of my worries were over. "How come he's back?" I asked Tanya.

"He got funding."

"For that wacky project of his? 'Immortality for the Immortals'?"

"Yep."

"Holy shit. The world has gotten even weirder than I thought."

I heard her chuckle. "Child, you ain't seen *nothin'* yet. You remember Heinlein's Future History?"

"Sure." In 1939 Robert Heinlein drew up a chart of several hundred years of imaginary future, within which matrix he eventually set a great many of his science fiction stories.

"What were the 1990s labeled?"

I visualized the chart. "Oh me. 'The Crazy Years.'"

"Fasten your seat belt. It's gonna get *nutty* out by and by. Few more years and the President of the United States won't be safe, I'm telling you."

Now there was a scary thought. I brushed it aside and tried to focus. "Okay, between your Isham and Omar I'd say we have serious muscle well covered. Long-Drink handles the wheels and boxes. Zoey and Erin do personpower recruitment. You got strategy and logistics. Eddie's the banker and general facilitator. The Lucky Duck does . . . what he does." I counted noses. "Hey—what about *me*?"

"I told you," she said. "You put everything you own into the boxes."

I began to hyperventilate.

"I hear you breathin'," she said. "Knock that off. Look, there's two ways to do this. One, you can examine every item, right down to the last piece of forgotten paper, and make the decision *do I take this or pitch it or do some third thing?* about a million times—and worry each time that you made the wrong decision, and sometimes *make* the wrong decision." I was sweating. "Or . . . you can just shovel things into boxes, without looking at them any closer than you have to to make 'em fit. If you do that, the load will be maybe twenty percent bigger and heavier, each person will end up lifting and carrying maybe two extra boxes—

but you'll have it ready in half the time, and you won't be an emotional wreck."

I felt obliged to make at least a token protest. "Heavier load means more gas." It came out kind of feeble.

"So I play an extra hand," Fast Eddie said.

"He's right, Jake," Long-Drink said. "Efficiency is much overrated."

I looked at Zoey. She shrugged. "We can sort the stuff as we unpack it, if we want."

I blinked and looked around me. "So then . . . the only thing we really have to do now is survive endless long days of unceasing brutal yet tedious backbreaking donkey labor?"

"Looks like," she said, and Tanya on the speakerphone chimed in, "*Now* you got it."

I like to sleep late in the morning. I don't like to wear no shoes. I despise all forms of exercise except sex, guitar-playing, elbow-bending, and talking. And thinking about sex. But there were clearly powerful karmic forces of some kind at work here that didn't give a damn what I liked or didn't like . . . and maybe I was even more wary of them than I was of manual labor. Or maybe I just wanted my wife and child to admire me a little. Bravery, I sometimes think, consists largely of faking bravery when necessary. "Well shit," I said, willing my voice not to quaver, "I thought I had a problem. This is merely a catastrophe."

Zoey appeared to relax slightly.

"You got it," Tanya said, chuckling. "Nothing you gotta do about it except survive it."

"So when should I get the truck for?" Long-Drink asked.

I had my breathing back under control now. "How long you figure it'll take, Tanya? To pack up this whole place and load it?"

"How the hell should *I* know?"

"Oh. Right."

Of course. Tanya had been in Mary's Place dozens of times. She'd even been in back a few times. But she'd never seen any of it . . .

Wrong. She went on: "I'll give you an estimate as soon as Zoey tells me how many warm bodies she and Erin have lined up to help." I suddenly realized Tanya could probably have produced a more accurate inventory of Mary's Place from memory than I could looking around at it.

I was getting tired of talking on the phone. "Okay," I said. "That covers everything I can think of. Anybody else got anything to contribute?"

There was a brief silence.

"Sounds like a plan," the Lucky Duck said. There was a general murmur of agreement.

"Right, then," I said. "Tanya, we'll get back to you tomorrow when we get a sense of how this is shaping up. Meanwhile, thank you from the bottom of my thorax."

"No sweat, cousin. Night." She hung up, and so did I, and somebody killed the speakerphone.

There was a brief silence, broken by Long-Drink McGonnigle. "I know the two things you should pack *last*."

I looked over at him. He was pointing to the two guns Erin had left lying on the bartop. "Aw, you heard the Doc: they don't use them much in Key West."

Long-Drink looked grim. "That may be . . . but just about the only thing I know about Key West is, you gotta go through South Florida to get there. You want those handy for show, to get respect."

As I was deciding that he had a point, I noticed something. "Hey—Erin!"

"What is it, Jake?" Zoey asked, hearing my tone.

"She left the safeties off on those things. There are nonbulletproof guests present. Okay, the Duck is safe enough, but what if Nikky took a round?" I went over and fixed matters, then looked around the room. "Erin?"

"I put her down just a second ago."

"Where the hell could she have—"

"Erin, where are you?" Zoey said in her command voice.

No response. Everyone else was looking around, too, but . . . wait a minute, not everyone. "For that matter, where's Nikky?" I said.

"ERIN?" Zoey called. *"NIKKY?"*

Erin rarely goes beyond earshot. Unlike most babies, she knows exactly how fragile and vulnerable she is. Just as I started to seriously worry, they came out of the back together, Erin in the crook of Tesla's right arm and a flat box in his left. "Forgive me, Zoey," he said. "Erin asked me to fetch this, and came along to show me where it was."

"I got bored with all the grown-up talk," Erin said. "I want to play some Scrabble." Sure enough, that was what the box was. Tesla set her and it down on the bar, opened the box, and began setting up the board. "Who'll play with me?" she asked, selecting her letters.

There was a silence. Everyone present loved Erin—but recent events had given us all a charge of adrenalin, and nobody seemed eager to sit down and lose at Scrabble . . . which was the usual outcome of playing with her.

"I'll play with you, kid," the Lucky Duck said, surprising me. He strode over, selected seven tiles at random, but he didn't bother to line them up on his rack. He just set them down on the center of the board without looking.

"Uncle Duck!" Erin cried. "*You*'re no fun!"

He had spelled out QUACKER. All seven of his letters. Ninety-four points, with the bonus.

"I'll play," Fast Eddie said, and the Duck made way for him, looking bored.

"Jake," Zoey said, "where are you going?"

I hadn't realized I was going anywhere. Sure enough, though, I was halfway to the door to the back. I interrogated my automatic pilot to find out why. Oh. Right. "Who else besides Zoey and me missed dinner?"

Zoey gasped. "My God, we *have* been busy."

"Come on," I said to the others. "I'm planning a this-and-that omelet—who's in? Speak up."

Eddie and Tesla and the Duck all admitted they could eat, and there was no point asking Long-Drink if he was hungry: he was awake. So I went back into the kitchen and made an omelet for six, and if you think that's easy, try it sometime. In fact, now that I think of it, if it's big enough for six people, it's not an omelet anymore: it's a full-fledged omel. I used our shallowest wok for a frying pan, and after I poured the egg mix into it I was as busy as a one-legged man at an ass-kicking contest for a while, and when it was finally time, Zoey had to help me fold the sucker with a second spatula.

Nonetheless, it turned out so well, I enjoyed eating it almost more than being complimented on it afterward.

Zoey and I were not permitted either to clean up afterward or do the dishes. We couldn't protest: they weren't guests, they were family, one and all.

As they worked, Zoey leaned over and murmured in my ear, "Thank you."

"For what?" I asked.

She just looked at me.

"It was my night to cook."

"Not for the meal, you asshole. For coming back from the dead."

"Oh." I blinked. "That."

I went up into my mental editing room and ran some flashback sequences of the last year or so. By God, she was right. Until that moment I had not fully realized what a waste of space I'd become lately. Zoey had been carrying me.

"I was scared," she said.

"Yeah," I said, "you must have been." I thought about saying I was sorry, and studied her face, and realized somehow that it would be a mistake. "I love you," I said instead.

She pulled her chair next to mine and hugged me very hard.

"Thanks for sticking around," I murmured in her ear.

"You're welcome," she said. Her voice was muffled.

We sat there together for a time, hugging, while a feeling slowly suffused me that had been so long absent it took me a while to recognize it: peace. It made me think of Chairman Mao's marvelous pronouncement, "All is chaos under heaven, and the situation is excellent." Soon everything around me would be coming apart . . . but right at that moment I had a double-armful of beautiful woman. For the millionth time I wondered why so many men find skinny women attractive. Why would you be drawn to a body that says, *I have either no physical appetites or inhuman restraint?* Masochism, obviously—but *why?*

Suddenly I had a flash, and grinned so broadly Zoey was able to detect it with the side of her neck. "What?" she asked.

"My brain has started working again. God, it's been a while."

"What?" she asked again, pulling away just far enough to see my face. "My, that's an evil grin."

It got even broader. "You know the Maloneys?"

"Sure. I introduced them to you. What about them?"

"Didn't you say they'd just lost their lease again?"

"Sure, and the sun came up this morning, so wha . . . oh. *Oh.*"

"We've got Tesla and Fast Eddie bankrolling us," I said, "but even so we're gonna have to unload this dump eventually, or they'll keep coming after us for taxes. I'll bet the Maloneys are sick of renting. What do you say we offer it to them for . . . oh, say seventy-five percent of what I paid for it, a thousand dollars down?"

If my grin was evil, Zoey's was satanic. "Oh, I think they would make *lovely* neighbors for Nyjmnckra Grtozkzhnyi. Make it fifty percent . . . and a hundred-buck down payment."

We smiled at each other.

"Rebirth, renewal, and revenge," Zoey said. "Could there be a more perfect day?"

Now *my* grin was satanic. "Wait until everybody leaves for the night," I said, "and I'll show you."

Her nipples stood up.

CHAPTER THREE

Railroading Time

"A low voter turnout is an indication of fewer people going to the polls."
—J. Danforth Quayle

BY LATE MORNING OF the next day, things were shaping up nicely. By late afternoon, they were completely out of hand.

The trouble wasn't that nobody wanted to help. The trouble wasn't even that *everybody* wanted to help—although there are few things that can screw up a move worse than having too many bodies to coordinate.

The problem was that everybody wanted to *come*.

I suppose it should not have surprised me as much as it did. But it did. Slowly, phone call by phone call by E-mail, I began to get it through my head that *none* of my friends and former customers were particularly happy where they were. If you've been telepathic with a large group of rather nice folks a couple of times, and now you're not, the Long Island/New York area becomes even more unbearable than usual, I guess. Whatever the reasons, it turned out

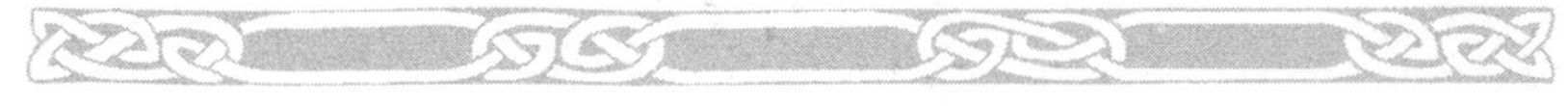

that in the fourteen months since we had been scattered, almost none of them had put down a root anywhere so deep that they weren't prepared to pull it up and leave on a moment's notice. And they all agreed that Key West sounded like a nice place to try.

Noah Gonzalez was sick of slipping on ice—he only has the one leg, you see. Tommy Janssen was a major Jimmy Buffett fan. Slippery Joe Maser was in the Merchant Marine, and the chances of his getting a ship before his ticket rolled over were considerably higher in Florida than in San Diego just now; also, one of his wives (Susan) was from there, and the other (Suzanne) had always wanted to go. Shorty Steinitz, having finally lost his driver's license for good—which even he admitted was only fair; Shorty once totaled a bumper car at a carnival—was suddenly in the market for a place where a bicycle was adequate transportation. Joe Quigley had finally lost *his* license, too—his private investigator's license, that is—and while that one *wasn't* fair, he and Arethusa were sick of the PI's life anyway and ready to chuck it. Ralph von Wau Wau had heard a rumor that *another* talking dog lived in Key West—a female!—and wanted to check it out. Bill Gerrity already had several friends in Key West, had been receiving invitations and job offers from the transvestite community down there for years. Josie Bauer had family down there. And so on, down the list of the former patrons of Mary's Place. For one reason and another, the answer always came down to, "Help you move? Sure, if you'll help *me* move."

Maybe it was just "railroading time."

What began in the morning as a series of pleasant surprises became apparent as a logistical problem of staggering proportions by late in the day. We were no longer talking about a move; we were talking about an invasion force.

And they all insisted they wanted to go together, as a convoy. It would be fun. A classic American road trip. A chance to all vacation together on the way to a new life in the sun. A memory to cherish for decades to come.

"Twenty-three people, Zoey! Just so far. *And* their families

and pets, and everything they own. Where in downtown Hell are we going to find twenty-three five-ton trucks? Not to mention gas and a hundred other—"

"It'll work out somehow," she said.

Everyone else I'd spoken to all day had said that, in just those words. "Look, I'm trying to get some worrying done here, and you're not helping."

"You're doing fine on your own," she said soothingly, and set two fresh cups of Kenya AA before us.

"Wait a minute," I said. "Wait, now. I seem to recall I was just as worried as this about something . . . uh . . . yesterday, it was. Yes, yesterday, I remember now. And then I thought of something and did that, and everything got all better. Now, what was it?" I smelled the coffee. "*Oh*. Right. Where's the phone?"

"You're resting your head on it, Daddy," Erin said.

I lifted my head and looked, and she was right. "Very good," I said. "I was just testing you."

She nodded. "I passed."

I blinked at the phone, wondering why I had wanted it. A long gulp of coffee. Oh yes, of course! The inspiration that was going to save my bacon, for the second time in two days. I picked up the phone and speed-dialed my mastermind, my Dortmunder, my Eisenhower: Tanya Latimer.

"Tanya? Jake. Listen, things have—"

"Jake? Hey, do you think McGonnigle could maybe come up with another truck someplace? Ish and I have been talking it over all day, and we figure after Nova Scotia, Florida sounds good . . . and besides, we're basically still packed, so—"

I held the phone away from me, stared at it, and passed it to Zoey.

She saw my face, sighed, nodded, accepted the phone, and I concentrated on finishing my coffee while she took on the chore of explaining to Tanya that the Latimers were the twenty-fourth party to join the wagon train, and agreeing that that sure was amazing, huh, and finally asking if by any chance Tanya had any thoughts to offer on exactly how to manifest and organize said wagon train. I couldn't hear the answer, but it was short. Zoey thanked her and promised to get back to her and hung up.

"She hasn't got a clue," I said.

Zoey shook her head. "She thinks it's impossible. She says 'Good luck.'"

Think about it. Call it two dozen vehicles—though it could easily run to twice that many. How do you keep them together, without everybody having to memorize two dozen license plate numbers? How do you coordinate stopping for gas? Stopping to pee? Stopping to gawk? Stopping for breakdowns? What are the chances of getting everyone to agree, even once, on where and what to eat? And if you scatter for meals, how do you re-form the convoy afterward without creating a public nuisance somewhere?

Try and calculate the theoretical maximum distance your caravan can cover in a day. Cut that in half, to get the probable real-world maximum. Now sit down with a map, and work out where you'll probably be stopping each night—assuming nothing goes wrong. Now phone motels, campgrounds, or hostels in each of those places, until you find ones that will accept a reservation for two dozen rooms, with kiddy cots in half of them. Allow a good ten minutes per call, and be prepared to be persuasive. Assuming you do get lucky, they will want the number of a credit card with a whopping balance—and if by inevitable mischance you should be held up on the way, and arrive five minutes later than you said you would, you will find that half the rooms you're paying for have been rerented already.

Hell, where do you find two dozen big trucks?

I got so desperate I asked Tesla to help me cheat, even though I knew better.

"Nikky, Mike and Sally taught you how to do that Transiting thing, right? Like, teleportation? Couldn't you just sort of . . . slide us all right down there, shazam, without covering the intervening distance?"

He left off playing Scrabble with my daughter and frowned. "Jake—"

"From what I hear, a hundred people appearing out of thin air in Key West is not going to cause that big a stir."

He shook his head, sadly but with finality. "I cannot permit humans of this time—other than yourself and your friends—to observe Transition, lest they suspect prematurely the existence of the forces which make it possible. It does not matter whether or not it would frighten them. It is a question of chronistic prophylaxis. To permit futuristic knowledge to enter the timestream at this historic locus would risk disastrous paradox, you know that."

I did know it, but was feeling stubborn. "Hell, the whole crew of us are walking paradoxes—*you* know *that*."

Erin picked that moment to lay down the word "QUANTIZE," on a triple word score, in such a way that it interlocked with two other existing and lengthy words. She giggled and selected seven new tiles from the box.

"See?"

Tesla smiled sadly. "Yes, but you are *indigenous* paradoxes, native to this ficton."

"Okay, but can't you bend the rules a little, just this once? Come on—to help save the universe?"

He smiled again, even more sadly. " 'To save the universe,' " he asked, paraphrasing that infamous line from the Vietnam War, " 'it was necessary to destroy the universe . . .'?"

I gave up. You quote that line to an old hippie, you're kind of hitting below the belt.

"I am sorry, Jake. This is not a rule, but a necessity. You must solve this problem using contemporary methods and materials."

"Like what?"

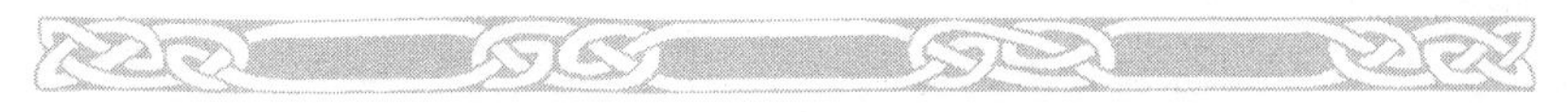

He spread his hands. "I will give it thought." He returned his attention to the Scrabble board.

Erin finished studying her own new letters, and looked up at me. "I know who can help you, Daddy."

"Who's that, Peanut?"

"Jorjhk."

"Zoey," I called, "get the barf-scarf. She's coughing something up."

"One drool-spool coming up," she said, coming in from the back with one.

Erin grimaced ferociously. "Daddy—*Jorjhk*!"

"Something stuck in her throat!" Zoey cried, and came at a gallop.

Tesla tried to pick Erin up, I believe with the idea of performing some sort of Heimlich maneuver, and got an elbow in the solar plexus for his trouble; Erin squirmed clear.

"That's his *name*, you mungle-bungles," she yelled. "The guy who can help you. *Jorjhk*. Jorjhk *Grtozkzhnyi*. Nyjmnckra's nephew."

Ten seconds of paralyzed silence all around, broken at last by the nearby sound of the Lucky Chuck, duckling. Excuse me: the Lucky Duck, chuckling.

"Jesus, Jake," Zoey said wonderingly. "She's right."

Damned if she wasn't.

Even the first time I saw him—before I had any conception of how much I would come to hate him—I thought Jorjhk Grtozkzhnyi was the ugliest man I'd ever seen in my life. (And very nearly the ugliest *person* I'd ever seen in my life. But then there was his aunt Nyjmnckra, you see, and femininity gives much greater scope for ugliness.) I believe a charging rhinoceros would stop in its tracks to gape at him. In fact, now that I think of it, in certain lights, his face would closely resemble the back end of a female rhino. In heat. (I watch PBS.)

It went perfectly with the rest of his exterior, too. He was built along the lines of a sidewalk mailbox, always dressed in off-the-rack polyester (the stuff everyone else had left *on* the rack), bathed insufficiently often, and had a complexion that made you wonder if there could be such a thing as spoiled putty. His walk reminded me of a little windup duck I'd had when I was four or so, scaled up to mailbox size.

But all these uglinesses were as nothing compared to his personality. I have known more than one person whose external ugliness masked an inner beauty. He was not one of them. He had *earned* that face.

He was a career bureaucrat, and he was proud of it. What else can I say?

I did not want him in my home, not even now that it wasn't going to be my home much longer. There was an impressionable child present. Not to mention the odd few rats, spiders, and roaches about the place, whose sensitivities ought to be considered. Also, the houseplants in the bedroom in back might die. So when I phoned him, I gave him the address of the Maloneys and told him to meet me there. He was willing to meet immediately, once I told him I was planning to sell Mary's Place and leave Long Island. But I made him wait until after supper. I knew from experience that dealing with him would destroy my appetite completely for at least twelve hours.

Long-Drink let me borrow his wheels. I arrived at the appointed time to find Grtozkzhnyi waiting for me, his inevitable polyester suit covered by a Robert Hall topcoat, his bald head covered by a small dead fur-bearing animal of some sort, whose death by electrocution had apparently been botched. He was standing in the street by the driver's side door of his car, staring over its roof at the Maloney residence, and the expression on his face made it, incredibly, even uglier.

Which did not surprise me. Especially not when I opened my own door and the full impact of the sound hit me too. I had timed our meeting to coincide with feeding time. Olga Maloney

boarded dogs. *Many* dogs. Her husband Frank had converted the basement of the house into a kennel for her. Twice a day, she let them all out into the enclosed backyard at once, for feeding and exercise. The evening feedings frequently coincided with Frank's band rehearsals, and this was one of those nights. They're a tribute band: they call themselves Redi-Wip, because they're Cream imitators. As I got out of the car they were just launching into "Toad." Since they all have day jobs, and don't have to earn their living from music, they can afford very good sound equipment. The outlines of the house visibly blurred every time Frank stomped on his floor-tom pedals—which, given the song, was more or less constantly. It kind of forced the dogs to talk louder so they could hear each other. The resulting cacophony pretty much blanketed the audible spectrum, and on up into the hypersonic.

We were a good fifty yards away; it was possible for us to converse without quite shouting. Nonetheless Grtozkzhnyi shouted. "Do you expect me to go *in* there¿"

I shook my head, and he relaxed slightly. He turned and looked at the house again. The front door opened, spilling light and *lots* more noise, then shut again.

"An uncle of mine lives on the approach to JFK," he said. "I wish I were there now." He shook his head. "I never thought I would wish that."

A little girl was coming down the walk toward us, maybe ten years old, pushing a bicycle. Frank's youngest daughter Bridget. She stopped just short of the sidewalk, stared at Grtozkzhnyi, and said, "God. You are . . . like, *so* ugly."

He frowned at her. "You are a very rude little girl."

Bridget nodded, studying his face. "Yeah, but I can be polite if I want. You always look like that." She seemed to reach a decision. "I'd kill myself," she said, and got on her bike.

Grtozkzhnyi growled and started to come around his car, angling to cut her off, but she stood her ground. "My daddy is a state trooper," she said. Grtozkzhnyi stopped in his tracks.

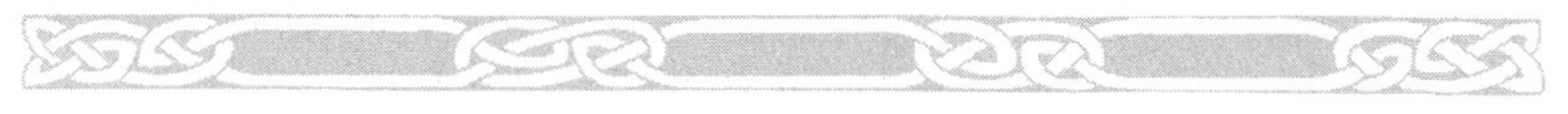

She noticed me for the first time. "Hi, Jake. Erin with you?"

"Hi, Bridget. No, not tonight."

My existence ceased to have meaning in her universe. She pedaled away down the block.

Grtozkzhnyi stared after her.

The background racket became, astonishingly, even more astonishing. It took me a few seconds to work out the nature of the change, because it seemed too weird to be true: the drum solo was becoming stereo. A second channel was fading up, *behind* me. Strangely, this one was in a different time signature. I looked around and suddenly it made sense. The approaching car, a 1970 Dodge Pioneer, did have a muffler—you could see it hanging beneath, like a desperate hobo clinging to the underside of a boxcar—but it did not appear to be connected to the exhaust system in any important way. The engine had bad valves, and at least two bad cylinders that caused it to misfire rhythmically—and, we soon learned, badly worn and misadjusted brakes. It came to a shuddering halt alongside us, and continued shuddering. With the engine idling, the car was *noisier:* now you could hear, or more accurately feel, the rap music from the car stereo. With all the windows rolled up, it was as loud as the ongoing drum solo from the house, and clashed badly with it. It sounded like "Fight the Power" or something with the same rhythmic structure and emotional tone, which narrowed it down to ninety percent of rap.

The passenger door opened—the rap briefly overpowered the heavy metal from the house; a generational triumph—and emitted a cloud of pot smoke and a fifteen-year-old male; that is to say, a lout. He was in full lout uniform: logoless baseball cap worn backward over a *faux* bowl haircut, nose ring, ten studs in each ear, T-shirt large enough to conceal a pregnancy, "shorts" long enough to conceal his calves and baggy enough to share with two friends, and sneakers that appeared to have been fashioned out of Cadillac Eldorado upholstery, dipped in Day-Glo paint, and inflated with helium. As a concession to the bitter cold, he had left the baggy sleeves of his T-shirt unrolled. He leaned and bellowed something back into the car, then slammed the door and stood clear. The Dodge's engine roared like Kong in his wrath, its tranny screamed like Fay Wray in despair, and it peeled away, backfiring as it went like Robert Armstrong hurling gas grenades, tires squealing like someone forced to sit through the De Laurentiis remake.

The lout threw me a wave—his other hand busy putting Walkman earbeads in his ears—then caught sight of Grtozkzhnyi. "Whoa," he said, frowning. "Bogus." He turned away and headed for the house.

Grtozkzhnyi turned to look at me. Now that the car was gone, the overall noise level was no lower; it was just monaural again, and the rhythmic discord was resolved. He opened his mouth to speak, then shook his head and gestured for me to join him in his Volvo.

Once we were inside with the doors closed, it wasn't any noisier than being in an overloaded 747 at takeoff. We both took a moment to savor it.

"Why are we here?" he asked finally, taking off his gloves.

"That," I said, pointing over my shoulder at the house, "is the home of Francis Xavier Maloney and his wife Olga. Frank is a sergeant in the state police, who moonlights as a drummer. His wife Olga runs the kennel. They have six children. You've already met the nice ones—that was Brian just now, and the one driving the car was Frank Junior."

"Why are we here?" Grtozkzhnyi repeated stolidly.

"Their landlady is evicting them."

He just looked at me. "No. Really?"

"She's been *trying* to evict them for more than a year. But Frank's been a trooper a long time, and Olga's family has owned a sizable chunk of the North Shore since the twenties. Between 'em they're so well connected it took the landlady a long time to find a judge willing to be bought, and a lawyer willing to be the bagman."

"But what has all this—*oh.*"

"As I told you on the phone, I'm planning to leave town, and I am looking for someone to sell Mary's Place to."

His eyes went dull with horror.

"And I thought maybe if you came along while I put the idea to Frank, you could fill him in, give him an unbiased assessment of the neighborhood, tell him what a swell place to live it is and so forth."

He began to curse in what I presume was Ukrainian.

"I was thinking of asking a hundred bucks for a down payment; does that sound high to you?"

He gestured with his hands, as if throttling an invisible throat. "You can't . . . I won't . . . you'll never . . . I'll . . ."

"You're a civil servant, Jorjhk," I said. "You have demonstrated to me that you have connections far and wide throughout the bureaucracy. You know more than I ever will about how the power structure works, the interlocking hierarchy of clout. If a state trooper with eighteen years on the job and five commendations and his old-money wife square off with a town inspector, who wins?"

He looked at me as if he were planning to paint me from memory at some later time.

"You know better than I ever will how many different licenses, permits, variances, and easements Olga must have to be able to run that kennel. Think about the lawyer who got them all for her."

He closed his eyes, put his hands in his lap, took several deep breaths, and regained control of himself. "What do you want?" he said without opening his eyes.

"Two dozen schoolbuses."

He opened and closed his mouth several times. I waited.

"Not new ones," he said finally.

I shook my head. "But roadworthy, inspected, with good paperwork. I'll want them at my place, gassed up, a week from today."

"Do I get them back?"

I shook my head. He looked unhappy, so I added, "Or us, either. And the Maloneys find their own place to live. And I sell Mary's Place, to you or your aunt or the town or whoever you like, for exactly what I paid for it a couple of years ago. Deal?"

"Hell," he said.

"A pleasure doing business with you," I said. "Say good-bye to your aunt for me, would you? I'm going to be busy packing, and I'll need my strength."

Did you know you can actually split the corners of your mouth from grinning too big? I arrived home with trickles of blood in my beard.

CHAPTER FOUR

Bus Bar

"I have made good judgments in the past. I have made good judgments in the future."
—J. Danforth Quayle

TESLA DISAPPEARED ON business of his own, promising to catch up with us after we reached Florida. Three weeks later, we were ready to roll.

Okay, I'm skipping over a lot of details. An *infinity* of details. And some of them were fascinating—at least to us, at least at the time. But I figure, how much do you really want to know about the practical details of converting a retired schoolbus into a moving van/Winnebago—on a budget, in snow season, mostly outdoors? Or the logistical processes of coordinating close to a hundred people who *all* tested out rather higher than usual in Rugged Individualism? Or the sheer brutal donkey labor of picking up a couple of dozen households in your hands and putting them on high platforms with the intention of taking them off and setting them down somewhere else later? Are these things you envision needing to know at some point in your life? Can't we just stipulate that miracles occurred and prodigies were performed, and let it go at that?

Perhaps some general outlines can be sketched. If a particular

task required technical or mechanical expertise, Shorty Steinitz and Dorothy Wu, our two resident master mechanics, generally handled it. If a breakthrough in lateral thinking was called for, most often it was Erin who took it on and solved it. If it involved broad-scale planning or people-managing skills, Tanya Latimer gravitated to it and found the right people to parcel it out to. If luck was required, we gave it to the Lucky Duck and forgot about it. If the job called for muscle, either Tanya's husband Isham or Jim Omar did it.

Omar had shown up the same day, in fact at the selfsame hour, that those two dozen remaindered buses were delivered to my parking lot. You couldn't help but notice a resemblance. Like the buses, Omar was big and solid and mostly bright yellow: lots of blond hair and beard sticking out of a long yellow fisherman's slicker, with white gloves suggesting headlights and boots roughly the color of tires. Also like most of the buses, he showed signs of impressive mileage. He too spent a lot of time out in the weather.

He arrived as I was in the middle of an argument with the delivery driver who had been least successful at denying being the man in charge. I was in the process of explaining to him that I required buses in good running order, which at least some of these manifestly were not, and he in turn was explaining that he didn't know shit about that and didn't give a rat's ass, that these was the buses they gave him, plus which they all had fresh valid state inspection stickers on them, and anyway they got here, didn't they? Gradually we both became aware of the presence of Omar, standing nearby at the starboard forequarter of one of the more suspect buses. He had broken out the bus's jack, and cranked its big tooth up to about four inches higher than the slot it was supposed to go into on the underside.

"Hey," the crew chief said, "don't mess with that, okay pal?"

Omar straightened from his work and smiled at him. "I just want to look at something."

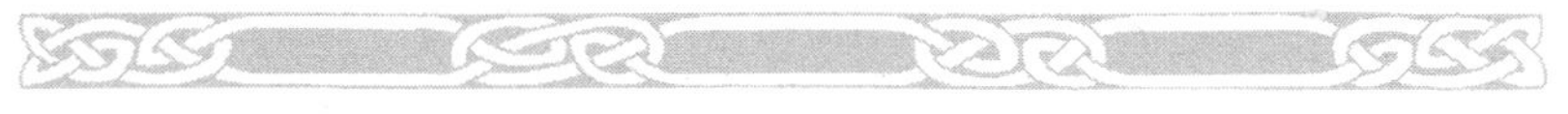

People almost always underestimate Jim Omar. He doesn't *look* like a Schwarzenegger, or even a Stallone. He's built about like a normal, reasonably fit human being . . . about eight percent *larger* than normal in all dimensions, but you tend not to notice that until he's up close. His face is quite pleasant, perhaps because he rarely needs to be anything else.

"As soon as Skinny here signs these papers, you can look at anything you want," the crew chief told him belligerently.

Omar nodded and turned back to the bus. He stood the jack up flush against the side of the bus . . . then crouched slightly, picked up the front end of the bus with his hands, kicked the jack an inch closer to it, and set the bus down on the tooth. The jack promptly sank three inches into the snow and the blacktop beneath it, leaving the wheel with an inch of clearance.

He saw us staring, and smiled pleasantly. "Quicker that way," he said, and turned back to his work. He popped the wheel cover off, with his fist, undogged the lugs with his fingers—two at a time; he had no trouble starting any of them—took the huge tire off, and held it at chest height without apparent effort while he turned it to inspect it. Then he set it down in the snow, and squatted and squinted into the exposed entrails of the bus. He poked at the widget, checked the play on the thingie, tugged experimentally on the whatchamacallit. Then he stood up and came over to join us.

"You should take this one back," he said politely to the crew chief.

You could see the guy become aware of the angle at which he had to hold his neck to look Omar in the eye. "Maybe so."

"Also that one there, and that one," Omar said, pointing to two other buses. "Otherwise somebody will lose his state inspection license. For openers; after that it gets ugly. You yourself could lose civil service, union status, end up a civilian. And not a popular one." His voice was soft, mild, inoffensive.

"Yes," the crew chief said.

"I'll put the wheel back on for you," Omar offered.

"Thank you," the crew chief said.

By the time Jim had dogged down the last two lugs machine-tight with his fingers, a small crowd of other delivery drivers had collected. A very quiet crowd. When he set his boot down on the plate of the jack to hold it, and lifted the bus up off it, setting the bus down on the ground so gently it didn't bounce even once, the crowd *transcended* quiet, and began to actually absorb sound. The three drivers who now had to drive their rejected buses back to wherever they'd come from obviously resented it—they'd expected to spend at least the last half of the job riding home in something *safe,* in one of the two vans with the rest of the boys—but none of them made any protest when their boss gave them their orders.

As one of them was about to board the bus Omar had just examined, Jim held up a hand to stop him. "With that front end," he said, "and those tires, I wouldn't take it over thirty-five." The man just nodded, and boarded the bus still nodding, and drove away still nodding. At thirty.

"The three replacements will be here this time tomorrow¿" Omar asked the chief.

He opened his mouth, left it open for a while, then nodded himself, once. He got into the nearest van of drivers without another word. It pulled away at once, spraying snow, and the other van wasn't slow in following it. As I watched them both make the right out onto 25A, I realized that at least the bus invasion had managed to finally clean out my damn driveway.

All the mahouts were gone now, leaving my parking lot extremely full of twenty-one shabby yellow elephants, steaming and ticking in the cold air. Omar's black pickup truck was visible at the outskirts of the herd, like a shepherd dog keeping them all penned up. He and I stood side by side, regarding the peaceful scene together, enjoying the silence.

"Hi, Jake," he said after a while.

"Thanks, Jim."

He bent and got a handful of slush, used it to wipe his hands clean of tire grease. "I hate long arguments."

"Welcome back to the States. What do you say we go in and get some Irish coffee in us and tell fibs?"

"We'd be fools not to. Let me get my gear and I'll join you inside."

"Need a hand?" I asked, and he smiled.

Over drinks, after the obligatory small talk with Zoey and Erin, he told me a little about his grant. "It's not much—but it's a start. At *last*. It'll allow me to begin systematizing the project, a little bit, anyway. Set up a facility, get a database started, maybe even hire a couple of field agents for a year or so. I've decided to start with writers."

I nodded. "Musicians after that, maybe."

"That was my thinking. Then if I get renewed next year, dancer/choreographers and so on from there."

"What is this project, Uncle Omar?" Erin asked. (She had decided, on what basis I cannot tell you, that "Uncle Omar" somehow sounded more right than "Uncle Jim.") "I asked Daddy about it, but he made a joke I didn't understand and changed the subject."

"Well," he said, "I've always believed I have a shot at living forever. I think we're going to lick immortality one of these days, and I think some of the first immortals are already alive now."

"Sure," she said.

"Well, last year Robert A. Heinlein died . . . and ever since, I feel just a little bit less like living forever. If there isn't going to be a new Heinlein novel coming out every year or two . . . well, it just isn't going to be the same, is it?"

She shook her head no. So did her mother and I.

"So okay, he's gone and we can't have him back. But what if we could have a little *piece* of him back? What if we could clone him, one day?"

"How?"

"Salvage his DNA. Before it's too late."

Erin's mouth dropped open. I was expecting it, and caught most of the drool in the barf-scarf I had ready. "You mrrm—*Daddy!*—you mean you want to dig him up and take a DNA sample?"

He shook his head. "Too complicated, and I wouldn't want to upset his widow. Besides, she had him cremated. Scattered his ashes on the water with full military honors."

"Then *how?*"

"Several ways. Let me give you a for-instance. Mr. Heinlein was a writer. That means he was a reader. You probably haven't noticed yet, at your age, but it's just about impossible for a grown-up to read a book without shedding hairs into it, even if they're careful."

"Oh, my God," Erin said. "I thought it was just Daddy."

"No, honey—even people with a normal amount of hair and no beard at all do it. Likewise dandruff and assorted kinds of skin flakes. A lot of people lick their fingers before they turn a page. Occasionally, other fluids get rubbed off on the paper, too. Some readers have the bad habit of using the corners of several pages at once to clean their fingernails, which are always full of dead skin cells. You'd be amazed how long you can keep a cell from deteriorating, if it's sealed up in a book. Especially one printed on acid-free paper—like serious readers own. If you have a man's books, the ones he actually *read*, you have his DNA."

Zoey gave me her cup to refill, and took over the job of keeping Erin's chin dry. "So you want to go around to the widows and widowers of great writers," she said, "and ask if you can vacuum out their late loved one's books . . . so you can re-create them out of their dandruff flakes?"

Omar beamed and nodded.

Erin had that happy-baby grin that makes her look like an advertisement. "You still have a couple of big steps to go," she said. "From DNA to stem cells, from zygote to embryo, then from infant to an adult weird enough to want to write books."

"Sure," he agreed, absolutely unfazed that a fourteen-month-

old might know such things. Some folks can take in stride the fact that Erin is able to talk articulately . . . and still unconsciously expect her to be as ignorant as most people her size. "And it's possible some or all of those problems will never be solved—not even in my anticipated long lifetime. But meanwhile, just *in case* they get solved, the important thing is to start preserving the database, before it's too late. That part can't wait. Hell, it's probably already too late to save Frank Herbert, and I'll have to move fast to get Theodore Sturgeon."

"What did you do before you got this grant, Uncle Omar?"

He shrugged. "Basically the same thing. Except not for people. For the last twenty years I've been wandering around the planet trying to establish a genetic library for as many endangered or extinct species of plants and animals as I could. All that's changed now is, I've expanded the definition of plants and animals to include writers."

"Fair description of some of them," I said, just to be saying something.

"How does it work, Uncle Omar? How do you do it?"

He shrugged again. "Go to some remote corner of the earth where a lot of species are circling the drain. Jungle up and get to know them. Collect DNA. When I either have all there is to get there, or get really homesick for indoor plumbing, I come back to the States and spend some time cataloguing and arranging for preservation and so on. Then when I get sick of civilization I find a new remote corner of the earth."

"Wow. What a great job. Working for whom?"

He smiled. "For me. Freelance."

More drool to be mopped up. "How did you pay for it, all these years?"

He spread his hands. "Scuffled. Hustled. Once in a long while, a small grant or stipend from someplace. Not much, not often. Aren't many funding agencies that consider the biodiversity of Gaia to be part of their mandate. And the job can't be done without stepping on political toes . . . which is better done by a pri-

vate individual with no affiliations and no fixed address. I can slip in under the radar."

"A guerrilla, you mean," Erin said.

He nodded. "Sort of," he said. "Except a basically nonviolent type. You know those Greenpeace guys, call themselves 'eco-warriors'? I'm kind of an eco-medic."

"Is it fun?"

His smile was a beautiful thing to see. "Yes, Erin. It is."

I put my oar in. "Let me get this straight," I said. "For twenty years hardly anyone would fund you to try and preserve thousands of vanishing species . . . and now you got a fat grant to try and preserve a handful of dead writers?"

He nodded. "Ain't humans a pisser?"

I shook my head at the wonder of it, gave Erin her bib, and went to The Machine to draw myself another Irish coffee. "If there is a God, I know why He hasn't been answering His phone lately: He's helpless with laughter."

"Look, Jim," Zoey said, "now that you've got this grant, can you really take time off to help a bunch of loonies move to Florida? We really appreciate the help, but what you're doing is *important.*"

"Oh, sure," he said. "No sweat. It's not even out of my way: the cold-storage site where I have my DNA library stashed is down in the Keys. Besides, one of the first targets on my acquisition list is John D. MacDonald. Plus Mrs. Heinlein lives down that way now."

The empty mug I had set on the conveyor belt emerged from the far side of The Machine filled with Kenya AA and Old Bushmill's and snowcapped with whipped cream. The aroma was angelic. Jim caught my eye and made a hand signal; I nodded and put a second mug on the belt for him.

"Wait a minute," Zoey said. "I heard you were down in Central America, this last trip."

"That's right," he agreed. "Belize."

"So if your facility is in Florida, how come you overshot so

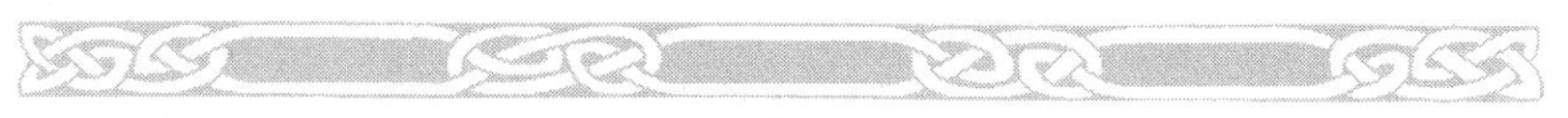

far? What brings you this far north, in winter? Just homesick for where you used to live?"

He laughed out loud as I set his Irish coffee in front of him. "Nostalgia for *Long Island*?"

"Then what?"

He looked up at me. "Word reached me down there that Mary's Place had closed."

I stared at him. "You never set foot in Mary's Place in your life."

He nodded. "Exactly. Always meant to; put it off. Wanted to see if there was anything I could do about that."

"Jesus." I shook my head wonderingly. "Of course. It's your thing. Preserving endangered species."

"That's part of it, maybe," he said, and took his first sip of coffee.

"What's the rest?" Erin asked.

He wiped whipped cream from his upper lip, gestured with his coffee mug, and said, "This is it right here, Erin."

"I don't get it. You came to Long Island for the coffee?"

He looked up at me again. "Jake, how long has it been since the last time we saw each other?"

The calculation took some time. "I make it three years and ten months."

He gestured with the mug again. "This," he said with the certainty of an expert, "contains Ethiopian Harrar and Tullamore Dew with double cream, a dash of nutmeg, and no sugar."

"Well, sure," I said. "You still like it that way, I hope."

He turned to Erin. "You see what I mean? He remembers my prescription. He hasn't laid eyes on me in almost four years, and he remembers how I take my coffee. I know he's got something different in his own mug, but for the life of me I can't remember what *he* likes, except that the whiskey will be Bushmill's. I can't remember how my *sister* takes her coffee, for Christ's sake." He turned back to me again. "When a friend like you needs help, Jacob, I'd come from a lot farther away than Belize."

What a fine thing to have somebody say in front of your wife and daughter. If I really deserve the friends I've got, I must be one hell of a fellow.

A little while after that, people of mechanical inclination began showing up, and when there seemed to be enough of us and we seemed to be sufficiently fortified with antifreeze, we all went outside together and began giving those buses a fairly close inspection. After an hour of that, we spent time going around to everybody's ride and inspecting the tools and materials they had fetched, and then there was an extended conference in the bar, most of which I missed through being busy constructing a makeshift toolshed outside in the parking lot with Omar and Shorty Steinitz. (Nails being about the only things on earth Shorty isn't terrible at driving.)

Shortly before midnight, consensus was reached. The job could be done. Guesstimated time, two weeks. Guesstimated budget, within parameters. Doc Webster being known to be a night owl, we placed a speakerphone call to him, and told him to expect us all in a month or so. I will not reproduce the conversation, as most of the puns were substandard—the Doc was just too happy to do his best work. He agreed to alert his real estate broker friend and apprise him of our needs: a property suitable for a discreet nontourist tavern, and temporary accommodations for about two dozen house hunters and their families, who would be arriving in a posse. We broke up in high spirits, and the next day we went to work.

Thank God I had spent the week we waited for the buses to show up in dismantling and packing most of my own household and bar. Not only was there no longer any time to do so—we needed the room! For cots and sleeping bags, to accommodate the ever-changing cast of those who were working too hard to drive back home again every night—and, during the day, as a makeshift day-care center for the kids and grandkids of those outside working on buses.

It was a very busy and very happy couple of weeks. Like I said, I'll skip over the, uh, nuts and bolts details . . . except that I must state for the record we would never have met either our deadline or our budget without Shorty Steinitz. Not to disparage the efforts or skills of Dorothy, who was also invaluable—but Shorty had special qualifications that proved crucial for our unique circumstances.

Maybe it seems paradoxical that the man generally acknowledged as the world's worst driver made his living restoring classic cars. Well, gunsmiths aren't necessarily crack shots, and some luthiers can't play an E minor chord. Shorty had carved himself out a fairly unique niche market: he would undertake to restore any automobile whatsoever to absolute mint condition . . . as long as it was at least thirty years old. All parts guaranteed authentic and chronistic: if you brought him a '57 Thunderbird with a broken headlight, Shorty would refund your money before he'd try and fob off a '58 T-bird lamp on you. He charged a medium-sized fortune, of course—but the 1980s were heavily populated with people who had more money than they knew what to do with: Shorty had all the work he could handle and a long waiting list. He claimed he was into it for political and artistic reasons, saying there could be no more socially subversive act than selling something utterly useless and horrifyingly expensive to a capitalist oppressor. I think he just liked the gig. And doubtless the money.

Anyway, the point is that his experience in restoring old clunkers, and his encyclopedic knowledge of sources for obsolete parts, came in more than handy in refurbishing all those creaky old schoolbuses. Even though they were a little out of his usual line, most of them were at least of a vintage Shorty was familiar with, and he enjoyed the creative freedom of being allowed to fudge and improvise a little for a change.

Three weeks later, each of those antique buses had been brought fully up to Shorty's and Dorothy's standards with regard

to roadworthiness, gas mileage, and emissions cleanliness. And each had been fundamentally reconfigured within, so that its interior was now roughly sixty-six percent cargo space and thirty-four percent passenger space/living quarters—with variations to fit individual family units or other groups. Each had, at minimum, heat, running potable water, a stove of some sort, and some sort of sanitary provisions. No two were alike; we scrounged parts from *everywhere*. My personal bus, for instance, had a surplus Greyhound toilet (with a smaller holding tank) and a microwave oven wired into the electrical system, whereas Shorty managed to fit a standard Winnebago plumbing system and stove into his, and Jim Omar, with characteristic quirkiness, built a wood-burning cookstove and a genuine antique water closet complete with pull chain into his own vehicle. (His ignition was literally a switch: a big old knife-switch like the one Frankenstein's monster throws to blow up the laboratory, sticking up out of the dashboard. He said he hated carrying keys. At one point on the trip, at a rest stop in Virginia, he and I would watch a young wannabe bus thief spend five solid minutes looking for the place where the key went, before we chased him off.)

One thing that kept me awake nights for a while was the problem of what the hell to do with all the *seats*. In converting those big yellow kid-haulers to big yellow cargo-haulers, we naturally had to rip out one whack of a lot of seats . . . and it turns out that the damned things don't stack neatly, and after a while there was an almighty huge heap of them. I was perfectly prepared to leave them for Grtozkzhnyi, let *him* figure out what to do with them once we were gone—but it got to the point where they were taking up so much space in the parking lot, there was scarcely room for people to park.

Then one morning Zoey let out a whoop while reading *Newsday* over her breakfast coffee. She had found an article about how the county was considering whether or not it could afford to replace several hundred park benches in county parks. She started working the phone, and by dusk of the following day

we were as seatless as Cher. You remember those plastic school-bus seats, don't you? Leave one out in the weather for a hundred years, it won't need replacing.

How did we keep track of who put in how much money, who contributed how much labor, who deserved how much cubic footage for his goods?

We didn't. It seemed too much like work. Of which we had no shortage.

Instead, we used basically the same scheme we've always used for bar-change. We just trusted each other.

See, back in the original Callahan's Place, Mike Callahan had a flat rate: every drink in the house cost a dollar—and if for some reason you decided *not* to smash your emptied glass in the fireplace, you were entitled to take two quarters' change out of the cigarbox on the end of the bar on your way out. The prices will give you an idea of how long ago this was. When I opened up Mary's Place after Callahan's closed (well, actually it didn't exactly close—what it did was more *open* a little too emphatically . . . owing to the detonation of a small nuclear weapon within its walls), the cigarbox was one of Mike's many traditions that I carried on—although naturally I had to raise the prices, to three bucks a drink, a dollar back if you returned your empty glass. Both Callahan and I made it a point never to pay the slightest attention to who took how much out of the cigarbox. We noticed its existence only when someone pointed out to us that it needed refilling . . . which didn't happen often. Mike said if he couldn't trust his customers, he didn't much want to tend bar, and I've always felt the same way.

If you're already accustomed to trusting your friends with small change, it's not much of a leap to serious bucks. A cigarbox wouldn't have served, in this instance, so Long-Drink solved the problem by bringing in a packing crate that had been used to ship boxes of cigars. He set it just inside the door and hung a sign on it that read "THE KITTY," and I tossed in a few hundred bucks to salt the mine, and after that we basically forgot it. If folks needed cash for materials or supplies, they took what they figured they'd need and came back with any change; if folks had cash to contribute to the caravan, they tossed it into the crate. Records of who put in how much do not exist—at least not with me, though I imagine most folks reported to the IRS eventually. But if I wanted to for some reason, I think I could probably guess pretty close. I already *know* which of my friends are how affluent and how generous; I don't need figures to tell me.

Neither did anyone else. Astonishing as it may seem for an enterprise involving human beings, there were *no* squabbles about money. To each according to his/her needs; from each according to his/her abilities, was our guiding principle. We had more important things to think about.

Hundreds of them. No, hundreds of thousands. *Everybody* had Special Circumstances. Kids (or grandkids or in some cases great-grandkids), or pets, or disabilities, or unique cargo requirements of some sort. Bill Gerrity, for example, owns a macaw. That affects interior vehicle layout more than you might imagine: your average macaw could easily chew his way out of a mahogany box, and for some reason they find steering wheels irresistibly attractive perching-places—not ideal when you're pushing several tons down the highway. Then there were the Masers. You would expect a household consisting of one husband and two wives to have unusual travel requirements—but what none of us had fully grasped after more than thirty years of drinking with Joe and Susie and Suzie was that between them they had *fourteen cats*. Tommy Janssen had gotten so heavily into computers lately that his bus needed special wiring and power supply. And so forth.

This was not something as simple as, say, planning the Normandy Invasion . . . unless you can picture a Normandy Invasion carried out by the inmates of a particularly easygoing asylum. Rugged we were not, necessarily, but we sure were individual.

Fortunately, we had Tanya Latimer.

How can I convey to you just how organized Tanya is?

Ah, got it. I stayed with her and Isham once, while my own place was being painted. Every Sunday she sat down and decided what she was going to cook for the following week, and made an exhaustive list—in Braille!—of all the necessary ingredients she lacked. Then she rewrote the entire list. In the order in which the required items appeared on the shelves of her local supermarket, so that she could start at one end of the store and shop straight through to the other without ever needing to double back.

You will appreciate that this required memorizing the entire inventory of the supermarket—something the manager probably could not have done. The week I was there, she ended up with *two* lists, because the store she usually gave most of her business carried a poor line of Mexican food, and she knew I liked that stuff. You guessed it: she had the other store's layout memorized too. There were people who knew her only as a fellow shopper at the market who had no idea she was blind.

If the Chinese had Tanya, they wouldn't *need* fire drills. With her help, the jillion impossible things we had to accomplish all got done somehow.

What I'm not sure I can explain to you is why they were *fun*.

Work sucks, right? Everybody knows that. *Hard* work *really* sucks. Endless backbreaking labor interspersed with countless impossible decisions must therefore logically suck The Big Hairy Pockmarked One. QED.

Well, maybe there's something wrong with the premise. All I can tell you is that hard, even backbreaking *shared* labor, labor toward a common goal earnestly desired, does not suck. At least, it didn't for us.

It was, in fact, some of the most fun I ever had out of bed.

CHAPTER FIVE

Drunkard's Drive

"If we don't succeed, we run the risk of failure."
—J. Danforth Quayle

FORTUNATELY, WE FINished before it killed us.

In spite of everything, there came a crisp morning in early March when Mary's Place itself was a hollow shell, the box a bar used to come in, and the parking lot outside was full to the brim with grumbling farting schoolbuses, all of them, in Theodore Sturgeon's memorable phrase, "packed to the consistency of a rubber brick" with everything we owned. Even at idle, that many engines made an impressive rumble. Amongst them, like pilot fish at a convention of yellow sharks, were occasional smaller vehicles: the cars and trucks and motorcycles of those of us so hopelessly addicted to internal combustion that they wanted to own a car even in Key West. Most of those lesser vehicles were shut off at the moment, since they'd already warmed up on the way over here.

Except for a few folks wandering hither and yon on last-minute errands, most of us had gathered by the doorway to-

gether. There was no conversation. We admired our caravan together in silence, thinking of what lay behind us, and what lay ahead.

Finally I turned to my Dortmunder.

"All right, Tanya," I said. "Let me have it."

She obligingly punched me in the stomach.

"No, no, dammit! The route!"

I pronounced it unfortunately, and she began to aim a second punch a bit lower.

"The route!" I repeated hastily, this time pronouncing it like the rout this conversation was becoming.

"Oh. Sorry, Jake. What route?"

I stared at her. "The route we'll be taking to Key West. Knowing you, I presume you have it all planned out day to day, with mileage estimates and fallback plans and projected gas consumption."

She smiled. "I planned a route suitable to this particular group of people, Jake. There is no route."

Several people laughed.

I blanched slightly. "You mean, we're faking it?"

"Jake, we'd be faking it even if I spent a month nailing down the itinerary. Be realistic."

"Is that absolutely necessary?"

"Look at this group of loonies." She gestured around for emphasis. "I can organize them all fine, individually, give them each a plan and more or less get them to stick to it. But get *all* of them to stick to the *same* plan? For days at a time?" She laughed. "I guarantee you, every state we pass through, somebody's gonna want to stop and gawk at some tourist attraction they always wanted to see, or visit some relative they haven't seen in years and are a little vague on how to locate precisely." There were rumbles of agreement. "There'll be flat tires, engine trouble, mechanical trouble, medical trouble, more than likely some cop trouble, and for sure there'll be just plain road fatigue—no way to predict *any* of it. Might as well face it, Jake: this is going to be a Drunkard's Walk—only on wheels."

I had to admit she was right. The only way to keep a convoy this size together—and I knew we all wanted to make the trip together—was to stay loose and be constantly prepared to improvise. But as Road Chief, I was a little dismayed. "Can you give me a hint, at least? For instance . . . do we want highway, do you think, or back roads where we can get 'em? Efficient trip, or scenic route?"

She shrugged. "Play it by ear. Literally. Everybody's got a CB aboard; I suggest you do whatever the hell you feel like, and if enough people don't like it, you'll hear about it."

She was sure right about that.

I sighed and bit the bullet. "Okay," I said. "We fake it."

I looked around for somebody to give the signal to board, and slowly realized that everybody else was looking at *me*.

"You want to say a few words, Jake?" Long-Drink asked.

"Uh—"

How could I possibly have failed to anticipate this moment? I'll say *too busy*, and you go with *too dumb* if you prefer. This was a Big Moment, a pivotal point in the lives of all of us. Something obviously had to be said. I obviously was elected. I hastily ransacked my brain for the right words . . . and realized that I could probably have spent the previous three weeks doing nothing else, and still not have found them. There was too much to say, and some of the words hadn't been coined yet. I looked around at all my friends and their families, and felt my eyes begin to sting. Then I saw others starting to cry outright. It made me smile, and the moment I did, my own tears spilled over.

Fast Eddie, of all people, spoke up. "Dis was a great place," he said. "Ya done good, Jake."

There was a strong rumble of agreement. I found that I had Zoey's hand in mine, and squeezed *hard*. She squeezed back.

"I love all of you, too," I said, and paused until I could speak again. They waited.

"Look," I said then, "we didn't get all weepy and sentimental when Callahan's Place blew up. We picked ourselves up and kept going. Now we're doing it again. Only difference is, this place didn't end with a bang. Well, I'm tired of whimpering. Let's go find ourselves an even better place. We got a universe to save."

A cheer went up.

"Let's have fun doing it, too," I added, and the cheering got even louder.

Long-Drink McGonnigle gestured for attention. "I got something I want to say before we go," he said. "Would those of you with impressionable children please cover their ears?"

He waited until this was done. Then he paused a moment for effect, took a deep breath, tilted back his head, and bellowed to the skies, *"Fuck Long Island!"*

"FUCK LONG ISLAND!" we chorused automatically, loud enough to make the world echo, and dissolved into laughter and cheers.

I raised one arm high. "All right, people," I cried, "mount up!"

And suddenly we were all in motion at once. Omar picked up a big sawhorse under one arm and trotted it out to 25A to block traffic for our departure. Zoey stuck the key in the front door, left it there, and headed for our bus, carrying Erin. I thought about taking one last look around, decided that what I was already looking at was more rewarding, and followed them both.

Ralph von Wau Wau had elected to ride with us, at least for today. I let him go first up the stairs into the bus; dogs are lousy at climbing stairs. I followed him, and opened the window beside his seat for him so he could ride the way he likes to: the way *most* German shepherds like to ride. "Sank you, Jake," he said, and stuck his head out the window, his tail already beginning to wag.

Zoey kissed me soundly before she'd let me sit down in the driver's seat. Then she strapped Erin into the special seat we had rigged up for her right beside me, where she could see everything. I reached past her and pulled the lever that shut the door.

The bus seemed eager to be going. Once Zoey had strapped herself into her own seat just behind Erin, I picked up the CB mike. We had all agreed on two channels, one for casual chatter and one for important traffic; I selected the latter. "Anybody got a problem?"

Silence.

"Okay then. Wagons, ho!" I put her in gear and gave it the gun, threaded my way through the maze and out to the highway, turned right on 25A, keeping it slow.

Nyjmnckra Grtozkzhnyi, my Nemesis, was standing by the roadside in front of her place as we rolled slowly past. Bundled up in an overcoat and babushka, she looked like some sort of squat evil prehistoric toad-god out of H. P. Lovecraft. She had clearly come out to gloat at our departure. It was the first time I had ever seen her smile. She was the only person I've ever seen whom a smile made uglier—and you have to understand, until I saw it I'd have said the trick was impossible. The sight disturbed me—and not just aesthetically: it was an ill omen for our journey. Not that I believe in omens. No sir. Nonetheless I stepped on the accelerator, wanting to be past her as quickly as possible.

But that bus was *loaded;* it took a while to answer the helm. There was plenty of time for little Erin to notice her, wave to attract her attention . . . and then carefully and deliberately give her the finger.

Nyjmnckra Grtozkzhnyi fainted dead away: threw her arms in the air and fell over backward and made an angel in the snow.

We were almost to the Expressway by the time Zoey and Ralph and I managed to stop laughing, and chuckles continued to come out of the CB for some time to come.

The trip started off kind of dull. Familiar roads, not much to look at outside that we hadn't all seen before. Two dozen schoolbuses traveling in a pack through New York City during school

hours attracted absolutely no attention whatsoever. No reason to pay any attention to us; none of us were spraying gunfire.

Without discussion, my family and I slipped into the pattern we would tend to follow all the way down the coast: me driving, Zoey navigating, and Erin dividing her time between gawking out the window, physical exercise of one kind or another, and trolling around the Internet with the souped-up laptop she had built with Tesla's help. (If you boggle at the phoneless net-surfing capabilities and high download speed of Erin's laptop in 1989, all I can tell you is, Tesla assured me there was no miscegemation involved, that not one piece of gear in that rig was a technological anachronism . . . though they might have been hooked up together in ways nobody else had quite thought of doing yet in 1989.)

All too soon we were in New Jersey, remembering the dullness of New York with nostalgic fondness. Erin had been chattering when we crossed the state line, but the sight of the Jersey Turnpike reduced her to silence. After a few miles of it, she said, "This is New Jersey¿"

"That's right, hon," Zoey said.

Erin shook her head. "God, I hate to think what *Old* Jersey must look like."

A few miles farther down the 'Pike, the CB speaker crackled and Jim Omar's voice said, "Smoky on the back door, Jake, gumball lit."

"Copy," I said, and swallowed something I happened to have in my mouth, and opened my window a little farther to air the bus out. So did Zoey. "Prepare for boarders, everybody." I didn't have to check, I knew I was doing precisely the speed we'd all agreed on in advance: a safe, rational five miles an hour over the posted limit. I eased on back until I was doing exactly the limit, glanced in my sideview, and soon saw the spinning flashers of a state police cruiser coming up fast on my left. A few seconds later the sound of the siren reached me.

I was not even faintly surprised. I had been expecting this to happen—and to happen just about now, too. As part of my research for the trip, I had dug out and reread Stephen Gaskin's wonderful old sixties memoir, HEY BEATNIK! It's the story of the longest-lasting hippie commune in American history (The Farm still exists *today*, albeit much changed)—and it begins with Stephen's account of the giant bus caravan that brought them all, hundreds of hairy freaks, to Tennessee from California. An important point he raises is that there exists a phenomenon he calls "cop teletype": an informal and mostly unofficial network by which state highway patrols exchange information with one another. Any kind of serious weirdness moving on the interstate highway system is just naturally going to be logged and passed along down the line—and a convoy of two dozen converted buses, containing people *not one* of whom is wearing a necktie or pantyhose, definitely fits the cop definition of serious weirdness. I had foreseen that we would probably show up on the radar the moment we left New York City (where *nothing* is considered seriously weird by the cops), and sure enough, here was our first ping. This encounter, Stephen's memoir suggested, would be crucial. Much, if not everything, depended on it going well.

The copmobile passed the whole convoy, came up alongside me, and matched speeds. I glanced over and down, and as I expected, the trooper in the shotgun seat gave me a hard look and the *pull over* sign.

I glanced away for a quick assessment of the situation. The shoulder here was really not wide enough to accommodate a schoolbus—two dozen of them in a row plus ancillary vehicles would be a major road hazard. Traffic was moderately heavy. We were just at that moment coming up on a road sign that read "REST AREA 1 MILE AHEAD." I could just make out the exit for it on the horizon ahead. "Get ready to stop, folks," I said into the CB mike. I turned back to the cop, pointed to the road sign, and pantomimed that we would all pull in at the rest stop.

Maybe he didn't have time to see the sign before it flashed past, didn't realize where he was on the road. Maybe he just hated mimes. Instead of nodding and telling his partner to pull in in front of me, like a reasonable person, he stuck a handgun out the window, cocked it, drew a dead bead on my face, and repeated his *pull over* gesture with emphasis.

I raised my hands in surrender, nodded as pacifically as I could, said, "*Heads up*, people—we're stopping *now*," into the CB mike, and took my foot off the gas; the heavy-laden monster began to slow at once. I eased over onto the shoulder, and the copmobile pulled in ahead of me. Way ahead: the driver, at least, was sensible enough to realize that I could not decelerate any quicker than whichever bus behind me happened to have the worst brakes, and gave me plenty of room.

Eventually we were all at rest. My bus was sticking out at least a foot into the road, and nobody else was any better off. The CB was full of indignant questions, complaints, and sulfurous curses. Braying car horns dopplered past. Zoey unstrapped and checked on Erin, cursing loudly herself. Ralph was in the doorwell, barking his own curses: he had slipped off his seat and slid under Zoey's into the well. I put the mike to my mouth and brayed, "SHADDAP."

Silence fell, in my bus and on CB, except for the continuous dopplering sound of horns from drivers whizzing past us.

"Is anybody hurt?" I asked. "Any injuries? Report!"

Nothing. Zoey signed that Erin was fine. Ralph growled, but softly, came up the stairs and went back to his seat.

"Okay. Everybody stay inside, sit tight, and stand by," I said, and hung up the mike.

This was not going as well as I'd hoped.

The cop car was about fifty yards ahead. The cop with the gun got out, holstered it with a flourish, and came toward me, doing Eastwood. The driver stayed behind the wheel; I was too

high up to see him, but through my open window I could faintly hear him pumping up a shotgun. His partner came around to my door—there was *just* room for him to stand between the bus and the ditch—and gestured. I cranked open the door.

"A fuckin' hippie," he said under his breath.

He was young, mean, and stupid. His face and body language and the meticulous perfection of his haircut and shave and uniform all loudly proclaimed the message *I am a hard-on, and would be very happy to prove it.* A quarter of a century of history melted away; suddenly it was the Sixties again. I was a hippie in a bus; he was a cop. Natural enemies.

"Good afternoon, Officer," I said politely.

"Step out of the vehicle please, *sir,*" he said, doing his best to make a fighting word out of the "sir."

I failed to notice. "Certainly." I unbelted, being careful how I moved my hands, and dismounted.

It really felt like being in a time-warp. The actual cops I had known back in the Sixties, those that weren't already retired, were probably wearing mustaches and hair as long as mine by now, and had nearly forgotten how much they used to hate longhairs. But pendulums do keep swinging, and this twenty-something throwback might have just stepped into Bryant Park, looking for fun. I could feel hairs standing up on the back of my neck. "Please take your operator's license out of your wallet and hand it to me, sir," he said.

"I don't have a wallet," I said.

He frowned. "You don't have a wallet?"

"Nope."

"Where the hell do you keep your credit cards?"

I sighed. "I don't have any of those, either."

Now he really scowled. I had confirmed his darkest suspicions. Hell, *drug dealers* had credit cards. I was not a normal human being, not a card-carrying citizen, not a decent respectable member of polite society.

Well, what could I say? He was right.

"Do you have an operator's license, sir?"

"Yes, I do."

"Please hand it to me, sir."

I took it out of my shirt pocket and handed it over. He backed off a pace or two, keeping one hand on his gun butt—a Glock 9mm—and studied the license. "You're Jacob Stonebender?"

"That's right."

"And this is your address?"

I sighed again. "Not since nine o'clock this morning."

He looked at me. "This is not your address?"

"Not anymore," I repeated.

"What is your current address, sir?"

"I don't have one yet. We're moving."

He scowled even harder. Not only was I not a card-carrying citizen, I was homeless. An Okie. He tucked my license into his shirt pocket, touched his shoulder mike, and recited the information he had so far to his partner in the cruiser.

I was getting more depressed by the minute. This was not going well at all. Soon, inevitably, he would want to search the bus . . . and then *all* the buses. Even if everybody else had hidden their stash as well as I had, by the time he was done making a nuisance of himself, there would, inevitably, be at least one fender bender: someone racing by would either clip one of the buses, or clip somebody to the left of him in avoiding one, or slow down to gawk and initiate a chain pileup. An inauspicious beginning for our journey. Furthermore, it was *freezing* out . . . and I was dressed for comfortable driving in an unusually well-heated bus, with no more than a sweater to keep off the chill.

"Hey, Jake," Ralph von Wau Wau said from above me, "Zoey vants to know if you vant your chacket."

The cop glanced up automatically, did a double-take, then made it a triple-take.

"Yeah, thanks, Ralph," I said.

"Gluffs, too?" asked the German shepherd.

"Sure," I said.

He ducked back inside for a moment, came back out with my pea coat in his teeth, and let it go with a flick of his head. I caught it and put it on. Throughout all this the cop was as motionless as if he had frozen solid, staring fixedly at Ralph.

"Goot day, Officer," Ralph said politely.

The cop made no reply.

To my left, Erin appeared in the open doorway at the foot of the stairs. "Don't forget your hat, Daddy," she said, and tossed my watch cap to me. I caught that too and put it on.

The cop tore his eyes away from Ralph with a visible effort, glanced at Erin . . . and stared at her just as hard.

"Good afternoon, Officer," she said. "Is this going to take long? If it will be a while, I really ought to shut the engine off and save gas. And pass the word back up the line by CB, so all the others can do the same."

The cop's left eye began visibly to tic. His hand on his gun butt began to tremble slightly. Other than that, he might have been carved from stone. You know the expression, *you could see the wheels turning?* Well, in his eyes you could see the wheels *trying* to turn—and burning out their bearings instead.

"Vould you mind iff I step out of ze vehicle too, Officer?" Ralph asked. "Ve haff sanitary facilities aboard, of course—but I haff never cared for litter boxes."

His voice drew the cop's eyes back to him.

"I assure you, I vill be discreet," Ralph told him.

Somewhere in the cop's head, a relay clicked over. *What to do when you're in over your head.* He put his free hand to his shoulder mike and said, "Marty, come here."

I was close enough to hear his partner's instant reply, though I couldn't tell you if it came from an external speaker or an overloud earphone. "Trouble, Joe?"

Joe took a deep breath. "Marty," he said, "that's not a simple question."

"It isn't?" Pause. "On my way."

He was as good as his word. I heard the cruiser's door open,

and a few seconds later he came into view around the fender with a shotgun at port arms, an older cop with a lot more miles on him than Joe had. Marty looked as if he might well have served through the Sixties—and had been thinking about it ever since. "What's the situation?" he asked his partner.

"I want to search every one of these goddam buses," Joe said. "These mopes are *wrong*."

"We have no problem with that, Officer Joe," Erin said. "But wouldn't it make more sense to do it at that rest stop just ahead?"

"Zat vouldt zertainly be more pragtical for efferyvun," Ralph agreed, laying the accent on even thicker than usual.

Marty looked at both of them, then at me.

"They're right," I said.

"You see what I mean?" Joe said. "It ain't a simple question."

Marty nodded. "I see what you mean."

"Look, fellas," I said, "I'm trying to be cooperative, but I'm getting goose bumps, and traffic's starting to back up. Could we hurry this along? How about if you go ahead and search my bus—and then after you come up empty, you let the rest of us pull up ahead to the oh *shit*."

Joe had been drifting over toward the door, probably to do just as I was suggesting—but suddenly he stopped in his tracks. I could see his nostrils flare, hear him sniff, imagine what he smelled in my bus, and feel my heart sinking. He was *exactly* the sort of young policeman who would have a hypersensitive nose for pot, and genuinely believe it to be a dangerous narcotic. I should have waited until *after* this known-to-be-inevitable confrontation to light up . . . but had foolishly allowed the ugliness of the New Jersey Turnpike to overwhelm my judgment. Bad mistake.

Sure enough, a second later he had me up against the side of the bus, a palm on my chest holding me in place, his Glock out and pointing at my face. "That's it!" he roared. "Everybody off the fuckin' bus, *now*."

For what happened next I accept full responsibility. I'd been suppressing annoyance ever since he'd first pointed that thing at me back out on the highway. My job as Road Chief was to stay cool under provocation. But now my irritation blossomed into anger. Perhaps I was politically offended by his assumption that pot smokers are presumptively armed and dangerous. Perhaps I was just an insulted ape. In any case, I did something stupid.

I reached out and poked my middle finger into the barrel of his Glock.

It was a snug fit. He tried to pull clear, and failed. "Get that finger out of there," he snarled, "or I'll blow it off!"

"I doubt it," I said.

"NO!" Marty cried.

Joe was young, and even stupider than anger had made me. He growled and pulled the trigger. The gun burst with a loud bang, and dropped to the ground. Joe yelped and lurched away from me, holding his wrist and gaping down at his gun hand. The thumb stuck out at an unnatural angle.

His staggering took him to the open door of my bus. Erin reached out a hand from the bottom step, caught hold of his belt, and reeled him in. Still staring stupidly at his injured hand, he let her take it and examine it. As preparation for our trip, she'd done quite a lot of reading on first aid.

"It's not broken," she told him, "but it's dislocated. This is going to hurt."

He blinked at her. She popped his thumb back in place, and Joe screamed. Then he looked down at the hand, and carefully worked his fingers, and looked back up at Erin. He opened his mouth, and after a few seconds managed to say, "Thank you."

"You're welcome," she said gravely. "You should get it looked at."

"Nice job, honey," Zoey said.

"Thanks, Mom. I just followed the book."

I turned to Marty. His face was blank. He still had the shotgun in his hands, but had clearly forgotten it. He was looking at what was left of Joe's gun, on the ground. "Lemme see your finger," he said to me, his voice hoarse.

Well, he'd asked. In a long and interesting life, it was the first time a cop had ever asked me to give him the finger. I held it up, as politely as I could.

Marty looked at it, and then me. For a fairly long time. Finally he said, "Where you folks from?"

"Long Island," I told him.

"Where you all going?"

"Florida," I said.

He lowered the shotgun. "Drive on," he said.

"Thank you, Officer," Zoey said.

I held out my hand to Joe, palm upward. He blinked at me and started to back away.

"I need my license," I said.

"Oh." He got it back out of his shirt pocket with his left hand and gave it to me. "Sorry we bothered you, Mr. Stonebender," he said dizzily.

"Good," I said, stepped around him, and began to board my bus. Marty put out a hand to stop me. "You gonna file a beef?"

I shook my head. "That was my fault. I'm glad your partner didn't get hurt bad."

He bit his lip and nodded slowly. "Nice of you to look at it that way," he said.

I picked Erin up, carried her up the stairs with me, and put her back into her seat. "Bye, Officer Marty," she said, waving to him.

"So long, miss," he said, and touched his cap. "I'll go make a path for you folks." He bent, scooped up the ruined Glock, and handed it to his partner. "Come on, Joe." I could see from his eyes that Joe was thinking about going into shock.

"Thanks," I said, and cranked the door closed. The cops got back in their car. Officer Marty put on his light, sirens, and emergency flashers, and when he got an opening pulled out onto the highway and stopped, blocking traffic from the right-hand lane.

I got on the CB. "Okay, folks, we're moving out. Stay on the shoulder until you get past the Smoky." I sat down and strapped in, revved my engine a couple of times.

A chorus of acknowledgments came back. "What was that noise, Jake?" Long-Drink asked.

"Nothing, Drink," I assured him. "Just shooting the bull." I put her in gear. "Let's roll."

We had no further trouble in New Jersey. Beyond having to look at New Jersey.

And we had no further police trouble the whole rest of the way down to Florida. Not highway cops, anyway. In state after state, they watched us roll by without putting down their donuts. The word had apparently gone out on the cop teletype: *Don't mess with them.*

Getting shot seemed a small price to pay.

I happened to get something in my eye just as we left Jersey and crossed into Delaware, so I missed that state almost entirely. I think we were in it for all of ten miles. That seemed adequate.

Just before we left it and entered Maryland, I had a brief instant of panic when I started seeing signs for Newark. For a moment I had the idea I had gotten us caught in some evil Twilight Zone loop, and now we were back in North Jersey again, condemned to spend eternity on the Jersey Turnpike. (That's the only way I can think of that would make the Jersey Pike even worse: turn it into a Möbius strip.) But it turns out Delaware has, for reasons I can't even imagine, a Newark of its own. I couldn't help but wonder what it must be like to be from there, and have someone ask you where you're from. First you have to admit you're from Newark . . . then you have to decide whether to humiliate yourself even further, or just let your listener assume you mean the one in New Jersey. They must have real cheap rent there.

We stopped for the night at a little state park slash campground just over the Maryland border. It was early in the day to

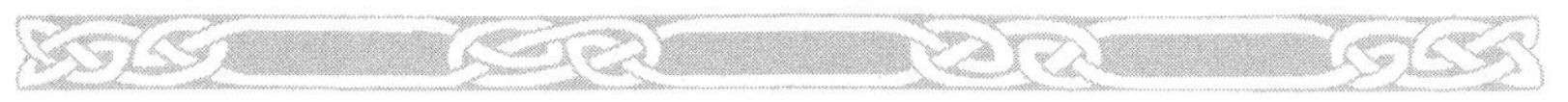

stop—we'd made pretty good time so far. But if we'd kept on going until the sun gave out, we'd pretty much have been forced to pass the night in Baltimore. We just weren't in that much of a hurry.

Also, I found myself captivated by the name of the town nearest the campground. It was called—you'll have to trust me on this—North East. I have no idea why. You could start there and go south as long as you like without ever coming to a place called East. There is no place to the west of it called North. Maybe it's just that everybody there wants to disassociate themselves as much as possible from sou'westers. Maybe the *big* town, East itself, just up and went west one day, abandoning its outlying region to fend for itself.

Perhaps one day population growth will force incorporation of a suburb of North East, called Southwest North East. I like to think so, anyway. That's just the way my mind works—or avoids doing so, if you prefer. I take great personal delight in inexplicable oddities, especially of nomenclature, and am always happy to add to my collection. One of my favorites, for instance, is the intersection in New York City where Waverly Place meets Waverly Place. (Honest—look it up! It's in the Village.) And I had only with difficulty been talked out of leading us all miles out of our way into Pennsylvania, just so I could take a quick look at Intercourse, the town Ralph Ginzburg went to prison for. (Do you recall the story? Back in the Dark Ages, Mr. Ginzburg published a pornographic magazine so tastefully camouflaged that several respectable authorities were willing to testify that it was Art—but the judge jugged him anyway. With an excess of what I can only call cockiness, Mr. Ginzburg had arranged for subscription copies to be mailed out from darkest Pennsylvania, so they'd arrive postmarked "Intercourse," and Hizzoner maintained that this demonstrated prurient intent. Anytime somebody does hard time for having a sense of humor, you better believe I'll make careful note of it.)

So there we were, slightly northeast of North East, with the wagons circled for the night, and a big communal barbecue thing just starting to happen in the center—ever have a barbecue in the dead of winter? It's more fun than you might think—and the air was full of tantalizing smells and happy chatter and the blessed sound of laughing children. The light was just starting to go, and you could sense a pretty good sunset building, and I had finally walked off all the stiffness in my legs. Several of the people standing around the barbecue area were strangers; we had kind of drawn attention when we pulled up in twenty-four school-buses, and a certain amount of mingling was going on. At least one of the strangers was carrying a guitar in a backpack, and another had that indefinable look that suggests a blues harp player; I was thinking about unpacking my guitar Lady Macbeth and seeing if I could get a jam going, when a car pulled up and parked nearby. As the driver got out, he looked oddly familiar, but I couldn't place him.

"Now where do I know that guy from?" I wondered aloud.

Erin didn't need me to point to know where I was looking; at the time she was about a foot behind my head, riding in her pack, which I had put on as a backpack in order to help stretch my lumbar area. "It's Officer Marty, Daddy," she said.

"Cushlamachree!" I breathed.

Sure enough. The plainclothes and unmarked car had fooled me. Hell, it wasn't even really an unmarked car, technically—not a Plymouth Fury at all, but a civilian vehicle, a Honda Accord. (Ever wonder why all cops drive Furies? Donald Westlake says it's the name. He says if they ever start making a car called "Kill," the police departments will all switch at once.) But that was indeed Marty getting out of it.

He spotted me almost at once and walked toward me, slowly and carefully. He seemed to be making a point of keeping his hands in sight and visibly empty. His body language told me he meant me no harm, and I believed it.

He stopped a few yards away, close enough so we could converse without raising our voices, and nodded. "Evening, Mr. Stonebender."

"Jake," I told him. "Evening, Marty."

He nodded again.

"And this is my daughter Erin."

"Hello, Erin," he said. "I'm pleased to meet you. I'm Marty Pignatelli."

"Hi, Marty. You look good in real clothes."

There was a brief silence then.

"So what brings you to Maryland?" I asked finally.

He looked unhappy, but determined. "I've been trying to think how to say this the last fifty miles. I still don't know."

Like I said, he was considerably older than his partner Joe, about my age or a little older. He might have actually been a cop back when I was a hippie—he was my natural enemy of old. Maybe we'd both grown a little, as we aged. I wasn't feeling any antipathy toward him that I could detect, and he wasn't showing any toward me. As Robert Heinlein said, sometimes it's amazing how much mature wisdom resembles being too tired.

Of course, it may have helped that I'm bulletproof.

"So say it wrong," I suggested. "Then we got something to edit."

He nodded. "That makes sense. Okay." He took out a pack of unfiltered Camels, offered me one, which I accepted though they're definitely not my brand, and lit us both with the inevitable Zippo.

"I been a cop a long time," he said, and exhaled smoke. "No, even longer than that. One thing I've learned. Anyway, it's always worked for me. If your brain tells you one thing, and your eyes tell you something different . . . go with your eyes. They're way less likely to malfunction."

"Sound," I agreed.

"So my partner really did shoot you today, and you really didn't much mind."

I nodded.

"Your wife wasn't even mad. And your dog talked to me."

I nodded. Not the time to explain that Ralph was not my chattel.

"I gotta ask you to explain," he said. "You don't owe me an answer—but I gotta ask."

I smoked his tobacco and thought about it. I could see in his eyes that he was as close as he was ever going to come to pleading. He needed to know. He *must* need to know, because I could also tell he was as close as he was ever going to come to being scared shitless. I began to see it from his point of view. One possible explanation—indeed, one of the more plausible ones—was that I was some sort of alien monster mutant out of the *X-Files*, or an unstoppable cyborg killer from the future. In the movies, people you couldn't hurt with a gun were hardly ever on your side.

Hell, what harm could it do to tell him? Even if he believed me.

Was there the slightest chance in hell that he would believe me? He did seem to have come a long way since the Sixties. I decided to run a small test. I took a joint from behind my ear and held it up. "Mind if I smoke?" I asked.

He took it from me, lit it with the end of his own cigarette, took a long deep hit, and handed it back to me. "Good shit," he said appreciatively after he exhaled. "Thanks."

So I explained.

It wasn't the first time I had told the story; I was able to cover most of the highlights in a little under half an hour. He listened carefully and well. From time to time he would make little involuntary interjections—"You set off a nuclear weapon you were holding in your hand?"—but always to confirm that he'd heard me right rather than to challenge what I'd said: basically he kept listening until I was done. Then he sat and thought for a minute or two.

"Like I said, I been a cop a long time," he said finally. "One

thing I know, it's when people are lying to me. Every word you just told me is the God's honest truth."

"I hate to admit it," I said. "It'd be such a grand lie, I wish I could claim it."

"You and your friends actually saved the fucking world."

I shrugged. "Twice, actually. But that was the first time, yeah."

He blinked, pursed his lips, and nodded.

It was starting to get dark now. "Hey, Marty—you hungry?"

"Yeah."

"Why don't we go get some of that food before it's all gone?"

It was the first time I'd ever seen him smile. "Thanks, Jake," he said. "I think I'd like to meet your friends."

"I think they'd like to meet you," Erin said.

So we strolled over to the barbecue area together, and I introduced him around.

The food was good, the conversation after was even better, and after a while I *did* manage to get a jam session going around the campfire that had been built, with the two guys I'd spotted earlier plus a few other camping musicians who'd been attracted by the noise and party atmosphere. Toward the end there we had three guitars, harmonica, tenor sax, alto recorder, and an autoharp going, and it got pretty juicy. We all had different repertoires and styles, so we set up a circle system: each of us got to pick a solo he thought the others might be able to jump in on, and in between each solo we'd do a Beatles number, since *every* musician knows at least a few Beatles tunes, and ought to be able to fake several more without too much strain.

Every so often I'd catch sight of Marty deep in conversation with somebody. Zoey first, then Ralph, then Long-Drink (who could talk the ears off a cornfield), then the Masers . . . he got around quite a bit in a short time. There was no vibe that he was interrogating anybody, not in the cop sense. He was just asking a lot of questions, and listening to the answers.

After the jam ended he wandered over to me and sat where I

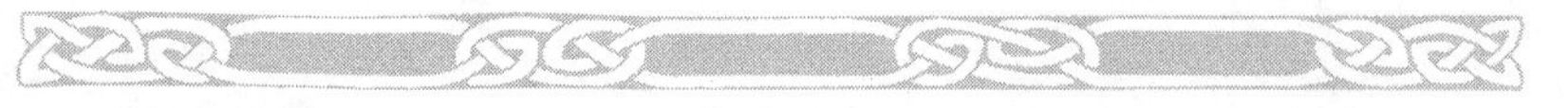

could see him. As soon as I'd finished putting Lady Macbeth away in her case, I gave him a questioning look.

"I got my twenty in," he said. "My wife got smart and left a long time back. There's nothing in Jersey to hold anybody, but there's less than nothing to hold me. There isn't even anything in my apartment I want. I always wanted to see Key West. Eddie Costigan says I can ride in his rig if you say it's okay."

If Fast Eddie had invited a police officer to ride with him, that was all I needed to know. Eddie has his own kind of radar. "What about your car?" was all I asked.

He exhaled with relief. "Next big town down the line is Aberdeen," he said. "I'll set off early tomorrow and try to peddle the heap there; it'll give me a stake to hold me until I can get my money transferred to Florida. With any luck by the time you people pack up and get that far, I'll be waiting for you on the side of the road with my thumb out. You're taking 95, right?"

"Actually, I was thinking of taking Route 40."

"Even better," he said. "Goes right smack through Aberdeen."

"You going to retire by phone?"

He looked embarrassed. "I already did."

I was startled. "Before you even came after us?"

He nodded.

"How come?"

"Two things," he said. "First, I figured if there's people around that don't mind being shot, maybe it's time to stop being a cop. The second thing . . ." He hesitated. "Well, I kept thinking if it *hadn't* been for you being bulletproof, an innocent man might have gotten hurt today. I *know* Joe is an asshole, I knew that when he made me pull you over, and I still let things get way out of hand."

"Like I told you before," I said, "it was my fault. In Joe's shoes, I might have pulled the trigger too."

He grimaced. "Well . . . then maybe you shouldn't be a cop either."

"Amen," I said, and picked up my guitar case. "Well, we both have an early start tomorrow."

He nodded. "Look for me just this side of Aberdeen on 40."

"I will. Good night, Marty. And welcome to the caravan."

He met my eyes and held them. "Thank you, Jake."

"Like I said, you're welcome." A thought belatedly occurred to me. "Oh shit, wait, I just thought of something."

"Problem?"

"Well . . . you'll have to decide. In the interests of full disclosure, I have to give you fair warning about something."

"Okay."

"We pun."

His eyes widened. "*All* of you?"

"To excess," I confessed. "If that's not redundant."

He paled slightly, but rallied. "Too late now," he said philosophically. "I already quit my job."

"You'll get numb and grow scar tissue eventually," I said.

"Oh, I'm tough enough," he said. "I don't even let my dentist give me Novocain when he's doing a root canal."

"Really? How do you deal with the pain?"

"Transcend dental medication," he said with a straight face.

I paled slightly myself . . . then awarded him a wince and a groan.

"So you folks are all like ambitious Southeast Asians?" he went on.

"Huh?"

"Taipei personalities."

I grinned, even though that's not really the proper form of applause for a pun. "Marty, I think this is going to work out. Wait'll you meet Doc Webster."

He was waiting by the side of Route 40 the next morning as we came up on Aberdeen. Whether our Triple A rating on the interstate cop teletype was all Marty's doing, I couldn't say for sure—I never asked him—but I'd be surprised if it wasn't.

CHAPTER SIX

Capital Offense

"I believe we are on an irreversible trend toward more freedom and democracy—but that could change."
—J. Danforth Quayle, May 22, 1989

THE NEXT DAY WE SPLIT up, by common consent.

It was only another fifty miles or so to Washington, and *everybody* wanted to sightsee, i.e., gawk, and of course no more than two buses could agree on exactly what to gawk *at*, so there was no sense in trying to stay together. Some of us wanted to see the White House, some the Mall, some the Capitol, some the Library of Congress, some the Smithsonian—some of us wanted to slip across the river to Arlington or the Pentagon—there were even a few who decided to skip the District of Columbia altogether, left the caravan at Baltimore, and headed down 97 to Annapolis. (Jim Omar went with that contingent . . . then left them behind and went on farther south to the Smithsonian's Institute for Environmental Studies, just across the bay from Beverly Beach.)

So we went our separate ways for a while. I will spare you the details of just which sites my family and I chose to gawk at, and note only that we had a good time.

No, I'll mention one small disappointment. I had been to D.C. once before, as a child back in the late Fifties . . . and I was dismayed to learn that nowadays the F.B.I. Headquarters tour no longer offers American children the opportunity to fire a tommy gun. I'd told Erin about how much fun it was, and promised her that I'd bully them into letting her have a crack at it somehow . . . and had to renege. I complained to the official who gave me the news, and he said the feature had been dropped from the tour due to lack of interest. I expressed polite incredulity—kids no longer wanted to operate a machine gun? "I think they all have their own now," he said.

That's all I feel like telling about our time in the nation's capital. When I'm on my deathbed, regretting my myriad sins and failures of character, one of my few proud consolations will be that I seldom made anybody look at my vacation photos. On that ground alone I believe I may just escape the fires of hell.

We had set up a rendezvous point in Falls Church, Virginia, where we'd been offered accommodation by a friend of Doc Webster's who lived there and had *lots* of parking room. The one thing we had all managed to agree on was that we could probably visit all the tourist traps on our personal target list within forty-eight hours.

Naturally we were wrong. *I* was there on time . . . and so were exactly two other buses (Fast Eddie's and Noah Gonzalez's). The rest took days to trickle in. One or two of them *limped* in, in need of repairs. And by the time the very last of the prodigal vehicles had finally showed up, several of the earlier arrivals had slipped away again, on assorted errands or excuses. I started to feel like I was running a traveling day-care center, and we were out of Ritalin . . .

I tried to force myself to be philosophical about it and not fret. Our host Ted was a pleasant gent, the area was tolerable, the company was good, and we were, after all, in no hurry. What was there to worry about?

I succeeded so well at not worrying that Zoey and Erin finally had to kick me in the ass.

"Daddy," Erin said, "you're acting my age."

"She's right," Zoey said.

I drew in a deep breath to bellow, "God damn it, I am *not*!"—and thanks be to God, I heard myself saying it before I actually said it, and decided it wouldn't help my mood any just now to sound like an asshole, and didn't say it. One of my rules of thumb is that if you hear yourself sounding like an asshole, there's a fair chance it's because you're *being* an asshole. So I let that breath back out, slowly, and took in and released a few more like it, and thought about the tantrum I was having. Or trying to have.

No, dammit, it still seemed to me I was *entitled* to this one. "That's easy for you to say, Pumpkin," I told my daughter. "You've never been responsible for over a hundred people. Over a hundred *irresponsible* people." Now I didn't sound quite so much like an asshole. More of a whiner. Erin squirmed on my lap, but said nothing.

"They'll all show up, eventually," Zoey said, and nothing in her tone or facial expression indicated that it was about the dozenth time she'd said it in the last hour. She was making herself a sandwich at the back of the passenger area of our bus, slathering honey mustard mayonnaise sauce on a roll.

"Sure—but *when*? And in what condition? You know how it works, Zo. It's not enough just to get everybody *here*. Oh no! We can't roll until everybody is here *and* has their assorted tanks pumped out and pumped full, *and* has all their shopping done and their flats fixed and their brakes tightened and their oil topped off, *and* every driver's had at least eight consecutive hours' sleep . . . and then, you watch: in the first fifty miles somebody will throw a rod, somebody else will want to peel off

and visit the great aunt he hasn't seen in thirty years, and two of them will just plain get lost because keeping track of two dozen big yellow buses right ahead of them will be too much of a mental strain for—"

"You're doing it again, Daddy."

Was I? Just in case, I stopped.

"So what?" Zoey asked. "What's the difference? We're on some kind of a schedule? The window for Key West closes soon?"

She'd very nearly poked a hole in my bag of wind, with those first three sentences . . . but the way she phrased that last one gave me some ammo. "No, but the window for the Shuttle sure does! You know how attached I am to seeing that."

"But they *always* hold, don't they, Daddy?" Erin asked.

"They usually do, yes, Pigeon—but no law says they have to. And the way my luck runs—"

"Do you believe in luck, Daddy?"

I blinked at her.

"Only when he's mad, honey," Zoey told her, and filled her roll with Bavarian ham and thick slices of Edam cheese. "Jake, relax. We've still got time. If we start running so late that it looks like we'll miss the launch, nobody will mind if we put the hammer down and go on ahead of them—we could be there in a day if we gunned it."

I snorted. "To be sure. To be thoroughly sure. Leave this collection of goofballs, weirdos, and nincompoops on their own, to take care of themselves? Half of 'em would never reach Florida, and the rest would trickle into Key West over a period of a month, after wasting weeks just trying to *find* each other."

"They'll probably do that even if you do stick with them," Erin said.

"The hell of it is, you're right! They're as organized as spaghetti, for Christ's sake. I must have been fucking *crazy* to take this on. Honest to God, it's like trying to herd cats—the toilet's about to fall out of my goddam bus and I can't even get anybody to help me *fix* it—" I was working my way back up to full-bore tantrum again.

"Mother?" Erin said. "Time for drastic measures?"

Zoey finished layering the avocado slices onto her sandwich and closed it up. "I think you're right, dear. Shall I take it?"

Erin shook her head. "No, you got it last time. My turn." She turned her face up to me, and gave me the full-bore impact of those eyes of hers, from which no man can turn away unless she wills it. "Daddy?"

I braced myself. "Yes, Princess?"

"You're not *supposed* to be Uncle Mike."

"Huh?"

"Nobody *expects* you to be."

I gave my head a little involuntary shake, like a dog throwing off water. "I don't get you."

She climbed off my lap, stood on the seat beside me so that our eyes were on the same level. "I'm going too fast, I guess. Let me back up. Look, when you get upset about something, you like to get mad about something else. That's okay, as long as people know how to read you, I guess. But Mom and I are getting tired of it right now. You're getting mad at everybody so you won't get mad at yourself. So why don't you just get mad at yourself and then forgive yourself, and then it'll be all over with, and we can have *fun* again."

"You go, girl," Zoey murmured.

I blinked at my daughter in silence for a time. It is always humbling to meet someone smarter than yourself . . . and when it's someone under two years old, it sort of transcends humbling and skips right on into humiliating. I still didn't know what the hell she was talking about—but I could already tell that she was right.

"You said it yourself once, Daddy. You told me. You said, 'Anger is *always* fear in disguise.' Always, you said."

Again, her words *felt* true. "But what the hell am I afraid of, then? Do you know?"

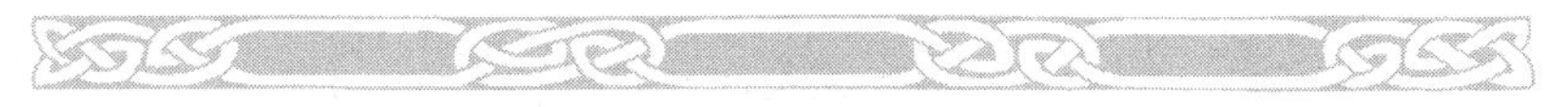

She turned to look at her mother. "You want to jump in? You know I'm not good at being tactful yet."

Zoey nodded serenely. "That's why you should take it, hon. I don't think it can be said tactfully—and he'll forgive you quicker."

Erin nodded and turned back to me. "You're afraid you're a shitty Road Chief. You're afraid you're a cheap imitation Mike Callahan, and everybody knows it. You failed, big time, and you're afraid that means you're a failure. You're afraid you're gonna fail again, only bigger. You're afraid you're gonna screw up *this* bar too, and then Mommy and I will decide you're a loser and go away. So if you get mad enough about something else to storm off and leave the caravan instead, then nobody but you will ever find out what a loser you were. At least, not as quick." I closed my eyes. "Believe me, Daddy, I know: you and I are at about the same emotional age right now. It's just about the way I'd feel if I were you."

I sat there in silence with my eyes shut and my mind revving in neutral. Each of her sentences was like being punched in the heart by a pro; in combination they were devastating. I felt a blackness opening beneath me. My right arm was resting on the back of the seat; I felt something touch my hand and realized Zoey had put a jigger into it. Automatically I drank the Irish whiskey that was in it, in a gulp. Zoey's unseen hand took the empty jigger away again.

Maybe she and Erin shared a glance. "One more part I forgot," Erin said. "You're superstitious. You know it's silly, but you have this idea that every time you take a wife and daughter out on the road, something bad is gonna happen."

The bulk of my adult life has been colored by the knowledge that I killed my first wife and daughter, Barbara and Jessica, by being cocky enough to do my own brake job and incompetent enough to screw it up. Pinned in the wreckage, unable to move, I'd watched them both die. By fire. It was to escape the shattering impact of that grief and guilt and shame that I had originally found my way to Callahan's Place almost twenty years ago. There I had met most of the friends I was traveling with now . . . and had slowly, over time, been healed by their kindness and caring and good fellowship, and by the wisdom of big Mike Callahan.

About five years ago, sort of as icing on the cake, I had had it *proved* to me by Mike's daughter Mary that while my grief was earned, my guilt and shame were not: that the brakes that had failed, and killed Barb and Jess, were *not* the two I had replaced after all.

But I realized now that Erin was right. Oh, the good news had probably percolated down to my subconscious long since . . . but it didn't matter: even though I knew better, part of me would *always* think of myself as The Guy Who Killed His Family, and I would *never* feel fully at ease while driving with my loved ones.

Even if Omar and Shorty *had* checked the brakes, this time.

"But don't pay any attention to that part," Erin said. "That one, you already know better than. Let's do the other stuff. Okay?"

I seemed to hear my own voice from far away. "Okay."

She leaned closer, took me by the hair, put her face a few inches from mine, and those incredible eyes of hers locked on. "Let's do the important part first."

"Okay."

She spoke slowly and distinctly. "Even if you are a failure, Mommy and I aren't going anywhere. We love who you are. I know it doesn't make any sense, but neither do John Tesh fans: it's just the way we are, that's all. You're stuck with us. Okay?"

"Okay." I felt something shift inside me. "That's good to hear."

"Next, you're *not* a failure. You're just not Uncle Mike. And Daddy, really—who *is*?"

I sighed. "Honey, granted he had certain advantages I lack . . . but Mike ran Callahan's Place for *thirty-eight years*. I didn't last a single year. Any way you look at it, that's poor performance."

"Compared to *what?*" she asked.

I said nothing. At least with my mouth, but she must have read something in my eyes. Without losing her lock on them, she spoke to Zoey. "Mom, put on that song he wrote."

I thought she meant the one about laughing when the joke is on you. But Zoey knew better, somehow, and found the cassette Erin wanted and slipped it into the deck. A song I had written years ago, long before I ever met Zoey, called "Perspective." My younger self sang it to me now:

A cop with any decency at all looks like a hero
A millionaire knows billionaires who think that he's a zero
The shoes a lord rejected are a godsend to the churl
And an immie in the sewer looketh mighty like a pearl

A million people kill themselves attempting to be stars
While stars go nuts with loneliness and smoke the highest tars
Businessmen competing, and the ones who do the best
Win the hatred of their neighbors and a cardiac arrest

So remember on those days when in your bed you shoulda stood
That somewhere there is someone who makes even you look good
It's only your perspective that has got you in a muddle
You ain't too small a frog—you just been in too big a puddle!

Erin let go of my hair and gestured; Zoey stopped the tape. "*Most* bars opened by human beings close within a year, you know," Erin told me. "I looked it up. And Uncle Mike isn't a human being."

"Don't tell *me* Mike isn't human," I said sharply. "He's probably the humanest guy I ever—"

"Oh, *Daddy*," she said, with the massive scorn only a small child can easily lift, "he is *not*—he just plays one on TV. You

know that! If he's a human being, you and me are *Homo habilis*. He comes from so far in the future, *they don't even have sad people*, Daddy! He told me he was over a hundred years old the first time he ever set foot in this galaxy. I asked him to show me where his planet Harmony is in the sky, once, and he told me the light from the birth of its star hasn't got here yet. How are you supposed to measure up to that? How could anybody?"

"He left the gang in my hands," I said, hearing my voice quiver but unable to control it. "He spent my whole lifetime building it, and then he handed them all off to me and went home. I scattered them to the four winds in a matter of months." I swallowed. "And then spent the next year wearing my ass for a hat, feeling sorry for myself." I tried, and failed, to pull my gaze away from Erin's eyes. "I used to ask myself . . . when things got tough, I'd ask myself, *What would Mike do?* I don't feel like I have the right to ask that anymore. You're right: I'm not him. And him is what I wanted to be."

She tugged gently on my hair, forcing my face to describe a small circle in the air. "Where are we going right now?"

"Florida. Key West."

"Who?"

"Huh?"

She bobbed my head again. "Who's going?"

I blinked. "You. Me. Mom. The whole gang. Eventually."

"Why?"

I opened my mouth.

"No, don't tell me a bunch of reasons why going to Florida is a good idea. Any of those people could have decided to move to Florida a year ago, just like Uncle Doc did. None of them felt like it then. How come they all happen to be on the road, more or less together, right now?"

I didn't know what to say, what kind of answer she wanted from me.

Zoey spoke an inch from my left ear. I hadn't heard her approaching. "Hint: *because you are*, schmuck! Just like me and the kid."

I heard white noise. Erin's eyes began to kaleidoscope.

"Because they know you can do what Uncle Mike did, Daddy," my daughter said. "You can help them get telepathic again. You *did* it, once. It took Uncle Mike thirty-eight years. It took you one. You think they care how good a businessman you are?"

Zoey was at my right ear now, speaking softly but overriding the white noise. "Doc told me about it. That night you were all standing around the radioactive crater that used to be Callahan's, and everybody said you should open up Mary's Place, and you said *why me?* And it was Long-Drink who answered you. He said, because you were always the merriest son of a bitch in the whole crew."

That was true. The Drink had said that. And there had been a rumbled chorus of agreement from everyone present at the time.

"That's important, Daddy," the girl with kaleidoscope eyes said. "That's really important. That's why you have to stop all this bull-grunty. Nobody *wants* you to make this trip organized and efficient. They want you to make it *fun*. So do me and Mommy."

"Lighten up, Stringbean," Zoey murmured.

Then she straightened up and backed off a few paces, and said in her normal voice, "I think that's enough for now, Erin. It's like making yogurt. Now we leave him alone for a while, for the yeast to work."

"Okay," Erin said, and powered down her eyes, and disconnected her gaze, and climbed over me. I presume Zoey picked her up and carried her off the bus; I was distracted. Anyway, when I emerged from the fog, they were both gone.

My God—they were right! The one trying to force unwanted adult responsibility on me was not them, or the group, or cussed Fate, or Tesla, or even Mike Callahan. It was *me*!

My only demonstrable talents were for fucking off and having fun—it was time I started playing to my strengths.

I didn't need to follow their tracks in the snow. My ears led me to Ted's house, where the crew—those who had showed up so far—had gathered to party. Even with half of us missing, the joint was rockin'. Ted obviously had a piano somewhere in his home, and Fast Eddie, deprived for so long, had seized the opportunity to take on his Aspect and raise up his Attribute: as I came in the door I could hear him playing an instrumental chorus of the rousing old John Koerner classic "Good-Time Charlie," with Zoey on bass and somebody I didn't know on banjo. I had Lady Macbeth in my hands, but discovered that Ted's piano was not tuned up to concert pitch . . . so I set her down on a couch, and walked into the room where Eddie was with my kazoo in my teeth, blasting out a raucous solo as I came.

Eddie made room for me, and we volleyed back and forth for a couple of verses, both of us standing on a flying carpet Zoey built for us with her big standup bass, while people cheered and clapped and danced. The banjo player, as I expected, turned out to be our host—and he was good, not one of those banjo players who tricks everything up. Erin and Ralph von Wau Wau were dancing together in the middle of the room, a sight that would make a cat laugh. She caught my eye and threw me a grin, and I sent it back with a blown kiss. Another verse came around, and I sang it to her:

Don't you try to dance like Snaker Ray—
The last woman tried it got thirty days!
Good-Time Charlie's back in town again . . .

She giggled and did a little parody of a bump and grind, and Zoey did a comic underline with her bass. I looked over at her, and cut to the last verse, the one you sing at the top of your lungs in your highest register:

Well, I lost my money and I lost my honey—
If I can't get happy, then I better get funny:
Good-Time Charlie's back in town again

—Eddie knew it was the last verse and was ready for my

Oh, yeah,

and so were Zoey and Ted—

Good-Time Charlie's back in town again!

And Eddie took us home and nailed it shut, and the room exploded in laughter and applause.

"Good news," Zoey called to me over the noise, and Erin ran over and hugged hell out of my leg, and I smiled so big I hurt my face.

Two extremely merry days later, we were assembled and ready to roll again.

I don't remember where we were, on the map. Somewhere well south of Falls Church, perhaps in one of the Carolinas. It was evening, I remember that much—after sundown, but before we got to wherever it was we were stopping that night. Everything else about it I remember very well.

The weather was good, road conditions nominal, traffic moving. Zoey was snoring gently, just loud enough to hear, in the curtained-off area at the rear of the living area that we were pleased to call "the bedroom," and Erin and I were sharing the drive together up front, with her strapped in beside me in her special seat.

We chatted in soft voices to kill the monotony of broken white lines coming at us out of the dark, covering a variety of subjects I can no longer recall. Then there came one of those natural pauses where you've used up the present topic, and somebody has to introduce a new one, and I let Erin take it because I had proposed the last one—but she took so long that I got hypnotized by the highway and forgot I was waiting for her to speak. When she did, it startled me a little. So did what she said.

"Is it weird, Daddy?"

"Yes, honey, it usually is," I said automatically. Then, "Uh . . . is *what* weird?"

"Having a freak for a kid."

I snapped my head around to look at her. She was looking back at me, her face expressionless. Bland little Buddha. It came to me for the first time that if she and I were about the same emotional age, then she could hurt about as profoundly as I could. Maybe all babies can, regardless of emotional age. In any case, I knew my answer was important to her. So I thought about it, real hard and real fast.

My first impulse was to say, "I wouldn't know"—to deny the question, in other words. But I was not in the habit of lying to my daughter—had not been since, when she was about a week old, I got it through my head that it was not only a bad policy but a waste of time. And there was no honest way to deny it: Erin *was* a freak. A freak's freak, in fact. I had considered *myself* a freak all my adult life, and was traveling in a company any one of whom could claim that title—if nothing else, by virtue of being bulletproof—but the Lucky Duck and Ralph von Wau Wau the talking dog were perhaps the only ones of us who could claim to be as much of a freak as Erin was.

Oncoming headlights tried to make shadows move across her face in time with the traffic, but her features were too young and smooth to give them anything to work with. Yet even the poor light could not hide the unmistakable adult intelligence in her big baby eyes.

Okay, Jake: it's a bona fide question. What's your answer?

"Yeah, it is," I said, with what I hoped was no perceptible hesitation. "A little."

She nodded. "I thought it must be."

"Be weird if it wasn't weird," I said, and put my own eyes back on the road to make sure we were still on it.

"What's it like?" she asked.

I was about to say that I'd never thought about it . . . when I discovered that I *had*. Sometimes the brain does some thinking—even a whole *lot* of thinking—without recording it in the Master File Directory the consciousness uses. Suddenly I realized that somewhere in the basement of my mind, a little thought loop had been running, like a set of Lionel trains with no way to escape its track, for quite some time now. I scanned it.

"Pretty strange," I heard myself say. "About ninety-nine percent of the time I'm scared for you. The rest of the time I'm scared *of* you."

The second sentence shocked me a little—but it made Erin break up. "You're scared of me?"

"A little," I admitted. "There've been a handful of science fiction stories about kids as smart as you—and in just about every one of them, the kid was ruling the world by the time she was old enough for junior high school. Usually with an iron fist."

She giggled. "Then they weren't as smart as me," she said. "Tyrants are *stupid*."

"Yes, they are, honey."

She stopped giggling. "Would it be so terrible if I ruled the world, Daddy?" she asked soberly.

My turn to giggle. "You know, it's hard to see how it could help but be an improvement."

"That's what I thought," she agreed, still serious. "Someday, maybe. Now tell me why you're scared *for* me."

I hesitated. A lifetime of cultural conditioning told me emphatically that a parent should *never* share fears for a child with the child. I mean, how's the kid supposed to react to learning that even the omniscient omnipotent grown-ups are scared?

But Erin knew I was neither of those things. And she was not a naive babe.

Dammit, that was the problem. A parent's job is supposed to be to preserve his kid, for as long as possible, in blissful ignorance of the human predicament. But for me and Erin, that had never been a possibility.

"Honey," I said, "it's real hard for *any* kid to grow up to adulthood with any kind of emotional stability. But for most of them, there are at least some guidelines, some rules of thumb, some handed-down wisdom. But you are unique. I have *no* idea how to raise you, to give you what you're going to need . . . and there isn't any authority on earth I can consult. You're going to have emotional problems nobody else has ever had."

"Like what?"

"How the hell do I know?" I thought about it—or rather, reviewed old thoughts I had not shared with myself until now. "Here's one of my guesses, though. The average kid, he's at least five or six years old before he notices that all the grown-ups are treating him like an idiot. You're going to have your intelligence insulted for *years* longer than most kids have to deal with. It'll be almost two decades before society grants you any civil rights or professional opportunities. That's bound to have an effect."

"Yeah. But I'm expecting it. I think I can handle it."

"Another one: most kids never do quite get it through their heads just how little and weak and clumsy and fragile they are—until they aren't anymore. You've always known. And you're *still* going to have to wait months and months to get strong enough and coordinated enough to do things you've been wanting to do for more than a year. That's got to be frustrating . . . and scary."

"You got that right."

Suddenly I was amazed at myself. "Jesus—we should have had this conversation *months* ago. Why didn't we?"

My daughter cleared her throat. A mile or so went by, and still she made no answer.

"Oh," I said, and then, *"Oh!"* I felt my shoulders slump. "I've been full of shit for a long time, haven't I?"

"Yes, Daddy."

"I'm sorry, Pumpkin."

I felt her little hand on my right arm. "Don't worry about it, Daddy. You were entitled. You had a lot to work out. And I was part of that." I started to argue. "I was," she insisted.

"Well, I'm sorry anyway," I said, taking my left hand off the wheel and putting it on hers. "I could have been a better dad."

"And you will be," she said. "But I could have been a better kid, too—and I never will be."

"What do you mean?" I asked, scandalized. *"How?"*

She pulled her hand loose from mine. "Oh Daddy, come on! Other parents get to *teach* their baby everything. They get to smile when the kid does something endearingly dopey, or says something charmingly wrong. They get to feel like every little thing in their child's head is something they put there. They get to bill and coo over this cute little helpless doll, and tell it soothing lies that make them feel better, and play infantile games with it, for years and years. You and Mommy got screwed. You don't get to have *any* of that. Instead of a baby, you got an uncoordinated midget that shits her pants sometimes. I've been beating both of you at chess and Scrabble since I was a couple of weeks old. It's *gotta* suck."

I thought about it. "Maybe it should. You're right: it seems like it ought to. But I've honestly never given it a thought."

"Is it because I'm not your biological daughter, do you think?"

"Definitely not," I said.

Her silence expressed her skepticism.

"No, really. Maybe it's because I've always known you."

"What do you mean?"

I wasn't sure myself, and struggled to put it into words. "I *did* play infantile games with you—when you were in your mother's belly—even before she started to show, I mean. When she and I got together, you were more of a zygote than a fetus. About the time you were growing your first brain cells and starting to knit them together, I was out there, a few inches away, blowing

Bronx cheers on Zoey's stomach at you and telling you dopey jokes. Probably the first things that ever tickled you were some of my sperm."

She giggled, and put her hand back on my arm.

"And then just before you were born, while Mom was in the middle of birthing you, we got telepathically connected. All of us, of course, but especially you and me. Remember?"

"Sort of," she said.

"You weren't even 'Erin' yet. You were 'Nameless.' That's what we'd been calling you for months."

Her grip on my forearm tightened. "I do remember," she said.

"There was a lot of other stuff going on. We were all trying to save the world. Mom was in labor. You were busy getting born. But while all that was happening, on another level you and I were in rapport, for . . . oh, a *long* time. Five minutes . . . a million years . . . one of those."

"Yes," she said dreamily.

"It was nice."

"You had space monsters coming in the roof, and you were so happy to be with me you didn't care."

"That's right."

"It was nice," she said again.

"And then, five minutes or a million years later, Tommy Janssen had a brainstorm and stuck a SCSI cable in his mouth, and Solace joined us all in the telepathic hookup. And a little while after that . . . well, everything changed, and you weren't a normal baby anymore."

Solace, the self-generated consciousness of the Internet, had sacrificed herself that night, died fighting to save the human race—most of whom did not suspect her existence, and would have hated and feared her if they had. And just about her last dying action had been to upload as much as she could of her own immense store of knowledge and intelligence into the tiny unformed skull of my daughter, and leave her a tutor-avatar: "Grampa Murray," an AI kernel smart enough to accelerate and oversee Erin's intellectual development, and small enough to run on a single enhanced Mac II.

"But you see," I continued, "all that normal-childhood stuff you were talking about that I won't get to have with you—I *had* all that with you. For five minutes, or a million years. At a level deeper than any other parent will probably ever dream of. Like I said, I've always known you. I even know what it was like to have all that data come flooding into your head at once, because I was there in your skull with you at the time, and I could see that it wasn't scaring you or hurting you."

"Yeah, you were," she said.

"I got to watch you grow up, like any dad. It just happened quicker, that's all. And also, to a lesser extent, I got to watch you grow up over the next few months—even if we weren't telepathic anymore by then. It took you at least a couple of weeks for your brain to process and structure all the information it got in that first big flash—and two or three months for you to start getting your motor control down. You were as endearingly clumsy and dopey as any daddy could have wished for: you just didn't keep it up long enough for it to get to be a pain in the ass." I broke off for a moment, as some road situation or other briefly claimed my attention. "And I'm going to get to *keep on* watching you grow up—and it's gonna be really cool."

"You think?"

I nodded firmly. "Definitely. Erin, the one lie every parent needs to believe, desperately, is that his or her particular child is somehow, in some way, unique and special. Most of them are whistling in the dark."

"Yeah, so?"

I turned and grinned at her. "So I'm the first father in the history of the world who knows for a fact that it's *true*. You're going to surprise me every single day of your life, and I plan to enjoy every minute of it. Face it, kid: unlike most babies, you ain't boring. I'm the luckiest dad that ever lived."

"Oh." She dimpled, and we smiled at each other until I had to put my eyes back on the highway.

I checked my gauges, checked my mirrors. A thought struck me, and I chuckled. "For instance," I said, "back when you were in Mom's womb, and I used to try and imagine what it was going to be like, being a dad . . ."

"Yeah?"

"Well, I didn't picture us having conversations like this until you were at least ten or eleven. You know, talking about real stuff. Father-daughter stuff." I chuckled again. "I figured then I'd be telling you stories about what you were like when you were a year old. Only you're probably going to remember."

There was a short silence. Then she said, "Daddy? Do you suppose when you're with that me—the eleven-year-old me—you'll really remember *this* me?"

"Oh, for sure. And I'll miss you."

"You think so?"

"Definitely. But it's okay . . . I'll have you right here: in my head, always. And the two-year-old you, and the three—all of them."

"Sure, but still, wouldn't it be neat if we could travel in time like Uncle Mike? Then I could visit you when I'm eleven and you're in your fifties—and you could pick me up and cuddle me again. And wouldn't you like to have a father-daughter conversation with the eleven-year-old me, *now?*"

"I don't know," I said dubiously. "That does sound like fun—but, honey, time travel isn't for human beings, like you and me. I wouldn't mess with it, even if I could. Just for a start, it's dangerous as hell. If you time-hopped to when you're eleven, there'd be two of you, two Erins, in the same ficton. Temporal paradox. That's supposed to be real bad medicine."

"What would happen?" she asked.

Why is the sky blue, Daddy? No matter how educated you are, your kid can find a question to make you feel like an ignoramus.

"I don't really know," I admitted. "Mike was always a little vague about that. But what I *think* might happen is exactly what Uncle Nikky is afraid of: the end of the universe."

"Oh."

"Or maybe worse. It's okay for Mike and Lady Sally and Mary to mess with that stuff: they're a thousand years more advanced than we are. And Finn seems to handle it okay—but he's an alien being, from a race that always sounded a lot saner and smarter than mine, and besides he's Mary's husband. But contemporary human beings? No, hon. You notice even Uncle Nikky doesn't fool with it—and he's been the smartest and boldest man alive for over a century now."

"I guess," she said, and suddenly yawned hugely. "Listening to Mommy sleep got me tired, Daddy. I'm going to go climb in with her."

"Okay, honey—need help?"

"I got it," she assured me, and unstrapped herself and went aft. Bedclothes rustled, and Zoey murmured momentarily in her sleep. Shortly Erin's own breathing sounds became as rhythmic as her mother's, and then fell into sync with them.

I drove on. For a while, I listened in to the ongoing chatter on the CB—a word game was in progress—but I couldn't seem to focus on it and switched off without contributing anything. I thought about putting on my Walkman and listening to music, but couldn't think of a cassette I felt like hearing. I was wide awake, not hungry or thirsty, not especially stiff or sore, the caravan was moving fine and all was well.

After a while I noticed I was gripping the wheel so hard my fingers hurt, and admitted to myself that I was terrified out of my mind for my daughter. Easily twenty times as scared as I'd been willing to cop to while talking with her just now. And absolutely helpless to do anything about it except hang on and keep playing it by ear, hoping for the best. I started to tremble and sweat, saw the road ahead of me start to blur.

And the moment I did I heard Mike Callahan's voice. In my

head, not in my ears; I knew the difference by now. It conveyed his personality, his *presence*, better than sound alone could have done, or even smell.

"She'll be *fine*, Jake," he told me.

And then he was gone again.

After a while I said, "Thank you, Mike," aloud to an empty cabin. And drove on, leading my family and flock through the darkness to an unknown destination.

A few miles later I put the CB volume back up again. Long-Drink was just saying, ". . . and an unpopular politician becomes devoted and debriefed," and Maureen Hooker answered, "Whereupon his secretary gets delayed."

"Not to mention dismayed, detailed, debunked, and bauched," I said, and the channel briefly overloaded as twenty people all groaned at once. "And a tone-deaf musician will soon be decomposed and disconcerted . . ."

And the miles went merrily by.

CHAPTER SEVEN

The Cat Who Walks Through Windshields

"I was recently on a tour of Latin America, and the only regret I have was that I didn't study Latin harder in school so I could converse with those people."
—J. Danforth Quayle

WHAT WITH EVERYbody and his brother peeling off from the caravan from time to time, to visit a relative or see some sacred site or other—and almost invariably screwing up their rendezvous back with us—we did not make terrific time.

As we went through Savannah, I was powerfully tempted myself: Albany, Georgia, the birthplace of Raymond Charles Robinson, aka Ray Charles, would only have been a three-hundred-mile detour to the west. Zoey was as tempted as I was. But Erin pointed out that Brother Ray wasn't there anymore, and we drove on. (Just as Erin's taste buds had not yet matured enough for her to find spicy food enjoyable, her musical taste had not yet evolved to R&B.)

We really ought to have stopped somewhere in southern Georgia for the night. But once we left that state and crossed into Florida, the only border we would have left to cross was the one between the U.S. and the Conch Republic. Somehow that gave

us all an extra charge of adrenalin, even though we knew it would still be a couple of days before we got to Key West. That was another consideration: two of the most anticipated highlights of the whole journey were coming up, the only two side trips *everybody* wanted to make, and it turned out we were all eager to get to 'em. After a brief CB conference, we agreed to press on. In the words of songwriter Tom Rush, "we crossed the Florida line movin' Special Airmail," just as the sun was going down . . . and then there was a small kerfluffle.

The idea was for us all to pull off I-95 well north of Jacksonville, take a small road east to the sea, and circle the wagons for the night at either one of two state park campgrounds, Amelia Island or Little Talbot Island, depending on which seemed best capable of accommodating an invasion by two dozen busloads of weirdos. The turnoff we wanted shows up clearly on the map, and I'm sure it's really there and adequately marked—but I never saw it, and neither did any other driver or navigator in the caravan. It wasn't the lousy light, either. We were all distracted.

Just at that interchange, where we should have headed east toward Yulee, a lost tributary of A1A (miles from the rest of it) heads *west* . . . toward a town called "Callahan" . . .

By the time we all finished discussing that over the CB, we came to the belated realization that we had blown right past our exit. The two choices were, try to U-turn and go back north again, or continue on and trust to luck. Being a pessimist, I favored the first alternative, and said so. But there was broad and strong resistance to the idea of turning around and retracing even a few miles. That same sense of urgency that had pushed us into crossing over into Florida in the first place was still operating, I guess.

Which doesn't make much sense. Of the two treats that lay ahead of us, one had no deadline factor, and we were now comfortably early for the second one. Nonetheless I felt it myself: the impulse to keep moving south.

Still, I hesitated. Darkness was falling fast, and Jacksonville seemed like a lousy place to look for a motel owner with a free spirit and a young heart. Too crowded, too built up and civilized. It would be a shame to come so close and get us all busted for vehicular vagrancy by the local heat. (Who were not plugged into the highway-cop teletype.) It could cost us the second of our anticipated treats—the one I personally looked forward to most eagerly, and the only point on our itinerary that came with a deadline.

"Jake?" It was Jim Omar, four buses back.

"Yeah, Jim?"

"You know how sometimes a gambler knows, just *knows*, that he's hot?"

"Yeah, I guess."

"Press on."

This didn't sound like ultrarational Omar to me. "Are you sure?"

"I've got a good feeling," he said.

"Me 'oo, Da'y," Erin's muffled voice said from behind me.

I glanced over my shoulder. "Well, of course you do, sweetheart: you've got Mommy's tit in your mouth."

She and Zoey exchanged an enigmatic glance. "They're such babies," she said to her mother, who nodded and told her, "Believe it or not, dear, there'll come a day when you'll thank God for that." I was facing forward again by then, but I could *hear* Erin looking dubious. "Keep going, Daddy," she said to me, and went back to her dinner.

"Yo, Stringbean," said another voice on the CB.

"Yeah, Ernie?" The Lucky Duck had no bus, had brought nothing whatsoever with him from Long Island, was driving an orange VW Beetle with more miles on it than the Verve Records catalog. The Duck has never owned anything much, or seen any reason to: all his life, anytime he needed something, it seemed to come along.

"How often do I give you advice?" he asked me.

I thought about it. "Can't say you ever have."

"Drive on," he said. "I smell good luck."

"That's good enough for me," I said. "Jacksonville, here we come."

We saw no place suitable before Jax, and things didn't look encouraging south of it on the map, so we left I-95 there and headed east for the ocean, hoping for a miracle.

And got one. Wandering around in the dark through one of those sleepy little seaside retirement communities, convinced we were doomed, we happened upon one of the cheesiest motels I've ever seen in my life. Years ago it might have been something nice, but huge gated townhouse communities for seniors had been developed on either side of it in recent years, cutting off its beach access, and now it was clearly teetering on the ragged edge of bankruptcy. There was *plenty* of room in the parking lot for two or three dozen vehicles, as long as we were prepared to pay the standard rate for a dozen motel rooms we had no intention of sleeping in.

Well, some people used them, and it's possible some of us even slept in one. Zoey and I went into one to use the shower, which was marginally better than the ones you find in campgrounds, and we might well have drifted off in front of the tube afterward. But while I was discovering there was nothing on I really wanted to watch despite ninety-nine-channel cable, I saw my first Florida cockroach come out of a baseboard, and so did Zoey, and that was it: we reboarded our bus and sealed it tight.

Which was a bit of a problem at first. Even with the breeze coming in off the ocean, it was a rather warm night by our Yankee standards. We talked about cracking windows—cockroaches, even ones that big, couldn't actually climb up the side of a bus, could they?—but when we finally got around to trying it, Zoey saw her first Florida mosquitoes, and that was the end of that idea. (A couple of them got into the bus, but fortunately I had a two-by-four and excellent reflexes.)

Shortly after that, fortunately, we had the epiphany that generally comes to northerners their first night in Florida: the stunning realization that, just as excessive cold can be mitigated by

putting on more clothes, excessive warmth can be ameliorated by their removal. Luckily, we were still so far north in Florida that the process reached equilibrium short of the point at which we'd have had to remove our skin. Soon we were all properly dressed for the climate—which meant pulling all the curtains, to avoid scandalizing the senior citizens who kept driving, strolling, hobbling, or wheeling by outside.

"This is really nice, Daddy," Erin said. "I like it when it's warm enough to be naked. Is it always warm in Florida?"

"Usually a lot warmer than this, from what I hear," I said. We were sitting side by side at the computer, a modified Mac II I'd wired up to its own 12-volt, playing games together. "Down where we're headed, I think they pray for nights this cool. Do you think you'll like really hot weather?"

"I don't know," she said. "I've never tried. Do you think you will?"

"Definitely," I assured her.

"How do you know?"

"For the same reason you're winning this game."

"I'm winning because you're not paying attention," she said.

"Exactly." I stopped sneaking peeks and stared frankly at my wife, who was curled up nearby with a Randy Wayne White novel. "Any weather that makes your mom dress like that is good weather." Zoey ignored me and kept reading, but she pinkened slightly, and I thought I heard a faint purring sound. "In general, the less clothes people have to wear, the better I like it. I'm a nudist at heart. Used to be a practicing nudist, once, but Long Island's just too cold for it."

"Really, Jake?" Zoey asked. Erin, sensing that I had lost interest in the game we'd been playing, quit out of it and opened up the paint program instead.

"Aw, just for a year or so, back in the Sixties. Bunch of us in this huge old house with a really good furnace, kind of a commune. We had a sign by the door on the way out, said, 'Did you remember to dress?' And another outside by the doorbell that said, 'Viewer discretion is advised.'"

"How did it work out?"

I thought I heard that purring sound again, and gave her my best leer. Odd, but pleasant, to know that my wife found it so enjoyable to imagine me walking around naked. "Very interestingly. Nudity did have a few drawbacks, though."

"Like what?"

"Well, when you play guitar naked, you end up with these really dopey-looking creases curving along your chest." She and Erin giggled. "And a cat jumping up on your lap unexpectedly can be a real, uh, catastrophe."

I expected Erin to complain about the pun. Instead she giggled again, and said, "I know what you mean. This one *tickles.*"

I glanced over and dropped my jaw.

There was a cat on her lap.

He—I was quite certain it was a "he"—wasn't a hell of a lot smaller than she was, the size of a bobcat but not as pleasant-looking. He was orange as an autumn pumpkin, with a white cross on his back, either his family coat of arms or protection against vampires. But I suspected the vampires were the ones in need of protection: he was muscled like a balrog. As I studied him, he yawned, displaying sabertooth fangs, and briefly unsheathed his front claws, which looked like he could dice a cucumber by simply flexing his toes. He had baleful yellow eyes with scalloped edges around the pupils. He was permitting Erin to adore his ears.

"How the hell did *that* get in?" I said. So *that* was where that purring had been coming from!

"What?" Zoey said, making a blunt instrument of her book and looking wildly about for mosquitoes. "Where?"

"That," I said, and pointed at the cat. "There."

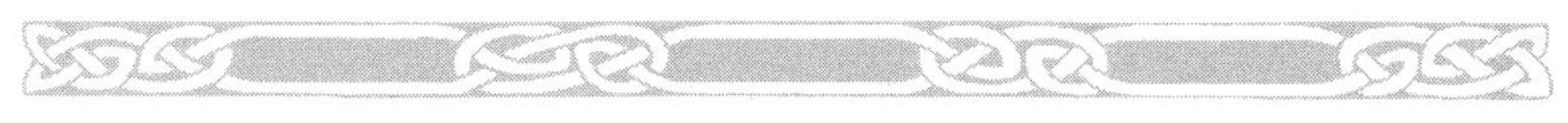

She looked where I was pointing. "Jesus." She put her book down and sat up. "I didn't see it come in past us when we got off and went into that motel room . . . and I'm *sure* it didn't come back aboard with us: I was looking close to make sure no cockroaches followed us in. He must have come in a window before we closed them."

I didn't buy it. "He couldn't have climbed up the side of a bus." I took another look at those claws. "Well . . . maybe he could, but we'd have heard him."

"Maybe he hopped up onto the engine compartment, then on up to the roof, and . . . no, that's silly."

"I can't see it," I agreed. "I've seen cats jump up into an open window, but I never saw one jump *down* into one. He'd have broken his neck trying. Erin, do you know how he got aboard?"

"No, Daddy," she assured me. "He just climbed up on my lap. I thought you guys found him somewhere. Can we keep him?"

"No, honey," Zoey and I said together. "He must belong to somebody, sweetheart," Zoey added.

"He's got no collar," Erin pointed out.

By golly, she was right. And the cat did have the faintly ratty look of the stray, did obviously need some love. Zoey and I exchanged a long and meaningful glance. We already knew we were doomed. For some reason we opted not to admit it, and wasted a good deal of time arguing with Erin. Of course she batted aside arguments faster than we could make them up. Diligent search with a flashlight, which the cat endured with massive patience, failed to turn up a single flea to bolster our case. Twenty minutes later the thing was tucking into a bowl of minced-up chicken leftovers and an adjacent bowl of water, purring like a chainsaw. (Erin, whose knowledge of cats was largely theoretical and colored by common mythology, wanted to give it a saucer of milk, but I explained the effect it has on the adult feline digestive system in real life, and the limited appeal, in an enclosed space, of a cat with diarrhea.)

Right up until then, Zoey had still been resisting, but as she watched the savage thing wolf down its food, she softened. "All right," she conceded. "What are we going to name the damn cat?"

"I don't know," I said. "What's its name, Erin?"

"I'll ask," she said. She reached out her little hand and stroked the cat's neck with unusual dexterity. "Excuse me," she said, "but what's your name?"

The cat broke off eating, looked over its shoulder at her—then got up and trotted across the bus. It stopped before the table the computer was strapped to, and leapt up onto it, unerringly picking the only possible clear landing spot, just to the right of the mousepad. For a wild moment I thought it was going to step over the mouse and start typing . . . but what it did instead made me giggle involuntarily.

It started playing with the mouse.

Just like a cat playing with a mouse—or so I thought at first. Its motions seemed random, alternating between batting it around and pressing on it. But onscreen, the cursor moved to the tool bar, selected a tool, moved it back to what looked like the precise center of the document window. The cat pressed one more time, and then stopped, nudged the mouse away, and looked over at Erin. I squinted at the screen. The tool the cat had selected had been the pencil. And in the center of the screen now lay a single dot.

"I get it!" Erin cried. "Do you get it, Daddy? Mommy? His name is Pixel. Hi, Pixel!"

The cat meowed, leapt down from the table, came right to her, and butted her with his head.

And I started to get a very strange feeling. My ears began to tingle, and I felt hair lift on the back of my neck. A sudden incoherent suspicion had come to me, one that filled me with something like superstitious awe, a kind of reverent terror.

But no—it *couldn't* be. It couldn't possibly. No way in hell. Not in a million years.

Could it?

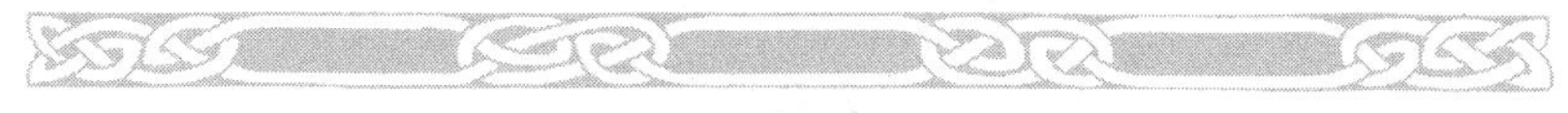

• • •

I couldn't even bring myself to share it with Zoey. I discussed it with Omar the next day, over a private CB channel, while she and Erin were in the back. I thought him the one best qualified of all of us to pour cold water on my astonishing conjecture. Instead, he agreed with me.

"It fits everything I know, Jake," he told me. "I corresponded with her. When the old man died and she decided to move east, she couldn't take a cat. So David Gerrold offered to take it for her, and she accepted. But after a couple of weeks, it took off from Gerrold's place, apparently to the immense relief of his dogs, and hasn't been reported since."

"Well, where did she move to?"

"About five hundred yards from where you were sleeping last night."

"What?"

"I didn't want to say anything. I'm sorry, Jake: I was dying to tell you, naturally, and everybody else too—but just think about it. *Everybody* would have wanted to go and visit her, you know that. You think she needs a hundred barflies and a talking dog showing up for tea?"

I had to agree, though I hated to. "Forget that for now," I said. "Are you telling me you think it could have followed her all the way across the country? With the trail at least two weeks cold to start?"

"Do you doubt it?"

Of course I didn't doubt it. Cats have been famously known to follow much colder trails much longer distances. I just *wanted* to doubt it . . . because the alternative was too awesome to encompass easily.

"God damn it, Jim, are you seriously telling me you think—"

"I can't prove it," he said. "But it fits the known facts. He answers to his name."

"I have *Robert Heinlein's cat* on my bus."

"The Cat Who Walks Through Windshields," he agreed solemnly. "Man, that's heavy."

"Jesus Christ."

"You mind if I pass the word?"

"Uh . . ." I pulled out and passed a senior citizen, an action that was becoming automatic. "Shit no, I guess not. Go ahead. I'm gonna need a while to deal with this."

"Ten four," he said, and was gone.

Pixel hopped up on the dashboard and looked at me. I looked back at him for a long while, and eventually noticed that I was smiling so broadly at him, my ears hurt.

"Welcome aboard, sir," I said. "We are honored to have you with us."

"Myert," he said graciously, and faced forward to watch the road.

"Hey, Zoey!" I called. "Come in here and sit down. Bring the kid."

"Are you out of your cotton-picking *mind?*" Zoey greamed when I told her. (Cross between a groan and a scream, remember? Similar to a scroan.) "Stipulate that a cat could make it from California to the Florida coast without being turned into road pizza or other ethnic food. Say he finds his way all the way to the new home of Virginia Heinlein. Why the hell would he *leave* her again? And hitch a ride with a caravan of escaped mental patients headed for the looniest corner of the land?"

"Beats me," I admitted. "Maybe that retirement community she's in now doesn't allow pets, and he doesn't want to get her turfed out—I don't know, Zo."

"Without sneaking in at least once to say hello and good-bye first? You said Omar told you the last he heard, Mrs. Heinlein hadn't seen any sign of Pixel. Her Pixel, I mean."

"He *did* sneak in, Mommy," Erin said.

We both turned and looked at her. "Say again?" I said.

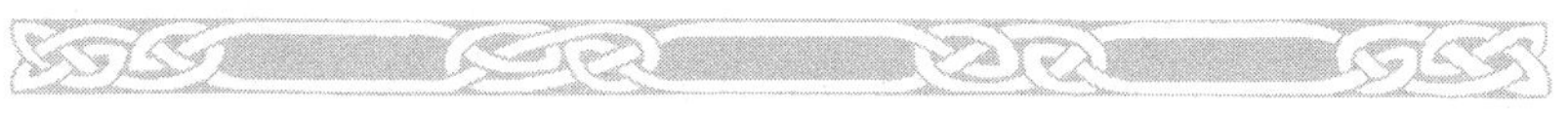

"He did sneak in and see her. He just didn't let her see *him*."

Zoey and I exchanged a glance.

"Why not, honey?" she asked.

Erin was already losing interest in the subject; she was hunched forward over her safety belt, inspecting her toes. "He knew it'd only make her sad if he moved back in with her. You know, remind her of *him*. Of Mr. Heinlein. Pixel came to check on her, because Mr. Heinlein asked him to, and then he saw she was just fine and he decided to come with us next."

"Oh."

Pause.

"How do you know that, Pumpkin?" I asked, already suspecting the answer.

"Pixel told me," she said. "When are we gonna get there, Daddy?"

It was the combination that floored me. The first statement was extraordinary, even for a child as unique as Erin; the question might have come from any child that ever lived. (And probably had.) It was clear from her manner and voice that she had vastly more interest in the second topic than the first. I couldn't help it: I broke into giggles, and she glanced up in mild surprise. "What's so funny?"

"Nothing, nothing. Uh . . . my guess is we'll be there in another four hours."

"Good. Pixel wants to see it."

Bemused as I was, that caught my attention. "Really?"

"I told him all about it. He says it reminds him of stories Mr. Heinlein used to let him read over his shoulder, by some guy named Varley. How come you never read *him* to me, Daddy?"

Zoey and I had a policy; every night, one or the other of us would read Erin to sleep. Naturally we had started with the best. (During waking hours, she often read other things of her own choice, generally nonfiction—though usually on the computer screen: she still found books a little awkward to handle at that age.) "We'll get to him after we work our way through all the

Heinleins and Sturgeons. We've still got a few of those left to go."

Zoey cleared her throat. "Uh . . . honey? They have pretty strict rules there. I'm sorry, but I don't think they'll let Pixel in. He'll have to wait outside with Uncle Ralph."

Erin finished admiring her toes and straightened up. "They can't keep him out," she said positively.

Huh. If she and Jim Omar were correct, and this was in truth and in fact *the* Pixel, she certainly had *that* right. I glanced around. "Where the hell is he, anyway?"

"Four buses back," Erin said.

"Oh. Well, as long as he—*huh?*"

"He went back to meet Uncle Ralph," she said.

"But—" Since last I had seen that cat, with my own personal eyeballs, on this bus, we had been continuously in motion—at fifty-five miles an hour. Ralph was indeed four buses back up the line today, riding with Fast Eddie.

"He says he wants to meet everybody. He's just starting with Uncle Ralph 'cause they'll be able to understand each other better."

I started to comment . . . then changed my mind. I had been deliberately staying off CB, because I didn't want to listen to fifty people asking me if I really thought that was Robert Heinlein's personal cat I had there with me, especially when I didn't know what to answer; *let Omar sort it all out* had been my plan. But now I nudged the gain up and picked up the mike. "Yo, Tricky Fingers, you got the Stringbean on the front door, come back?"

"Yeah?"

Eddie hates CB lingo; I only use it to tease him. "Say, good buddy, how's the pussy situation at your twenty?"

"It's him, Boss. No shit."

"Say again, good buddy."

"Quit it, willya? He's Pixel."

"He's really there, then?"

"Him and Ralph are rappin'. Damnedest ting youse ever hoid.

Ralph growls. Pixel meows. Den Ralph translates." He lowered his voice. "I tink Ralph is scared shit of him. I don't blame him, eeda."

I could hear a little of it going on in the background. "Jesus," I said. "How the hell did he get from here to there?"

"He's Pixel," Eddie repeated. "G'bye." And he signed off.

I couldn't blame him. The conversation there was probably more interesting. I shut down the CB again and met Zoey's eyes. "My God," I said. "It's true."

She sighed, and relaxed slightly. "I guess it is."

"Omar called it. The Cat Who Walks Through Windshields."

Her face broke into a broad smile, as warm and nourishing as the Florida sun itself. "Holy shit. What an omen."

"I don't believe in omens," I said.

"Neither do I," she agreed happily.

I found myself smiling back. "But what a fucking omen!"

Four hours later our ragtag caravan pulled into Disney World.

Erin had been right: Pixel had no trouble at all getting in. Nor did we. We'd phoned ahead, and learned that the Disney booking office was absolutely unfazed by the prospect of accommodating a party of slightly over a hundred people arriving in some thirty vehicles, most of them extremely eccentrically modified schoolbuses. I got the impression we were the fifth or sixth such group that day.

And that is about all I propose to say here about my time at Disney World. I won't even say we all had a wonderful time, because if you've ever been there, you already know that, and if you haven't, you won't have a clue what I mean. I know there are a lot of folks of my age and general hairiness these days who feel a knee-jerk need to put Disney down. Fuck those people. I know there are good and several reasons to question some of the goals, strategies, and tactics of the Disney corporate empire as a whole. I don't care. In my life I have managed to see both

Disneyland and Disney World . . . and I will remember both a lot longer and a lot better than I'll remember, say, Washington, D.C.

The only improvement I would suggest would be a more flexible policy regarding number of legs. I understand why they need to keep out dogs, but I wish they'd make an occasional exception for sentient ones who have taught themselves to use human plumbing. (Really—I've seen it.) Ralph insisted he didn't mind waiting out in the parking lot, and later loudly claimed to have had a splendid time with a cute little Airedale in the same fix, but we all knew better. It's just not fair, that's all.

On the other hand, since there were no other dogs inside, there was nothing for Pixel to cause a commotion by killing.

The rest of us, though, all went to bed that night happily exhausted. It's so rare in this life that you feel like you got what you paid for. We'd only scratched the surface, of course—you could spend a *month* at Disney World and not see it all—but somehow that awareness only made what we *had* experienced the sweeter. We could come back. When my head hit the pillow, one of my last thoughts was *it doesn't get much better than this*.

And then the next morning, of course, we all got up early and went to see a genuine miracle.

CHAPTER EIGHT

Static Test Site Road

"For NASA, space is still a high priority."
—J. Danforth Quayle, September 5, 1990

WE LEFT DISNEY WORLD just before dawn, in the most orderly and timely departure of our trip to date. A good thing, as I got us lost twice on the way. Jim Omar and the Lucky Duck had left even earlier, at high speed in the horrid little VW, and of course since the Duck was involved the timing worked out perfectly. Just as I was standing at the edge of the traffic jam from hell, trying to breathe pure carbon monoxide and having one of the most surreal conversations of my life with a Florida state trooper who wanted me to *move* all those ugly friggin' buses right God damn it *now*, Omar and Ernie came roaring up along the shoulder, back from Merritt Island, waving from the passenger window the stack of magic orange stiff-paper rectangles they'd managed to wheedle out of a guy Omar knew from his college days. It's always pleasant to watch a hard-on in a uniform detumesce. Clout can be a beautiful thing—when you've got it.

The orange cards were distributed one to a bus, placed

prominently in their front windows, and one by one we pulled onto the shoulder and drove slowly and smugly past hundreds of other stopped vehicles full of envious strangers. When we came to the huge barrier that was stopping them all, beefy cops horsed it out of our way and gestured us through. We were waved through a couple of checkpoints, stopped and very briefly questioned at a third, then passed over a small bridge and found ourselves on a two-lane road through flat tidal plain country. Deep drainage ditches on either side of the road, nothing much visible in any direction except wet-looking tall grass. The sun was up by now, and there was fog on the ground here and there.

Shortly we found ourselves on the tail end of a slow-moving line of cars, most of them considerably more expensive-looking than anything we had. We tooled along for a while at about twenty miles an hour, and once or twice the line stopped altogether for a minute or two, when more important vehicles up ahead had a use for that particular road.

I didn't mind a bit. My hands were trembling so badly from excitement that I'd have had trouble controlling my bus at anything over twenty. I heard my own pulse playing a Krupa solo in my ears, I could feel myself grinning like an idiot, my voice when I spoke sounded to me like a chipmunk on methedrine. Zoey and Erin were equally buzzed, and probably so was everyone in the caravan. Even Pixel felt it; he sat rigid on Erin's lap with his head thrust forward, staring out ahead and purring as loud as the bus in low gear.

And then suddenly we were there.

Find a spot, pull approximately into it, brake to shuddering halt, slam her in neutral, set brake, kill engine, leave keys, crank open door, spring for the stairs, bounce off wife, spring for stairs again, trip over cat, fall backward, land heavily, whack skull, feel daughter leap down onto chest from car seat and run down torso to stairs, curse feebly, spring for stairs again, fall down stairs onto hard blacktop, whack forehead, get up, postpone checking for broken bones or concussion and join thundering herd sprinting

uphill past the souvenir stands and portable toilets to the viewing area—

—where, like everyone else, I stopped in my tracks and stared, gaped, gawked, slack-jawed as a country yokel seeing his first transsexual hooker, awestruck as an atheist in Paradise, silent on a peak in Florida—

—stared, with my own personal eyeballs, across no more than a couple of miles of stunningly beautiful country, at an honest to God spaceship, right there at the edge of the shining sea.

Apparently Omar's friend had prudently concluded that our caravan was just a little too flagrantly weird for the Kennedy Space Center's main VIP site; the passes he'd supplied us were for the secondary VIP viewing area on Static Test Site Road. I didn't give a damn. I was forty-something years old and I was *standing in a fucking spaceport.*

The weather was less than ideal; there was a good deal of ground fog, and the air was on the chilly side. I didn't give a damn about that either. Let 'em hold! I was prepared to wait—to stand right there in that spot without shifting my weight or shitting my pants—for a week if necessary.

Suddenly I let out a squeak, spun in my tracks, and sprinted back downhill to the parking area, for the binoculars we had all forgotten when we'd spilled off the bus. I collected all three pairs, plus a reference book, the camera, and a collapsible tall chair for Erin to sit in, so I wouldn't have to carry her on my shoulders to let her see over the heads of the crowd. Then I sat on the bottom step and waited for my breathing and pulse to return to normal—it seemed a poor idea to die just now—then I got up and trudged slowly back up the hill. Stopping along the way at a tourist-vacuum to load myself down further with two coffees, an apple juice, film, postcards, a NASA sunhat for Erin, NASA ballcaps for myself and Zoey, and three pairs of sunglasses. Fortunately I was able to offload an awful lot of money.

With my total mass thus lowered, I was able to achieve escape velocity, and reached the top of the hill before my main engine ran completely out of fuel.

While I was setting up Erin's high chair and lifting her into it with the last of my strength, Pixel drank about a third of my coffee. I claimed it from him and finished it, then aimed my binoculars across the Banana River at Pad 39-B, and began serious gawking.

She was fucking gorgeous.

Discovery, she was. Flight STS-29, the twenty-eighth Shuttle mission. (STS-28, *Columbia*, had developed serious problems, we were told, and would not lift until the following August.) A heartbreakingly beautiful sight, standing there against the sky. This would only be the second launch since the Great Hiatus that had followed the *Challenger* Tragedy—the horrid pause that might well have turned into the end of the space program, if blessed Richard Feynman had not thought of a novel use for a glass of ice water. For a while I had feared I might never have a chance to see such a sight as this again.

All my reading had not prepared me for how *big* she was. Oh, I know the Space Shuttle is a midget compared to the old Apollo Program boosters—from where I stood, I could see that the immense doors of the Vehicle Assembly Building off to the left were almost twice as tall as they needed to be to pass a Shuttle. But knowing that brontosaurs once walked the earth does not diminish the impact of your first close-up encounter with an elephant. I could not believe they proposed to hurl that enormous massive object into the air, so high that it wouldn't come down until it was damn good and ready. I felt an enormous thrill of pride to belong to a species that could even conceive of a thing so splendidly arrogant—let alone pull it off.

There were maybe two hundred or so of us scattered across that bluff. Some were sober serious professionals, busy setting up complex and obviously expensive equipment of various kinds. Dozens of others had set up simple tripods, and were

mounting and testing either cameras or video gear. An equal number was preparing for handheld work—and perhaps half the total crowd had come simply to watch. Two boomboxes could be heard, one softly playing anonymous music, one somewhat louder tuned to a local newsfeed. Two giant and powerful loudspeaker towers were supplying us with live transmissions between Mission Control and *Discovery*'s flight deck, but at this point in the launch sequence, exchanges were infrequent and usually incomprehensible.

I had my breath back under control, but my heart was still hammering like mad. I could feel it.

"Can you see okay, Pumpkin?" I asked my daughter.

"It looks foggy down there, Daddy," Erin said. Sitting there high on her aluminum throne in her yellow sundress and sunglasses, she looked quite regal. "Do you think they'll launch on schedule?"

She was right: *Discovery* stood somewhere between ankle-deep and knee-deep in ground fog. But the sun had risen well above it by now. "Hard to say, honey. They never have once, so far. But they might—or they might come close, anyway. The sun will burn that off pretty quick, I think."

Behind me, Jim Omar's voice said, "Two-hour hold, max—if nothing else goes wrong."

"Well, tell 'em not to hurry on *my* account," Zoey said, tugging at Erin's yellow sundress to straighten it. "This is a nice place to sit and be."

"Amen," Omar said.

His diagnosis was prophetic: that bird was scheduled to lift at 8 A.M., and it was only a little after 10 when they went into the final countdown.

Okay, you've probably seen film or video footage on TV. But if you haven't been to a launch, at least as close as the thousands

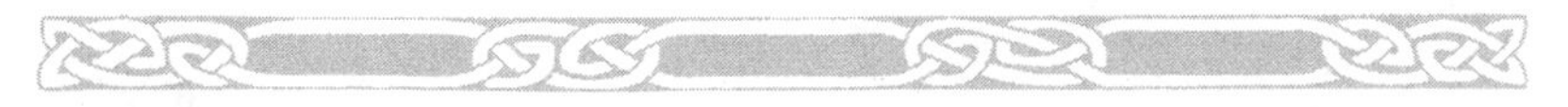

of cars stacked up back out on the highway, you just don't know anything about it.

At first the world is nothing but horizon, endless ocean and sky, all of it still, tranquil, serene. Three-hundred-and-sixty-degree Spielberg, rich and vivid. Lazy clouds overhead, a flight of birds just visible gliding low over marsh flats in the distance, a few boats out on the water. The stillness is not perfect—there is the countdown bellowing out of those superb speaker horns, and there is the internal thunder of elevated pulse—but basically the world is as it has always been: at rest, indifferent to anything any of the scurrying ants on its surface might come up with.

Then Hell breaks loose.

A dirty white explosion spreads in all directions. At its center, beneath the stacked array, a Beast is born. It is mighty. And angry. Its roar shatters the world, splits the sky, echoes up and down the Florida coast and miles out to sea. You thought you knew what to expect, but this is louder. The sound is tangible, hits you with physical force, vibrates up your legs from the ground beneath your feet, scares the living shit out of you. Your first thought is that you are witnessing a disaster even more awful than *Challenger:* an on-the-pad explosion.

Then the Beast's two big brothers wake up—the giant solid rocket boosters—and Heaven, Hell, Purgatory, and Limbo all break loose together and start to argue. The sound is indescribable, just short of unbearable. So insensate is the rage of this new Beast that the world itself will not have it. No matter that something the size and weight of an apartment building is sitting on its back: it lifts from the ground on a raving column of its own fury and rises impossibly into the air, becomes a thick growing tower of white smoke, the 128-ton Shuttle stack balanced on top like a Ping-Pong ball on the stream from a firehose. The bonds of Earth can be as surly as they like: the Beast is surlier, shrugs its terrible shoulders, and slips them clean.

You realize that you are pounding your hands together and

screaming *"Go, baby, go!"* like an idiot at the top of your lungs, and you gather that everyone around you is doing the same, but you can't hear any of it. Part of you wishes you had control of your hands so that you could take photos like you planned to, and another part is amused at the audacity of the notion that this literally earthshaking event could possibly be squeezed through a pinhole and captured on a piece of celluloid smaller than a matchbook. Instead you watch in reverent terror as a utensil built by bald apes flings ninety-seven tons of metal and plastic two million miles.

With five live men aboard.

You can read about something like that, and see it on television, and spend a large portion of your leisure hours trying to imagine what it must be like and thinking about what it means, and you think you get it. You're a space buff: if anybody gets it, you do. And I suppose you do—as an intellectual concept. Then you go there and see it with your own eyes, feel it with your own bones . . . and are astonished to discover that only now, for the first time, do you really Get It. Until now space travel had been real to me in the same sense that World War II was real to me, or China: I'd been told about it and had no reason to doubt what I'd been told. Now I *got it*.

My automatic pilot reminded me I hadn't checked on Erin in too long; I snatched a glance, saw her just behind me, in her chair where she belonged, and turned back to the spectacle.

For two million years it had been only a fantasy, a monkey dream. For the first fifteen years of my own life it had still been only a fantasy, something a teacher or a scientist might laugh at you for believing in. For the next quarter century it had been a news story—one that seemed to bore most of my fellow citizens silly. But now it was reality—*real* reality; that is, the part experienced by *me*—and the two-million-year-old dream had really come true:

The species I belonged to had figured out how to climb the biggest tree there is. We were already becoming familiar with its lowest branches.

In that moment, I *knew*, as fact, with utter certainty, that one day we were going to climb all the way to the top. Nothing was going to prevent us. Not presidents, proxmires, press, public opinion, economic forces, or nuclear winter.

No, it could be delayed, but it could not be stopped. This was evolution in action, before my eyes. As surely as we had come down out of the trees, as surely as we had crawled up out of the tidal pools in the first place, we were going to do this thing.

As long as we don't end the universe first, came the thought, and suddenly I was terrified.

When Nikola Tesla had first told me I had to save the universe I thought I Got It. Hell, I'd helped save the world, twice: what was the big deal? Glibness, flipness, denial. Now I *got it.*

Sometime in the next ten years or so, I was going to be involved in something alongside which this paradigm-shifting world-shaking thing I was now experiencing was an utterly insignificant event.

This had only required billions of dollars, millions of people, and a few centuries of scientific advance. But for my immensely more important and difficult task, *I* had access to . . . my wife, my kid, and a bunch of rummies personally known to me to be collectively about as reliable as an Internet connection.

The big white beanstalk rose toward heaven, carrying a truck, carried it so high that it appeared to dwindle away to nothing at all, while I stood there and felt myself sweating.

I was snapped out of my fog by the sound of Long-Drink McGonnigle's annoyed voice behind me. "Where the hell are they *going?*"

Low Earth Orbit, of course; what the hell did he mean? I turned to him, saw him looking around and glaring. So I looked around myself.

The crowd was leaving.

Half of them were already gone, disappearing down the slope

past the souvenir stands and portable toilets toward the parking area. The rest were in the last stages of disassembling tripods, packing gear, collecting possessions, clearly about to depart. Some were taking their time about it, but clearly only because they knew there was going to be a jam-up out in the parking lot: none of them watched the white beanstalk anymore, and none of them appeared to pay the slightest attention to the two speaker towers, which were still broadcasting live transmissions.

I couldn't believe it.

Three college kids near me finished strapping up their packs and started to amble away. I put out a hand to stop one of them. "Excuse me, but where the hell are you going?"

He stared at me. "Daytona Beach. Why, you need a ride?"

"No, I mean . . . I mean . . . how the hell can you *go?*" I gestured helplessly at the curving white beanstalk above us, and the glowing dot still visible at its tip. "Now?"

He turned and glanced at it, turned back to me. "It's over," he said, as one stating the obvious.

"Over?" I scroaned. "Are you out of your fucking *mind?* The SRBs are still firing! It was later in the flight than this when the . . ." I trailed off, superstitiously unwilling to speak the *Challenger*'s name while there was a bird in the air.

Zoey tugged my arm. "Jake—"

"For Chrissake," I told the kid, "they haven't even reached the first abort point: at this point we don't know if they're going to Low Orbit or Portugal—"

"Thirty seconds to SRB separation," the speakers brayed.

"—you see? It'll be at least five more minutes before MECO—before we'll know whether those five poor bastards are gonna live through the next four days or not." I pointed to the nearest speaker tower. "When we do, we'll know it before anybody else in the country. How can you possibly *leave?*"

He looked at me as if I were a penguin at a zoo, with mild interest and just a trace of pity. "The show's over, Pop," he explained, and took off to catch up with his friends, who had paused to see if he needed help kicking the old hippie's ass.

"Jesus, what's *wrong* with that generation?" Long-Drink asked. "Do they think all this is, like, a rock concert? One big spectacular special effect? And as soon as it's off the screen it doesn't exist anymore? Is this what comes of putting on Pink Floyd laser lightshows down at the Planetarium?"

"It's nothing to do with age," Tommy Janssen said. "Look around."

He was right. People of all ages were leaving. Even people who looked intelligent, seemed educated. Everybody but me and my hundred-odd friends, most of whom were looking just as baffled as I was.

"Screw 'em," Isham Latimer said. "Look up, quick."

Just as we did, the SRBs broke away.

I'd seen it many times, on film or on TV, much more clearly through very good telephoto lenses. No matter: the beauty of it struck me dumb.

The boosters pinwheeled away; the Shuttle kept climbing.

After a while my neck hurt, and there was no longer anything much to see, so I looked down and divided my attention between the reference book I had fetched along and the loudspeakers, translating their cryptic acronyms and following the flight in my imagination, as happy as I've ever been in my life.

Some indeterminate time later, I was rudely yanked back to the lower world by the unmistakable smell of an approaching civil servant. Sure enough: a twenty-something android with NASA patches on his shoulders. He looked harassed. Somehow his bureaucratic intuition told him I was the closest thing to a leader he was going to find in *this* group. He approached me, powered down, opened his oral cavity, and played the prerecorded tape for this situation.

"Youpeoplewillhavetocleartheareanow."

I had been expecting him to say something stupid, but this

seemed excessive. "I beg your pardon," I said politely, "but are you on drugs?"

Confused, he replayed his tape, with an addition of his own that I took as a cry for help. "Youpeoplewillhavetoclearthe-areanowplease."

I pointed to the nearest of the loudspeaker towers. "It's almost four minutes to MECO," I explained. The term baffled him; I paraphrased. "This launch is not *over* yet. We can't possibly leave now."

Treating him like a rational being was poor tactics; the word "can't" triggered him to go to DefCon Two. He lowered his brows the prescribed amount, swelled his shoulders, made his jaw muscles squirm, and said, "SirI'mafraidI'mgoingtohavetohave thisareacl—"

"Do you know who you're talking to, son?" Omar's deep voice rumbled from off to my left.

It's one of the interrupt codes. The kid turned toward him and waited for a password to be entered.

"That," Omar said, pointing solemnly at me, "is Neil Armstrong."

To my mild surprise, the kid recognized the name. His apprenticeship for that job must have been giving tour spiels at the visitors' center. The password was valid; he had to step back down to DefCon Three.

"Sorry, Mr. Armstrong," he said, relaxing his shoulders and jaw muscles.

He'd omitted my rank, but I let it pass. He'd also forgotten Armstrong never wore a beard, long hair, or glasses. "That's all right, son. Now fuck off, okay?"

His eyebrows remained lowered. "Uh . . ."

I sighed. "What is it, mister?"

"Well, sir . . ." He gestured vaguely toward the souvenir stands and potties, where a few other androids were staring at us in bafflement. "We all been out here all morning. You know, the crew. Is it okay if we—"

At last I understood. We were all at a holy event. He and his mates were at work. And wanted to split. "Son," I said patiently, "I don't care *what* you do as long as you leave us alone until MECO. That's when they turn off the big motor in the sky-car up there."

"I mean, we're not supposed to remove the portable sanitation units until everybody's—"

"I authorize you to leave," I told him. "If any of us shits after you go, I promise we'll cover it up, okay?" I turned away, triggering his dismissal protocols. He thought about saluting, couldn't decide, settled for a sketch of one, and buggered off.

We went back to monitoring the flight. When they finally announced MECO, just under nine minutes after takeoff, we all heaved a sigh of relief, gave each other high fives, turned around—and found absolutely no visible sign of life but our own vehicles, waiting in the parking lot below. Not even dust clouds settling in the distance. We didn't see another human being until we reached the visitors' center. There were dozens of them there, buying expensive souvenirs to commemorate an event most of them had neglected to finish observing.

I'll never understand people. Even being one doesn't seem to help.

CHAPTER NINE

Bus Turd Flush

"What a waste it is to lose one's mind. Or not to have a mind is being very wasteful. How true that is."
—J. Danforth Quayle's version of the United Negro College Fund motto, "A mind is a terrible thing to waste."

PERHAPS YOU'LL THINK it paradoxical that our group, the space buffs, left the visitors' center and were back out on the highway well *before* the rest of the tourists.

Well, of course we wandered through the Garden of Spacecraft, just like everybody else—real spaceships, who wouldn't?—but we didn't have to keep stopping to read the plaques, and puzzling over the big words: we *knew* what we were looking at. We'd been marveling at those utensils all our lives. We spent some time in the gift shop like the other tourists, too—but a surprising portion of what was for sale there came down to packaged information, which we already knew or had in our libraries. A few souvenirs and we were done. There was a tour of the Kennedy Space Center complex itself we could have taken, that sounded tempting as hell. A Titan booster, a full-scale LEM mockup, a Shuttle simulator—riches!

Nonetheless, at a little after noon we held an impromptu in-

formal conference outside the gift shop and unanimously agreed to hit the road.

Part of it, I guess, was a touch of something that had hit us at Disney World as well. Overload. Do something you really enjoy long enough, and your circuits fry a little. I've been fighting the impulse to say it for three sentences now, but there's no way around it: we were all a little . . . uh . . . spaced out.

Another part of it may have been that seeing Michael L. Coats, John E. Blaha, James P. Bagian, James F. Buchli, and Robert C. Springer get into a big metal can and head off on a journey of two million miles reminded us all subconsciously that our *own* metal cans were still a long way from MECO. The weather forecast for tomorrow was ideal, sunny, no clouds: it would be splendid to begin that last and most glorious leg of our trip, the run down the Keys, early tomorrow morning, and reach Key West in midday. But to do that, we had to camp somewhere well below Miami that night, ideally at least as far as Key Largo. And to accomplish *that,* we had to leave right away.

Oh, if we had put the hammer down and had good luck with traffic we could probably have done it handily—but we wanted to leave a cushion. There was still one more pilgrimage to make, one more holy shrine we all wanted to be absolutely sure we'd have time to visit. Even though we weren't absolutely sure it was there.

But it was.

We reached Fort Lauderdale a little after 4:00, and in its spaghetti-tangle of traffic we got separated briefly. Ever try to get two dozen fully loaded buses and a mess of smaller vehicles all through the same green light in rush hour?

By the time I found the place, there were only two other buses still with me: Long-Drink, and the Quigleys. Twenty yards or so after I turned in off the road, we had to stop at a gate, overhung with palm fronds. A muscle-bound beachboy stuck his head out of the booth. "Who are you here to see, sir?"

"We just want to look around a little," I told him.

He looked me over, looked my bus over, and I could see him reach the conclusion that we did not belong here.

So could Erin. By the time his gaze got back to my window, she had unstrapped herself from her seat, climbed onto my lap, and stuck her head out past me. "We'll just be here a little while, sir," she said, "and I promise we won't hurt anything. It's real important to my dad and his friends; they've been talking about it for *miles*."

The attendant blinked up at her. "I," he began, and was distracted by blaring horns. Long-Drink and Joe Quigley had both pulled into the driveway behind me, and Joe's bus had half its ass sticking out onto the road, blocking rush-hour traffic. The Drink couldn't even pull up alongside me on the left to make more room for Joe, because the outgoing lane was studded with those damned Severe Tire Damage teeth intended to keep out terrorists. I could see the beachboy realizing that at least one of those angry drivers out there on the street was liable to fire up his cell phone and start beefing to management soon. And there was no way for me to back out: even if he denied me entry, I'd have to drive through the gate, turn around, and drive out the exit—followed by two more buses—then take *forever* to reenter the traffic stream and unblock his driveway. Simpler to just let us in. He brought his agonized gaze back to me. "Low profile?" he pleaded.

"Subterranean," I promised him. More horns outside.

He gave me a blank pink Visitor's Parking Slip. "That'll be five dollars."

"Mom?" Erin said. Zoey handed her a bunch of bills from the glove compartment, and Erin reached past me out the window and offered them to the attendant. To reach, he had to leave his booth; he triggered the gate-lift as he did so, to save time and get us off the road as quickly as possible. He came to my window, made a long stretch, took the cash from her little hand, started to unfold it, and froze.

"That should cover all of us," Erin said.

"But . . ." He stopped and recounted the money. "But this is . . ."

He recounted it again. It kept coming out a hundred and fifty bucks.

"We'll be as unobtrusive as possible," I assured him, slipping the bus into gear. "You'll hardly know we're here."

Too late, he realized he'd been had. He began to say something, but by then we were in motion and the engine drowned him out. "Tell everybody to come straight on through, Drink," Zoey was saying into the CB mike. "We already paid the parking fee." In my sideview mirror I saw the kid think about blocking Long-Drink's way, and wisely decide against it. (By that point in the trip, Drink's brake shoes were kind of down to brake sandals. Flip-flops.)

There were a *lot* of places to park. Pocket after pocket of parking spaces, with winding little speed-bumped roads interconnecting them. There was even one mammoth section that looked large enough and empty enough to accommodate all of us—right by the water, which settled it. I drove all the way down to the far end and parked. As Zoey and Erin and I got out, Long-Drink and Joe pulled in on either side of us and disembarked as well. We stood there together a moment in silence, both eager and unwilling to proceed.

"This is it," Long-Drink said, an entirely unaccustomed reverence in his voice. "This is the place."

"It's really here," Joe's wife Arethusa said.

"The marina is, anyway," Joe conceded skeptically.

We were standing near the corner of an enormous L-shaped dock, at which were moored a great number of very expensive-looking shiny boats of every imaginable type and size. The sun was low in the sky, and somehow the light was magical, gave everything crisp edges. Colors seemed slightly more vivid, the way they sometimes look through binoculars.

"Do you suppose—" Zoey began.

"I'm almost afraid to find out," Long-Drink whispered.

"Look!" Joe commanded, and pointed.

We all did—and an electric thrill went through us. "Oh, my God," Zoey said.

There was a sign at the corner. The section of dock that directly abutted the parking lot was labeled "E." The part that stuck out into the water and had boats moored on either side of it was labeled "F."

We began to walk out onto that section, and then to walk very fast, and then I scooped Erin up and we trotted, and before we even had time to reach outright running, we were there. It was there. The place we'd all spent countless happy hours in, and had never laid eyes on before.

Not a lot to see, really. A parking space for a boat, like hundreds of others here. An empty one, at that: no vessel was moored there now. But there was *something* to see. Someone had placed a ceremonial brass plaque there on the dock, just in front of one of the shoulder-high wooden pilings, bolted onto a white concrete plinth that came up to my chest. We stood around like pilgrims and read it silently together.

The plaque read:

SLIP F-18
BAHIA MAR MARINA
DEDICATED TO THE "BUSTED FLUSH"
HOME OF TRAVIS McGEE
FICTIONAL HERO AND SALVAGE CONSULTANT

CREATED BY JOHN D. MACDONALD, AUTHOR

1916–1986

DESIGNATED A LITERARY LANDMARK
FEBRUARY 21, 1987

For the second time that day, I found myself grinning and leaking tears at the same time.

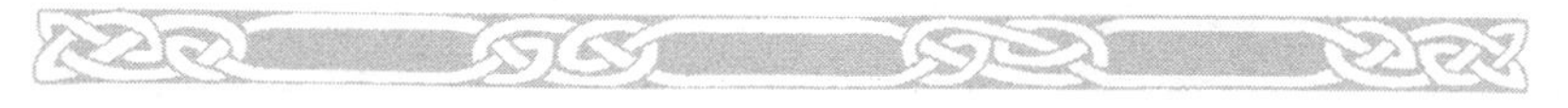

◆ ◆ ◆

Sometime later, Zoey broke the silence with a happy sigh. "Isn't that *nice*?" she said.

"Maybe there *is* some justice in the world," Joe said.

"I wonder who owns this slip now," Long-Drink said.

"Somebody cool," Erin said, "or he wouldn't have let them put that on his doorstep."

"Where do you suppose he is?" Joe asked.

"On his way down to the Keys with a houseboat full of congenial companions, I hope," I said.

A stranger came along, and the dock was narrow enough that we had to make room for him to pass. Everyone else kept their eyes on the plaque or the slip, but I was so profoundly happy I wanted to share it with the world, like a new acidhead, and caught his eye. A stocky, extremely hairy man in shorts and an eye-searing Hawaiian shirt, carrying a newspaper under his arm. He saw me looking at him, saw my maniacal grin, and smiled back pleasantly at once. I gestured at the slip behind me. "It's empty," I heard myself say.

He nodded. "It is always empty. It will never be rented again. His friends no longer own this marina, but they made that an iron-clad condition of sale, in perpetuity."

"That's *cool*," I said.

"Yes," he said. "Yes, it is." And he passed on.

"Did you hear that, guys?" I asked my friends.

"What, hon?" Zoey asked absently.

"This slip will never be rented out again. It's permanently reserved for Travis. Isn't that great?"

"Really?" Arethusa said.

"Yeah. That guy just—oh . . . my . . . *God*."

"What is it, Jake?"

My heart was hammering. It couldn't be. It just was not possible. "I—he—just a minute." I spun on my heel and raised my voice. "Excuse me?"

The stranger kept walking away.

"Sir? Excuse me?"

He was almost out of earshot now.

"Ludweg?" I bellowed desperately.

He stopped in his tracks, turned around, and looked at me. At all of us. Slowly, reluctantly, he came a few steps back toward us, until he was close enough to talk without shouting.

"You are an unusually astute reader," he said to me.

I nodded.

"Even the most devoted fans hardly ever seem to know the first name, for some reason."

I'd noticed that myself, and always wondered why. It's right there on the page in black and white. "Then . . . you're really—"

He grinned. "Heavens, that's not my *real* name. John would never have done that to me. But yes, I am who you think I am."

I lost my voice.

Long-Drink spoke up behind me. "It's an honor to meet you, Professor. How's the *Thorstein Veblen* holding up?"

"Reasonably well," he said. "Would you good people care to join me for a drink there?"

We all turned and looked at each other. I saw the same expression on every face but Erin's. We wanted to so bad we could taste it. And we knew we couldn't. Behind him, we could already see more buses pulling into slots out in the parking lot—half a dozen of them, with a lot more to come.

"Thanks," I said, "but there's over a hundred of us altogether."

"Really?" he said. "Well, another time, perhaps."

"I can't tell you how much I hope so," I said.

He nodded politely, turned, and started to go.

I felt a sudden telepathic communication with my companions. "Wait!" I called.

He turned again.

"Is Travis . . ." I wanted to say, *alive?* ". . . all right?"

He smiled. "Always," he said, and went on his way. As he

reached the end of the dock and turned left he went by Fast Eddie, the Lucky Duck, and a few others. None of them gave him a second glance.

I turned to Zoey, Erin, Long-Drink, and the Quigleys, and we all exchanged a look in which we agreed that none of us was going to say a word about this to the others. Not today, anyway.

Meyer had a right to his privacy.

Like I said, it was kind of a narrow dock. And it did, after all, constitute the sidewalk to the homes of a whole lot of rich people. Rich people do not like to look out their porthole and see a hundred fishbelly-pale strangers on their sidewalk, gawking. I was waiting at the end of the dock by the parking lot for Security when they arrived. (Sure, organizing things and sending folks out there in small groups, ten or so at a time, might have been smart. But possible it wasn't, so I never gave it a thought.)

They'd tried to make it look as much as possible like a real police car, but there's only so much you can do along those lines with a Jeep. It looked like what clown cops would drive in the circus. They'd done a better job of making themselves look like real cops. Like De Niro, they'd been willing to put on weight for the part. The one on my side of the Jeep ignored me for a moment, sizing up the crowd out there on the dock, then aimed his opaque sunglasses up at me.

"Y'all haul ass, nah," he said. His voice sounded like warm shit being stirred with a wooden spoon.

"We're here to see the literary landmark," I saw myself saying to him in those twin reflective lenses.

He considered the remark for a moment, found nothing there for him. "Ah *said*, shag ass out o' here."

From somewhere down around my knees, Erin spoke up. "Officer, we came a long way to see that place. It's special to us. We're not hurting anything. We won't even leave cigarette butts or flashbulbs or gum wrappers or anything. I promise."

He aimed his sunglasses down at her for several silent seconds, trying to decide whether he'd really heard her speak or not. No, of course not. He returned his Ray-Bans to me and, since he didn't seem to be getting through to me, raised his voice. "G'wan, git, nah!"

From somewhere down around my *other* foot, I heard a hissing sound. I glanced down. Pixel, back arched, hair lifting, teeth bared. He didn't like Erin being dissed. The situation was deteriorating fast.

"Look," I said to the rent-a-cops, seeking a logic that would appeal to them, "there's *got* to be a bookstore in this marina complex, right?"

Both rent-a-cops stared at me.

"A gift shop?" I suggested, pointing over at a cluster of buildings in the near distance.

"Thur's a gif' shop," the one on my side admitted grudgingly.

"Well, there you go. Undoubtedly they stock the works of John D. MacDonald there, and I can promise you these folks are going to buy out every copy, just so they can boast they've got a copy they bought *here*. We're money on the hoof to Management."

"Ever' copy o' whut?"

"Books! Books by John MacDonald, the man memorialized by that plaque out there. The creator of Travis McGee, for heaven's sake!"

He turned to his partner. "They got any books in thet gift shop? Ah never seen none."

The driver shrugged. "Half a dozen books on fishin' is all. This Johnny Donald McGoo write fish books, boy?"

I opened my mouth, and was too shocked and scandalized to speak. I felt a gentle hand on my shoulder, turned to see Long-Drink McGonnigle. "Meyer said the place was under new management," he reminded me.

"Sure," I said angrily, "but he didn't mention the new owners aren't bright enough to put a bucket under a waterfall of money."

"Think about it, Jake," he said. "I kind of *like* it that way."

I did think about it—and saw what he meant. If the present

owners were that smart, we'd have arrived to find not a respectful plaque off the ass end of the parking lot, but some horrid sort of McGeeLand, commercialized to the hilt in the classic Florida style we were already becoming familiar with. T-shirts with Trav's picture on them. Little plastic models of the *Busted Flush,* accurate down to the oversize shower stall, and of Miss Agnes the electric-blue Rolls-Royce pickup truck. Hairy Meyer action figures. Disposable heroine dolls. Thermal beach cups with the Plymouth Gin logo. Acres of books at inflated prices.

Extra money for Mr. MacDonald's widow, I suppose—some tiny percentage of it. I can only hope she doesn't need extra money that badly.

"You're right, Drink," I said. "Let's split before somebody notices us and wises up." I turned back to the security thugs. "We're leaving now. Take us a couple of minutes."

Badly confused by our exchange, and my surrender, they took refuge in nods. "Yew got fahv," the driver said, and peeled away.

So I left Pixel to calm down and went back out on the dock and explained the situation to everybody, and with gratifyingly little argument was able to start the herd moving in the general direction of the buses.

"Come on, Daddy," Erin called a few minutes later from her chair in the front of the bus. "Everybody's ready to go but us!"

"Be out in a minute!" I was as good as my word, slid into my seat and buckled my seat belt before the flushing sounds behind me had ceased. "Roll 'em, baby," I told Zoey.

"Key Largo, here we come," she agreed, and put the beast in gear. As we moved slowly through the parking lot, I stared out my window, trying to memorize the place. I felt a strange, bittersweet sadness. How ironic, to find myself glad that so few people cared about John D. MacDonald's memorial. He himself might have appreciated the humor in it.

"Daddy," Erin said.

"Yes, honey¿"

"The toilet's still flushing."

"Oh, my God—"

Suddenly there was a horrid sound from below, a kind of bass screeching, as if God were trying to log on to the Internet. Zoey took her foot off the gas at once, but it was already too late: with a final loud *skrunk* suggesting a successful connection, the sound stopped before we could.

"Was that what I know it was?" she asked calmly.

I unstrapped and went to look, just to be certain. Pixel came along and stared with me, licking his paws. "You know that plumbing problem we developed?" I called back.

"Intimately," Zoey said.

"We don't have it anymore."

"Uh-huh."

"Now what we have is more of a *no*-plumbing problem."

There was a silence in the bus that lasted perhaps ten seconds. And then all three of us, simultaneously, broke up—laughed so hard we rocked the bus.

"Talk about your *Busted Flush*," Zoey roared.

Through the open windows, we could hear the laughter traveling back along the caravan. For a minute there, the whole parking lot echoed with it.

Then after a while the smell drifted in the windows, too, and at first that just made us laugh harder, but finally it reminded us that the rent-a-cops would be back to check on us soon. Still chuckling, Zoey put it back in gear and pulled out. The others followed us, detouring daintily around what we had left behind.

And the CB was suddenly full of congratulations.

Look, I'd been having trouble with that inboard sewage system the whole trip, okay? To this day, more than a decade later, despite repeated denials by me *and* my family, there is not one of my friends who doesn't believe I did it deliberately somehow. There's no justice.

On the way out the gate, Zoey handed the beachboy another wad of cash from the dwindling stash in the glove compartment. "For the mess," she explained, and drove on. I couldn't see his expression from where I was sitting, but I could imagine it.

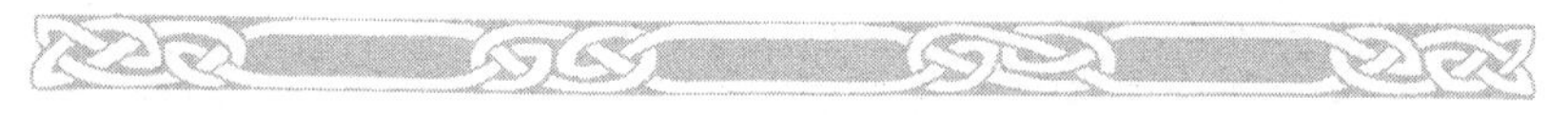

Traffic outside was, if anything, worse. By the time the last bus finally made it back out onto the road (miraculously without any accidents), Zoey and Erin and Pixel and I were already outside Lauderdale city limits and getting back on the highway. We all met up at the first rest stop, where Omar and I did what repairs we could to the underside of my bus while everybody gassed up, and then we were back on the road again.

Zoey drives faster than me. Better, too. She put the hammer down, and we managed to reach the state park at Key Largo about five minutes before everyone was too tired to drive another mile.

There was no party tonight; it was too late and we were all too exhausted, from the emotional impact of the day as much as from the long drive. Everyone had already eaten, aboard, on the way. Nonetheless a few of us got out and milled around together briefly, speaking of all we had seen since sunup.

"What's that smell?" Maureen Hooker asked suddenly.

Conversation ceased while we all sniffed the air and tried to identify it. I realized I'd been smelling it for some time now, without quite being aware of it.

"Salt," Slippery Joe Maser said. "The sea."

"Sure," Maureen said. "But what else?"

"Iodine," Fast Eddie said, "and mildew."

Everyone slowly nodded.

"Limestone," Long-Drink said. "Crushed limestone." A few more nods.

"Zawdust," Ralph von Wau Wau said positively. "Burnt zawdust. Unt somevere nearby, oysters."

Jim Omar was just getting down from his bus. "Hey, Jim," I called, "what's that smell, do you think?"

He lifted his head, and his nostrils flared. He smiled. "That's South Florida," he said.

He was right. We smelled it again when we woke up the next morning, and occasionally throughout that day, and after that we hardly ever noticed it again. But it was always there. It still is today.

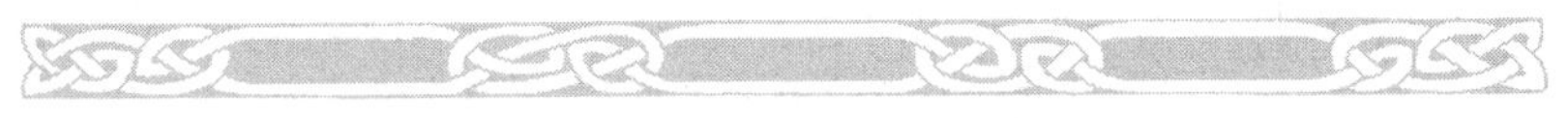

CHAPTER TEN

The Goldbrick Road

"May our nation continue to be the beakon [sic] *of hope to the world."*
—the 1989 Christmas card of the J. Danforth Quayle family

I WAS AWAKENED JUST after dawn by a loud crash.

Oh God, I thought, sitting up in my bunk, *the damn sewage system fell out.* Then I remembered it already had. Besides, the noise had come from the wrong place—from up at the *front* of the bus. Now I was fully awake. Had we slipped our parking brake and hit something? I'd have sworn Zoey parked us on level ground. I climbed over her sleeping form and went to investigate.

Through the windshield I saw the front hood was open. No, it was *missing.* I'd been told Florida assayed out about as high as New York for sneak thieves—but could someone possibly be trying to steal my *engine?*

I dismounted carefully, and saw no one around. I located the hood panel lying on the ground beside the bus, with a dent in the middle. I hunkered beside it and looked around. There were no footprints visible in the sandy earth anywhere near it—nothing at all but a broken pair of sunglasses, two coconuts, and a ciga-

rette butt. I squatted there, tapping my thigh with a large wrench I happened to have in my hand and trying to figure it out.

WHANK! Thonk! Thabibble . . .

Once I'd gotten back to my feet and brushed off the sand and recovered the wrench and combed the cigarette butt out of my hair, it wasn't hard to figure out. *Another* fucking coconut had fallen from the palm tree overhead—just like the one that had woken me.

This one had flattened the air filter, ripped one of my spark plug wires loose, and was presently wedged between the radiator and the engine. Down near the bottom where it would be almost impossible to get at: the *thabibble* at the end had been it wedging itself in there good. I looked up at that palm tree, with the intention of cursing it, and may even have opened my mouth to do so—but all of a sudden it hit me.

I was looking up at a palm tree.

Oh, we'd been seeing the damn things for days, even before we crossed the Florida line. But this one was different. Don't ask me how I could tell, I knew diddly about palm trees, but I was sure. Those other ones had been props, transplants, brought there from somewhere else to con the tourist or amuse the wealthy. This was the real deal. This one had just grown here.

The sun was coming up. The air was warm and damp and spicy. I was where palm trees grow. And heading south. Well, southerly. All at once I was too excited to even consider going back to sleep.

Just as well. By the time everyone else was up, I'd managed to get the damn coconut out of the engine compartment and make repairs. Only got hit by one coconut, and it almost completely missed my head.

It was a happily chattering group that pulled onto U.S. 1 that morning and headed off down the Keys, and our mood improved with every one of its hundred-odd miles.

Basically it is a highway through the ocean, which occasionally intersects lumps of sand-covered coral on its way west. These are the fabled Keys, where the people called Conchs live, and they range in size from mounds that a couple of kids with dirt-bombs could defend against their whole neighborhood, to comparatively enormous islands nearly as big as the Disney World parking lot. When you do cross a Key, the strip along either side of the road briefly becomes heavily encrusted with restaurants, burger stands, motels, boating and fishing and diving and tanning service industries, souvenir joints, swim-with-real-dolphins places, and assorted other tourist-milking apparatus. Nonetheless each Key was welcome, as the road usually briefly widened out to more than two lanes for a while, allowing at least a few cars to pass our elephantine caravan. I think that may be why we never actually drew any automatic weapons fire.

Only a lunatic could ever have dreamed of connecting all those featureless heaps of coral, sand, sawgrass, and mangrove flats with a 105-mile road to nowhere, and only an incredibly rich lunatic could have pulled it off. The longest and most expensive coral necklace on earth. Florida had produced a man who did it *twice*.

Evidence of his first effort, the one he had lived to see completed, kept appearing on our right as we drove: a second trestle bridge, much like the one our highway sat on and parallel to it. But the other one had nothing much visible on it but pelicans. It had *gaps* in it, every now and then, some of them big enough for a couple of Staten Island–sized ferries to pass through at once, with Conch kids fishing off the ends. Every once in a while it went away altogether for a few miles. It was the fabled Railroad That Went To Sea—or what was left of it.

One day around the turn of the century, the lunatic, Henry Morrison Flagler (the man who made Florida what it is today; John D. Rockefeller's closest associate), took it into his head that Key West would be the finest resort destination in America . . . if only there were a way to *get to* it from America without get-

ting seasick. There were no cars, then—but there was a railroad, from Daytona all the way down to a tiny-but-growing hamlet called Miami, and by an odd coincidence Flagler happened to own that railroad. (Among others.) So he gave orders, and men died in the mud, and by 1912 there was a reinforced concrete railroad bridge running the whole length of the Keys. You could get from Miami to Havana in twelve hours by train and boat. The terminus, Key West, until then primarily a place where the pirates and moonrakers kept their bars and brothels, began to boom.

But Mother Nature outboomed it. The Labor Day hurricane of 1935 (they didn't name them in those days) came raging in off the ocean and tore that railroad to pieces, smashed forty miles of track and trestle into the sea, killing over six hundred people in the process. Today, more than seventy-five years later, the railroad bridge has never been repaired or demolished: either is more trouble than it's worth.

The highway bridge that replaced it three years later is better built, and has outlasted many hurricanes. (Some three hundred of those killed by the '35 'Cane were WWI vets working on the highway at the time.) I never felt a twinge of worry anywhere along its length: compared to the best-maintained bridge in, say, New York City, it was the eighth wonder of the world.

And I'll tell you this: if there is a more beautiful drive anywhere on the planet Earth, I don't want to take it. I don't think my heart could stand it. But I don't see how there could be.

It's one of those things that can't be described; you'll have to take my word for it. I wasted several miles of the drive ransacking the English language for a word that might adequately convey to someone who'd never seen it even so basic a thing as the color of the water, there. It was a different color, a different *kind* of color, than any other ocean (or for that matter, thing) I'd ever seen before, a pale, translucent, jewellike, somehow subtly *glowing* green-blue, somewhere between turquoise and the color of lime juice. Here and there you saw large irregular darker green

patches in it that had to be the coral reefs just under the surface. The weather was absolutely perfect: endless blue sky, with just enough majestic clouds to decorate it. Florida sunshine felt good on Long Island skin. The wind kept bringing pleasant smells in the window as we went. That ever-present South Florida smell I mentioned earlier, which we still found strange enough to register and savor, plus small piquant accents that came and went. Barbecuing meat. Suntan lotion. Woodsmoke. Limes. Bug spray. Beer. Neoprene. Just breathing got you high. Looking out the window and breathing at the same time was enough to make you see God.

The CB buzzed with happy talk as we drove.

"I can't believe it," Long-Drink said. "There's hardly anybody here! And the ones that are, most of 'em look like actual human beings. I thought it was gonna be wall-to-wall rich people, in giant condo towers—but look: actual houses and stuff. Man, it's like Montauk, thirty or forty years ago before they fucked it up."

"It isn't anything like Orlando was," Maureen Hooker said. "I mean, most of the people along here milk tourists for a living too, obviously . . . but the Conchs don't seem as—I don't know—as *desperate* about it as they did back up there."

"This is hard to take," Slippery Joe Maser said. "It's so damn pretty it makes me suspicious. Ow!" That last was doubtless one or both of his wives kicking him.

"Jake¿" Fast Eddie called.

"Yeah, Ed¿"

"Ya made a good move."

There was a brief hash of sound as everybody tried to agree at once. I felt warmer inside than the sunshine on my arm. "We all did," I said when the commotion paused long enough.

"Fuckin A," Eddie agreed.

"Hey, where are we up to now¿" the Lucky Duck asked.

"Uh . . ." I peered out the window ahead to see . . . and cracked up.

"What's so funny¿" he asked.

"You'll see," I promised as we flashed past the sign that said we had reached Duck Key.

Next after that was Grassy Key, which prompted Long-Drink to say nostalgically that he hadn't seen a key of grass since the Seventies. It was followed by Fat Deer Key—Slippery Joe wondered aloud if that was a misspelling, and got kicked again—and Vaca Key—"Not the one in Hawaii," Omar said deadpan—and when Boot Key gave way to Hog Key, Joe Quigley said, "Oh, of course: you gotta tighten up your skate boots before you can play hogkey" . . . it went like that. As I say, the air and the scenery were getting us high, and any silly little thing became hilarious.

Just a little farther on, at Little Knight Key (don't ask), that damn road gathered itself, picked itself up by its bootstraps, flung itself into the air, and didn't come down for seven miles. Swear to God. The Seven-Mile Bridge: it passes above Pigeon Key on the way but doesn't come down until it reaches Little Duck Key. (More ribbing for the Lucky Duck, who took it with less ill grace than usual.) Damnedest view in the world: Florida Straits on the left, Gulf of Mexico on the right, infinite universe above, vast ocean below.

For a while we kept up the joking, turning to the map for inspiration—for that road connects a mere handful of the *hundreds* of Keys, and some of them have goofy names like Monk Key, Drink Key, Drunk Key, Waltz Key ("B flat, isn't it, Eddie¿"), Knockemdown Key, Little Knockemdown Key (but no Setemup Key at all, oddly), Rattlesnake Lumps, Snipe Keys ("You really gotta hunt for those."), and Women Key ("The trick is getting close enough to wind it," Slippery Joe said and got kicked a third time. He seems to like it.). Isham Latimer pretended to be offended by Coon Key and also by Eastern, Western, and Middle Sambo, and Tommy Janssen said it seemed wrong to have both a Squirrel Key *and* a Rock Key, but no Bullwinkle Key to accompany Moose Key. Fast Eddie, in a rare burst of loquaciousness, suggested that we'd seen so many camera-bedecked Japanese

tourists, there ought to be one where they could hold sing-alongs, named Carry Oh Key.

But after a couple of miles of that, one by one we all fell silent, shut up, and just *dug* it.

The Seven-Mile Bridge. Don't pass up a chance to drive it.

Four little Keys past the end of the bridge, on a fairly sizable and undeveloped one called Bahia Honda Key (Shorty suggested that Laheasa Honda was much better advice), we came up on the entrance to a big state park, on the left. We'd only been traveling a couple of hours or so, it was still before noon, but the sun was high enough in the sky to be hot as hell. All of a sudden I couldn't stand it anymore and put on my turn signal.

"Where you goin', Jake?" Long-Drink inquired behind me.

"You guys can do what you want," I said. "I'm going swimming."

Erin and Zoey cheered. Long-Drink echoed it on the CB, and as I pulled off the highway I could faintly hear the cheer echoing back along the caravan. I imagine the first fifty drivers behind us cheered just as loud when the last of our big yellow monsters finally got off the road.

The sign said campgrounds to the right, beach to the left. I took us left. Winding road through dunes thick with grass, speed limit of 15, speed bumps every few yards to enforce it. Then a seemingly infinite succession of blacktop parking areas on the right. No one of them had twenty-four open slots, but we managed to fit most of us into three adjacent areas. Fifty yards away was a line of shaded picnic tables with barbecue stands, occasionally broken by a large wood-frame shower-and-washroom building. Fifty yards of white sand beyond all that was that impossibly pale green ocean.

Body temperature, it felt like. When you were in up to your shoulders, you could look down and see your feet.

I'm not saying the Hawk Channel beach at Bahia Honda State Park is the finest place to swim on the planet. Just the finest I've

ever immersed my personal body into, so far. (A friend of mine says good things about the beaches north from Cairns in Queensland, North Australia . . . at least, at the time of year when the box jellyfish aren't running.) We had so much fun, at one point we got up a volleyball game, unhampered by our lack of a ball. Ralph von Wau Wau had some fun I think I won't describe. I myself spent lazy happy time shielding my wife from the sun with my own body, and found the pay most agreeable. (Sunburn wasn't a factor. Thanks to Mickey Finn, we're both radiation-proof.) A warm, slippery, sleepy wife is a nice thing to kiss. Erin built herself a Sand Bar—that is, a sand castle in the spitting image of Mary's Place—which struck several tourists dumb: as tall as she was, quite lifelike, and flanked by half a dozen little Sand Cars parked higgledy-piggledy. I looked at it and knew the tide would come in and dissolve it, eventually . . . and found I didn't mind a bit. I got my daughter's point, in other words—and so did many of my friends. The sea and sky and sun scoured a lot of scar tissue off a lot of souls that morning. We did a lot of grinning.

When I could sense that we'd have to leave soon, I fetched Lady Macbeth from the bus, and sang exactly one song: "Hey Jude." Most of my companions had jumped in by the end of the first verse, and I don't suppose more than eighty percent of the people on the beach that day joined in on the coda. We might be there now if I hadn't broken two strings.

Anyway, half an hour later we were all desanded, desalted, partially dried, regreased against the brutal sun and the flying carnivores called "mosquitoes" by the natives thereabouts, fed and watered, beginning to itch in unaccustomed places, and back on Highway 1. To my astonishment, traffic in both directions halted long enough to allow our entire yellow boa constrictor to leave the park as a unit.

Maybe five miles later, on Big Pine Key, one of the largest of the Keys, Willard Hooker lost a wheel. Fortunately he managed to

coast to a stop without tipping her, and there was plenty of shoulder there, and we all pulled off the road to wait while he and Omar and Shorty dealt with it. It turned out to be good luck, of a kind. By the time Shorty reported that it was going to be a good hour, someone had spotted the sign we'd otherwise have driven right past, discreetly pointing the way north to the National Key Deer Refuge. Several of us decided to kill the time by checking it out. Luckily Omar knew enough about the place to head off our stampede with a brief lecture. He made us all squeeze into his bus—which since Omar owns almost nothing was the only one with most of its passenger space and seats intact—and made us promise to be "tantric," as he called it. Respectful, that is, and quiet as churchmice. He impressed it on us so emphatically that the ranger who stopped us at a gate part-way up the trail could read it in our faces, and passed us through on foot. And so we got to see a few of the fabulous Key deer.

Full-grown deer—no bigger than dogs . . .

Swear to God; if I'm lyin', I'm dyin'. Perfect little miniature horned Bambis, somehow unmistakably adult; the elves of the quadruped world. They were the most breathtakingly beautiful animals I've ever seen, and I'd say that if Pixel were here. They'll remain that until the day it is given to me to see my first unicorn. Erin, *most* uncharacteristically, seemed to regress emotionally to normal level for her age, fell daffy in love with the little things, and had to be firmly talked out of luring one aboard to take with us. The thing that made me uneasy was that Zoey didn't contribute a word to the argument.

Never mind; Pixel rubbed against my shin approvingly all the way back to the highway.

Little Torch Key, Ramrod Key, Summerland Key, Cudjoe Key, Sugarloaf Key, Park Key, the charmingly named Perky Key, the Saddlebunch Keys, Shark Key, Big Coppit Key, Rockland Key, the huge Naval Air Station complex on Boca Chica Key—all flashed by in the next half hour. Maybe twenty-five miles after we left the Key Deer behind, the road made one last lunge into the sea for a mile or so, landed safely on Stock Island—primarily known as the home of the tallest known mountain of garbage in the world, Mt. Trashmore—skipped once, across Cow Key Channel—

—and poured us into Key West in glorious early afternoon.

We had left the United States behind and, with an appropriate total lack of border formalities, entered the Conch Republic.

Maybe you never got the straight of that. A surprising number of people haven't. Back in April of 1982, the federal government became embarrassed by the enormous number of illegal aliens and drug dealers it had justified its budgets by claiming were streaming up U.S. 1 into Florida every day. It had overplayed its hand a bit, and some people were demanding something actually be done. What the government of, by, and for the people decided to do was put a border crossing at the top of the Keys, just as though there were a border there, and then require anyone entering or leaving that hundred-mile strip of America to prove his or her citizenship—and, if he or she looked weird, to submit to a search. Hard to believe, I know, but it really happened. Those were strange and savage times.

Anyway, the Keys nearly went up in flames, as normal commerce in both directions ground to a near halt—but the reaction way down at the ass end in Key West was both typical and admirable. They decided that since Conchs weren't being treated like U.S. citizens, they wouldn't be. They seceded, and formally declared the Conch Republic. Issued passports, designed a flag, opened an embassy and everything. I believe they even applied to the U.N., though they may not have gotten as far as actually *mailing* it. The head rebel was really good with media, very dryly funny on camera. The Conch Republic got so much good ink, around the world, that the feds finally scrapped the border-crossing scheme, and instead solved the problem by simply not inflating their estimates of northward alien-and-drug flow quite so outrageously for a while.

That the Conch Republic concept is still alive today, and celebrated with a large and popular annual festival in which local boats pepper a "Coast Guard" vessel with rotten fruit until it surrenders, will tell you something about Key West.

Our first ten minutes in town told us almost as much.

At Doc Webster's advice, we hung a left as soon as we crossed Cow Key Channel, and took the A1A loop that runs down along the southern shore of the island. The first street we passed on our right was called Duck Avenue, which everyone agreed was a favorable omen. We went by the small airport (which Erin seemed to study particularly intently), and then saw on our left a remarkable strip called Houseboat Row. It's just what it sounds like: a long row of squatters living in houseboats, moored to public dock. Some of the houseboats were exquisite and elegant, with little trellised entrances from the dock to their gangplanks, and some were run-down and listing and half-awash. I'd seen a houseboat community before, back on Long Island, but it was nowhere near as interesting as this one.

But the people were even more interesting. Between Houseboat Row and the end of Smathers Beach, I saw just about every imaginable kind of human being there is, all sharing the sidewalk and sand and hot-dog wagons without friction or tension—and a startlingly high percentage of them fell under the loose general heading of My Kind Of People. Queers. Blacks. Cubans. Asians. Hippies. Drunks. Drag queens. Weirdos. Artists. Writers. Musicians. Beach bums and bunnies. Hustlers. All of them with an odd, indefinable shared quality that teased at the edges of my understanding.

There were also scatterings of yuppies in uniforms, and a few rich lizard people with their young trophy pets, from the luxury hotels and condos on the north side of the road—and of course something like half the total throng were tourists, half of whom

seemed to be drunken college students—but all of these seemed to be treated with great tolerance and forgiveness by the citizens.

There were as many bicycles and mopeds as there were cars—but most people seemed happy walking, and why not? You could walk across the whole island in an hour. If you were impervious to beauty, that is.

Past Smathers Beach we deked north and rejoined Route 1, now that it was safely past the mall district, and headed into the heart of town at a stately 20 mph. The colorful, raffish aspect of the people we drove past did not change; if anything they got a little funkier. And they still all had that ineffable shared quality in common, which I finally realized was *fearlessness*. None of them was remotely afraid that a cop was going to drag him into an alley and tune him up. The drunks knew they weren't going to be rolled. The gays weren't worried about being bashed. Beautiful women strolled along dressed in almost nothing but the confidence that they would not be raped. The few cops I did see wore short pants, rode bicycles, smiled a lot, and got smiled back at a lot.

"Jesus," Long-Drink said on the CB. "It's okay to be strange here."

"Roger that," Noah Gonzalez agreed.

"I thought we were gonna start a riot, rolling into a place this size in two dozen yellow elephants—but look: nobody even notices us!"

"Doc says per capita, this town has *both* more bars and more churches than anywhere else in America," I told him. "We should fit right in, Drink."

"I wonder what that must be like," he murmured.

You could sort of sense the main drag, Duval Street, coming up—the tourist quotient rose to near saturation as it neared. A few blocks short of it we turned north again and followed that street to the end. Just short of Key West Bight, I pulled into a trailer court, followed by the first eleven buses behind me, that being the court's capacity. The rest continued on a few blocks to

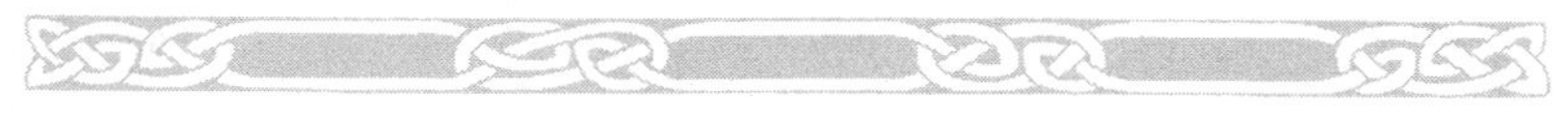

Trumbo Annex, U.S. Navy territory, where Doc had arranged additional temporary accommodations for some of us.

The Doc himself came bustling out of the trailer court office as I shut down the engine. Somebody came out the door with him, but all I could see was Doc. I'd known him for twenty years, and my first sight of him took my breath away. He had, as advertised, dropped at least fifty pounds, lost at least one chin—and his perennially pale skin had turned the color of mahogany. He wore a white straw fedora, wraparound shades, a pale green short-sleeved shirt, khaki shorts, and sneakers with no socks. Formal dress by Key West standards. He looked healthy and fit and happier than I had ever seen him. In that first glimpse of him I *knew*, way down deep in my bones, that I had made the right choice in bringing my family and friends here.

My loves and I swarmed down from our bus and gang-hugged him: I hit him high, Zoey hit him low, and Erin got him around the knees. There was a lot of laughing and squeezing and rocking back and forth, and everybody was probably saying something but nobody was listening to anybody.

Then Long-Drink hit, hard, and I had a rush of brains to the head and got out of that hug just before it turned into a pileup, scooping Erin up out of harm's way too and carrying her out of range with me.

I found myself facing Doc's companion, and blinked at him in mild astonishment.

My first thought was *Saint Popeye*. He had the bowlegged stance, battered skipper's cap, corncob pipe, weatherbeaten face, and hyperdeveloped tattooed forearms of a fisherman—but the sparkling wise eyes and dreamy closed-lipped smile of a serious acidhead.

Which would have explained the rest of his wardrobe. Put a rainbow in a blender for three seconds on high, spill it on cotton, nuke it till it glows, and you've got his shirt. I was wearing those new self-polarizing sunglasses, and that shirt made them darken. He wore it unbuttoned, displaying a broad tanned hairy chest and washboard abs. Instead of shorts, he wore what I guess was a sarong, or possibly some self-invented variant: a lot of loosely gathered cloth that covered him almost to the knees and looked airy as hell. His feet were bare, and appeared to have been bare for a very long time. He wore a small, tasteful gold ring on his left big toe.

Back up to those glittering eyes. They were ice-blue, and locked on to mine like tractor beams. I already *had* a big goofy grin on my face—not just from greeting Doc; I'd had it more or less since we'd left Key Largo that morning—but the sheer benevolence of his answering smile made me grin even wider. This, I could already tell, was a Buddha.

"Hi," I said, shifting my grip on Erin so I could offer him my hand.

"Good idea," he said in a resonant baritone, and put something into my palm instead of his. I blinked down at it, and my keen jungle-honed senses quickly identified it: a split second after my eyes told me it was the thinnest joint I had ever encountered, my nose told me it was also probably one of the best.

I looked back up to find him holding out a Zippo. My smile muscles were starting to *ache*, a little, and I found I liked the sensation. What athletes call a good burn. One good burn deserves another; I leaned into the flame. *Thhhhhhppp*—

Oh, my . . .

"Welcome to the Island of Bones," he said as I passed the thing back to him.

Seeing my puzzlement, he explained. "That's what Ponce de León named it. *Caya Huesos*, the Island of Bones. The Calusa used it for Boot Hill at the time." He took a hit. "Things have picked up a little since," he croaked, and handed it back to me.

"I'm Jake Stonebender," I told him, because I could already tell that if I took a second hit of this stuff without introducing myself first, I would never get around to it.

He held up a finger, listened to the cosmos a moment, then exhaled. "I'm Double Bill."

"You mean like a parrot?" Erin asked him. "Or a deerstalker cap?"

He looked at her with obvious delight. "Naw, it's my name. William Williams. My folks thought they were funny."

"So do mine," she said sympathetically, grinning back at him.

"S'cuse me," I said, and let out my breath. "Double Bill, allow me to present my daughter Erin."

"I'm fifteen months old," she told him, "and I'm kind of a genius."

"Sure you are," he said happily. "Is it fun?"

"So far."

"Well, good."

Everything had begun to sparkle, just perceptibly. I could tell I had about thirty seconds of responsibility left to me, max, and made a token effort. "Look, there's a lot of stuff I ought to do before I relax. I should go in and get us all registered here—"

"Covered," he said.

"—and meet our host, and thank him for taking on this many—"

"You already have. You're welcome."

"—oh." Shift gears. Cap'n Buddha manages this trailer park. Of course. No wonder they'll take us. "Far out. Then I guess the only priority flag left on my list is to make a start on permanent housing." I gestured toward the exuberant throng with Doc at the center, making atrocious puns. "All those folks need homes, and I got another load just as big over at Trumbo Annex—plus I need to find a nice place for us all to hang out together. Doc's got a friend who's supposed to be a big-time realtor, but the sooner I give him an idea of just what he's dealing with—"

"Don't sweat it," he said. "I've had bigger challenges."

Shift gears again. Double Bill is the big-time realtor. He probably *owns* the trailer park.

This is what a *realtor* looks like down here. I can't wait to meet a beatnik. Interesting people, these Conchs.

"Far out," I said, and gave up. "Then I guess I'm off duty."

"I'm also an attorney," he said, "and my best advice to you at this juncture is to let me relight that for you."

I shook my head. "Thanks—but let me see if I can pull Zoey out of that scrum and see if she'd—"

He held out a fistful of joints just as slender and potent as the first. I have no idea where he got them from; he didn't have a single pocket I could see. "Have her pass these around, and then come back and we'll finish this one. I want to hear about just what kind of a bar you have in mind to run."

"Well . . . okay." I set Erin down. "Be right back, love."

"She'll be fine," Double Bill said, and held out his swollen forearms. Erin hopped up into them without hesitation and nestled in, staring up into his sparkling eyes.

A couple of hours later the whole gang, both contingents of us, assembled at the Schooner Wharf, a splendid waterfront bar roughly between our two sites.

We were home at last. And already beginning to realize it.

CHAPTER ELEVEN

The Hip Square

"People who are really very weird can get into sensitive positions and have a tremendous impact on history."
—J. Danforth Quayle

"BOY," I TOLD DOUBLE Bill, "I can't help thinking this bar right here would be a hard one to beat."

The Schooner Wharf was (and still is) an open-air oasis overlooking Lands End Marina, an agreeable boat basin packed with ships of all kinds, including one custom houseboat that fit my personal mental image of Travis McGee's *Busted Flush*. The bar itself was a mahogany racetrack oval with a roof overhead to keep the sun and rain and seagull shit off, and three bartenders dressed as shipwreck victims were working *very* hard in there. An adjacent shack produced decent finger food and housed supplies and washrooms. There were plenty of tables around, shaded by huge folding umbrellas advertising exotic beers, and there was a covered stage nearby, empty now, but piled with equipment that suggested a blues band would be playing there that night. Looking around me, I saw as many obvious Conchs as obvious tourists—a hard trick to pull off. Neither group

seemed to even notice the arrival of a hundred more people who knew each other. The air was full of happy laughter, and canned music that alternated between island music and blues, and the scents of beer and oysters and fried food and rum and drinks involving citrus fruits.

"It's in the top ten," Bill[2] agreed. "But I have a few spots in mind I'll show you tomorrow. Not on the water, of course, the kind of money you're talking."

"That's okay," I said. "I like ocean—but I don't completely trust it."

"Smart."

Doc Webster's familiar booming voice was heard then, and a pleasure it was to be hearing it again. "All right, everyone who came here with Jake, the Mary's Place gang—can I have your attention a minute¿"

Like all of us, I turned in my chair and gave him my attention. I assumed some kind of toast was coming, and wondered where we were supposed to smash our plastic cups when we were done.

Beside the Doc stood a striking woman, striking even in this context. She was a mix of some kind of Asian and something else, I guessed black. There are no ugly interracial children, and she brought up the average. I estimated her age at about thirty, give or take. Petite and slender but not frail, and definitely female. She was showing a lot less skin than most of the women present, but she didn't need to. If you'd seen her go by wearing a chador, she'd have caught your attention. Amazing pale eyes. She wore a lovely low-cut lime green dress with tasteful diamond cutaways at the waist, a matching hairband, a matching purse slung over her left shoulder, and brown low-heeled sandals. She seemed just a little nonplussed at having accidentally strayed into the midst of such a huge group of pale strangers, just as the speeches were about to begin, but she hid it well, I thought. There was something odd about the strap of her purse, where it crossed over her shoulder; my first stoned impression was, *four brown bullets in a bandolier*. I looked closer.

They were Doc Webster's fingertips. He had his arm around her.

"—wanted to wait until I had all of you together," he was declaiming, "so I'd only have to say this once."

Even the other customers were listening now.

"Now, nobody's asking you for a quick decision or anything," he went on. "I know you all just got here, and you're all disoriented and tired, okay? And I know you've all got a lot to think about already, and it's damn near impossible to think about *anything* your first week in Key West, I can testify to that—" Rousing cheer from the locals. "—but I feel a certain urgency about this matter, and I figure the sooner you start to at least consider—"

The woman turned her head and looked at him, and he stopped speaking.

A silent shockwave went through our group. None of us had ever seen, or ever expected to see, Doc Webster cut off in midsentence.

"Right," he said to her, and then to all of us again, "Uh, folks, this is Mei-Ling. She . . . uh . . ."

Doc Webster at a loss for words? That was it: *anything* was possible.

The moment I heard her clear strong contralto voice I had to abandon a perfectly rotten pun I'd been hatching: if she'd been a recent immigrant, I could have done something with *Webster's new American*. But her accent made it immediately clear she'd been raised in the States, possibly even in New York. I was so busy mourning the lost opportunity, I almost missed what she said.

"Sam says you people are the ones I have to ask for his hand in marriage," she announced.

There, you see? *Anything.*

She might as well have set off a grenade. No, a grenade wouldn't have startled us nearly as much, most of us were immune to them. We gaped at her, in dead silence, for what seemed like an eternity. She stared back at us with her jaw firmly clamped and her face as expressionless as she could make it.

And then she lost it, and laughed in our faces.

We all broke up too. So therefore did all the eavesdropping locals and tourists, and the bartenders started up a round of applause that soon swept us all.

The Doc and Mei-Ling stood at the center of it, and as we all saw how they looked at each other, the applause swelled to the point where they probably heard us back in Key Largo, a hundred miles to the east.

When it finally wound down, Mei-Ling murmured in the Doc's ear, and he pointed me out. She took him by the hand and marched directly up to me, looked me in the eye, and smiled. "Hi, Jake," she said.

"Hi, Mei-Ling," I said. "This is my wife Zoey, and our daughter Erin."

She nodded at each one. "Zoey. Erin. I'm pleased to meet you both. Welcome to Key West." She turned back to me. "Well?"

I stared at her, and blinked a lot.

"How soon can I have an answer?" she persisted. "I want to nail him down before he can change his mind."

I looked to the Doc. "I'm the Dad, am I?"

He raised one eyebrow and shrugged. "That's about the size of it, son. You speak for the group, everybody knows that."

I glanced at Zoey. She too lifted one eyebrow—the other one—and shrugged.

So I turned back to Mei-Ling and looked her up and down, as politely as that can be done. Now that she was up close, I could see that the red trim at the bodice of her dress was actually little red letters, spelling out the words "Mei-Ling, Duval Street," across her chest. There was a certain natural tendency to keep exploring the area, but I pulled my eyes back up to hers.

"Are you sure you know what you're doing?" I asked her.

"Is anyone?" she asked me.

Good point. "Uh . . . can you cook?"

"That's what the cabdrivers all say," she said, pokerfaced.

I was beginning to like her. "And you fully understand that Sam is the only retired doctor in Florida who *isn't* rich." Doc's hospital on Long Island, Smithtown General, had been blessed with an anonymous benefactor who sent in regular donations for over thirty years—right up until the month the Doc retired and left the state.

She nodded. "Not a problem. I am."

Mild alarm bells were starting to go off. She was beautiful, smart, quick, twenty to thirty years younger than the Doc, *and* rich? And anxious to nail him down? You didn't often meet either rich people or beautiful people who were wise enough to cherish a man like Doc that much.

But what else could she be after? He didn't *have* anything to steal, except his time and company. Her Long Island accent and Americanized manner said this could not be some kind of immigration scam. He no longer had any drug access. Even fifty pounds lighter, he was not Adonis.

Well, there was one good way I could think of to test true love.

"And you *have* been properly warned? He has fully and freely disclosed to you the nature and extent of his . . . behavior, and you understand that he is powerless to change?"

She glanced at Doc, looked back to me, and lifted an eyebrow inquiringly.

I leaned closer and lowered my voice discreetly. "He makes puns," I explained.

She rolled her eyes. "*Tell* me about it. That's how we met."

I nodded. "Typical. Sad case, really."

"We passed each other on the street one night, and I had this dress on, and three steps past me he turned on his heel and bellowed, 'I *get* it!' So naturally I turned around, and he pointed at these—" She indicated the letters that ran along the top of her bodice. "—and said, 'That's your Mei-Ling Ad Dress you're wearing! Have I cracked its unZip Code?' Well, he was the first one who'd ever got it, so what could I do? I took him home and put him on my Mei-Ling List."

Light began to dawn. "You *like* puns."

She nodded. "I used to work for someone who cherished them; she corrupted me, and I've never been able to kick."

Now their relationship began to make sense to me. Doc Webster is the finest improvisational punster it has ever been my misfortune to try and compete with, certainly the best that ever walked into either Callahan's or Mary's Place. Olympic class, in other words. They wanted to put him into Guinness, once, but he politely explained that he'd rather put *Guinness* into *him*. (Stout fellow.) If Mei-Ling was one of those poor perverts, like myself, who actually enjoyed horrid puns, she had certainly found the father-lode.

What *he* saw in *her*, of course, I could not guess.

Zoey spoke up. "What do you do, Mei-Ling?" she asked politely.

Mei-Ling smiled warmly at her. "I'm a hooker."

"Oh, what a coincidence!" Zoey said. "Four of our group are hookers, too; you'll have to—well, look at this: here they are now."

"Hi, Mei," said four voices at once.

Mei-Ling's eyes went wide with shock and joy. "Mo! Professor! Arethusa! Joe! Oh, this is *wonderful*. I didn't know you were with this bunch, I never saw you—Sam, why didn't you *tell* me?" The five of them embraced at once.

"I didn't know you knew them," the Doc explained to the air, and perhaps to me.

"Oh, it's been so *long*—"

The penny was just beginning to drop. "Mei-Ling—you used to work at Lady Sally's House?" I asked.

"Too long ago," she agreed, returning to the Doc's side. "I had to leave a few years before the Lady closed down, and I've always regretted it."

That explained why I'd never seen her there. I knew I'd have remembered her if I had. Lady Sally's House—closed these fifteen years now, more's the pity—had once been the finest brothel in the

eastern United States, run by Mike Callahan's wife, Lady Sally McGee. It was where I had met Doc Webster myself in the first place.

"Us too," Maureen said. "Mei was *solid*, Jake—we could have used her, there at the blow-off." I said nothing; from what I hear, they could have used a Ghurka division that day. "Mei, did you really manage to bag Sam?"

Mei-Ling looked around. "Well, from the general reaction, I'd say I've got a shot. This was his last excuse. Nobody's said 'no' *so* far." She was looking at me as she said the last sentence.

"Forget it," Arethusa told her. "You're in. If anybody does object, we'll make 'em go back to Long Island." She seemed to be looking at me, too. "This girl is something special, Jake. *Everybody* at Sally's took a crack at Sam, at one time or another. Mei-Ling's the first one of us who ever set the hook." She turned back to Mei-Ling. "And I'm *dying* to hear all the details."

Mei-Ling said nothing, kept looking at me.

It suddenly came to me that in all the years I had known Sam Webster, it had never once occurred to me to wonder how he was in the sack.

"Hey," I said, "the issue is settled. Mei-Ling, if you're good enough to work for Lady Sally, you're good enough to marry our Doc. Bless you, my children—may you be as happy together as Zoey and me."

The cheer started out local—then Maureen turned and announced, "It's a done deal," and the whole place went up. Tourists from Dortmund, Singapore, and Johannesburg began competing to buy drinks for the wedding party, loosely defined as all of us gathered around the Doc and Mei-Ling, which over time became *all* of us, and we might still be there swilling down free piña coladas if Tom Hauptman hadn't noticed that the sun was going down.

He got us organized, and Doc and Double Bill led the way. Maybe a quarter of the Schooner Wharf's other patrons tagged along with us. As we turned onto Caroline Street and started heading west, I saw lots of people heading in the same direction, some ambling and some in a hurry. I felt a tug at my short sleeve, and looked over to see Double Bill offering me a smoldering spliff. I did the indescribable eyes-and-face dance that means, *Is this really cool?* and he smiled. "It's not considered polite to do it in the Square itself. Making a cop ignore a crime while geeks from Milwaukee are pointing camcorders at him would be, like, *inconsiderate,* you know?"

I could see the logic—it was the concept of having cops it was worth being considerate of that boggled my mind just a little bit. But not enough to keep me from helping him destroy the evidence before we accidentally embarrassed a policeman. The six-block walk seemed to take a long time. I didn't mind. I was at the head of a company of glory, marching to the sea to pay it our respects.

Nonetheless we got to Mallory Square with plenty of time to spare: the sun was still well above the horizon. First an overfull parking area and a public washroom facility used by almost all of us, then a phalanx of chained-up bicycles and mopeds, then a swarm of sunburned humanity milling around in the Square itself, a stone pavilion right at the water's edge. Some were inspecting the wares of local vendors, spread out on tables or blankets: handmade jewelry, clothing, and ceramics; paintings, sculpture, and other objets d'art; food and drink of several exotic kinds; your fortune told or portrait painted or cards read—nothing that looked junky or tacky or purely mark-up commercial. (Clearly a co-op of some sort was at work here.)

Another sizable segment of the crowd was watching the live entertainment—which included a unicyclist dressed like Uncle Sam who rode around giving out $22 bills, a first-rate bagpiper in full clan kit, a sword-swallower (they're always more impressive when you can walk around them and satisfy yourself they're not using sleight of hand), a fire-eater who kept belching enormous fireballs into the air, a couple of clowns, a balloon artist in a tall top hat, a bed-of-nails guy who doubled as a glass walker, a strolling female violinist, an incredible guy named Frank who filled a shopping cart with truck tires and then balanced it on his chin, two folksingers with beat-up Martins and an endless repertoire of upbeat and slightly off-color songs . . . and, of course, the informal king of the Square, Will Soto. With his gunfighter mustache and long ponytail, he looked like a Hell's Angel in tights. He held center stage, right at the seawall itself, performing unlikely feats of juggling, general legerdemain, and Robin Williams–like improvisational comedy—on a tightrope, balanced high above water that had not yet made up its mind whether it was Atlantic Ocean or Gulf of Mexico. As tourist boats, powerboats, and yachts came gliding slowly by to show off their wealth and leisure to the poorer tourists on the dock, Will would shout abuse at them, or pull down his tights and moon them, to the immense delight of the crowd.

The third general component of the melee was the shutterbugs. Every square inch of seawall that had not been appropriated as some performer's stage area was *packed* with photographers and videographers, shoulder to shoulder and craning to see over and around each other. Nearly every lens was trained in the same direction: at the sun, sinking down just to the south of Sunset Island, a little spit of land a little ways out that had been placed there by God specifically for the purpose of making a congenitally stupendous sunset even *more* photogenic. A few mavericks were taking shots of the seagulls and pelicans that squatted out on two or three concrete cruise-ship pilings about fifty yards from the dock. A constant parade of watercraft went by, slowly and gracefully.

I looked around for a while with a New Yorker's practiced eye, and failed to spot a single pickpocket working this ripest of crowds.

One of the clowns went by me, a sort of psychedelic Santa whose hat was labeled *Amazin' Walter*, and I found myself beaming like an acidhead at him and asking, "Does all this really happen *every night?*"

Amazin' Walter grinned and shook his head at once. "Hell, no. Only when it ain't snowin'." He passed on.

In my ignorance, I believed that particular sunset must be one of even Key West's finest. I've since learned it was about an eight on a scale of ten. At least one percent of the visible color spectrum was not represented anywhere in those pastel clouds that evening. A lot of us wedged their way in among the shutterbugs to get a good view of the spectacle. I'd like to say I was cleverer than that, but actually I just couldn't drag myself away from catching Will Soto's act, and stayed to gawk. As I should have expected, he timed it to end about three minutes before the sun touched the island, hopped down off his tightrope-frame, and began passing the hat—and now I had a peachy view. So did Erin, perched on my shoulders. As Will came by with his hat, I had her grab hold of my hair while I reached down with one hand and dug a twenty out of my pocket. I dropped it in the hat, caught Will's eye, and said, "You're as good as the game, brother."

He nodded graciously. "Are you with it, friend?"

"Not presently," I told him. "Folksing a little."

"Just get to town?"

"Yes," I told him, a little surprised.

"You'll stay," he said, and went back to working the crowd. His hat filled with cash quickly, very little of it coins.

"He's nice, Daddy," Erin said.

I started to nod, and that reminded me that she was still clutching my hair. "Yes he is," I said, and locked my hands around her fanny again so she could let go.

"Want me to take her?" Zoey asked beside me.

"I'm fine," I assured her. And then I looked around—really looked around, and took it all in, setting and sunset and happy people and honest merchants—and added, "In fact, I left 'fine' in the dust a long ways back. I'm *great*. How about you?"

Her arm went around me, and her hand settled on my butt. "I left 'great' behind a long ways back. Jake, what the hell *took* us so long?"

Erin and I somehow worked it out wordlessly that she'd take hold of my hair again so as to free up one of my arms to go around Zoey. "Who knew?" I said.

"True," Zoey said.

We watched the sun drop the last few increments. At the last moment, Zoey nudged me and gestured with her chin. I picked out the Doc and Mei-Ling nearby in the crowd. They were kissing, oblivious to crowd and sunset and everything but each other. Just then the bottom edge of the sun melted and spilled down into the water just below, an odd optical illusion that made it look a little like an incandescent flat tire, and a cheer went up, and flash units and horns went off, and a zillion cameras and camcorders began to chatter like a locust orgy. Zoey and I stood arm in arm and watched until the last gleam of sun disappeared . . . and then we turned to each other and we kissed too. When Erin finally made us break it up, I looked around to find that half the crowd was gone already.

Including half of *our* crowd. But it didn't matter. The trip home was a straight six-block walk, no chance of getting lost—and getting lost in Key West didn't sound very scary anyway. So we stayed long enough to introduce ourselves to Will Soto, and found the conversation illuminating.

"In the late Seventies, early Eighties," he told us, "vendors and buskers were setting up here illegally, and the tourists loved us, and the merchants loved us too, but the city had eyes to put a cruise-ship dock here, so they started hassling us. Recognizing the levity of the situation, we got organized about five years ago. Karen and Richard Tocci and Featherman Louie and Marylyn the Cookie Lady and Love22 and Sister and me and a bunch of others formed the Key West Cultural Preservation Society in '84, and managed to cool the clem. We got a great show of support from the nearby merchants, and that helped a lot. We finally cut a deal with the city, where the Society leases this dock for four hours every night, and then turns around and rents space to the various artisans and performers. We clean up after ourselves, we keep out the drunks and dealers and dips, everybody's happy."

"There's a living in it?" Zoey asked.

"The Society breaks even, the members all make a living."

I shook my head. "Jesus. A town that makes a fair deal with its buskers, and then keeps it. I'm gonna like it here."

Will grinned like a pirate. "Don't get too starry-eyed, Jake. They got idiots here like everywhere else. No place is perfect." Then he blinked. "No, I take that back: this place *is* perfect." He sighed faintly. "But no place can *stay* perfect."

"Then we should dig it while we can," Erin said. "And try and keep it perfect for as long as we can."

Will did a small double-take. Erin was down at ground level by then, and for an instant he thought perhaps I was doing a ventriloquist routine. Then he located Erin's eyes, looked closely at them . . . and directed his response to her. "You said a mouthful. Erin, right? I wouldn't mind having those words carved on my headstone, Erin. So what are you guys gonna do down here, to help keep it perfect?"

"We came to save the universe," Erin said.

He pursed his lips judiciously. "*Really?* Big job. This is the place to do it, though." He looked up to me. "Is she serious, Jake?"

What the hell. I nodded.

It didn't seem to faze him. "What's your first move?"

I searched his face carefully for hints that he was either being sarcastic or politely humoring us. I didn't find any. "Well, first I'm going to open up a bar—"

"Good luck," he said. "This town's already got more bars than it has drunks—and it has a *lot* of drunks."

"Well, see, I sort of brought my clientele with me," I said. "It's a long story, but there's about a hundred of us."

He nodded. "That'll help."

"Can a musician make money in this town?" Zoey asked.

"If they're good," Will said carefully. "What's your ax?"

"Standup. Any kind of music."

He grinned broadly. "You don't even need to be good, then. A bass player, versatile, and pretty as you—shit, you'll have more gigs than you can handle."

Zoey beamed.

"Okay, so your nut's covered and you open your bar. What then?"

I floundered, unable to come up with a way to explain it. Erin jumped in. "Daddy and his friends will work on getting telepathic, and then they'll all talk it over with Uncle Nikky and make a plan, and then they'll save the universe."

He blinked at her. "Uncle Nikky?"

I sighed, knowing how this was going to sound. But what could I do? "Nikola Tesla," I said.

His eyes locked on mine and stayed there for several long seconds. "Look," he said finally, "I have to break down and stow my gear now. But you and me have got to talk."

I told him where we were staying for the time being. "And I know where to find you."

"Everybody does," he agreed. "Nice meeting you, Jake. You too, ladies."

"You were great," Erin told him. He flashed her that pirate grin and was gone. I could see why they'd named a whole school of Zen Buddhism after him.

As we went by Duval Street on our way back to the trailer court, it was just beginning to gear up for the evening ahead, and you could already sense the energy starting to build. It reminded me a little of the French Quarter in New Orleans, and a little of

Commercial Street in Provincetown—sidewalks spilling over with tourists and hustlers and colorful drag queens, storefronts blaring music, pedicabs and tour buses and endless bicycles crawling down a narrow street together. But in many ways it was unlike either the Quarter or P-Town. For one thing, the smells were different, tropical and haunting. Everything was cleaner and less garish and in better repair than the Quarter; it didn't have the cramped feeling or upscale pretensions of P-Town. I saw a minimum of neon. For a Main Stem, it was pretty okay.

And the farther we got away from Duval, the nicer and quieter and prettier it got.

Scents came and went in the night air. Jasmine. Limes. Swimming-pool chlorine. Flowers whose names I didn't know yet, hibiscus and bougainvillea and frangipani and a dozen others, all intoxicatingly sensual. Cooking smells. Cat pee. Fish off to the left somewhere.

The side streets on our right got more and more tempting-looking as we left Duval behind, too, but we were all too weary to explore, and stayed on Caroline all the way back home. A block away from the trailer court, Pixel met us, loudly demanding dinner. As we walked, Erin told him about the guy we'd seen at Mallory Square named Dominique, and his truly amazing three trained cats, Sara, Piggy, and Sharky. Pixel seemed properly impressed, and Erin told us he would be coming with us next time to check them out.

The sight of our own familiar yellow submarines was cheering. The party was already under way, and we joined right in. The Doc and Double Bill were barbecuing ribs and burgers in massive quantities. Tom Hauptman had set up an impromptu bar on a folding table under a coconut palm, and was passing out cold beer, margaritas, piña coladas, and other liquids. Fast Eddie had somehow acquired an upright piano in reasonable tune (it turned out to belong to Double Bill) and was letting his fingers out for a walk after their long confinement. Long-Drink was juggling Key limes. Mei-Ling had organized the kids into a treasure hunt. The Lucky Duck was pitching dimes in the air, had a stack of about eight, on edge, in front of him, and looked about as happy—at least, as little unhappy—as I've ever seen him.

We jumped right in. Fed our faces for half an hour, made music for a couple of hours—Double Bill turned out to have a fantastic singing voice, and a great repertoire—then put Erin to bed and talked for another hour or so, over Irish coffees—finally climbed aboard our own yellow home and went to bed. An hour after that we went to sleep, and I distinctly remember thinking as I drifted off that today had been, without question, the happiest day of my life.

The next day was better.

CHAPTER TWELVE

The Place

"It isn't pollution that is harming our environment. It's the impurities in our air and water that are doing it."
—J. Danforth Quayle

I WAS AWAKENED BY A familiar weight on my chest, and opened my eyes to find my daughter's angelic face an inch above mine, an expression of solemn disapproval on it. "Daddy," she whispered, "you're missing the party!"

The sun was already high. I was naked, and had kicked off the sheet, and I was neither too hot nor too cold. I realized I had been vaguely aware of divine scents and happy sounds somewhere nearby for some time. Now they came into focus. Subdued laughter. Happy but not manic conversation. Gentle bluesy piano chords, like Charles Brown in an introspective mood, unmistakably Fast Eddie. Giggling children. Soft clattering noises and crackling noises and bubbling noises.

And let me give the smells a paragraph of their own. First, the underpinning: sea salt, a hint of iodine, just a dash of windblown coral dust, and the blossoms of some lewd tropical flower I didn't know yet. Then, floating over this base: bacon. Sausages.

Onions. Eggs, with which some sharp cheese had been mated in some intriguing way. The never-before-tasted or even -imagined, but somehow unmistakable, tang of fresh-picked avocados mashed with fresh-squeezed Key lime juice. And overriding all these, like Charlie Parker soloing over the orchestra, the smell of smells: *coffee*. Even better: a kind of coffee I'd never had before, which I could already tell I was going to like a lot, and take with a lot of sugar. I guessed, correctly, that it was Cuban. I could picture the beans: dark and oily and round, like the berries I'd seen the Key deer leave behind.

Erin was right. Brunch was nearly served.

I turned to Zoey and gently touched her hair. Her breathing changed. She opened one eye halfway. Then one nostril. (On the same side as the eye.) Then she opened *both* nostrils, wide, closed the eye again, and smiled. "If you bring me a cup of that," she said, "I will marry you."

"You already *did*, Mommy."

"I'll do it again."

"Now that," I said with great sincerity, "is a nice thing to hear. It's a deal." I removed Erin from my chest and sat up and got dressed. Key West style: a pair of shorts and, just in case it was formal, a pair of sneakers and the NASA ballcap I had picked up at the Shuttle launch.

Diplomatic relations had clearly been opened with the incumbent residents of the trailer park, and the vibes were good. Even the lesbians were smiling at everybody. Some of the cooking gear was ours, some was unfamiliar, and all of it was busy. Over at the far end of the common space, under a scaly tree that looked to me like it was from Alpha Centauri, Pixel the cat rode regally on the back of Ralph von Wau Wau, both of them surrounded by an awestruck mob of adoring Conch children. Ralph is real good with kids; back home on the Island, they were about the only people outside of Mary's Place who'd talk to him. Here at my end of the clearing, most of our kids (who were used to

Ralph and Pixel by now) were gathered around a splendid snow-white cockatoo that talked. It was talking to Bill Gerrity's macaw, which did not. The macaw looked lovestruck. Doc and Mei-Ling were at the center of a crowd too, gathered in a rough circle of lawn chairs and chaise lounges, eating and talking and laughing easily.

I set Erin down, and she scampered off to join the crowd around Ralph and Pixel. I located the coffee urns immediately . . . but even closer I could see something even more urgent: a bus with its door open. I'm not sure whose it was, but it was empty, and where mine had a gaping hole in the floorboard, it had a toilet. Bladdest, bladder, blad . . . aaaah.

I met Double Bill at the coffee urn table. Also on it were huge pitchers of fresh-squeezed orange juice, iced tea, and ice water with Key lime slices floating in it. "Do you know," I told him, "that this is the first time in ten years I've smiled *before* coffee?"

He grinned. "Get used to it."

"Won't be easy," I said, filling a mug and adulterating it. Then I stopped with it halfway to my lips and looked around. "No, wait a minute. It *will* be easy."

"Well," he said, "we'll see what we can do to help you exercise the facial muscles involved today, get them in shape for it. After we eat, I'll take you downtown and show you your new saloon."

"Uh—" I already liked Double Bill a lot—but I *was* from Long Island, and he *was* a realtor; my instincts fought with my intuition. I sipped coffee to cover, and thought fast. "Gee, Bill, I haven't even had a chance to really sit down with you and talk about exactly what I'm looking for yet; maybe we ought to do that before—"

He held up a work-worn hand. "Sam spent about, oh, I guess fifty hours outlining your requirements to me, this last month. How about I just show you the place I have in mind, and then all you'll have to tell me is what details he got wrong?"

I had to admit that made sense. "Is it far?"

The question delighted him. "Son, no place on the Rock is far. It's about the same distance as Mallory Square; we'll bike over after brunch."

By now I had enough caffeine in me to be civilized. "Thanks a lot, Bill. That'll be fine. I appreciate."

"Go bring some of that java to your lady," he advised. "The food won't hold out forever."

"You're a kind man," I told him.

"Naw. I just like the way she looks in shorts."

Maybe he *did* know my tastes. "Astute, then."

I usually sleep much sounder than Zoey. It was a rare treat, a kind of privileged intimacy, to bring her coffee in bed, to be allowed to witness her transition from sleeping animal to sentient human. I developed the theory that Cuban coffee cures morning breath, and proved it empirically on the spot. The kiss progressed to the point of a promissory note, and then we allowed the food smells, and Zoey's bladder, to pry us apart. As she was dressing I said, "Double Bill likes the way you look in shorts."

She grinned over her shoulder at me and tugged them all the way up. "Doesn't everybody?"

The food tasted as good as it smelled. We found two folding aluminum lawn chairs nobody else was using, and dug in. As we ate, Jim Omar came up, with a guy I didn't know: a tall white-haired eagle-beaked senior citizen in shorts and a magnificent pale green linen shirt. He carried something that looked like a deflated football at his right hip. "Somebody I want you to meet, folks," Omar said. "He's a friend of Doc's, and I think he's going to be a big help to us. Bert, this is Jake and Zoey."

"Hewwo, Mert."

Bert waved his free hand. "Finish eatin', kid," he told me. "Pleasure, Zoey." Since he couldn't shake her hand, he took it in his left, bent with an old man's care, and kissed it. Zoey turned pink and her eyes softened.

"Bert thinks he can help us get rid of our buses," Omar told us.

"Really, Bert?" Zoey asked. "All of them?"

Bert shrugged. "I'll call a guy."

This was one of the many nagging little worries I'd been sweating: one of my last responsibilities as Road Chief for Callahan's Caravan. Assuming Double Bill really did have accommodations for our tribe, what the hell were we going to do with two dozen converted buses at the ass end of nowhere, once we were done unloading them? Waste days making cattle-drive runs up to Miami and try to peddle them there? "That sounds great, Bert," I said, having cleared my mouth by then. "You do know there's two dozen of the damn things?"

He nodded, and shifted his grip on the object at his hip. "Jimmy tells me once they're empty, ya got enougha the original seats left ta make like a dozen regular schoolbuses again, anna dozen hulks for pahts, am I right?"

There was something odd about his voice, besides a slight hoarseness. "Yeah, that sounds about right, I guess."

He shrugged again. "I know a guy has, like, interests in transportation, plus he's got a certain relationship with the school district. Ya got paper on alla buses?"

"Yeah, they're legit."

"Fahget aboudit. Chollie'll give you a price."

I finally got what was strange about his voice: there was nothing strange about it. He was the first stranger I had met in days that didn't talk funny. He talked normal, like a person. "You're from Brooklyn, Bert?"

"President Street," he agreed. "You was born inna Bronx—Bainbridge Avenue?—but you been out onnee Island since. Zoey, you're from the Island too, am I right?"

"Huntington," she told him. "You have a good ear, Bert."

Another shrug. "People talk ta me. Fuck else I got to do but listen? S'cuze my French."

She started to tell him not to worry about it, but just then the thing in his hand opened up two gummy eyes and revealed itself to be an ancient chihuahua so ugly it qualified for Nyjmnckra Grtozkzhnyi's class, canine division—if such a distinction is made. It was smaller than Nyjmnckra, but that was the only visible improvement. Bert was carrying it upside down like a football; it blinked up at me mournfully and blew a long dry fart. He glanced down at it and frowned. I believe there's a Carl Hiaasen novel in which a psychotic spends several chapters wandering around with a dead pit bull attached to his wrist; that's the kind of look Bert gave this dog, as if he'd been carrying it like a ball and chain all his life. "Jesus Christ," he said to it softly. The dog blinked up at him, sighed, and farted again. "Look, I gotta go," Bert said to us. "This millstone around my neck has gotta have his flaxseed. Ya get the buses empty, you're ready, lemme know, I'll give Chollie a call. Maybe we get together sometime afta ya get settled in. Nice meeting ya, Zoey; take it easy, Jake; later, Jimmy." And he was gone, shuffling away through the sunlight with his dog at his hip.

"Old bullet wound in his thigh," Zoey murmured to me.

I nodded and finished my eggs. "I'd say he looks like a retired Mafioso, if there was such a thing."

"Sounded a little like one, too. God, just hearing Brooklyn spoken gave me a funny feeling, you know?"

"Me too. Like I'm an expat in Singapore, and just met someone from jolly old England. Listen, Double Bill has a place he wants to show us, possible site for the new bar, says we can bike over after we eat."

"Jesus, it's already starting, isn't it?" she said.

"I don't know," I said. "I think it started a while back up the trail, I'm not sure exactly when. But yeah, we're committed, and the ball is in play."

Erin came bustling up, impatient enough to spit. "Come *on*, you guys—let's go see the new place! Bbiillll says there's a *parrot* that shits in a *toilet*—"

"Wait a minute," I interrupted. "Say his name again?"

"Bbiillll," she repeated.

I nodded. "Just wanted to be sure I heard it right. Carry on."

"Bbiillll's got bikes for you guys, and I can go in the backpack, let's *go*."

"I don't know if that sounds safe, honey," Zoey said.

"It is if you're a good driver," Erin pointed out.

Zoey and I exchanged a glance. "I'll take her," I said. "The traffic I saw last night at rush hour was candy. This time of day we should be fine."

Word spread as we got ready to leave, and of course *everybody* wanted to come. Fortunately, there was a finite limit to the bikes immediately available for borrowing, and I was able to hold us down to roughly platoon strength. We finally got under way a little before noon.

It took most of us about a block or so to get our "bike legs" back—especially those of us who had been bike riders already. We were used to the fancy hi-tech bicycloid things everybody rode up north nowadays, which had thirty-seven gears and motorcycle-style brakes on the handlebars and weighed four pounds. These were *bicycles*, like the first one I ever rode: one-speed clunkers that you braked by reversing the pedals, with fat tires and a basket atop the front wheel to hold your baseball mitt and homework. You didn't hunch forward over the handlebars; you sat up straight like a human being. I found it almost eerily enjoyable to ride one again. They weighed a ton, steered *hard*, and took forever to get up to speed—which made them perfect for pool-table-flat, slow-motion Key West. Modern magnesium-alloy bikes tempt you to *use* their truly amazing capabilities . . . and the next thing you know you're rocketing along so fast you might as well be in a car, too busy to see what you're passing.

Instead we tooled along through the sleepy funky streets of Old Town like kids playing hooky, pedaling like mad and then coasting for a block or two, rubbernecking to either side, peeling off from time to time to check out something interesting, or just swooping back and forth for the hell of it. Tourists were doing the same thing, at the same lazy pace; the only way to tell us apart was that their bikes had prominent number plates identifying the rental source. I got back that childhood feeling of being on a magic flying carpet sailing through space. I remembered for the first time in decades how much fun it was to fold your arms across your chest and steer by posture alone—would have tried it, if I hadn't had Erin on my back.

It was her first time on a bike, and she loved it, if anything more than I did. By the time we reached our destination, she had browbeaten me into promising that I would get her a bike of her own and teach her to ride it . . . and not some little baby *tricycle,* either, but a scale model of a grown-up bike. I finally agreed I would . . . just as soon as she could walk, run, jump, and somersault proficiently, *in the opinion of her mother.* I knew even that proviso wouldn't help me for long; Erin had pretty much quit crawling for good before we'd left Long Island, and by now was walking and running more like a child than like a baby. But I could already see that this was a town in which even a normal baby could safely ride a miniature bicycle.

Even on Duval Street, the main stem. It was crowded and busy at noon on a weekday, but we had no trouble at all crossing it: car and truck drivers were all alert for confused strangers on bicycles or on foot. This was so far back in history that no more than half of the stores on Duval were T-shirt shops, then, broken up occasionally by an art gallery or bookstore or craft emporium.

Once we crossed Duval, things almost instantly became quieter and less commercial; within half a block everything was residential again. And the kind of residential where chickens run free in the street. Wood-frame houses with unenclosed porches, all snuggled close together, no two alike; white picket fences everywhere, the whole neighborhood overgrown with lush green foliage that tended to red flowers.

We came to a long stretch of head-high picket fence, lined with coconut palm trees; at its center was a little gate with a

sloped roof over it. Double Bill braked his bike to a stop there, and began chaining it to a parking meter. Zoey and I followed his example, and Erin made me take her out of the backpack and put her down, and we waited there on the sidewalk until the rest of our strung-out group had arrived and secured their bikes too. There was no conversation; we were all too nervous. I kept trying to sneak peeks over the fence while I waited, but everywhere you could get a leg up somehow, there seemed to be a bush in the way. Doc Webster kept grinning at me.

Finally we were all assembled in a rough circle around Double Bill. In the noonday sun, his Shirt of Many Colors seemed to shimmer with Cherenkov radiation, and the gold ring on his big toe shone. He smiled at us around his Popeye pipe, reached into a nonobvious fold of his sarong, and produced a key.

"Take as long as you like, folks," he told us. That was his entire sales pitch. He unlocked the gate, and stepped aside.

Nobody moved. I gestured for Zoey. She gestured back, *Don't be silly: you first.*

Erin zipped through the gate.

So I stepped through after her . . . stopped almost at once . . . and was pushed all the way in by the pressure of the crowd behind me. When we were all inside, we stood in a group and stared, taking it all in.

Fast Eddie finally broke the silence. "Jesus Christ," he said, "it's poifect."

"Oh, Jake," Zoey said beside me, "it really is!"

Behind me, Doc Webster made a small rumbling sound of contentment. And possibly just a touch of relief.

We were in a large private compound, enclosed on all sides by either picket fence or walls of riotous tropical growth. Spaced around its perimeter were five pleasant-looking cottages that needed painting, but not too badly. Here and there tall palms provided large patches of shade. Off to the left was a small coral-

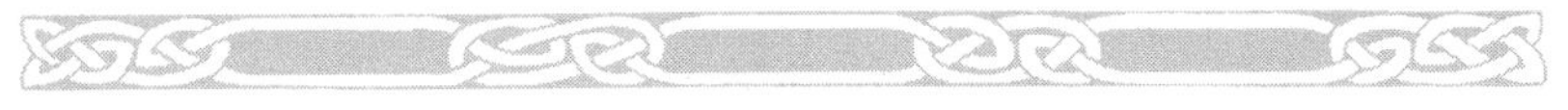

gravel-surfaced parking area accessible from the cross street below. And in the center of the compound was a round swimming pool, beside which stood a large, thatched-roof-covered, open-air bar setup—very much like that at the Schooner Wharf, save that it was a U instead of an O, surrounded by wide swaths of lawn covered with assorted chairs and tables. The bar was stripped bare now, but the pool had clean water in it, sparkling invitingly.

"Yeah," I said, "but what about—" And then I saw it. On the grass at the far side of the bar area, way at the back, well away from the swimming pool and facing toward it: a huge outdoor brick fireplace. Its interior was parabolically contoured, and big enough to barbecue a porpoise. You could smash glasses in that fireplace all night, no problem. A concrete walkway with a sloped tin roof joined it to the bar enclosure, and I could already see that Eddie's piano would fit in very nicely under that roof.

"I think we're home," I said wonderingly.

The Doc chuckled aloud.

We moved forward and began inspecting the place, chattering excitedly to one another as we made little discoveries. Omar went to check out the power and phone boxes; Zoey made a beeline for the cottages; I homed in on the bar, went around behind it and began inspecting its facilities. There was a countertop just the right size to accommodate The Machine and its conveyor belt, with power and water supply close at hand. Behind the bar area, concealed by the high bottle shelves that formed its back wall, I saw a small hedge maze that I could tell would provide several relatively private conversation areas back there.

I looked in the other direction, out over the bartop at the pool and the rest of the compound, trying it on for size. I watched my friends roaming around exploring, and tried to picture us all here of an evening, drinking and laughing and making merry around the pool. It wasn't hard at all. I realized I was facing west, toward the sunsets. That wouldn't be hard to take, either. I could smell the sea, only a few blocks away, see gulls wheeling in the sky.

I wandered back outside, located Zoey and Erin just coming out of one of the cottages. "This one's ours," Zoey said.

"Really?"

She and Erin both nodded positively. That was good enough for me. "Let's find Bill," I said. "I gotta find out how this place comes to be available. It's just too perfect. I mean, if it only turns out to be radioactive, no problem, but what if it has plague? We're not immune to plague."

Double Bill wasn't hard to find. He'd parked himself in a chaise lounge at poolside and fired up a joint. Everyone else seemed to wander his way about the same time I did, drawn by the same obvious question.

"This used to be a sort of private club," he said. "A nudist compound. There's a few of them around Key West, either nude or clothing-optional . . . but this was one of the oldest and most exclusive. Then a few years back, Duval Street started to really build up, and it's just too damn close to here. The word got around, and pretty soon every night drunken college kids would fall out of trees trying to peek over the fence, and finally the folks here all got fed up and moved the whole operation about a mile thataway."

"How long ago?" I asked.

"Last year. They held out as long as they could stand it."

"How come the place is still on the market?" Long-Drink asked, trying his best not to sound suspicious.

Double Bill opened his mouth to answer—

—and was drowned out by a high feminine voice, shrieking, *"Fuck me in the ass!"*

Bill smiled wryly. "That's part of it, right there," he admitted.

"There he is!" Erin cried happily. "I *told* you, Daddy."

I followed her pointing finger. A brilliant blue parrot, with green and red highlights around his head, almost as big as she was, standing by the side of the pool.

"God, it's so big!" he screamed, this time in a high *masculine* voice. *"Put it in slow."*

"Before it was a nudist retreat," Bill said, "this used to be a whorehouse. Harry there used to belong to the madam, and he stayed on when she left. Just refuses to go. He figures this is where he lives. The nudist folks got used to him, eventually anyway, but other people frequently seem to have a problem with him."

"Squeeze my balls," Harry said. Feminine voice this time. Go figure.

"Why is that?" I asked.

Bill shrugged. "Well, he's a little loud, I guess."

"Where's his *potty*?" Erin asked.

"On top of the fireplace."

"Show me," she demanded.

So Bill had to pick Harry up, put him on his shoulder, and carry him over to the outdoor fireplace beside the bar, followed by Erin and half a dozen of us grown-ups. Sure enough, sitting on top of it was an object so silly I had simply refused to see it earlier: a miniature toilet bowl, of the old-fashioned water-closet type, just like the one on Omar's bus, bolted down to the brick. Without any prompting, Harry hopped from Bill's shoulder onto the pot, used it for its intended purpose, and then tugged on the pull-chain with his beak: rainwater that had collected in the overhead tank dropped down and flushed the goofy little thing. (I looked, and discovered it drained down the back of the fireplace into a small coral-gravel leaching area at the base.) Harry accepted our thunderous applause as his due, with feigned nonchalance, but you could tell he was pleased. Erin just about went mad with joy.

"I don't know who taught him to do that," Double Bill said, "but you can see it makes him a more desirable neighbor than the average parrot."

"Get it wet first," Harry shrieked. (Feminine.)

"Makes it a little harder to run him off, too, eh?" Long-Drink suggested.

Double Bill's eyes twinkled. "Well, where else is he going to find a bog his size? Chase Harry off, he'd probably drown in somebody else's loo."

"Bill," Long-Drink said, "are you telling us this place is still on the market because every time a buyer comes around, old Harry freaks them out?"

Double Bill grinned. "Well, he don't help, that's for sure. But mostly the thing is, this site is your basic in-betweener. It's zoned to allow residential and commercial—but it ain't really appropriate for either one. Nobody's gonna get rich on five houses on a parcel this size, and for various reasons you can't put any more in. By today's standards it's too small for a motel, too cheesy for a resort, too close to Duval for a trailer park, and too far from Duval for a bar. Couple of times I had a guy thought it was *almost* right for him . . . and then he'd come around and meet Harry, and that was generally that. What the place really needs is something like a cult."

"He was pissing and moaning about it to me," Doc Webster said, "and suddenly it dawned on me I *knew* a cult that was looking for a temple. That's when I called you, Jake."

"You're sure we can get a liquor license?"

"You already have one. Grandfathered."

I turned to Double Bill. "And you know our top dollar."

He nodded. "I can get them to take that much—on one condition."

"What's that?"

"Would you be willing to sign a codicil guaranteeing Harry lifetime residence, and access to the facilities, there? The nudists got kind of fond of him. They'd have taken him with them, if he'd have gone, and they want to make sure he doesn't end up on the street, shitting on cars like a common parrot."

I approached the fireplace, held out my arm experimentally. Harry hopped up onto it at once, and fixed me with a particularly beady eye. He was lighter than I'd expected, thank God. "Harry," I told him, "you're welcome here."

"Oh God that's good, you slut," he bellowed triumphantly.

"We're taking the place, then?" Zoey asked me, and the low buzz of conversation all around us chopped off short.

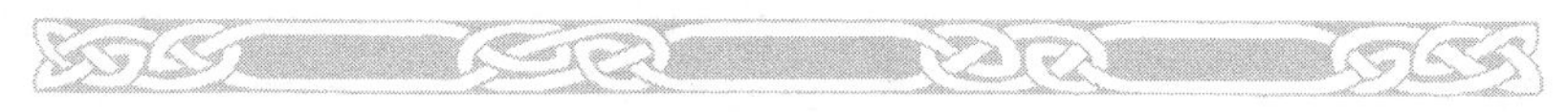

The question brought me up short. I had forgotten, for a moment, the magnitude of the decision we were making here. Suddenly I felt weight on me—the weight of all the people whose lives and hopes were involved here, and more. Would this be a good site for the battle to save the universe? Was this a congenial setting for experiments in group telepathy? Would it be a good place to drink, in the meantime? Was it where Zoey and I should raise our freak child?

In retrospect it sounds intimidating. But the weight that came on me then was not all oppressive—there was a steadying weight, too, a grounding weight: a sense of the mantle of Mike Callahan descending on my shoulders and anchoring me to something even deeper than the ground. I knew I was up to making this decision—and so it was only a matter of making it.

I looked around me. Not at the place; I'd seen all I needed to see of it for now. At my wife, and my daughter, and my friends. One by one I met their eyes and tallied their votes. Finally I turned back to Double Bill.

"We're home," I said, and shook his hand.

A cheer went up. Quite a long and loud and enthusiastic one, and just as it was starting to make me a little teary-eyed, it slacked off just enough to allow us all to hear Harry screaming, *"Oh God oh God oh God YES, Jesus YES—"* and we all broke up.

"Jake! Hey, Jake, point of order!" Long-Drink McGonnigle's voice cut through the hubbub.

"What is it, Drink?"

"I want to know what the *name* of the new place is."

Sudden silence.

For some reason, I had never given this a thought. We'd all met at Callahan's Place, then we'd all built Mary's Place together. Both were gone, now. This was neither. What was it, then?

"Jake's Place," Fast Eddie said, and there was an instant rumble of agreement.

A flood of blended pride and humility washed over me. I shook my head at once.

"Jake and Eddie's Place," I said. Again there was immediate general approval.

Eddie stared at me. "No way," he said flatly.

"Hell," I said, "you came up with most of the dough."

"Fahgeddaboudit."

I shrugged. "Fine. Zoey's Place, then."

Again the crowd tried to ratify the nomination, but Zoey cut them off. "Not a chance. Two time travelers and then me? Uh-unh. How about Erin's Place?"

This too was a popular suggestion. But Erin would have none of it. "This isn't *my* place, Mommy. This is your place, yours and Daddy's. I won't find my place until I'm grown up."

The group trailed off into baffled silence, wanting to approve *some* choice.

"Come on, Jake," Long-Drink said, "we gotta call it something, and you're the logical candidate. You're the one that brought us all down here."

I shook my head firmly, pointing at Harry where he sat on his throne. "No place that has a cute little comedy toilet in it should be called 'Jake's,'" I insisted. "Besides, I didn't bring us all down here, Nikky did." We all pondered that for a moment, and I could see *Tesla's Place* was not going to be a popular choice. "No, wait a minute, I'm wrong. He didn't bring us down here; Nikky doesn't know Key West from Cuba. He just told us we all needed to be someplace. The one who brought us all down here was the Doc."

Another instant rumble of spirited approbation.

And *again* the candidate declined his party's nomination. "Forget it," Doc Webster said. "I'm even less suitable than Jake. This town is all waterfront: you can't say, 'Hey, let's all go down to The Doc's,' nobody'll know where you mean."

"Dat makes sense," Eddie agreed reluctantly.

"I do, however, have a couple of suggestions," the Doc went on, "one serious, and the other catastrophic."

"Better give us the catastrophic first," Long-Drink suggested.

"Well . . ." The Doc hesitated.

"*That* bad?" Long-Drink asked, suddenly nervous.

Doc decided to take the plunge. "You know how they give show dogs big long dopey official names, and then a short version? Like, the dog competes as 'Snow Princess Magnificent,' but she's known around the house as 'Maggie'?"

"Sure," Long-Drink agreed.

"Well, I've been thinking about this for months, and I'll grant you it's horrible . . . but it may just be too horrible not to use. Bear with me, now: suppose this place was informally known as 'The Stoop.' 'Let's go down to The Stoop and get a beer'—how's that sound, for short?"

Long-Drink considered it. "Not too bad, I guess. What's the full name?"

" 'See Conchs to Stupor.' "

Several seconds of awed, horrified silence gave way to a spontaneous outcry of horror and revulsion. People spat, held their noses, clutched their bellies. Long-Drink, pokerfaced, reached out a trembling hand and flushed Harry's toilet. At last we had a name *nobody* liked.

"All right, all right," the Doc called over the tumult. "I *said* it was catastrophic. I know most of our customers probably won't be Conchs, too. Now let me tell you my *real* suggestion." And with that he began unbuttoning his shirt.

Fast Eddie and I exchanged a glance. Call our new bar "Fat Stripper"?

"You might have noticed on the way here," Doc said as he worked his way down his ample belly, "a lot of the stores on Duval sell T-shirts. The general theory is, it's some kind of Mafia money-laundering front. Anyway, they get distress consignments in all the time. This particular batch came from some science fiction convention huckster who went broke up north somewhere, and I have no idea what they meant to him . . . but they seem to work for us, and there happens to be enough shirts in the batch for all of us." By now he'd undone the last button. He pulled his shirt open, to reveal a simple black T-shirt, unadorned except for words in white at the left breast:

The Place
. . . because it's Time

"Huh," Long-Drink said.

"Shit, Doc, dat ain't bad," Eddie said.

"It's *right,*" I said wonderingly. "This isn't anybody's place in particular. It's just . . . The Place. I like it, Doc. I can live with that. How about the rest of you?"

Without planning it, about a dozen people all said it aloud experimentally, at the same time—"The Place"—and then *all* of us chorused, *". . . because it's time!"* as one, and Long-Drink let out a rebel yell, and applause became general.

It was agreed without dispute that the five cottages on-site would be occupied by 1) my household, 2) Doc and Mei-Ling, 3) Tom Hauptman and the Lucky Duck, 4) Long-Drink McGonnigle and Tommy Janssen, and 5) Fast Eddie by himself in the smallest one. Double Bill already had other homes lined up for most of the rest of the gang, working in cooperation with a friendly colleague/competitor of his named Joey Delgatto, and was confident that between them they could accommodate everybody. (There you go—that's Key West right there: the realtors got along with each other.)

Naturally, a party was held at Double Bill's trailer park to celebrate, that night, and we let out all the stops. Conchs came from all over town to see what all the excitement was, and kicked in a little of their own. I met at least six first-rate musicians, and Eddie and Zoey and I succeeded in impressing them all a little, and in between sets I tasted my first piece of *real* Key lime pie (you can tell the difference easily: the crap they sell

tourists is green; the real stuff is yellow), and what with one thing and another, fun got had.

And didn't stop just because the party finally did, either. I don't know if you're familiar with the phenomenon—I wasn't—but when a woman has been on the road for a long time, and then she locates where home is going to be from now on, and finds it good . . . well, let's just say she feels really celebratory. And so, shortly, does her lucky partner. Anticipating this syndrome somehow, Doc and Mei-Ling had graciously offered to take Erin for the night, and Zoey and I nearly finished off the suspension system on that noble old bus.

As we drifted off to sleep sometime around two in the morning, my last thought was, *Nine more years or so of this, and then I gotta start gearing up to save the universe? I guess I can handle that . . .*

So I shouldn't have been as surprised as I was to wake the next morning and find Nikola Tesla standing over me, frowning prodigiously. Some days you're the pigeon; some days you're the statue.

"Morning, Nik," I said, speaking softly so I wouldn't wake Zoey. "I was expecting you sooner or later, but—"

"I made a serious error," he said.

I blinked up at him, still only half-awake. "Oh, really?"

"In my estimate of the lead time you would have before the crisis."

Now I was awake. "How big an error?"

"Nearly ten years, I think."

Wide awake, now, and ready to shit the bed. "*How* near, Nikky? How long have we got?"

"Perhaps as little as five months, Jacob. I am sorry."

CHAPTER THIRTEEN

Because It's Time

"I stand by all the misstatements that I've made."
—J. Danforth Quayle to Sam Donaldson, August 17, 1989

I DISCOVERED I WAS holding my breath, and let it all out in an explosive sigh. "Christ, you had me worried for a second there." I shook my head. "That could have waited until after breakfast. You have woken a man for insufficient reason, Nik: prepare to die."

"I apologize, sir—but I felt you should know at once."

Deep breath. Maybe it wasn't absolutely necessary to try and assassinate the most dangerous man alive before coffee. He *had* apologized. "Well, I'm probably not going to be able to get back to sleep now anyway, so killing you is pointless. Okay, put the coffee on. In fact, fire up the urns outside—I'm going to have to call a council." I sat up and put my legs over the side of the bunk.

"No!"

His voice was pitched low, but so urgent that Zoey stirred in her sleep. "Whibbis¿ Hib sommel¿"

I hesitated. Tesla shook his head and made frantic *no, no* motions with his hands. "Go back to sleep, baby," I murmured to

Zoey. She made a little nickering sound like a horse and went back under at once. Tesla shot me a grateful look.

I eased to my feet and led him out of the sleeping area, pulling the curtain closed behind us and switching on the coffee machine as I went past it. I pointed Tesla to a seat, got my sunglasses from the dashboard and put them on, and slid into the seat across the aisle from him. The bubbling sounds of coffee being made reminded me that even pain is transitory. It helped.

"Nikky," I said, "as I understand it, the point of this exercise is for us all to eventually get telepathic. Anything you tell me, you're telling everybody. So why don't I call a council, and get it over with?"

Tesla looked uncomfortable. "For one thing, Jacob, there are strangers present in this trailer court."

"Okay, so let me go quietly round up the inner circle, at least: Doc, Eddie, Long-Drink, the Duck, Omar, Tom, Josie, Tommy Janssen, a couple of the others. We'll button up this bus, tyle the lodge, and discuss the fate of the universe in privacy."

"Eventually, of course," he said.

"Come on, Nikky, how many times do you want to tell this story? If it was worth waking me up, it's worth waking them up too."

He did not answer.

Light dawned. "Jesus." Nikky was embarrassed. He didn't want to tell this story at all. Forced to, he wanted to tell as few people as necessary. I felt a sudden burst of empathy. Nikola Tesla was a proud and accomplished and profoundly weird man, and what he had to say was not going to make him look good. I could relate. "Okay, Nikky, have it your way. Run it by me first. If I don't think I'm competent to relay it to the rest of the gang, I'll tell you."

"Thank you," he said, relief apparent on his craggy face. "First, you must understand Coleman's crucial observation regarding Guth's inflationary universe theory—"

"Christ, not *yet*!"

"Oh. I beg your pardon."

A few minutes later, my caffeine level finally rose up out of the red zone, and I felt safe in removing my sunglasses. "Okay. *Now*. Slowly."

He nodded, took a long sip of his own coffee, and began. "Alan Guth's theory of the inflationary universe requires, at a fundamental level, the assumption that very early on in the history of the Big Bang, empty space itself, what physicists call 'the vacuum,' had some very unusual properties for a short time, and then underwent what is called a 'phase transition'—something like what happens when water freezes, a radical change of state—into its present form. Are you with me so far?"

"For an indescribably short time, nothingness was indescribably weird; then it settled down into nothing at all, and has been that ever since. Am I close?"

Tesla nodded. "Close enough. But we may be hasty in assuming it is nothing at all. Sidney Coleman was one of the first to make the point that *there is no way for us to be sure our present vacuum is in the lowest possible energy state*. It might, in theory, be possible for space to undergo a *further* phase transition, to a different, lower-energy vacuum state."

"Things can always get worse, in other words."

He nodded. "Indeed."

I tried to imagine a lower-energy vacuum. "Let me guess what a lower-energy vacuum is like. Everything really sucks, right?"

Nikky likes puns, but he didn't care much for that one, didn't crack a smile. "In a different vacuum state," he said, his voice flat and harsh, "all the laws of physics would be changed. All particles as we know them, and everything we see around us, would be destroyed. Instantly."

I could think of absolutely nothing to say except, "Uh-hunh."

"Do you know what supercool water is, Jacob?"

I nodded at once. "Irish whiskey."

Again he ignored my feeble levity. "If you have *very* pure water, you can cool it to below freezing temperature and it will not

freeze. Then, if you introduce a single speck of dust, the whole mass freezes over in an instant. Cosmologist Sir Martin Rees speculates that our universe could be in such a state, its vacuum 'supercooled'—and that, given the proper trigger, a bubble of 'new vacuum' might be accidentally created, which would expand at the speed of light to engulf the universe."

"And something that human beings do could cause that?" I shook my head. "Nikky, I'm going to try very hard throughout this discussion to avoid saying, 'That sounds fucking crazy,' but that sounds fucking crazy. Humanity just isn't that powerful. Hell, not even close."

"Jacob, humans have already produced conditions that never existed naturally anywhere before."

"Name one," I challenged.

"Refrigeration. So far as present human knowledge extends, there was never anything in the universe colder than 2.7 degrees above absolute zero, the present temperature of the microwave background—until we made refrigerators."

"Huh."

"And in the other direction, we are equally ambitious. The kind of thing that might create dangerous conditions with regard to the vacuum would be a collision between very high-energy particles in a big accelerator. Such a collision could conceivably create a large local energy density of just the kind that might trigger a phase transition in the vacuum."

"Whoa." I got up and refilled my coffee, then his. "I mean, I'm second to none in my admiration for the high-energy physics boys, but if you're trying to tell me those guys with the big racetrack in Texas have something powerful enough to destroy the universe ready—"

Tesla frowned ferociously. "No. I thought that was going to be the trigger—that is where I got my original ten-year parameter—but I was mistaken. The Superconducting Super Collider is not only incomplete, I have just learned that it will never be completed. It will be canceled by Congress in just a few years."

That sidetracked me. "*What?* How could they *possibly* pull the plug on the SSC? They've already spent gazillions, and the damn thing's like 75% built already!"

Tesla shrugged irritably. "There is no rational reason. That is why I overlooked the possibility in my thinking. Trust me: it will be aborted four years from now, 80% complete."

I felt the same frustration I'd felt a little over a year earlier, when Tesla had told me flatly, again from his authority as a time traveler, that shortly the Soviet Union was going to cease to exist. I *knew* I could believe him, but it just didn't seem conceivable.

Still didn't, in fact: at that time, in March 1989, the Soviet Union was still there, still apparently healthy and vigorous—finally out of Afghanistan, having a little trouble in outlying provinces perhaps, but pressing on with *glasnost* and *perestroika*. Nobody knew the game was over yet but Callahan's gang . . . and maybe Mikhail Gorbachev. *Certainly* not the CIA.

"Second time, Nikky: 'That sounds fucking crazy.'"

"It is fucking crazy," he said irritably, "but it is true nonetheless."

I waved the distraction aside. If I couldn't trust the facts Nikola Tesla gave me, there was no point in going any further. And all he was asking me to believe was that the U.S. federal government could be monumentally stupid. "Okay, so the trigger won't be the SSC. How about that international Linear Collider I read about?"

"That," he agreed, "will be able to reach collision energies even higher than the SSC . . . and it *will* be built, eventually. But not for—" He frowned again, and stopped speaking.

I sipped coffee and waited.

"Nikola," I said softly after a while, "if I'm following you, you believe that sometime this coming August, something is going to trigger a phase transition in the vacuum, or, as I would phrase it in layman's terms, Fuck Up Everything. It won't be the big ring at Waxahacie, and it won't be the Linear Collider they haven't even drawn up plans for yet. Fine, I got that. So what's going to do it?"

He looked up at me from under those craggy brows, his eyes full of pain. "I fear it will have been me," he confessed.

He got up and began pacing up and down the aisle, absentmindedly juggling small balls of electric-blue fire—a nervous habit of his for over a century, which had delighted Mark Twain. I shut up and watched him and waited.

Outside, I could hear people stirring, exchanging sleepy morning greetings. Smells of sea and mildew were borne on a steady warm breeze. Parts of the old bus creaked and ticked as sunlight found holes in the shade that shielded it. Pixel the cat either had been aboard undetected all night, or now pulled his trick of walking through walls; all at once he was on my lap, quietly but firmly demanding attention. I scratched him behind the ears and under the chin without taking my eyes off Tesla, and Pixel seemed willing to tolerate this perfunctory service; he settled firmly in place and began to purr just audibly. We waited together.

Finally Tesla stopped pacing and made his blue fireballs disappear. He resumed his seat across from me, slid back against the wall of the bus, and put his legs up on the seat, crossing his ankles. He folded his hands on his lap and addressed a point about a foot above my head.

"Eighty-one years ago," he said, "I sent a message to Robert Peary at the North Pole."

I nodded sagely, as if this made any sense to me at all, and kept my mouth shut.

He lowered his gaze briefly to meet mine. "You must understand, Jacob: at that time I was perhaps as frustrated and desperate as I have ever been in my life."

I nodded again. He looked back up at the ceiling behind my head again.

"I had been trying to complete Wardenclyffe for eight years. The crowning accomplishment of my life, and it was like chasing the horizon: as I approached, it receded. The world was hailing that treacherous fop Marconi as the inventor of radio, and I was determined to show him up as a dilettante, but I could not seem to get my feet under me. J. P. Morgan completely abandoned his support, when he learned that my real purpose was the broadcast transmission of power. A financial panic five years earlier had ruined me personally—and just about any investors I might have hoped to find. I was being sued by several creditors back in Colorado Springs. Even my friend George Westinghouse, who had become rich from my patents for alternating current motors and generators, declined to help me. Like the SSC in Texas today, Wardenclyffe was 80% completed, needing only the 68-foot dome itself to be placed atop the tower—it had been for five years! But the workers would not work unless I paid them, and I could not. Then the architect, Stanford White, was murdered by Harry Thaw, his lover Evelyn Nesbit's husband . . ." He broke off.

"So you sent a message to Peary," I prompted gently.

"On June 29, 1908," Tesla agreed. "He was then in the midst of his second, ultimately successful attempt on the North Pole. I told him I knew he was quite busy, but that I would appreciate it if, the next day, he were to take special notice of the sky, and report any interesting observations he might make."

I was still puzzled, but hanging on gamely. "Okay. And the next day, Peary reported . . ."

"Nothing," Tesla said flatly. "He and his team saw nothing at all. They never guessed how very fortunate they were."

He clammed up again.

My first impulse was to be irritated with him for dragging this out. I squelched that and thought hard instead.

Let's see. Nikky is trying to signal Peary somehow, and for some reason it doesn't work. Visualize the geometry. Here's Wardenclyffe—about twenty minutes from where I used to live, on Long Island's North Shore, at Shoreham. There's Peary, somewhere damn close to the Pole. Connect them with a dotted line representing the failed signal . . .

Wait a minute. What if the signal didn't fail? Suppose it simply *missed*? Extend the dotted line . . . and *what* did he say the date was?

"Holy, fucking, *Christ*—"

Frowning like an Old Testament prophet, Nikola Tesla nodded at me. "That same day," he said, "in central Siberia, there was a loud noise, and half a million acres of pine forest near the Stony Tunguska River all decided to lie down for a while."

"Jesus, Nikky!"

Pixel was gone from my lap, taking several gobbets of my flesh with him; I would have to apologize to him later. I'd woken up Zoey, too; another apology due. I sat frozen, marinating in awe and horror.

"The explosion was heard 620 miles away," Tesla went on. "Whole herds of reindeer were destroyed. Several nomadic villages vanished utterly. To this day, no plausible explanation has ever been adduced."

My voice sounded funny to me. "Nikky . . . you're telling me that *you . . . caused Tunguska?*"

He hung his head. "I overshot by more than a thousand miles. Fortunately for Peary and his companions. Unfortunately for an indeterminate number of Siberian nomads. The beam was much more powerful than I had anticipated."

For many years, the officially accepted explanation for the stupendous destruction at Tunguska—the most powerful recorded energy event in history—had been meteorite impact. When a 1927 expedition failed to find an impact crater, or any trace of nickel-iron shrapnel (down to a depth of 118 feet!), they decided that a 100,000-ton fragment of Encke's Comet, composed mainly of dust and ice, had entered the atmosphere at 62,000 mph, and exploded just above the surface, creating a 15-megaton shock wave. *That* story held up for decades, until somebody got around to working the figures—at which time they decided it hadn't been a chunk of comet, but maybe a mini-black-hole, which just happened to dissipate just before it struck Siberia. As a layman, I'd never been much impressed with any of these theories . . . but had been forced to admit that the best I could come up with myself, a crashing alien spacecraft, was also low-probability.

Somehow I'd never thought of a Nikola Tesla publicity stunt gone haywire . . .

The implications began to sink in. "Oh my God, Nikky—is this to do with that stuff the feds supposedly took out of the hotel basement after you died, and then classified forever? Papers and working models? Your Death Ray?"

Still looking down, he nodded. "A type of particle-beam weapon. Quite unconventional . . . and quite powerful."

"How powerful? After almost fifty years of secret government development, that is?"

He shook his head, still declining to meet my eyes. "There is no way to say. I myself never made a second test."

I shook my own head. "Jesus, you must have freaked when you found out what had happened. How long did it take for the news about Tunguska to get around?"

"Weeks," he said. "Within two or three, I had a fairly clear idea."

"What did you do?"

"I had a nervous breakdown. I entered a state which would today be called clinical depression. I abandoned my business interests, my friends, even my correspondence, retired to my bed. Scherff continued to look after my interests for me, bless him, even filed my tax returns . . . but there was nothing he could do, and nothing I would do. Eventually I was forced to sign over Wardenclyffe to George Boldt, to cover my bills at the Waldorf . . ."

"And now Wardenclyffe is a factory or something," I said finally, just to break the silence. "I went over to take a look at it once, but there wasn't much to see. The tower was gone."

He sighed and sat up straight, but he still wouldn't meet my eyes. "Not a single ounce of metal anywhere in that tower, and it

still took three successive demolition crews over a year to bring it down. All three used dynamite, too. But only the third used enough."

The subject of demolition put me, at least, back on track. "Okay, so the government has a Tesla Death Ray, forty-odd years more advanced than the one you took out half of Siberia with. Why are you acting as though all this were your fault? *You* didn't give it to them, for Chrissake."

"But I *did*," he said, and *now* he looked up and met my eyes.

"You did? How? Why?"

"For the most ludicrous reason imaginable. Insufficient arrogance."

I hesitated, but decided to keep going with brutal honesty. "Nikky, I've heard you accused of a lot of things, but never—"

He nodded. "I will try to explain. When Lady Sally McGee offered to rejuvenate me, to make me immortal, and required me to publicly appear to die first . . . I *knew* those papers were in the hotel safe. I could have destroyed them easily before staging my death. I thought it was safe to leave them there, for some hypothetical posterity perhaps."

"Why?"

"Because I had by then spent over thirty years trying as hard as possible to discredit myself, and believed I had succeeded."

I blinked at him several times.

"Have you studied my biography, Jacob?"

"Several of them," I agreed.

"Then perhaps you have noticed that during roughly the first half of my life, I produced a steady stream of novel discoveries and successful products . . ." Yeah, and Shakespeare wrote some interesting plays. ". . . and during the latter half, I essentially produced a steady stream of increasingly grandiose and wild-sounding pronouncements, concerning devices which I never actually offered for examination."

I had to admit he was right. Impenetrable city-sized force fields, broadcast-powered aircraft, antigravity, charging the ionosphere to a glow so it would never get dark again anywhere—all these had been publicly announced by Tesla at various times in his "last thirty-five years" of life, and none ever shown. By the time of his supposed death, it was true that most of the world considered him a loopy old bird who rated lip-service respect for half-remembered accomplishments in a prior century, but was not to be taken seriously anymore—basically, an especially entertaining eccentric.

"The dividing point was Tunguska. By the time of my death, most of my true accomplishments were either misattributed to others, or largely forgotten. My eventual vindication by the Supreme Court, which awarded me primacy over Marconi in the question of radio—eight months after I 'died'!—was almost universally ignored, and is forgotten today. The general consensus of the scientific community at the time of my death was that I was an old humbug, a mountebank who had for decades been coasting on a reputation achieved by luck, bolstering it occasionally with absurd, empty boasts. Everyone knew that Edison had invented electricity, and Marconi had invented radio; I was the man who had invented the special effects prop for the second *Frankenstein* film, the Tesla coil. Lady Sally had already informed me, as a wry joke, that I would not be inducted into the Inventors Hall of Fame until 1975. It simply never occurred to me that I had enough credibility left to be taken seriously by anyone in authority.

"I underestimated the desperation in Washington in January of 1943. The war was not going well; the Manhattan Project was not going well. It was decided to explore even wild-card alternatives—and so the FBI seized all my papers and equipment."

"But they didn't *do* anything with them, then?" I had a sudden wild vision of Truman sitting in a room with his advisers, and saying, "Fuck it, let's go easy on them. Start with the atom bomb . . . and if that doesn't work, then get tough."

"No," he agreed. "Not then. Even if they understood what they were reading, at that time it would have required another

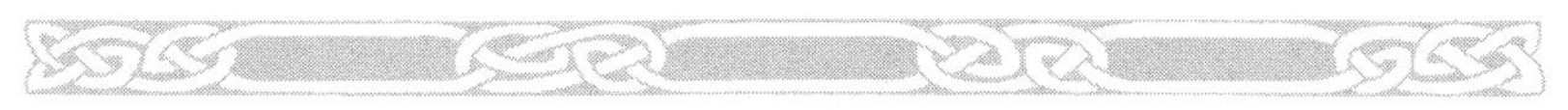

Manhattan Project merely to re-create Wardenclyffe, and without me that would not have been enough. Not within the time-frame they envisioned. My papers and artifacts were all inspected, classified, and set aside." His face changed. "But not forgotten."

Zoey shuffled into the passenger area, wearing a passable counterfeit of her face, hair combed, silk robe tied. "Morning, Nikky. How've you been?"

You would not think a man that long and tall could levitate from a reclining position on a bus seat to standing vertical in the aisle so quickly, without losing dignity. Especially not at age 133. He came erect with an almost audible *click*, and instantly bent at the waist to kiss the hand Zoey had no choice but to give him. "Well enough, dear lady—and yourself?"

"Better than that," she said. "Have you eaten?"

"Perhaps later, thank you. I apologize for awakening you."

"I'm sure you had reason to."

"Thank you for taking it that way. May I pour you coffee? It is reasonably fresh."

"Thanks," she said, and sat down to get out of his way. "So," she added as he went by, "I take it all hell has broken loose?"

"Not yet."

"Not quite," I said, getting up myself and heading for the door, "but you were barely in time, darling. There *was* about to be a catastrophic explosion in here. Chat with Nikky: he'll bring you up to speed. I'll be back in a flash."

"Jesus," she said, "can't you give me a quick synopsis? I gotta pee myself."

I danced in the doorway. But it had been hard enough to drag it out of Tesla the first time. "You know about Tunguska?"

She furrowed her brow. "Siberia? Long time back? Big boom, big mystery?"

I nodded vigorously. "Very big, both. Eighty years ago. Nikky did it, by accident, testing his Death Ray."

"Okay."

Before coffee. What a woman. "The feds have it now. They've been upgrading it for forty-six years. That's as far as I got. I'll be back as fast as I can. Entertain Nikky."

She caught the change in my tone on the last two words. Her eyes widened slightly, and she nodded just perceptibly. "Sure. Go."

With a wife like that, anything is possible. I hated to leave her to make small talk with a full bladder of her own . . . but I did not want to leave Nikky alone just now. I could tell we were only partway through this story, and the rest of it wasn't going to be any easier to tell than the first part had been. I don't even remember whose bathroom I borrowed, or much of what I did there, save that it was energetic and comprehensive; I was too busy thinking.

How were we well-intentioned civilian goof-offs and misfits supposed to assault the federal government of the United States? Where the hell would they *keep* their Death Ray—anywhere near Key West? It seemed unlikely. Though you could time it for sunset at Mallory Dock, and maybe nobody would notice the slight increase in pyrotechnics. I couldn't seem to make myself believe it. I knew Tesla made mighty magic; Tunguska said so. But it still seemed a *big* jump from something that simulated a 15-megaton explosion to something that could seriously threaten to zap the entire universe. You'd think that if the numbers were anywhere within five or ten orders of magnitude of that kind of power, even the Defense Department would have the sense to see this was a weapon too powerful to have any conceivable use.

Come to think of it, I'd *seen* a Tesla Death Ray once, briefly. He'd produced it that final night at Mary's Place, at Mary Callahan-Finn's request, for use in the firefight we anticipated with The Lizard . . . though fortunately it had not proved necessary for him to actually fire it. Had he really been prepared to incinerate the universe if necessary that night, and just forgotten to

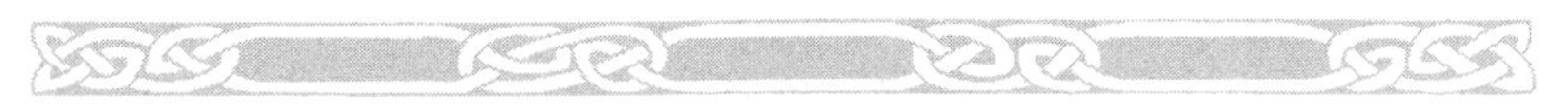

mention it? Or did his have a low-power setting that the government model omitted as a cost-saving measure?

I didn't stop to wash my hands until I was back on my own bus and had relieved Zoey to . . . well, to relieve herself. (I made a mental note to see about replacing our toilet—then remembered I was moving out of this bus soon. The new owners, the school district, probably wouldn't *want* their schoolbuses to incorporate facilities that might inspire a young man to drop a cherry bomb down them.) Before she left Zoey told me she and Tesla had worked it out that what he was really feeling was not so much guilt as frustrated anger. (My wife is capable of amazing things before coffee.)

"It was by far the hardest thing I have ever done," he explained to me. "Certainly the most galling. I have a large ego, Jacob. For me—me, who powered the world!—to spend the last half of my life playing the part of a blowhard . . . never again to publicly demonstrate another of my achievements—" He broke off and looked down at his lap. "And worst of all," he went on in a softer voice, "to have all that humiliation and self-abasement turn out to have been useless, wasted . . . and all because I was arrogant enough to believe it was sufficient protection . . ." He shook his head, looked back up at me, and smiled one of his rare smiles. "It is infuriating."

I shook my head. "I think it's one of the most heroic things I ever heard of, Nikky."

"It did not work."

"It kept the Death Ray off the world stage for eighty years," I insisted. "Imagine what *that* would have done to the doctrine of Mutual Assured Destruction! From what you tell me, in another year or two the Cold War is *over*. I say you done good."

"But not good enough," he said.

"Something else to think about," I said. "You ever wonder why Lady Sally made you immortal?"

He blinked at me.

"Because you're a genius?" I said, and shook my head. "A *lot*

of geniuses passed through Lady Sally's House at one time or another, and to the best of my knowledge, she never made any of *them* immortal, let alone taught 'em how to time travel."

"Then why—"

"You've got an ego as big as your talent; the combination could have destroyed civilization; you saw that, and subordinated your ego, for the good of your species. That's heroism, Nikky. Unprecedented in history, as far as I know. I think you succeeded in impressing Lady Sally. Genuine heroism gets ladies wet."

He colored slightly. "Jacob, I hardly—"

"Now it turns out your heroism was 'only' sufficient to protect us all for eighty-one years, and earn you immortality. Okay, fine. Being immortal, you're still on the case, and being intelligent, you have wisely hired the most experienced world-savers around to help you. You have led us to the Promised Land, where working conditions seem ideal, and we have five months. Why don't we just get on with it?"

His face went blank, his eyes dulled. He "went away," I guess to that place inside his head where his visions came. He was gone maybe half a minute. When he came back, his eyes were less haunted, his brow did not refurrow; his shoulders relaxed slightly. "Thank you, Jake," he said.

"You're welcome, Nikola."

Zoey reboarded the bus, carrying Erin. "He over being pissed at himself?" she asked me, gesturing at Tesla.

"Yeah," I said.

"Good."

I held out my arms and she put Erin in my lap. "Have a seat: we're just getting to the good part."

"Mommy told me about your Death Ray, Uncle Nikky," Erin said, "but you couldn't blow up the whole universe with *that*, could you?"

It had taken me several minutes' thought to get that far; Erin leaped there instantly. Smart, my kid.

He smiled at her sadly and shook his head. "No, Erin. Even the most powerful variant theoretically possible could not come close. The event we are threatened with must be the result of a *combination* of causes. My weapon can be only one of them—necessary, but not in itself sufficient."

She nodded. "What are the other factors?"

Tesla's face slowly changed. At no time so far had he looked anything remotely like happy—but now he looked desolate.

"I do not know," he admitted.

None of us said anything for a minute or so.

"Can't you cheat?" Erin asked finally. "You know, time travel ahead five months, and peek?"

He shook his head with great finality. "No."

"Not permitted?" We had always gathered from the Callahans that there were certain fundamental restrictions of some sort on time travel, but they'd carefully left the matter as vague as possible.

"No," he said. "Not possible."

"How come? Oh, wait—I get it."

I sure didn't. "Explain it to old dad."

"Remember, Daddy? You can't time travel to a ficton where you already exist. There can't ever be two of you at once."

True. I had been told that. Suddenly I saw what she meant.

And Nikky confirmed it. "I could never abandon my post during a crisis. I will surely be there when . . . whatever it is happens. So I cannot peek."

I was beginning to boggle again. "Nikky, wait a minute now. You have no real idea what's going to cause the crisis—but you're sure your Death Ray will be involved. Why?"

He sighed. "Are you familiar with Heinlein's felicitous phrase, 'I could be wrong, but I'm positive,' Jacob? I cannot prove, in the scientific sense, that my weapon will be a factor in this. But I am intuitively certain."

"Well, look," I said, "nobody has more respect than I do for your intuition, Nikky, but—"

"Two things support my conviction," he interrupted. "First, I theorize universal disaster must require human action of some kind—"

"Why?" I interrupted.

Erin looked up at me to see if I was kidding. "Daddy," she said gently, "the universe is *old*. If it was possible for it to destroy itself naturally, without human intervention, it would have done it a long time ago."

That made sense. I remembered Tesla telling me earlier that nothing in the universe had ever been colder than 2.7 degrees above absolute zero until humans came along. "Okay, I got you. Say for the sake of argument that you're right, that destroying the whole universe probably requires the special talents of human beings or equivalent. But not necessarily *you*, Nikky. Granted, you're the greatest Mad Scientist we've ever produced. But you're not the *only* one."

"But my weapon is, to the best of my knowledge, the single most powerful energy-producing utensil of which the race is presently capable, by a wide margin. And will be, well into the next millennium. Nothing else comes close, not even H-bombs. It *must* be involved."

"But it's not powerful enough to destroy the universe by itself. Something else is involved too."

"And I do not yet know what," Tesla agreed.

"Then where the hell do you come up with this five-months-from-now figure for a deadline?" I asked, exasperated.

"That is a minimum figure," he said. "It could take much longer than that for . . . whatever it is . . . to occur. But that is the soonest it could happen. If it is possible for a universal destruction machine to be accidentally created, and if my weapon is a necessary component of that machine, then five months from

now is when that machine will first be possible. That is when the doomsday clock starts ticking."

"Why?" I insisted. "What happens in five months?"

"STS-28," he said. "It is scheduled to lift off on August 8th, and return on the 13th."

STS-28? Hell, I'd just *seen* STS-29 launch myself, with my own personal eyeballs, only a few days ago. I did vaguely recall hearing that the Shuttle mission just before it, scheduled to go up in January, had been postponed indefinitely, for obscure reasons. I tried to remember what we'd been told about it.

Oh my God . . .

We'd been told almost *nothing* about it. Except that it would be a dedicated DoD launch, the fourth so far. Classified payload . . .

"The Defense Department is going to orbit a Death Ray?" I greamed.

Tesla nodded. "The news has just now reached me."

CHAPTER FOURTEEN

On the Case

"We are all capable of mistakes, but I do not care to enlighten you on the mistakes we may or may not have made."
—J. Danforth Quayle

"BUT WHY?" I SCROANED. "In another year or two the fucking Cold War will be *over* . . . oh shit, they don't *know* that, of course . . ."

"Actually, the problem is that they do," Tesla said. "Therein lies the irony. At this point, certain decision makers in the U.S. high command now know that the Soviet Union is in serious, fatal trouble. It is inconceivable to them that it could ever simply opt to peacefully dissolve itself. They cannot imagine the Evil Empire accepting defeat until it has sacrificed the last *kulak*. For many years now, the only real card the Soviet generals have had to play was the possibility that they were genocidal lunatics, and they bluffed a little too well. Key thinkers at the Pentagon and NSA believe that soon they may launch a desperate first-strike, while they still can. And so this summer—"

"—they're going to put one of your Death Rays in orbit," I said again. I still couldn't believe it.

"A stealthed satellite, carrying an utterly top secret particle-

beam weapon," Tesla agreed. "Once they do, the universe-destroying trap must be considered armed. The final trigger, whatever it is, could occur at any time during the satellite's expected twenty-five-year lifetime . . . but it could also occur in the second it reaches orbit. So we must plan on the assumption that it will. And it will probably occur *before* the Soviet Union dissolves, hence within two years."

"What's the other thing?" Erin asked.

"Beg pardon?" Tesla said, confused. He wasn't used to the way Erin can *veer*, sometimes.

"You said two things supported your belief that your particle beam is involved in the end of the universe. Then you told us one thing: namely, 'how could it not be?' What's the *other* thing?"

"Ah, I see." His eyes widened slightly as he took her meaning . . . then they narrowed again. "The other thing . . ." For a long moment I thought he wasn't going to answer. Then he sighed, and let his shoulders slump, and said it. "The other thing is that when Michael Callahan gave me this commission, charged me with the local defense of the universe, he stated that it was my 'responsibility.' That was the word he used. And he said it in Serbian, so he must have wanted his meaning quite clear to me. He did not actually use the word that corresponds to 'redemption,' but I felt it was implied. It was clear in his face: I, Nikola Tesla, must undo this thing . . . because it is at least partly my fault."

My head was starting to ache dully. "Where the hell *is* Mike, anyway?" I asked irritably. "Why the hell aren't he and Sally here helping? This is more their line of work than ours."

Tesla sighed. "As Erin said a few minutes ago, even a Callahan cannot be in two places at the same time. At the moment, Michael and Sally are engaged elsewhere."

I stared at him. "In something of higher priority than the destruction of the universe."

He shrugged. "What can I say, Jacob? Some things I simply cannot discuss with you."

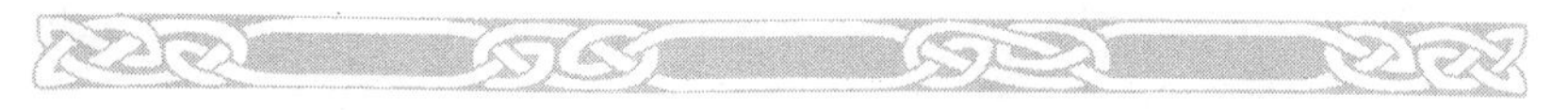

It was hard for me to swallow. Okay, Mike wasn't really a human being, he just played one on TV, as Erin had said—nobody knew that better than I. But he'd done so for over forty years! He came to this ficton in the first place and opened up his bar for the specific purpose of saving the human race from destruction. Hell, I'd been telepathic with the man: I *knew* he loved me, loved us, loved the human race—and loved Earth, ancestral home of his earliest forebears, too. It just didn't seem reasonable that he'd see us through two major crises, and then when the really *big* one came along, bug out and leave us to our own devices.

All I was sure of was that he must either have a damn good reason, or not have any choice. I tried, briefly and futilely, to imagine what it must be like to have problems more pressing than the End of Everything, and gave up. It made my head hurt to try. Mike and Sally were out of the picture; accept it and move on.

Move on *where?* I cudgeled my brains.

For a while, the only result was bruised brains. Then I got a glimmering. "Hey, Nikky—you say the Death Ray—"

"Jacob," he interrupted, wincing slightly, "could we not call it something else? Please?"

"You say the Tesla Beam alone isn't powerful enough to deflate the vacuum."

"Definitely not."

"Suppose you aimed two of them at each other, and fired them both at once, at maximum power?"

"But there is no other."

"Suppose the Russians have one, too."

For a moment his eyes widened. But then he shook his head. "No, they cannot."

"How can you be *sure?*"

"Daddy," Erin said patiently, "if the Soviet Union had something more powerful than H-bombs, which didn't have to go by ICBM, couldn't be seen coming, acted instantly, left no radioactivity, and probably couldn't ever be positively traced back to its source . . . it *wouldn't* choose to dissolve peacefully."

I sighed. No arguing with that. "Who, then? China?"

Tesla and Erin both shook their heads firmly. "There is no other, Jacob," Tesla said. "And even if there were, and you set them up facing each other and fired both simultaneously, you still would not produce enough energy to destroy the universe. Something else is needed."

"What?"

"I do not know," he confessed. "We must find out. Before 8 August—assuming STS-28 actually launches on that day as scheduled."

I got up and got some aspirin, washed them down with the last of my second cup of coffee. "Well," I said, "I'll put it to the group as soon as I can, and see if anybody has any ideas."

Tesla looked alarmed. "Jacob—*only* the group! And please make very sure each of them understands this is secret information—"

"Jesus Christ, Nikky," I said indignantly. "Do you think there's one person in that bunch who'd betray a confidence? Considering what's at stake? Besides, this is Key West: around here you could tell people the universe was going to end this summer and nobody'd even—"

"You prove my point!" Tesla shouted.

All three of us were frozen with shock. Nikky has a lot of voice in him, and a face admirably constructed to express anger. I had never seen him angry before, or heard him shout.

"Always, you and your friends have kept clan secrets well," he said. "And why not? All of you were weird in some way, in a place where weirdness is not well tolerated: that is what brought you together. And the things that happened to you were so weird themselves that no one else who was not as weird as you would have believed them even if you *had* told of them. *But now you are in a place where most people are weird*. I fear that you will cease to fear."

I began to see what he was driving at. "Shit."

Tesla lost his anger all of a sudden, and only looked sad. "I hear my own words and see I am a fool. Of course you good people should cease to fear. If you want to let all your new neighbors know that Erin is not a normal infant, and Mr. von Wau Wau can talk, and Mr. Shea can roll sevens as long as he cares to, and so on—that is your affair. By all means tell them you know several time travelers and an alien cyborg, and have survived a nuclear explosion. If it suits you to charge tourists money to shoot you with handguns at close range, who am I to say you should not? Leave your doors unlocked if you enjoy the freedom to do so in safety."

He leaned forward in his seat, and somehow managed to look all three of us in the eye at once, spoke quietly but with great intensity. "But no matter how relaxed you become, you must never disclose to any stranger anything you have learned through anachrognosis, from a time traveler. The secrets of time *must* be kept. Or things could happen which . . ." He hesitated, then went on. "I cannot explain this so you will understand it . . . but there can be things worse than the destruction of the universe. And the tearing of the fabric of history is one such. Even in Key West, it is not safe to risk that."

"Okay," I said, considerably chastened. "I hear you. Family only."

"What about new family?" Erin was bold enough to ask. "Aunt Mei-Ling? Uncle Bbiillll?"

Tesla started to answer, then hesitated and looked pained. "I cannot tell you you may not expand your group," he said. "But until you are sure a new member is discreet, please do not speak in their presence of the Tesla Beam, or STS-28, or the end of the universe, or the collapse of the Soviet Union. I do not know either of the people you mention, Erin . . . but I will trust anyone you and your parents trust. I only ask that you do not relax your vigilance in that regard, simply because you are now in a place where trust is more easily given."

I had to agree that was good advice.

He stood up. "I am going to make certain investigations, and see what I can learn of the Defense Department's intentions and

capabilities. I will be back in a week, and we can share what we have all learned and conjectured."

"Okay," I said, and was going to add some last-minute question, I forget what, but it doesn't matter because all of a sudden he just . . . wasn't there to ask. No sound, no flickering lights, no apparent disturbance of air currents, even. Zip, gone.

"I *love* it when he does that," Erin said.

A sort of daytime party was already getting under way outside the bus when I emerged. I probably couldn't have stopped it if I'd tried, and why try? The gang had been cooped up in buses forever, they were in the Promised Land, there was basically nothing for us to do until the various real estate deals closed and it was time to start unloading buses and moving in. Meanwhile their new neighbors were friendly and savvy, and everybody was in the mood to put out little roots of friendship. Food was made, beer was drunk, music was made, talk was talked, and so on.

So what with one thing and another, it took me until late afternoon to cut the Inner Circle out of the herd and take them aside for a briefing.

I use the term ironically of course; we have never been organized enough, or hierarchical enough, to have an Inner Circle—and if we had, none of us would have wanted to be in it. The group members I picked were pretty much just the first couple dozen I happened to run into that day whose opinions I really wanted. The oldest veterans of Callahan's Place, mostly. The cover story I used was that we needed to plan the details of setting up our new bar, which of course we actually did.

At Double Bill's suggestion, we took everybody down to one of Key West's best-kept secrets. It is kept secret by leaving it right in plain sight, big as life, right on Duval Street: the Holiday Inn La Concha. It's plainly one of the tallest buildings in Key West, but there is no clear sign at street level to alert tourists walking past that its observation deck is open to the public free.

Therefore it is seldom crowded up there—and it offers perhaps the best view to be had on the Rock. You can see *everything* from there, in all directions, walk around the building and take in the whole island—or sweep your eyes across the Atlantic, the Florida Straits, the Caribbean, and the Gulf of Mexico in one glance. They say on a clear day you can see Cuba. From up there the sunset is, if anything, even more beautiful than it is from Mallory Square; certainly more peaceful and quiet. Plus they serve booze.

It was getting on toward sundown by the time we got there, too. The few people who were already present, mostly hotel guests and a few savvy locals, had already gravitated to the west side of the building. So we gathered on the south side, where we could have privacy but still get a fair shot at the sunset. By happy chance it was also the downwind side; Double Bill lit and passed around a handful of what looked like filter cigarettes but weren't. Present were me, Zoey, Erin, Fast Eddie, Doc Webster and Mei-Ling, Long-Drink, the Lucky Duck, Tom Hauptman, Jim Omar, the Latimers, Josie Bauer, Tommy Janssen, Shorty, Slippery Joe and both his wives, Margie Shorter, Dave and Marty, Dorothy Wu, Ralph von Wau Wau, and two of our newest members, Acayib Pinsky and Pixel the cat.

I began the discussion by stressing Tesla's warning that all of this was Top Secret, Eyes Only material; then I went on to give them a summary of everything he had told me—starting with the news that the end of the universe was not ten years away, but something closer to five months. After I was done, they were all silent for a time, thinking.

It was Long-Drink who broke the silence. "Jesus Christ," he said, so softly it was almost a prayer. "The man who gave the human race just about everything it's got—and got *nothing* in return—spent the last half of his life deliberately making himself look like an idiot. For their benefit. A proud guy like Nikky."

"God damn," Tanya Latimer said. "That's a *man*." There was a general murmur of agreement.

"What I can't believe," Zoey said, "is that even that sacrifice wasn't good enough. He *still* got bit on the ass . . . by his own genius."

"So we gotta fix it for him," Fast Eddie said. Another rumble of common agreement.

"Okay," Doc Webster said. "Let's get down to business. What do we know?"

"Not much," Zoey said.

I said, "We know that Ragnarok is coming. We know the Tesla Beam is involved—"

"*Do* we know that, Jake?" the Doc asked.

I shrugged. "I don't know, Doc. Do you doubt it?"

"No," he said, "I'm just pointing out that our certainty is intuitive rather than empirical. We're expecting a high-energy event, and the Tesla Beam is the highest-energy utensil we know of. Besides, if we assume it *isn't* involved, we're left with nothing much to think about. But we ought to remember we could be all wet. For all we know, on August 9th an alien god will appear out of a hole in the tenth dimension with something that makes a Tesla Beam look like a firecracker, and use it to clear this annoying universe out of his way."

"Fine," I agreed. "But I *am* intuitively certain. I intend to assume that the trigger for Ragnarok, whatever it is, involves the Tesla Beam—plus other factors yet to be identified. Therefore we know that whatever happens, it could come any time after August 8th, and won't be sooner. What I don't know is where the hell to go from here."

Tanya Latimer spoke up. "We have to try and figure out what the other factors are."

"If Nikola Tesla doesn't know and can't guess—" the Lucky Duck began sourly.

Acayib Pinsky cut him off. "Dr. Tesla is an intelligent and heroic man, and very learned. But he is *not* an expert in the present state of human science or technology. It seems to me to be a simple problem of research. We investigate high-energy technologies, and rank them in order of the probability of their interacting somehow with the Tesla Beam—"

Omar cut *him* off. "Why not save that until after we've solved the problem?"

Several people asked at once what the hell he was talking about. I was one of them.

He stared around at us, honestly puzzled. "Look, I appreciate the theoretical beauty of this situation as much as anybody. I'd love to know what combination of circumstances could destroy the universe. But first I want to stop it from happening."

Margie Shorter exclaimed, "How the hell can we do that unless we find out what we're trying to stop, Jim?"

He held out his hands palm upward. "Are we all agreed that Tesla's weapon is not sufficient, but is necessary, to destroy the universe?"

Nobody disagreed.

He turned his palms over. "Then we just take it out of the equation, and all is well. We can figure out what the other factors would have been at our leisure."

"Huh?" is sort of the vector sum of all our exclamations.

"Kill that satellite, or disable it, or keep it from being orbited in the first place."

Brief silence.

"Jim," I said, "we're a bunch of barflies. Furthermore, at the moment we're barflies from out of town, about as local as a fish in a tree. I don't even know where the Post Office is. Are you seriously suggesting we should try to take on the U.S. Defense Department?"

"Why not?"

I had trouble framing my answer.

"Jake, look," he said. "Take a worst-case. Say we fail, big-time. What's the worst that could possibly happen?"

"They could *shoot* us!" I said. Then I heard what I had just said, and had to grin. "Oh. Well . . . put us in prison for the rest of our natural lives, then."

"For interfering with the secret Death Ray they put into orbit?" he asked gently.

It did sound like a hard headline to sell.

"This is nuts," Shorty said. "We couldn't even beat a town inspector on Long Island. How the hell are we supposed to take on DoD?"

"I didn't say it was going to be easy," Omar said. "But has anybody got a better approach?"

Everybody tried to talk at once.

After considerable discussion, Tanya Latimer sorted it out. We ended up forming two committees. One to try and identify candidates for Other Contributing Factors. And the other to figure out a way to put that damn Deathstar out of operation, without being caught at it. Omar was right, it made sense. Maybe the first committee would come up empty. Or maybe whatever the other factors were, they would turn out to be even *harder* to influence. You work with what you've got.

The sun was well down, by then—sad to say, we had been too distracted to fully appreciate the sunset—and we all left in a thoughtful mood.

Most of us headed back to whichever of the two trailer parks was their present temporary home. Or in Double Bill's case, his permanent one. But a few of us—my family, Doc and Mei-Ling, Fast Eddie, Long-Drink, Omar, and Pixel—decided to stay downtown and do the Duval Street Crawl. It was a Friday night, in the middle of March, between the main assault waves of college students: viewing conditions would never be better.

And a colorful and interesting experience it turned out to be. In a way it was like a watered-down version of the French Quarter of New Orleans—watered down in that the Quarter's ever-present spices of genuine danger and true sleaziness were missing. Duval Street was just as decadent and lively as the Quarter . . . but somehow more life-affirmingly so: the cops traveled solo, rather than in threes, and the hookers did not, in the presence of your wife, ram your hand down their pants and then under your nose. You walked two blocks outside the French Quarter unarmed, you were asking to die; walk two blocks off Duval and there are fearless chickens on the sidewalk and a stranger will come down off his porch to offer you a beer.

Also, most of Duval's funkiness was genuine, come by honestly, not painstakingly faked from old photographs the way it was in the Quarter or in Provincetown. It was just too mildewed, moldy, warped, and rusted to be a Disney re-creation. And an astonishing proportion of the things it had to sell tourists were actually worth the money. In particular, at that point in history Duval Street had not yet succumbed to the plague that within ten years would blight it beyond recognition: so far there were no more than one or two T-shirt shops per block. Today, in 1999, apart from bars and a restaurant or two there's almost nothing else *but* T-shirt shops on Duval—many of them, oddly, owned by Russian immigrants—even though the market cannot possibly support half that many. It's hard to figure. But back in '89, the T-shirt emporia were still an admittedly gaudy minority, interspersed frequently with things like art galleries, jewelry stores, clothing stores, handicraft co-ops, sidewalk restaurants, head shops, bookstores, comic book shops, antique stores, record stores, no-taboos porn stores, massage parlors, a hundred different kinds of exotic fast-food outlets—and, of course, dozens of bars, including Jimmy Buffett's original Margaritaville, which was not to burn down for years yet. The sidewalks were crammed, and not just with pedestrians: every available space seemed to hold some kind of vendor's wagon or souvenir stand or blanket array of trinkets for sale; people walked past it all in a slow amble, most of them cheerfully tipsy, better than half of them smiling.

Hustling went on, but it was good-natured, low key. Again, it wasn't like the Quarter, where angry-looking black kids got in your face, demanding to "betcha dolla I know where you got them shoes," and getting ugly if you didn't want to play. (If you did, the answer was, "You got the lef' one on your lef' foot, right one on your right, gimme a dollar, chump!") Instead, a grinning Cuban would catch your eye and call out, "Hey Cap'n—you can't keep a woman as pretty as that without a opal like this here." And when your wife answers, "If he had to buy me, he couldn't afford me," the Cuban just laughs and waves you on.

Every twenty yards there was a bar. Three of them claimed to be the genuine original place where old Papa Hemingway used to get faced, and I later learned all three were lying. Just about every joint had some kind of music—in the space of three blocks, we heard rock, country, folk, jazz, reggae, heavy metal, salsa, blues, and R&B. And here at last was something the French Quarter had over Duval Street, head and shoulders over it, in fact: the music wasn't as good. None of it actually sucked, nothing we heard was unprofessionally bad—but let's face it, *no place* has music as good as New Orleans. There wasn't anything to touch, say, the Famous Door.

This was good news to Zoey. The longer we strolled, the happier she got. It was clear there would be plenty of work in this town for a really good, versatile bass player who could play any style and sing. And although I'd only be available to join her one or two nights a week, our trio act with Fast Eddie was easily better than anything we heard on Duval that night.

Erin had a ball, too. She spent most of the walk on Long-Drink's shoulders, he being the tallest of us, and from time to time she would demand that we pass her up a mango ice cream or a bite of Cuban sandwich or a sip of peach juice or a forkful of Key lime pie or a bite of pizza. Whenever her mouth was empty, she drove Zoey crazy demanding explanations of the obscene jokes and mottoes on the T-shirts in the shop windows.

Finally we ended up at an open-air Cuban joint at the far north end of Duval. A competent trio pumped spicy salsa out of a synthesizer, congas, and an accordion, and because the house knew gringo tourists were usually timid and ignorant, it em-

ployed shills: a pair of pro dancers who alternated exciting demonstrations of salsa with patiently persistent importunings of the audience to get up and join them. The girl was so beautiful Zoey found her attractive, the boy was so handsome I found him attractive, and both were really good dancers.

And really persistent proselytizers: the next thing I knew, I was dancing with Rita.

I do not, repeat, do not dance—and if I were going to, would certainly not choose salsa. But Zoey *does* dance, and an opportunity to dance with a pro like Enrico—as stunningly handsome as Enrico—was just too good for her to pass up; she didn't even pretend to resist when he took her hands and pulled her up out of her chair. So I let Rita draft me too. My feeling is, I'm perfectly willing to make a fool of myself in public, if it'll get me a good seat when my wife is dancing. Rita found it hilarious and touching that I kept looking past her splendid bosom to get a glimpse of my wife, and forgave me my ineptness. And turned out to be very good at leading a dumb Anglo with two left feet through at least a few of the intricacies of beginner salsa; by the time the tune mercifully ended, I was doing well enough to garner a smattering of applause (enthusiastically led by Erin) for my courage. The applause for Zoey was a lot louder, and included me. Rita kissed me soundly, on the forehead, and Enrico bent low over Zoey's hand and kissed it, and then the two of us, both bright pink, collapsed back into our chairs and sucked piña coladas until we had enough breath back to kiss each other for a minute or two. Other volunteers took our place on the dance floor eagerly.

We left Duval well before midnight, just as things were going into high gear, and the walk back home was glorious. Dark, quiet streets, for one thing, even when we were still only a block or two from Duval. It was still Friday night; we passed places where parties were going on. But Key West locals didn't seem to party as frantically as the tourists did. You'd hear laughter, but not the kind of desperate hyena laughter that signals a party back in New York, which sounds as if the participants are having fun

at gunpoint. Even the party music hadn't been turned way up to make the people laugh louder. The air was no temperature at all. Soft warm breezes came and went, bearing smells of jasmine and coral and frangipani. A star-spangled sky soared over us.

That last especially impressed Erin. "I never *saw* so many stars," she kept saying. "So *clear*."

"Too much crap in the air back on Long Island," I told her.

"You should have been here a couple of weeks ago," Double Bill said.

"How come?" Erin asked.

"We had Northern Lights."

We all stopped walking and stared at him.

"No, really," he said. "Swear to God. Sheets of fire in the sky. Mostly green, but a lot of red, and a little purple even."

To our surprise, Doc Webster backed him up. "He's not pulling your leg, Erin. Genuine Aurora Borealis. Old Stan Wedermyer, this astronomer I know, said something about the biggest solar maximum in three hundred years. Didn't you guys see any up New York way? It was reported all over the South."

"Hell, maybe we did get Northern Lights," Long-Drink said. "How could we tell, through the smog?"

"True enough," the Doc conceded. "Pity; it was something to see."

"Well, this sky is spectacular enough for me," I said.

"Me too, Daddy!"

We walked another block or so, all craning our necks to look up at the stars. It was worth a stiff neck. The difference between what you could see in the night sky back on Long Island and this was like the difference in sound quality between a 1965 monaural transistor radio and a modern CD player. It made me think of the first time in my life I'd ever heard high-fidelity stereo, on headphones: that astonishing, almost frighteningly beautiful moment when Paul McCartney suddenly appeared, magically right in the very center of my own personal skull, and began singing.

Would people still be willing to live in cities, I wondered, if they fully grasped the extent to which they're turning down the brightness, contrast, and color controls and minimizing all the equalizer settings of their lives by doing so? Now that I came to think about it, they accepted the muffling of *all* their senses. Not just sight and sound. Few of them ever got to taste really fresh food: to them, fresh meant "only three days old and never frozen." Their senses of smell *had* to shut down, in self-defense—I once read a great science fiction novel, I forget the author's name, where a mad scientist increased everyone's sense of smell, and civilization fell overnight. And as for the fifth sense, the one Theodore Sturgeon says is the most fundamental, touch (". . . all the other senses are only other ways of touching . . .") . . . well, city people just didn't. Not even with their eyes, if they could help it.

Was that why they seemed to need to stimulate themselves so strongly and so relentlessly? Do filters on all your senses make you need to party hearty, just to be feeling something?

No. Key West was an anomaly. Even people in rural areas of North America tended to be manic these days, to pursue pleasure like it was the six-fingered Count who'd killed their father Domingo Montoya. City people just had better utensils. And a bit more anonymity in which to safely disgrace themselves. The night skies had probably been clear and crisp over the Spahn Ranch when the Manson family lived there . . . and I bet they had an excellent stereo, grew tasty carrots, and could smell a cop a mile away. By all accounts, they did a *lot* of touching. So much for simplistic insights. I gave up philosophy and just dug the stars, until my neck made me quit.

When we got back to Double Bill's trailer park, I invited everybody aboard my house for God's Blessing, and they all had the sense to accept. Seven adults, a baby, and a cat packed into a third of a schoolbus made a nice intimate conversational group. We chatted surface pleasantries while I whipped the cream and brewed the coffee and poured in the Irish whiskey. But once I'd served us all (except Erin, who contented herself with the

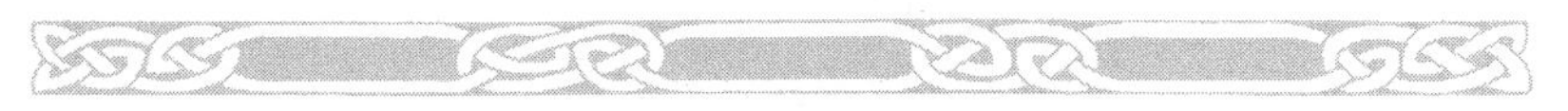

whipped cream), within a couple of sips the conversation had turned serious.

"Jake," Doc Webster said, "you contracted with Nikky to get the whole gang telepathic again within ten years. You really think we can pull it off in five months? Without Callahan or the McDonald brothers around to help?"

"In a place like this, maybe," Long-Drink said. "What do you think, Jake?"

I shook my head. "I think that's the wrong question."

"What's the right one?" the Doc asked.

"I don't know anything about telepathy," I said. "I've *been* telepathic three times now—each time with assistance from a special talent, and for a period measurable in minutes. I honestly have no idea if we can all figure out how to find our way back there again by ourselves . . . in five months, or ever. I strongly suspect we can, if we try hard enough, but I don't know. That ain't what's worrying me."

"What is?" Zoey asked.

"Say we pull it off—come this August, we all achieve telepathic rapport again. Say for the sake of argument we figure out how to do it anytime we want, for as long as we like. *How does that help us take out a satellite?*"

There was a startled silence. Two or three people started to answer, but none of them got as far as producing an actual word. Instead we all put our faces in our Irish coffees.

"You know," Omar said thoughtfully after a while, "engineers have a saying. When the only tool you have is a hammer, it's amazing how every problem that comes along seems to look like a nail."

"What are you saying?" Long-Drink asked.

"Just that maybe we've got carpal tunnel vision." The Doc winced slightly. "We saved the world twice using telepathy, so we assume that's the way you save the universe, too—like it's our only parlor trick."

"Jim," I said, "it *is* our only parlor trick. We're a bunch of rum-

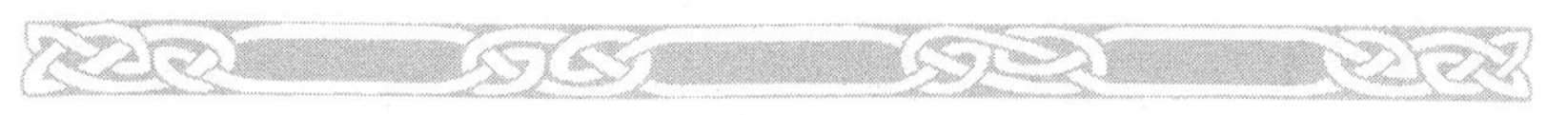

mies, far from home. Our time travelers are gone. Our alien cyborg is gone with them. Our cluricaune hasn't been seen in over a year. As far as Special Talents, we're down to a pookah, a talking dog, and a computer genius—"

Erin hugged my leg for that last one and said, "—plus we're mostly all bulletproof, Daddy."

"Granted," I said. "Nonetheless, I don't see us taking on the Joint Chiefs of Staff and winning, because we're all telepathic with each other. I just don't see our role in this."

"I've never been telepathic," Mei-Ling said, "so pardon me if this is a silly question. But is there any possibility that if the whole group were in rapport, you'd be able to . . . reach out, to another mind?"

"What, and take it over, like?" Long-Drink asked.

"Not necessarily. Could you all . . . could we all perhaps plant suggestions in certain key minds? Without their realizing it?"

All of us who *had* been telepathic—everybody except Mei-Ling and Double Bill, that is—exchanged a long look. Finally I spoke for all of us.

"I don't *know*—but I doubt it. I doubt it a lot." The others murmured agreement.

Omar settled his big shoulders. "I think you're right, Jake. I don't think telepathy can help us just now, even if we get it. Maybe we will, someday, if the universe doesn't end first. I hope so, since I missed the last time. But I don't think we should focus on it."

"But what the hell else have we *got*?" I said.

"Brains," he said simply. "Guts. Good intentions. Hell's own luck."

"Against the Department of Defense," I said.

"Hardly seems fair, does it? All they got is a lousy Tesla Death Ray."

CHAPTER FIFTEEN

The Devil's Luck

"I am not part of the problem. I am a Republican."
—J. Danforth Quayle

THE NEXT WEEK WAS very eventful for all of us. A million things had to get done, in an environment where your natural instinct was to curl up in the hammock with a margarita. Double Bill took me by the hand and led me through the closing on the property, business license, transfer of the liquor license, and similar rituals and formalities of commerce. I looked upon it as my penance, for fucking up the last time and costing us all Mary's Place. And at that I got off easy. The stack of paperwork required to sell booze legally in Key West was no thicker than the Manhattan phone book. The corresponding heap back on Long Island had literally been taller than me—and I'm six one.

Zoey meanwhile ran around at various speeds, none of them low, performing a variety of tasks and moving gracefully between them. While setting up the utilities, phones, and cable TV, she also arranged everything from furniture to flowers. She even managed to scrounge an ISDN fast Internet connection for Erin,

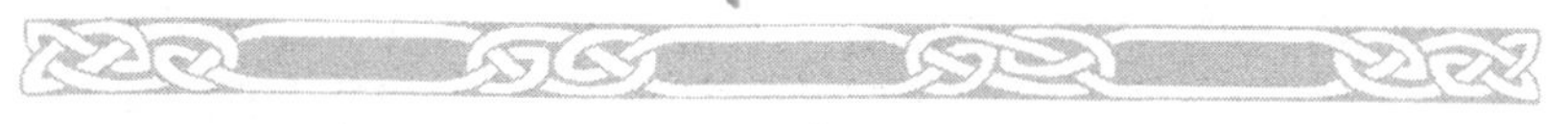

through a friend of Doc's and Mei-Ling's—a real godsend, as it allowed her to access the Net at 128,000 bps on our Mac as well as on her Teslafied laptop.

Erin herself used that connection to prowl NSFnet, ARPANET, MILnet, and a few other networks with our highly modified, massively souped-up Mac II—and on the side she voluntarily organized several small but important group projects, such as compiling all the now-useless overcoats, gloves, fur hats, and snow boots we'd all brought with us, and packaging them to take out to Mount Trashmore. Ever since we'd decided to move here, she'd seemed to relish finding physically challenging things to do, even on the long trip down, and now that we'd arrived, Key West was perfect for the purpose, warm and safe. She was already much stronger and more coordinated than she'd been back on Long Island, roughly equivalent to a normal four- or five-year old.

A lot of us were busy with similar moving-in tasks of their own, and the rest were busy helping them, while waiting for their own house negotiations to close. Every day was like a barn-raising party. Much like the weeks we'd spent fixing up and loading all those buses in the first place, only in better weather. You fell into bed each night utterly exhausted and totally exhilarated—and woke every morning starving and eager to get started again.

All of us, and a couple of dozen sympathetic locals, spent all day Thursday at The Place, unloading. Incredibly, we managed to empty all five relevant buses before collapsing—despite considerable harassment from Harry the parrot. It helped a whole lot that most of the bar equipment we'd fetched south with us had, by happy chance, ended up distributed among those same five buses. Having the Lucky Duck on your packing crew is a good idea.

(One moment memorable enough to be worth reporting was the first meeting of Harry and Pixel. When we first arrived, Harry waddled forth to greet us, squawking—and stopped dead in his

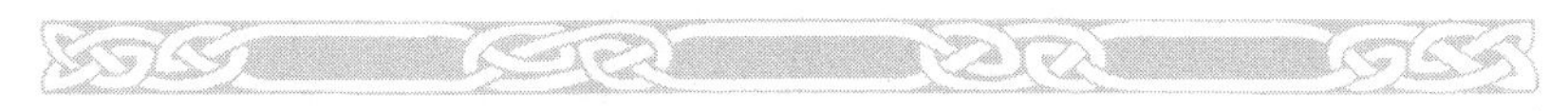

tracks when Pixel got off the bus. Pixel approached slowly, stopped a few yards away. Harry stood his ground, feathers ruffling slightly. Erin looked to me and I shrugged helplessly, already mentally composing Harry's eulogy. Pixel lowered his ears, made a noise deep in his throat, and crept closer. When he was a foot or two away, without any warning Harry suddenly screamed, *"Oh, what a gorgeous PUSSY!"* right into his face. Pixel did a sudden back-flip . . . and glared around at all of us. Nobody laughed—then—and everybody found something else to look at. Harry turned his back on Pixel and strutted away, and after a moment's consideration, Pixel visibly decided parrots were beneath notice and turned away himself. From that point forward, the two of them maintained a stiff, uneasy truce. Most of the time, anyway.)

Then the next morning, without even so much as pausing to hook up The Machine, we left everything there in boxes and went to help four other busloads of people off-load at *their* new homes, and got *that* accomplished just after sundown. It being a Friday night again, the temptation to party was enormous, and many of us yielded to it.

Nonetheless, the informal council I'd formed the previous week convened at my (new) place after supper. There'd been too many volunteer locals around all week for me to have a chance to safely discuss the end of the universe with anybody, and I wanted to get everybody else's thoughts and ideas before Tesla showed up. There was enough room on the porch for eight or ten of us, seated on assorted boxes and crates; a couple more perched on the railing; the rest gathered on the little patch of lawn in front of the porch, some on blankets and a few on folding chairs.

To my surprise, progress had been made. Instead of having no candidates for Cause of Ragnarok, we now seemed to have two competing theories.

The first, unsurprisingly, came from Acayib Pinsky, our resident physicist.

Barring Marty, Acayib was the most recent member of our

caravan: he'd wandered into Mary's Place for the first time on the last night of its existence, fifteen months earlier—just in time to get plugged into our telepathic hookup and help us defeat the Dark Side of the Lizard. He suffers from a quite rare hereditary condition called Riley-Day Syndrome (three hundred cases in the whole country), which leaves him with several major deficiencies. The first is definitely the most spectacular: he is and has always been absolutely unable to perceive physical pain.

Think of that: a man who has never once in his life said "Ouch."

Until he met us, anyway. Perhaps understandably, he had always had an irrational yearning to *feel* pain, to know what all the fuss was about, to be like everyone else. In that first timeless moment of entering telepathic rapport with the rest of us, he had learned better. He told me once later that pain had struck him as so utterly *outrageous* that he could not understand why people who believed in God had not put a price on His head. In the end, he decided that maybe Riley-Day Syndrome wasn't such a bad deal after all.

Does it seem that way to you? Consider what comes with the package. As Tom Waits said, "The large print giveth . . . and the small print taketh away." Perhaps because they never got any exercise, Acayib's tear ducts never developed: he can cry if he's sad enough, but is quite unable to produce tears. He's prone to ghastly skin rashes and profuse sweating and sudden spasms of vomiting. His blood pressure and temperature fluctuate like the Dow Jones index. He can't keep his balance well and tends to fall down a lot. And, of course, he's a mass of scars and badly knit bones—for fairly obvious reasons. The scars are worse on parts of his body that are outside his field of vision, but he has lots on his hands, too. He used to see his doctor for a checkup four times a year—but then one time the doctor found a bullet in the meat at the back of his thigh, and Acayib didn't even have a guess as to when or how he'd acquired it; ever since, he got himself looked over monthly.

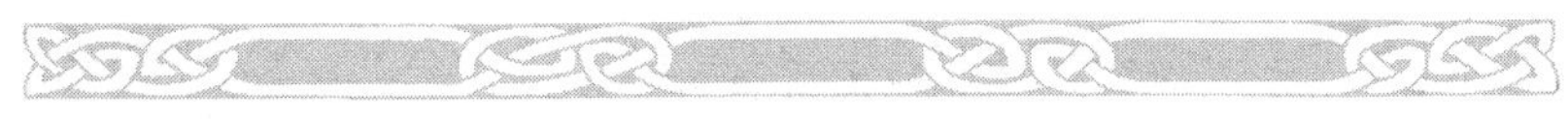

He had also developed a constant ongoing *alertness*, an almost Zen state of awareness of himself and his immediate surroundings that never flagged. It gave him a great personal presence and charisma that even profuse sweating, big purple blotches on his face, and a tendency to vomit without warning could not entirely erode. And though he was only twenty-six at that time, he exhibited a maturity far beyond his years.

Well he might: Acayib knew that statistically he was most unlikely to see his fortieth birthday. Fully half of all Riley-Day babies are dead before age twenty.

Sorry for the digression, but Acayib's an interesting cat. Take it all as background, to give you the full benefit of the horrid hilarity in what he had to tell us. You see, Key West's warm damp air had been paradoxically good for his rash: the only blemish still visible was a dark purple patch on his forehead . . . that made him look just like an underweight Mikhail Gorbachev. And what he had to say to us was:

"Is everyone here familiar with the expression 'God is an iron'¿"

Most of us were, but Mei-Ling raised a hand and shook her head no.

"A person who commits felony is a felon," Doc Webster explained. "A person who commits gluttony is a glutton—"

"—and a person who commits larceny—" Slippery Joe began, but his wife Susie stepped on one of his feet and his other wife Suzie stepped on the other. Suzie's maiden name is Larsen.

"—therefore," the Doc went on, ignoring the interruption, "God is an iron. Acayib is telling us to brace ourselves for some sort of punchline. Acayib¿"

"Wait," I said, "let me guess. We're looking for the missing Second Half of the Armageddon Trigger. The first half is an energy beam devised by Nikola Tesla. So the second half has to be some forgotten secret invention of Thomas Edison. It uses DC current, I bet—right, Acayib¿"

He shook his head. "That *would* be a good joke," he agreed. "But I have a different irony in mind—one that pivots not on who created the two things, but on who deployed them, and why." He waited, in case anyone else wanted to try and guess.

Jim Omar was the first to get it. "Oh my God . . . you mean—"

Acayib nodded, wiped sweat off the purple blotch on his forehead, and said, "The first part of the trigger is an orbital weapon secretly deployed by the Defense Department. So naturally, another part will—I think—be a perfectly legitimate, aboveboard, purely scientific satellite . . . orbited by the Soviet Union."

"*What* satellite?"

"Mir."

Acayib explained. Unfortunately, he began to do so in Physicist . . . but we were able to head him off and get him to summarize in Layman. The gist was this:

He had been researching the current state of the art in high-energy physics, searching for something that, in combination with a Tesla Beam, might disrupt the vacuum—and had pretty much come up empty. It was hard to be sure, because the only baseline we had for the Tesla Beam was a large eighty-one-year-old hole in Siberia—but as far as Acayib could tell, no known particle accelerator even potentially operational by August could deliver enough power to do the trick, probably not by a few orders of magnitude. But in researching the literature, he had run across a snide reference to one of the devices in Mir's Kvant-1 module.

The experiment was a real long shot . . . but on the other hand, it was pretty cheap, and the potential payoff quite high. High-energy physics is done by whacking very fast-moving, powerful particles into each other, and observing the results of the wreck. On Earth it is very difficult and thus expensive to get the particle going that fast. But space is full of *very* high-energy particles: cosmic rays. Oh, they vary considerably—but some of them are the most energetic known things there are in the universe.

Just not many of them. And there's no way to tell when the really zippy ones will arrive, or from which direction.

The Soviets figured what the hell, and put a particle detector aboard Mir. Perhaps before it got so old it fell out of orbit, the space station would chance to intersect a really high-energy cosmic ray or two at just the right angle . . . and then Soviet science might see things even the mighty canceled SSC could not have shown. So far, as expected, no dice—the author of the article Acayib read had been pretty snotty about their chances.

"That article started me thinking in two directions at once," Acayib told us. "First, as I said, some cosmic rays are extremely energetic. They are also extremely tiny—but I believe that if an ultrahigh-energy cosmic ray were to meet with a Tesla Beam coming in the opposite direction, the impact might very well produce a pinpoint of a high enough energy density to perturb the vacuum. If Tesla and Coleman are right, even a pinprick in the vacuum would be enough: the new, lower-energy vacuum would expand at lightspeed."

Rooba rooba rooba.

"This naturally led to the question, why would a Tesla Beam be coming in the other direction? What might the Deathstar be firing on? And as I said, I had begun by thinking of cosmic rays hitting the detector on Mir . . ."

"I think I see where you're going," Omar said excitedly. "Say a really high-energy cosmic ray hits the Mir target. Maybe it's one of the really rare ones, much more powerful than they anticipated, and it . . . I don't know, wrecks their detector."

I began to see where he was going, and felt the blood cooling in my temples. "Wrecks it in such a way—"

"—in such a way that the American Deathstar satellite might well misinterpret it as a nuclear weapon, arming. And fire on it."

There was a *rooba rooba*, a sonic collage of exclamations of dismay, and Acayib tried to get the floor back. But Doc Webster's booming voice overrode everyone.

"Wait a second," he insisted. "Hold on, now. If that happened . . . well, I wouldn't want to be on Mir at the time . . . but I'm damned if I see how it could destroy the universe."

"Sounds good ta me," Fast Eddie said.

"Think about it, Ed. The superparticle hits Mir. All hell breaks loose. This news leaves Mir, and has to travel at least *some* distance—admittedly at lightspeed—to reach the Deathstar. Then some computer on the Deathstar has to misidentify it, and issue the firing command. Even if the Tesla Beam requires zero warm-up, fires *instantly,* it still has to take some time to reach Mir. At best, it arrives late for dinner—at least a second after the superparticle has been destroyed. So where's your Big Bang?"

"Right here, big boy!" Harry the parrot screamed.

By now we had all gotten pretty good at ignoring the bird. But it was harder to ignore the hole the Doc had just punched through the logic of Omar's scenario. "Maybe *two* cosmic rays, one right after the other?" Omar said, but without any conviction. We all fell silent—for long enough to allow Acayib to grab the floor again.

"I'm sorry, Jim," he said, "but I think your basic premise is flawed. Cosmic rays can be powerful—but as I said, they are also very tiny phenomena. And good detectors are dense, inert things. I don't believe even the most powerful imaginable particle hitting the Mir detector would so much as cause it to seem warmer to the touch, let alone destroy it spectacularly."

"Huh." Omar wrinkled his forehead in thought. "Okay, I give up. Why *would* the Deathstar fire on Mir, then?"

Acayib shrugged, and wiped sweat from his forehead. "I'm not sure. Perhaps it will fire at something else. But Mir feels plausible to me. It must be very high, if not number one, on the Deathstar's list of preprogrammed targets. Most of the other Soviet-orbited objects have long since been checked off as harm-

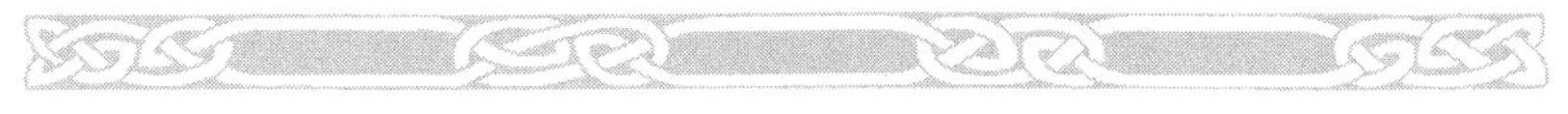

less—have been observed to perform functions that would simply not leave sufficient room aboard them for additional military gear of any consequence. If the Deathstar is to fire at anything, Mir is a likely bet."

"Yeah, but why?" Long-Drink insisted. "The guys on Mir aren't dumb: they've got to know they're being scrutinized. Why would they do something threatening, just as their government down below is getting ready to pack it all in?"

Acayib shrugged again. "Madness? Mutiny? Malfunction of some kind? We know Soviet space technology is fairly primitive. Uranium would make an excellent cosmic-ray target; perhaps they've shipped a large quantity up to Mir, and the shielding is bad."

I agreed with Long-Drink: it sounded pretty unlikely. The boys on Mir wouldn't put up with leaky uranium-shielding for very long.

And looking around me, I saw a lot of other dubious expressions. But nobody had anything else to suggest.

Except Erin.

"Uncle Kay," she piped up, "there's another factor you may be overlooking."

"What's that, Erin?" he asked.

"Uncle Bbiillll told us a few weeks ago they saw the Aurora Borealis here in Key West. I thought he was pulling our leg—but I did a little research on the Internet, and he's right. You know how sunspots run on an eleven-year cycle? At the moment we're right in the middle of the biggest solar maximum in three centuries—and there have been all sorts of odd phenomena reported. Garage doors opening and closing by themselves in San Francisco. Northern Lights sightings all over the South. And they say it looks like it hasn't peaked yet. The Earth's magnetic field is *all* out of whack, just now. Could that . . . I don't know, cause something that would make Mir temporarily look like a target to the Deathstar? Or maybe even just trigger the Deathstar all by itself—at just the wrong time?"

Acayib started to answer . . . then caught himself, closed his mouth, and started thinking hard. As he was doing so, Nikola Tesla appeared on the lawn in front of him.

Happily, he materialized between Long-Drink and Fast Eddie, who are so used to him by now they didn't even flinch. Eddie dipped a can of cold beer out of the ice bucket and passed it to him. Nikky glanced down at it, poked at the pop-top ring . . . turned the can over, produced an old-fashioned church key, and punched a tiny hole in the bottom. In 1989, you could still do that. Pressure equalized, but no spray emerged. Then he punched a larger hole on the far side, and drank deep from it. "Thank you, Eddie," he said, wiping foam from his mustache.

I recapitulated the results of our thinking to date for him, with occasional assistance from others, and Tesla listened carefully, without interrupting. When I ran down, he sat a moment in thought. Then he finished his beer, and nodded. He gestured with the can, and it went away.

"You have done well," he told us. "Any or all of these things could be factors in the catastrophe. And I fear I have identified at least one other candidate."

"Jesus Christ," Eddie said. "*Anudda* one¿"

Tesla nodded. "There is a phenomenon just beginning to be noticed in this time, which will not be fully understood for many years to come. Did any of you know that hurricanes sometimes produce gamma rays¿"

Rooba rooba rooba.

"It is true," he assured us. "X rays as well, but especially gamma rays. Sometimes in beams, sometimes in rings that rise like smoke rings from the top of the hurricane—sometimes even in more exotic configurations. And sometimes at very high energies."

"Harder!" Harry the parrot shrieked—but softly. For him, anyway.

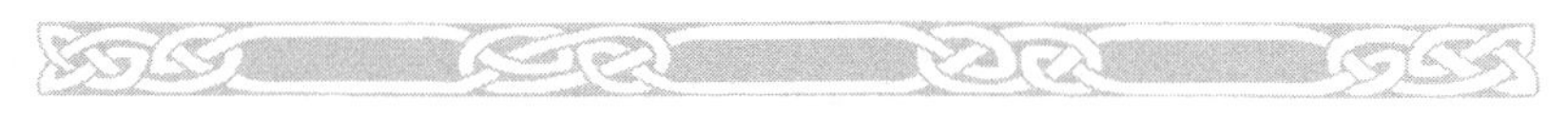

Now that I thought about it, just about the only way you could detect such a thing as a blast of gamma rays rising from the top of a hurricane—and live to report it—would be from a satellite. We haven't been putting the damn things up for all that long . . . and I imagine the first few gamma-ray detectors placed in orbit were trained either on the stars or on military targets—not on hurricanes.

Doc Webster cleared his throat. "You're saying a hurricane could maybe turn itself into a natural gamma-ray cannon, firing straight up . . . and the Defense Department may not have *known* that when they programmed their Deathstar? And maybe it misinterprets what it sees as a blast of gamma rays and X rays coming *down* from Mir?"

Tesla didn't reply. He didn't need to. His face answered for him.

"And the fucking Deathstar is going up in August, right smack in the middle of the season," Double Bill said softly.

Rooba rooba.

"That still does not mean a hurricane is necessarily involved in the end of the universe," Acayib pointed out. "We already have sufficient . . . what is it, Nikola?"

Tesla started to speak, hesitated, then tried again. "As I told Jacob, I cannot prove that my own weapon is involved in this—but I am intuitively certain. It is too ironic not to be true. This is like that."

"What is?" Zoey asked patiently.

"Lemme get it wet first!" screamed Harry.

Tesla sighed. "I hate anachrognosis. Information should never be passed from one ficton to another."

"You peeked to the back of the book," Erin said.

Tesla nodded. "Hurricanes cannot yet be predicted well . . . but once they occur they are public record. I time-shifted forward, and looked up the tropical storm records for this coming summer. One will occur just after the object we are calling the Deathstar is orbited—and, at several points, directly in the path of Mir." He stopped talking and looked away from Erin.

There was more. Somehow I knew there was more. "And?" I prompted.

Tesla said, "It will be officially designated 'Hurricane Erin.'"

Rooba rooba rooba.

I wished The Machine were hooked up. As a working substitute for this meeting I had scrounged half a dozen Black & Deckers, and they were lined up in my new kitchen, all primed with Tanzanian Peaberry grounds and waiting to be triggered. I started to get up and do so, but Erin saw me and waved me back into my chair. "I'll get it, Daddy," she insisted, and scampered up the porch steps as quickly and gracefully as Pixel could have managed it, which I know because the cat followed her in like a furry shadow.

Zoey and I exchanged a glance. "I don't like this," she muttered without moving her lips.

"Me either," I said in the same prison-yard murmur.

But I did understand Tesla's conviction. This was the way things tended to work in my slapstick world. The only surprise was that it hadn't been Hurricane Jake.

I wished it had been. I told myself the unease I felt was mere superstition, primitive magic thinking. But my precious baby daughter was, let's face it, already entirely weird enough. Not too weird to suit me, mind you . . . I *like* weird . . . but I definitely did not want her name associated with the end of the universe, did not want her, even nominally, any more involved with it than she already was. She already represented, to me, everything we had to lose; it didn't need underlining.

"So let me summarize," Tanya Latimer said, cutting off the rumble of chaotic talk. "We have not one, not two, not even three, but *four* possible factors for our catastrophe trigger. One: Tesla Beam. Two: especially energetic cosmic ray. Three: solar storm. Four: hurricane gamma-ray cannon. Question: Is there any way for us to pin down just which ones, or which combination?"

"They're all good!" the parrot shrieked. Pixel padded out of the house, and stared at him. Harry backed up a few steps, and ruffled his feathers.

"They're all nuts," Long-Drink said. "I'm not buying any of this."

"Do you science guys," Tanya went on, ignoring him magnificently, "know a way to assign relative probabilities for any of them, so we'll know which ones to study first?"

Several people all began to speak at once. Acayib, Jim Omar, Long-Drink, Doc Webster. But Tesla held up a hand, and all of them yielded the floor. His expression was strange: solemn, somber, but with a wry ironic twist at one corner of his mouth.

"I do not anticipate that this will be a popular suggestion," he said. "But Mrs. Latimer, I think that Harry the parrot is correct."

"Huh?"

"With regard to your first question, 'which are the operant factors,' I believe the only possible answer is . . . *all* of them, in combination."

"Huh?"

He was right. It wasn't a popular suggestion. I myself, for one, thought he was nuts. I mean, I knew perfectly well he was nuts—but for a moment there, I wondered if he had ceased to be *usefully* nuts. Again, everyone tried to talk at once. This time Doc Webster won, as he usually does in such cases. "Nikola, with all due respect . . . I know there's no better hunch-player in the world, not in this century anyway, but—"

Tesla shook his head. "Here at last I am working with something other than intuition, Sam."

"Aw shit, Nikky," Long-Drink said. "Are you serious? I've been sitting here letting you jokers pull my leg for a long while now, but it just disconnected completely from my hip. Look, here's the most plausible scenario I can construct out of what you science types have given me. Mir happens to pass over Hurricane Erin—just as it sends up a gamma-ray fountain. Just then, it gets bollixed by sunspots. The Deathstar's targeting computer, seeing all this, goes Hal 9000 and decides to fire on Mir. Just then, a cosmic ray hits the detector on Mir—which even the Russians don't really expect to happen. Not just a cosmic ray, mind you, but a Giant Wamba cosmic ray. And it happens to come in at precisely the right angle to oppose the arriving Tesla Beam, at just the right microsecond, and so the universe ends."

He was right. Put that baldly, it sounded ridiculous. A gazillion to one five-cushion shot. Our faces fell.

"I mean, I believe in bad luck . . . but Jesus Christ, Nikky, have you calculated the *odds*—"

Tesla nodded.

"They've got to be infinitesimal!" he said almost indignantly.

Tesla nodded again.

Long-Drink was baffled by his serenity. "That's the most unlikely . . . not one chance in . . . I mean, even *Hollywood sci fi* wouldn't ask you to swallow something like . . ." He trailed off. All of a sudden, he got it.

The rest of us stared at him, waiting for him to explain. And then one by one we all started to get it. You could see it in our faces, like wind passing over a large field of wheat: the sudden dawning of comprehension.

This once, the Cosmic Author was not only permitted, but *required*, to stack absurd coincidences one upon another.

"Oh shit, of course," Doc Webster said for all of us. "In this case, the more unlikely the answer . . . the more likely it is to be correct."

"Substantially true," Tesla agreed.

"I don't get it," Fast Eddie complained.

"Try harder, asshole!" Harry screamed. Pixel stirred, but did not—quite—look in the parrot's direction. Harry subsided.

"Think of what we are talking about here, friend Eddie," Tesla said. "We are discussing *the end of the universe*. The universe is . . . well, for now, let us say it is something on the order of

twelve *billion* years old. It contains uncountable trillions of stars. It must, by now, have produced at least dozens of intelligent species—perhaps hundreds of thousands."

"So?" Eddie said stubbornly.

Tesla spread his hands. "If it is *possible* for the universe to end, Eddie—if there is *any* combination of circumstances which can accomplish that—then plainly it must be an extremely unlikely set of circumstances. Else the universe would have ended long ago. By definition it must require conditions so rare that they only occur a few times in billions of years."

Some of the wrinkles smoothed from Eddie's simian face as he absorbed the point.

Then they returned . . . and he turned slowly. To stare at the Lucky Duck. Soon we were *all* staring at him.

He was absolutely unperturbed. Under the weight of our combined gaze, he blew gently on the fingernails of his right hand and buffed them on his shirt, the picture of nonchalance.

And slowly we all relaxed too. We knew perfectly well Ernie can't help what he does, what he is. He doesn't control Luck. The other way around, if anything. Furthermore we knew that while things could get decidedly chaotic in his vicinity, the safest place to be while it was going on was always standing right next to him.

"I don't buy it," he said.

"I sympathize, Ernie," I said. "It does go against the grain. If I came across a stack of coincidences like this in a story, I'd just figure the author was making it easy on himself. But like Nikky says, in this one special case—"

He shook his head. "You ain't hearing me, Stringbean."

"You must not be speaking clearly, then," I said. "Try again."

Quick flicker of a grin. The only way to get to see that is to insult the Duck right back. It can get wearing, but I'm willing to indulge him to a point. "I know a little more than most of you science whizzes do about probability. I ain't got the book learning, but I got a feel for it."

"You won't get an argument out of me," I agreed. "So?"

"So I just don't buy an unstable universe that collapses *once* every twelve or fifteen billion years. It just doesn't *feel* right. If it can happen at all, it's already happened. A thousand times, maybe. And the universe seems to still be here. So, no offense, Nik, I say it can't happen. We can all go on vacation now."

We all looked to Tesla for his rebuttal.

He had nothing to say. He looked like he wanted to, but his expression was as clouded and sealed as if Thomas Edison had been in the room.

I was shocked. Was it even remotely possible that the Duck's intuition was right—that Nikola Tesla was wrong—that we had all left our homes and come a couple of thousand miles on a wild-goose chase? The silence stretched, and still Tesla said nothing.

Harry must have sensed the tension. *"Eat my pussy!"* he screamed helpfully. Then, suddenly—instantly—he was four feet above his previous location, flapping frantically, and on the exact spot where he had been sitting was Pixel, staring fixedly up at him, clearly inviting him to come back down and discuss his choice of words. Harry flapped harder, achieved escape velocity, and took refuge on Omar's shoulder. Pixel started in that direction. Then he and Omar locked eyes for a long moment . . . and Pixel remembered something he had to do in another part of the forest.

Nobody laughed. We were too busy waiting for Tesla to answer the Lucky Duck.

"Nikky—" I began, and I've often wondered what I'd have said next. But before I got to find out, Mei-Ling sat bolt upright and said, "Gamma ray bursters!"

I had no idea what that meant, but she had said it in an *aha!* voice, and Tesla's expression told me she had hit a bull's-eye of some kind.

She and her fiancé were exchanging a look, now, and slowly the Doc lost his frown of incomprehension. "Oh," he said, and then, *"Oh!"* and a few seconds after that, "Oh *wow*."

Until that moment I'd have bet cash that I would never in this

life hear Doc Webster say, "Oh wow." I cleared my throat, and caught his eye, and raised an inquiring eyebrow.

He glanced back at Mei-Ling, and then both of them looked at Tesla, and then back at each other. Mei-Ling nodded just perceptibly. He turned back to me, and although he addressed me, his voice was pitched to reach everyone, and did.

"Back in the Sixties," the Doc said, "DoD put gamma-ray detectors in orbit, to look for clandestine nukes. As far as I know, nobody thought to aim them at the eyes of hurricanes—but they did notice something they didn't expect or understand. Stan Wedermyer and Mei-Ling and I talked about it once. Gamma ray bursters." He glanced over to see how Tesla was reacting.

"What's dat¿" Fast Eddie prompted, to keep things moving.

"Think of 'em as God's Flashbulbs, Eddie. Sudden, short, and *very* bright. Powerful photons, up at the gamma end of the scale, *lots* of them in a burst. They last a few seconds at most . . . then there's a sort of faint afterglow of X rays that can go on for minutes, even hours sometimes. And then they're gone."

"Fuck ah dey¿" Eddie asked.

The Doc glanced at Tesla again, and then shrugged. "At this point, nobody's even absolutely positive *where* they are."

Eddie looked baffled. "I t'ought ya said dey could see 'em."

"Sure. Pinpoint them on a star map, no sweat. But *the map is two-dimensional*." He pointed to the canopy of stars overhead. "Say you spot one right there, right now, bright as hell . . . and then it's gone again by *now*. Okay¿" Several of us nodded. "Now: what did you just see¿ A bright light somewhere in or around the solar system¿ A *very* bright light somewhere else in the galaxy entirely¿ Or a *Jesus* big light way out on the other ass end of the universe¿ How can you know¿"

There was a short silence while we considered that. I could tell from Acayib's expression that he knew the answer to that question, but wasn't going to volunteer it because he was too busy thinking about something else. Bubbling noises came faintly from inside the house, and I wondered how Erin was do-

ing with the coffee, but decided not to offer help unless she asked. Omar was just about to venture a reply when the Doc continued.

"First thing you do is plot them. Do they cluster around the plane of the ecliptic, like just about everything else in the solar system but comets and dust? No. Do they cluster around the plane of the *Galaxy*'s ecliptic, like just about everything else in the Milky Way? No. The damn GRBs are randomly distributed throughout the sky."

"So they're cosmologically far away."

"Probably," the Doc said. "People with pocket protectors will keep arguing about it for at least another ten years, Stan tells me—but yeah, the smart money says whatever gamma ray bursters are, they happen all over the universe. But do you see what that implies?"

I was tired of sitting like an English major. "If they're coming from that far away, then they're really, like, incredibly powerful."

"Let me put it this way," the Doc said. "They make supernovae look like sparks. Stan told me a couple of them were observed to *outshine the entire visible universe*. Okay, for only a quick flash. But think of that! Think of the energy involved. To suddenly outdo the combined results of at least a dozen billion years of sustained fusion. And then vanish in an instant, with a brief faint echo. I think of 'em as Cosmic Pop Stars."

There was a smattering of applause.

"Or perhaps 'Warhols,'" Mei-Ling said softly.

The applause redoubled, and included a few "Oooh"s.

"Oh, *lovely*, darling," Doc said joyfully, taking both her hands and kissing her on the forehead. "That's just beautiful! Black holes, brown holes, wormholes, and warhols."

I admired her pun better than his myself. Doc had chosen his mate well.

"And also," I went on, since I hadn't made a fool of myself the first time, "if they're at cosmic distances, and the light's just get-

ting here, then whatever they are, it happened millions or billions of years ago."

"Very good, Jake," the Doc said approvingly.

"Doc?" Fast Eddie said.

"Yeah, Eddie?"

"Fuck do we care?"

"Oh." The Doc recalled himself and let go of one of Mei-Ling's hands. "Well, Eddie . . . we've seen about a thousand of these damn things so far. I think Stan said they come at a rate of roughly one a day. Mind you, they vary greatly: some GRBs are just little blips, some are monsters. Nobody has any idea what the hell they are, but all kinds of guesses have been made, some of them fairly science fictional. Black holes colliding. Star drives switching on. Wormholes eating galaxies."

"Doc?" Eddie said patiently. "Fuck we care?"

Doc Webster exchanged another uneasy glance with Tesla. "I got to wondering," he said, "where the hell Mike and Sally were, just now."

Rooba rooba rooba. A lot of us had been wondering that, in our idle hours, for a long time now.

"Just why they're too busy to attend the end of the universe," the Doc went on. "I wondered if maybe . . ." One last glance at Tesla, and he took the plunge. ". . . if maybe that's what they're already doing."

ROOBA ROOBA.

"Suppose," he boomed over the noise, "that warhols—some of them, anyway—suppose that's what you see when there's a sudden phase shift in the vacuum, and the universe starts to end. Suppose they're the muffled death cries of the plenum. Fossil evidence of past disasters—hundreds of them, maybe thousands. Which were snuffed out within instants of their occurrence." The longer he talked, the more people shut up and listened; he was able to lower his voice to normal level by the time he got to, "I think maybe I finally figured out, after all these years, exactly what Mike and Sally and all their immortal, time-traveling colleagues from the distant future *do* for a living, when they're not slumming on backwater planets for sentimental reasons." And there was dead silence as he finished softly, "Maybe they're Cosmic Firemen."

After a while Omar spoke up. "So then—"

"So the reason they left this particular warhol to Nikky and us to deal with is, they must be *busy* somewhere else, just at this moment. Guarding some *other* hot spot, that is for some reason at least as dear to Mike and Sally as Old Home Terra. Even a time traveler can't be in two places at once, and they had to choose."

I was watching Tesla. "And Nikky," I said, "told them, 'You go ahead. It's covered. This was my mistake; I'll fix it.' I won't ask you to confirm that, Nikky, because I know a lot of this constitutes miscegemation, information people in 1989 aren't supposed to have—and I know you hate that, so I won't ask. But if I'm wrong, fart in B flat."

Nikky met my eyes . . . and grinned briefly in spite of himself. But he said nothing, and the grin vanished quickly.

"So now," I said gently, "I begin to understand why you're so tense lately, Nik. Shit, I don't blame you. You stuck your neck out, sent the cavalry away, and now it's five months to zero hour and you haven't got a plan. Well, don't worry, we're gonna put our heads together and . . . what's the matter?"

Tesla had been looking unhappy since he arrived. Now he looked positively stricken.

"What is it, Nikky?" Zoey asked, alarmed.

"I don't need any help," Erin called as she came through the doorway.

And by God, she didn't. She was carrying a metal tray that held Bushmill's 1608, a sugar bowl, a large bowl of fresh-whipped cream, and a mess of spoons, and was having no trouble at all with it. I spotted how much concentration it cost her to pull it off, but I've been living with her all her life; a stranger

might easily have taken her for a short six- or seven-year-old. All the exercise and training she'd been doing on the trip south was paying off. She set the tray down on a small porch table, scurried back inside, and came out again pushing ahead of her a wheeled trolley on which were all the coffee machines and enough glass mugs for everybody. It took everything she had to move it, but she steered it pretty well.

Well, I thought, maybe a short recess will help Nikky decide to open up and tell us whatever's bothering him. I got up and began making Irish coffees and passing them out—pausing first to put my hand on the top of Erin's head and tell her what a good job she'd done. I was quite pleased to find that I could still effortlessly recall everybody's individual prescription: which whiskey they preferred, how much sugar, and so on. Tending bar must be like riding a bicycle: after a year out of action, I was ready to go again.

Suddenly that washed over me. After more than a year out of action, I was ready to go again. I looked around me and saw all my friends, my oldest friends, reaching out to me for cups of black magic healing potion, and it was as if I suddenly *clicked* into place. Into The Place. Into my new life. As of this minute, The Place was open, however long it took me to get the napkins stacked and the taps drawing right. All at once I was quietly, sublimely happy.

Finally everyone had been served, and I realized they were all waiting for me to propose the first toast. I couldn't think of a thing. Mike Callahan told me once, if you're stuck for a toast, think of the person in the room that's hurting worst, and try for a toast that will make them feel better. So I did.

"To Nikola Tesla," I said. "Guardian of Terra."

"To Nikola Tesla," came the chorus, and we all acquired whipped-cream mustaches.

"Now then, Nikky," I said when I'd wiped mine off, "now that we've drunk to you, why don't you have a gulp yourself and tell us what you're looking so worried about?"

He tried to answer—three times—but couldn't seem to get the words out.

"It's what you said wrong before, Daddy," Erin said.

I glanced down. "What was that, honey?"

"Uncle Nikky *has* a plan. He's had it for a *long* time. Weeks." She blinked up at me gravely. "Only you're really really gonna hate it."

I looked at her. I looked at Zoey. I looked at Tesla. I looked back down at my daughter. I thought like mad, reviewed everything I knew. And all of a sudden, in one of those blinding gestalts of insight that Nikola Tesla was famous for getting all the time, I got it. The whole thing, complete and fully formed. Unimaginable in one moment . . . and then, once you knew, inevitable.

I looked at Tesla, and saw it in his eyes. He did indeed have a plan to save the universe. It was a fine plan. A logical plan. A clever plan. Maybe even a workable plan. I stood up and threw my Irish coffee at him, missing his famous head by maybe an inch.

"No!" I roared. *"NO FUCKING WAY IN HELL, you Serbo-Croatian son of a bitch!"*

CHAPTER SIXTEEN

I Have a Plan . . .

"Republicans understand the importance of bondage between a mother and child."
—J. Danforth Quayle

MOST OF THE COFfee had impacted on Acayib. It scalded him like it would have anybody, but at least he didn't mind. Somehow that made it even worse.

But I was too enraged to register guilt just then. Anger is always—always—fear in drag. I was as scared as I've ever been in my life, and consequently mad enough to kill. I moved toward Tesla, and I'll be honest, I have no idea what I intended to do when I reached him. But the point is moot, because all of a sudden there seemed to be an awful lot of Jim Omar in the way. And when I tried to deke around him I ran into a wall of Doc Webster, and in the other direction a tangle of McGonnigle blocked the path, and just then Zoey moved in from behind and I was boxed.

"What's wrong with you?" she hissed in my ear, just as Omar said, "What's the matter, Jake?"

For an instant I considered blasting them all and about an acre of surrounding countryside into cinders with a Tesla Beam of pure rage. Then I felt the tugging at my pants leg.

"Daddy," Erin said, looking up at me with those huge eyes, "you're allowed to feel anything you feel. You're allowed to scream if you have to. You're not allowed to hit."

My rage deflated. It did not go away, but a relief valve popped open somewhere, and just enough of it escaped to keep the container from bursting. I stopped trying to muscle past my friends, and looked around at them instead. They were all concerned, all alarmed—and all baffled. "You guys don't get it, do you? You don't see what he's asking of us."

"I ask nothing," Tesla whispered, looking down at his lap.

"Tell us," Omar suggested.

Another increment of my anger converted itself to its less unstable isotope, exasperation. "What's the matter with all of you, for Chrissake? Think it through!"

"Help us," Mei-Ling said gently.

"What do you need, a goddam diagram? Think about our fucking problem! Think about what we all just got finished saying. What is it we have to do next?"

They all tried . . . but it was clear they didn't yet see what was now transparently obvious to me.

So I spelled it out. "The universe is in danger because of an event with four causes. These are: a solar maximum, a hurricane, a Soviet science experiment, and a DoD satellite. We have contracted to save the universe, so we have to eliminate one or more of those factors. So where do we start? Come on, anybody."

"The satellite," three people said at once.

"Naturally," I agreed. "We haven't got access to the remote control for the sun. All of us put together aren't blowhards enough to affect a hurricane. There's no way we're going to influence the Russians. That leaves the Deathstar."

Nobody disagreed.

"Now: how do we neutralize a Deathstar? Bearing in mind

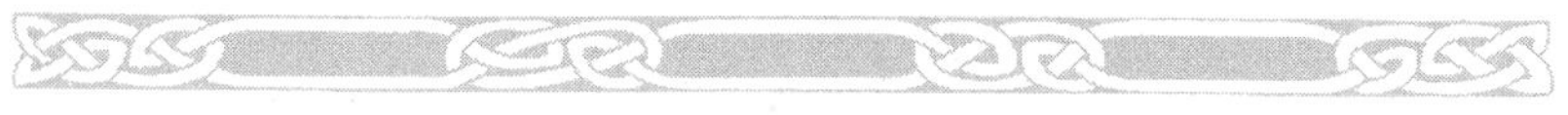

that whatever we do, we mustn't get caught doing it—mustn't enter the record of history."

A lot of blank looks. A lot of frowns. A few thoughtful thousand-yard stares.

"Once it's in orbit, we can't affect it without building and launching our own spaceship, which I think we can all agree would be difficult to pull off in five months, and would probably get us talked about. Plus we'd need at least one spacesuit, and EVA skills that you can't get out of a book."

No disagreement.

"While the Deathstar's still here on Earth, we can't affect it without infiltrating DoD or its contractors, and let's face it, none of us is the type."

"Wait a minute, Boss," Fast Eddie said. "How 'bout Nikky does dat Transit ting? Beams one of us inta da satellite factory wit a monkey wrench?"

Tesla stayed silent, looking down at his lap.

"Eddie," Omar said, "the very last thing they'll do before sending that satellite out the door and shipping it to the Cape is test it from top to bottom, hardware and software. Then just before they load it aboard, they'll test it again."

Tommy Janssen spoke up. "So what we need to do is figure a way to reprogram it: hide a bug in the software that won't show up until just after the thing is inserted into orbit. Very tricky . . . but not impossible." He glanced down at Erin. "Not for *us*."

I held my temper. "And when exactly do we do this?"

He looked blank.

I sighed. "Jim? You and Shorty and Acayib are the real space buffs. You know more about it than me. Is there ever a time when a satellite that's being built and readied doesn't have at least a few people standing around looking at it? Especially in the last five months before launch, when they're working on it round the clock?"

"Well, no," Omar agreed reluctantly. "Not reliably, anyway. I mean, there might be a random hour or two, but how could we know *when*? You're right: a satellite is pretty much under continuous observation, right up until . . ." He trailed off, and his face changed. "Oh." Then it changed even further, and he said, "Oh, *man*," and I knew he got all of it. His eyes met mine, and his big hand settled on my shoulder.

"Till what?" Eddie asked.

"Until it's loaded onto the Shuttle for launch," I said.

"The crew probably don't even glance in its direction from the time they climb aboard until the moment they're ready to inject it into orbit," Omar said. "Could be as much as forty-eight hours."

Silence, while everyone pondered all this, looking for a booby trap that would turn me into a raging madman.

"Jake," Doc Webster said, "I admit it: I'm stumped. You have succeeded in redefining our specific problem admirably. A few minutes ago, I didn't have the slightest clue *what* the hell we were going to do. Now, if I understand you, it seems all we have to do is somehow place one of us on the Space Shuttle, have him bollix the Tesla Beam, and bring him back to Earth again, without being caught at it. I grant you that sounds like a hell of a problem . . . but for the life of me, I still don't see what you're so *upset* about. We'll think it over, we'll take our best shot, and what the hell, maybe we'll get lucky."

"Dat Transit stuff, Boss," Eddie insisted. "All we do, we . . . aw, *shit*."

Eddie got it too, now. Not an articulate guy, Eddie, nor a knowledgeable space buff—but he tested high on intuition. And others of us, I could see, were beginning to suspect now.

"One of us," I said, spelling it out for the rest, "has to Transit aboard the Space Shuttle, and remain aboard undetected, until there's a chance to reprogram the Deathstar's computer without being spotted."

Rooba rooba. "How?" Long-Drink asked for the group. "They monitor the launch weight on a Shuttle down to the pound—they have to. You know that. And exactly where the hell do you hide on one? The part that's pressurized ain't very big, and it's damn full." Several people looked equally skeptical.

I didn't say anything. After a moment Omar took a deep breath and answered. "I'd have to check some specs to be certain . . . but I'm 90% sure there's only one possible place. The stowage lockers. Over a hundred identical Kevlar boxes—and they hardly ever actually use more than a dozen or two in flight; the rest are empty. They're in five different locations. The forward flight deck, where the crew sits for takeoff and landing. The aft flight deck—where the payload controls are. The middeck, where the tunnel to the payload bay is. The equipment bay, where the crew don't normally spend much time. And the airlock. If you could Transit directly from one site to another, you could be pretty sure of staying out of sight almost indefinitely."

"But what about the extra *weight?*" Long-Drink insisted.

Omar sighed. "Well, Drink, that's not too big a problem. No pun intended. Those lockers measure eleven by eighteen by twenty-one inches—call it two cubic feet. So anybody who could fit into one in the first place just isn't going to weigh a whole lot."

There was a collective gasp, as the implications sunk in, and everybody started to get it.

"You've told me yourself a thousand times, Daddy," Erin said. "*I* can't help it if I'm little."

With a bellow of primeval fury, Zoey flung me aside like a curtain and went for Tesla's throat.

Fortunately Omar was able to contain her long enough for Isham and Tanya Latimer to arrive. She strained mightily in their grasp and screamed hair-raising obscenities at Tesla, her face so red I was afraid she was going to have a stroke or a coronary. Tesla cowered in his chair, deathly pale, eyes wide, hands half lifted as if to fend her off, and I suddenly remembered that this was a man who could pull balls of fire from his pockets and produce Death Rays on request. I clambered to my feet and wondered what to do. And then a strange and wonderful thing happened.

Harry the parrot came sailing out of nowhere, landed on Tesla's head in a riotous flurry of color, and began shrieking equally hideous obscenities right back at Zoey, obviously overjoyed that at long last, somebody else wanted to play.

Even Zoey, in her condition, simply could not help joining in the avalanche of laughter that ensued.

I laughed with everyone else—it *was* funny—but by the time the laughter faded, I had gotten back a second wind of anger. I opened my mouth to take my second turn at abusing Tesla, and perhaps Zoey and I could have rotated indefinitely all night long. But again I felt an insistent tugging at my pants leg.

"Daddy," Erin said, once again using those baby blue tractor beams of hers to hold my gaze immobile until she was done with it, "it was *my* idea, not Uncle Nikky's. He spent hours trying to talk me out of it. You know how he feels about little girls."

I closed my mouth and opened it again.

"Could *you* have talked me out of it?" she asked.

I closed it again.

"That's why you're scared, right? 'Cause you already know I'm gonna do it, no matter what you say."

I nodded, and thought about bursting into tears.

"Then stop blaming Uncle Nikky, you jerk." She released me. "You too, Mom! If anybody else comes up with a better plan, I'll go for it in a shot. But nobody's going to, and it's not Uncle Nikky's fault, okay? He feels shitty enough that they're using his Death Ray."

I looked at Tesla—and did suddenly feel as if I'd been beating up a child. He really looked whipped. He wouldn't meet anybody's eyes.

"Besides," Erin said, "think about the first American to try and

go to space, the one that didn't really do it, but everybody said he did anyway. What was his name, Daddy?"

She knew it as well as I did. "Al Shepard," I said.

"Well, I only have to do one thing he didn't. I just have to travel a little more than three times as far in space as my height above the center of the earth. What do they call that ratio again, Daddy?"

I was too shocked to answer.

Doc Webster and Long-Drink and Jim Omar and a couple of others did it for me, gleefully chorusing, "Shepard's Pi!"

My daughter wanted to reach me so badly, she had made a pun. A little more of my anger melted.

Which did *not* end the discussion—not by a long shot. Just the tantrum part of it.

Zoey, of course, tried to discuss next whether or not we did or would ever allow this thing. But she was ruled out of order by Doc Webster, on the grounds that there was no point considering that until we had settled whether the trick was actually possible, and just how we'd go about it. Until then, he pointed out, Zoey and I didn't really know what we were being asked to assent to. His strategy worked: we got so involved in the intellectual puzzle of how to pull this off that we tabled indefinitely the question of whether or not to permit it.

Tanya the organizer broke it down into parts for us, the first question being: *Could we get Erin aboard the Shuttle without being caught at it?* To my surprise, that part turned out to be trivially easy. In less than five minutes, Omar and Tesla had devised a strategy that seemed to have every chance of success. I hated it, of course—because it involved placing Erin on board just before liftoff, and retrieving her after the Shuttle landed.

"Why should she have to endure blastoff, and risk landing—and risk discovery by the crew for days?" I argued. "Teleport her aboard when the damn thing's already in space, and wink her back home as soon as she's finished the job."

It sounded reasonable, and still does. The problem was, we couldn't do that. And I'm not sure I can explain why not, because I don't really understand it myself.

Mike Callahan could have done it, blind drunk. Lady Sally could have done it without working up a sweat. Their daughter Mary would have had no trouble. But none of those people were available. All we had was Tesla, to whom they had imparted some, repeat *some*, of their magic before they left for parts unknown. He could Transit himself and/or an inorganic load to just about anyplace with known coordinates. He could *not* Transit Erin, or any other living thing—not and have it arrive at its destination still alive. But what he *could* do—what he had already in fact done, long since—was teach her to Transit herself. Turned out she'd been practicing all the way down the East Coast, whenever Zoey and I both happened to have our eyes off her for a moment or two. It explained a few things.

She demonstrated for us. One second she was standing there talking to us; the next second she was gone, and her voice was coming from inside the house. Just as we turned that way we heard her climbing out of the pool behind us. As we turned and saw her there, she disappeared again, and this time played possum until someone happened to look up and spot her at the top of a palm tree. To my horror, as soon as I saw her she simply stepped off the tree and dropped. But before I could draw breath to scream, she was on the ground—instantly, without having covered the intervening distance, landing so lightly that her knees barely bent. She drew thunderous applause from the crowd, and curtsied beautifully. Pixel the cat couldn't take his eyes off her, and there was new respect in them.

The problem, Erin explained to us when I began to renew my objection, was that even after a great deal of surreptitious practice, she couldn't Transit reliably *to a rapidly moving target.* Not reliably enough, anyway.

"Think about it, Daddy. There goes the Shuttle overhead, 200-odd miles up, doing just under 17,000 miles an hour, *woosh.* I determine its position and vector as precisely as I can—and I can maybe even do that a hair better than NASA can, with Uncle Nikky to help. Then I Transit, and try to work it so I come out the other end not only in precisely the right spot, but traveling at the right speed in the right direction. I can't tell you just how I do that, but it's real hard. If I make a very small error, I end up in vacuum, which sucks." Two puns in one day. A lifetime record. "If I make even a *teeny-weeny* error, maybe I end up materializing in the same spot as some solid object aboard the Shuttle, and blow us out of the sky. If I make only a nanoerror, maybe I come out in the wall between the locker I want and the one next door, with the same result: boom. Trust me, it's a lot safer if I do it when the Shuttle is standing still, relative to me, and I don't have a long distance to go."

"But will there—"

"—be enough room in that locker for me *and* enough padding for liftoff? Of course, Daddy. And I can bring along all the food I want. Any wastes I produce, I'll just Transit over the side and forget about them."

Zoey spoke up, her voice tight. "Honey, a Shuttle takeoff is really . . ." She trailed off, and I saw her dilemma. Somewhere deep inside she knew we had already lost this argument, and Erin was going to go. Therefore, why frighten her?

Tesla spoke up for the first time in a long while. Still looking down at his lap, he said quietly, "Zoey, I guarantee there will be no *Challenger* disaster this time. This Shuttle will launch and return safely."

We all knew how much he hated to pass along information from the future. Zoey bit her lip, and said, "Thank you, Nikola." He nodded.

Omar spoke up, to argue that Erin didn't absolutely have to

stay aboard the Shuttle until it landed. Once her work there was done, he said, she could always Transit back out again right away—if she did it in two stages.

"Pick an arbitrary spot a mile above the Earth's surface, aim for an arrival vector matching the planet's rotational speed, and live with any small errors that crept in. From there, Transiting the rest of the way down to the surface ought to be easy."

"Not without a backup parachute!" I insisted.

"And how small an error are we talking about?" Zoey demanded. "She hasn't got any damn tiles on her, you know."

"It may be simpler and safer if I just stay aboard," Erin said. "The worst problem I'll have is to keep from being bored. Five days is a long time."

Tanya ruled her first question settled, for now at least, and proposed the next one: *Could we communicate with Erin while she was on the Shuttle, without NASA overhearing?* Tesla spoke up, plainly happy to finally have something he could say besides "I'm sorry," and told us that part was a boat race: with gear he would furnish, we could definitely talk with her, even during the eight-hour intervals when she was around the other side of the planet, with better audio fidelity than NASA could have provided, and a few microseconds faster.

The third question—*Could Erin reprogram the Deathstar without getting caught at it?*—took a little longer to settle, but the prognosis was just as positive. The reason it took time was, the only one of us who really knew what she was talking about was the one the rest of us were all arguing with, and we were too ignorant to understand her answers. But we all knew perfectly well that Erin had been interfaced with the world's first Artificial Intelligence literally *before* she was born, and posthumously tutored by it ever since. If Solace had been able to outhack the NSA—and she'd had to, to survive in cyberspace as long as she did—then surely her star pupil and protégée Erin could outhack NASA and DoD combined, at least for long enough to get us through the present crisis. Tommy Janssen was able to follow her arguments, and she convinced him: that was good enough for the rest of us.

The last question raised that night was: *What equipment would she need?* That produced a technical discussion between her, Tesla, Omar, Tommy, and, of all people, Double Bill. Bill knew a guy named Gordon who lived just off Route 1 up in Titusville, and who could, he assured us, supply us with just about any conceivable tech gear. The guy was apparently a fanatic collector, specializing in esoteric radio and aerospace stuff, and his collection covered over a dozen acres. Bill called it The Surplus Store of the Gods: everything from eight-foot dishes on tracking mounts, to a complete three-story optical tracking station blockhouse, to—Bill swore on a stack of cocktail napkins—an honest-to-God Titan booster. The excitement this produced among Omar and the other techie types lasted long enough for everybody else to start noticing how late it was getting, and how long we had all been talking, and that there was no Irish coffee left. People began to drift away, a couple at a time, and by the time it was settled that Erin's sabotaging needs could be met, there was pretty much nobody left but the people who lived in the compound.

They all helped clean up, and then one by one they too made their excuses and wandered off to their own wickiups. And then there were just me and Zoey and Erin, sitting there in silence on the porch.

With Tesla.

"Nikola," I said, "please accept my apology."

He looked up and met my eyes. "Jacob, I accept."

"Thank you," I said, and meant it.

"I'm sorry, Nikola," Zoey said. "I shouldn't have—"

He waved her off. "You had little choice, either of you. From an evolutionary standpoint, you both *exist* to be irrationally protective of your child. The part of you that understands the universe is more important than Erin is constitutes no more than eight million neurons, out of the hundred billion in your brain. It is hard to override 99.992% of yourself quickly, particularly when that part controls the adrenal glands." He stood up suddenly. "You will all have much to discuss, and it grows late. Thank you for your hospitality." He bowed to her, bowed to Erin, nodded to me, and turned to go.

"Nikky," I said.

He turned back. "Yes, Jake?"

"It isn't your fault. What DoD is doing."

He looked at me. "Isn't it?" he said softly.

"It was a good scam, what you did. The 'Purloined Letter' bit was beautiful, if you ask me. It should have worked."

He took a deep breath and slowly let it out. "I have often been a clever man," he said sadly, "but I have rarely been a lucky one."

"Yeah, well—"

"I had a responsibility to remember that."

"Shit, Nikky," I said, "you lost the gamble, okay, but how many would have even taken it? Just about anybody else who'd invented what you did in 1908 would by now probably be the tyrannical Emperor of Earth."

He literally shuddered. "Of all the petty territorial squabbles on this sorry planet," he said, "there is only one of the slightest interest to me . . . and I have absolutely no idea how I could resolve it even if I were the Emperor of Earth. I have always been equally proud of both my Serbian blood and my Croatian birth. But when I attended my own funeral in disguise, I found all the Serbs sitting on one side of the chapel, and all the Croatians across the aisle. Very soon, events will occur in my homeland that will tear the heart from my body—and the only thing I am even faintly grateful for is that there is nothing I can do about it."

I didn't know what to say. The pain on his face was hard to look at. For the first time I really understood that the upcoming collapse of the Soviet Union was not going to be an unmixed blessing. "Well," I tried, "at least maybe you can preserve them a universe in which to kill each other, if that's what they insist on doing."

"I suppose that's true."

"Give 'em a chance, and maybe in another century or two they'll wise up. Hell, give it another thousand years or so and who knows? Peace could even break out in Ireland."

"Imagine: a boring Ireland," Zoey said.

I nodded. "Their new slogan would be, 'Erin go blah.' "

My daughter pointedly did not groan or wince.

Tesla smiled faintly. "Perhaps so. Thank you, Jacob. Good night."

"G'night, Uncle Nikky."

"Good night, Nik."

And he walked away, summoning up a small, softly crackling fireball out of nowhere to help him pick his way through the unfamiliar terrain in the darkness.

Zoey and I exchanged a long look, in which about ten gigabytes of compressed information were silently exchanged. And then we turned as one to Erin.

It struck me, as I regarded my daughter, just how seldom I had ever seen her look defensive.

"Look, you guys," she said, "just because I happened to think of it first doesn't make it 'my' idea, okay?"

"Erin," Zoey said, "do you *want* to do this?"

Erin stared at her. "Are you nuts? Or do you think I am? That 99.992% of the brain Uncle Nikky talked about, mine is scared to *death*. I've never been away from you guys for one day, let alone five. I just can't think of another solution. If anybody else does, believe me, I'd love to hear it."

Zoey looked at me.

"This stinks," I said quietly. "I mean, I am overjoyed to hear that you're scared to death . . . and that stinks."

"I want to be sure you're scared *enough*," Zoey told her.

"I am, Mom," Erin assured her solemnly.

Zoey looked dubious. "We all know perfectly well that when you look all solemn and sincere like that, you're probably full of shit. Part of you thinks this is going to be a fun adventure. I want you to promise me: *no teasing the astronauts*. This'll be a *DoD* flight: they could stuff you out the airlock without it ever entering history, and they just might. And what would your father and I do about it, complain to the *Miami Herald*?"

"It'd take a busy astronaut to stuff *me* out an airlock," Erin said darkly . . . and I couldn't help but agree with her.

"Promise me," Zoey insisted. "Or you can't go."

Erin slumped and stuck her lower lip out. "Aw, okay. No teasing."

"We mean it," I said. "No weaseling, no sophistry. Stay out of sight. And sound and everything else. Or you won't be allowed to Transit again." I turned to Zoey. "Does this conversation seem to be getting at all surreal to you?"

After a moment, all three of us giggled.

"You mean I'll be grounded?" Erin said, and cracked herself up.

Zoey and I exchanged a glance. Three puns in a single night. Our daughter was changing.

Around four A.M., I finally got to sleep. I don't know if Zoey ever did, that night.

Many things happened in the ensuing days and weeks and months. Just about all of them were good.

A week later, for instance, we held the official, though absolutely informal, opening of The Place. It went as splendidly as any of us could have hoped, one of the more memorable parties even for us, who had more or less made a career out of partying together. Zoey had done a magnificent job on the decor and ambiance, with some help from Margie Shorter: everything really looked nice, tasteful, conducive to merriment. Nearly all of us were happy with our new living arrangements, pleased at our sagacity in moving here, in a mood to celebrate. In addition to our own ranks, we drew a small number of curious locals, most of whom seemed pleasantly surprised by what they saw and heard, and thanks to our discreet location and my fixed no-sign–no-publicity policy, the tourists never noticed our existence. It was a nearly perfect night, except for three things.

One of them, of course, was the ongoing underlying awareness that in a few months my baby girl intended to go to space and try to outwit the Defense Department. A little thing like that can nag at your mind, if you let it.

But the second thing that interfered with my joy a bit on opening night was an observation I made about halfway through the evening: the first evidence I'd seen that Key West was perhaps not really the magical Disney paradise it appeared to be on first glance, but just a very nice place in the real world, inhabited by human beings. We were situated only a few short blocks from Bahama Village, which I had several times been assured was not the black/Cubano *ghetto,* but the black/Cubano *district*—and indeed, if it is a *ghetto,* it is one of the nicest, cleanest, happiest, most self-respecting ghettos I've ever seen in my life. Isham and Tanya had sort of opened diplomatic relations on our behalf with the B.V. community, whose leaders had been vaguely dismayed by yet another goddam bar opening in their vicinity, and we had succeeded in allaying their concerns well enough that a few of those community leaders came to our grand opening, and ended up enjoying themselves greatly.

But about halfway through the evening, when it became clear that folks from Bahama Village were welcome there, some of the Caucasian locals drifted away, and did not return.

Well, at least the problem was self-correcting. I consoled myself that we had found a cheap supply of asshole-repellent.

It was the third invisible worm in the apple I found hardest to get past.

As Tesla had requested, we'd all thrashed it out in a special meeting I'd called the day before Opening. The discussion had been spirited and lengthy, but finally we had all reached consensus, if not agreement, on one difficult but important point: security. Here we were in Key West, suddenly surrounded with a plethora of people just as weird and whimsical as ourselves, and the temptation was to drop all shields and welcome in as many as were interested. At the same time, we were engaged in a criminal conspiracy to defy the Joint Chiefs of Staff, in order to prevent the destruction of the universe, and every new person we allowed into the conspiracy sharply raised the odds of something going catastrophically wrong. Any local who walked in was already wired into a superb grapevine that we had no way to control. Reluctantly, but necessarily, we concluded that we must never speak of the situation when an outsider was present, even if he or she seemed to be "our kind of people." At least until it was all over, anyway, and possibly forever if something went sour.

So there was, for the time being and for the first time in our history, a strong, if thin, invisible wall up between us and anyone we didn't know who walked in our gate. For the first time, we were not wide open to new recruits. I knew it wouldn't last forever: if the universe was still here in six months, we could all relax again. But in the meantime it . . . well, not "spoiled," but it *colored* things a little, for me at least. I've never been comfortable keeping secrets from people I like.

But there was no choice, so I did it, and managed to transcend it and have a good time at my opening. Zoey and I played two sets with Fast Eddie, one in the early evening and one at the end, and both were gratifyingly well received. There was no shortage of music the rest of the time, either, as rumor of my house policy had gotten around: anyone Eddie was willing to tolerate as an accompanist drank free, for as long as they were on the stand. An ever-changing cast took advantage, and they ranged from good to scary. My favorite was a fat Bermudan kid from Bahama Village with a cheap Harmony Sovereign guitar who had obviously studied the work of Joseph Spence very carefully, then built on it: he could have made a statue tap its toe.

At the very end of the evening, I identified at least one respect

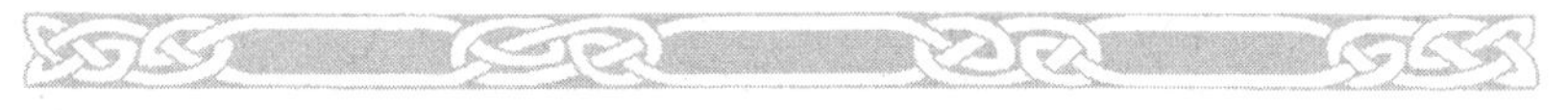

in which The Place was clearly superior to its predecessor. Back at Mary's Place, if you took a drunken notion to look at the stars and think deep thoughts, you had to put on your overcoat, climb the stairs to the roof, find a vacant chaise lounge, and be prepared to cope with cold winds. At The Place, all you had to do was fall down.

Over the next few weeks, Zoey and Erin and I spent our nights presiding over the festivities at The Place, "keepin' our good friends high," in Joe Dolce's memorable phrase, and our days bicycling around Key West, getting to know the place. It's full of fascinating spots. Hemingway's old place, now a reasonably tasteful museum, still patrolled by descendants of his original seven-toed cats. Houseboat Row. Harry Truman's Little White House. The splendid sleepy streets of Old Town. The famous, oft-photographed marker at The Southernmost Point . . . which is not. About a dozen really first-rate bookstores. A great aquarium where Erin was permitted to feed a shark. The gardens at Audubon House. Several good beaches—Smathers, Higgs, South Beach, Fort Taylor—though none approaching the Platonic Ideal we'd found back up on Bahia Honda Key. A day trip out for snorkeling on the Reef. An entire fascinating day at the City Cemetery, examining generations of aboveground mausoleums—necessary for the same reason they are in New Orleans: because the local water table lies about a foot below the surface. And, of course, the Shipwreck Museum. Shipwrecks loom large in the early history of Key West: they say the first local industry of any real economic consequence was the systematic use of false lighthouses to lure passing ships onto the reefs, where they could be conveniently salvaged.

In addition to the plethora of interesting things to see, there were so incredibly many good cheap restaurants that four months was just about long enough for us to complete the census, and enough good bars that I *still* haven't visited them all.

And of course, you didn't need to do *any* of that stuff to have a fine time. A day spent in your shorts lying in the shade in a rope hammock reading a book is a day well spent. The weather was not always perfect. Every so often it would rain for as much as an hour. Some nights you'd need a sweater. Some days were *too* hot.

I exaggerate slightly here. The heat was very agreeable for me—but then, I'm six-one and weigh 140. Zoey, who weighs more than that, sometimes found the temperature a bit oppressive. On the other hand, the longer she lived in it, the less she weighed, which pleased her. And didn't bother me *too* much, though I'd liked those extra pounds. I would rather have a wife who feels good about herself than one whose frame conforms to my precise fantasy ideal.

And whatever her weight, anything that encourages my wife to walk around in a minimum of clothing is a good thing, whether it be climate or self-image. I routinely got to see a lot more of Zoey's surface area than I had been able to back on Long Island—often all of it—and I enjoyed it, and she enjoyed that, and often enough we did something about it. Amazing how much more romantic a moment can be without gooseflesh and the constant white noise of a space heater roaring away.

Me, I've *always* been a nudist by inclination, on grounds of sheer laziness if nothing else—and I was living in a former nudist colony. Zoey finally had to put a sign up beside the door on the way out of the house, reading, "Did you remember to dress¿" just like the one back in my old commune.

We filled in the time, is what I'm trying to say. We did not spend every hour of those months constantly worrying about what was going to happen in August.

No more than half of them, maybe.

One night Tesla and I found ourselves alone together on my porch, and I tried to get him to agree with a theory I had been

working up: that our success was guaranteed. I liked the theory a lot—and like all new lovers, I could discern no flaw in it.

"It stands to reason, Nikky. You try not to commit miscegemation if you can help it—but you've already told us several things about the future that imply we simply can't lose. The Soviet Union collapsing, for instance: that's supposed to come months *after* August. So logically, if you've been to points in time after August, the universe isn't going to end then. Right?"

He sighed deeply, and shook his head. "Logically you are correct. But logic was never built to handle such matters. I cannot explain this in any terms you will find meaningful, but I ask you to take my word for it: if the universe ends this August, what will be destroyed is not only its present, but also its past, *and its future*. It might be said that even paradox requires a universe in which to exist."

"Aw, Jesus," I said.

"I am sorry, Jacob," he said. "I do not wish to alarm you. I think there is every chance we will be successful. Truly I do. But there are no guarantees."

I was sorry I'd brought it up.

The worst part about the actual preparations for the event was that nothing went wrong. There were no hitches, no glitches, no problems identified that we weren't able to solve. There was nothing for worry to get a purchase on. It started to feel as if all the bad luck was saving itself up.

Erin studied details of Shuttle layout with Jim Omar and Shorty, ran endless computer simulations with Tesla and Tommy Janssen, and discreetly practiced Transiting under Tesla's tutelage. She soaked it all up like a sponge. Actually more like a flower, which proceeded to bloom. I slowly began to realize that for most of her short life, her adult-sized brain had really had very little more challenging to do than play Baby for me and her mother. It made me feel old. But then, I was.

She also did some physical training with Margie Shorter and Maureen Hooker, but less than you might think. In zero gee, strength can actually be a handicap. One of the most common gripes of the Skylab astronauts was that they wished they weren't in such damned great shape: over and over again they would push off *too hard*, and crack their skull when they reached their destination, or bash their knees on the way through a hatch. Erin's exercise regimen aimed at increasing coordination and flexibility, rather than strength or muscle mass.

We never did manage to fake up a really satisfactory way for her to practice moving in zero gravity. Underwater just ain't the same thing, and neither is balancing on an air-blast column. But we did, twice, drive her back up to the Cape, so she could take the Shuttle Simulator tour—she drove the tour guide crazy—*and* do a little discreet, highly unauthorized, and massively illegal inspection of certain other parts of the Kennedy Space Center that were decidedly not open to the general public, using her . . . uh . . . letter of Transit.

Like I said, we filled in the time. All of it, however busy it sounds, took place on Key West time—that is, in dreamy slow motion—and we rarely felt stressed. By day we worked at the details of our plan, and by night we drank and laughed.

And then all of a sudden I blinked, and it was early evening on August 7, and I was standing on a high octagonal platform telling outrageous lies to a man with a heart of gold, with the fate of the universe, aka my daughter Erin, strapped to my back.

CHAPTER SEVENTEEN

Big Bird

"Welcome to President Bush, Mrs. Bush, and my fellow astronauts."
—J. Danforth Quayle

USING THEIR NASA connections and a pack of lies so outrageous that I will not recount them here—both because I am ashamed of them and because who knows? I might need to use them again someday—Jim Omar and Shorty Steinitz had managed to pull enough strings to get me certified as a bona fide VIP visitor to the Kennedy Space Center, under a name and identity I think I will keep similarly obscure. A VIP of the highest possible civilian clout, in fact, entitled to get up close and personal with a multimillion-dollar spacecraft the night before its classified launch.

There it was, only a few hundred feet away, towering above us, larger than life and twice as natural: an honest-to-God Space Shuttle. *Columbia* she was, nearly ready for her eighth flight. I was standing on Pad 39-B, at the base of the immense Fixed Service Structure, a place I'd yearned to see close up for decades, had only a few months earlier been thrilled to death to see from two miles away. I should have been happy as a pig in Congress.

But I was too conflicted to fully appreciate it. The man who had been conned into vouching for me, whose identity I will also suppress, stood beside me on my right and pointed out features of particular interest to me, smiling in a way so benignly avuncular that I felt like a Commie spy. On my left was the guy from NASA Public Affairs, who despite his professional smile was obviously watching me like a hawk, afraid I'd do something incredibly unauthorized and stupid. Which I planned to do. I could also see at least four armed men who, if they ever figured out my true intentions, might very well shoot me, at least in the legs.

Also, it was very damn windy up there, four or five stories above the ground, and I was distracted by the unfamiliar and unpleasant sensation of cool breezes on my chin and upper lip and ears and the back of my neck. It had been decided by a committee of which I was not a member that my chances of passing as a VIP would be much higher if I lost the beard and long hair. It was the first time I'd had my bare face hanging out in over a quarter of a century, and it didn't help a bit that the first time Zoey had seen it, she had laughed for a solid five minutes. I was going to get her for that, someday.

Also, I was distracted by the weight strapped to my back. All two-year-olds weigh more than you'd think they would—and since Erin was currently pretending to be sound asleep, all of it was dead weight. Not the phrase I wanted recurring in my mind, just then.

And Erin was not the last of my distractions—for while I was listening to my host tell me things I really wished I could spare the attention to follow, I was also listening to two other people he could not hear, only one of whom was there. I had a magic Tesla receiver in each ear, both cunningly disguised to look like particularly repulsive ear hairs. The left one brought me the faint voice of Nikola Tesla, who was then sitting in a schoolbus out on I-95, parked in the breakdown lane. The right fed me the amplified subvocalizations of Erin. Anything I subvocalized was picked up and broadcast to both of them by a Tesla transmitter on my throat, cunningly disguised to look like a shaving cut you wouldn't want to look at for very long.

". . . sound pressure at liftoff is so incredibly horrendous," my host was saying, "it'd tear apart both the Shuttle and the pad if it weren't muffled by that."

Obediently, I looked where he was pointing—straight ahead past the Shuttle, at the 290-foot-tall water tank that would drop 300,000 gallons of sound-absorbing water under the Shuttle at the moment all hell broke loose tomorrow morning.

Even excluding the mighty spaceship itself, it was by no means the most impressive artifact visible on that platform. The Fixed Service Structure, at whose base we were standing, was taller (347 feet tall with the lightning mast), and the complex Rotating Service Structure that hinged on it, while less than 200 feet tall, was infinitely more complex and interesting than what was, when you came down to it, just an overgrown pull-chain toilet. And to either side of it I could see what, if you allowed yourself to think of the Shuttle as a phallic symbol, appeared to be its shrunken testes—large ball-shaped tanks at the northeast and northwest corners of the pad. If testicles they were, they were definitely of the brass monkey variety. Each was basically a big thermos bottle: the one on the left held almost a million gallons of liquid oxygen at about 300 degrees below zero, and the one on the right kept nearly as much liquid hydrogen at better than 400 below zero—between them, the hypergolic fuel for *Columbia*'s huge external tank.

The whole preceding paragraph has absolutely nothing to do with this story—except to illustrate my predicament. I was in a place that was just entirely too damned interesting. Everywhere I looked was something that tugged—no, *yanked*—at my attention. It was a rotten place in which to sustain an elaborate deception.

"Well," I said, "that's the way I leave a lot of places myself."

My host looked puzzled.

"Baffled," I explained. *Come on*, I added subvocally, *aren't you guys ready yet?*

My host grinned. The NASA PR guy did not. There are PR guys with senses of humor, but working for NASA generally cures them.

Almost, Tesla reported in my left ear.

Daddy, that was awful, Erin murmured in my right.

Thank you, honey. "Can we go over to the far side and look over the drop-off?" I asked aloud.

The PR guy clenched his teeth, and my host looked sad. "I'm sorry."

"Too dangerous?" I asked. *Let's go, let's go!*

"A matter of timing," my host explained. "In about fifteen minutes they start putting the payload aboard—and it's classified, I'm afraid, so they really don't like civilians standing around rubbernecking. And as soon as that's done they start loading up the external tank with the hypergolics: trust me, you don't want to be around then." *Ready!* Tesla said.

"I suppose not," I agreed. *Are you ready, Erin?*

Ready, Pop!

Okay: phase one on "three," phase two on "zero," just like we rehearsed it. Everybody synch on me. "I've already imposed a lot," I said to the flack, handing him my camera, "but could I ask you for one more?"

He sighed, affixed his smile, and took the camera with every appearance of delight. "No problem at all." I used the posing dance that ensued to cover my subvocal countdown.

Here we go! Erin and Tesla chanted along with me: *Number* five *jet fire; number* four *jet fire; number* three—

"Smile!"

—Nikola Tesla Transited a large heavy wrench to a point in space just to the east of us, and about a hundred feet up in the air—

—jet fire; number two *jet fire; number* one—

KLANG!

"Jesus!" cried the PR guy, my host, and two of the armed men, and they all spun as one toward the sound, the PR guy dropping my camera to do so.

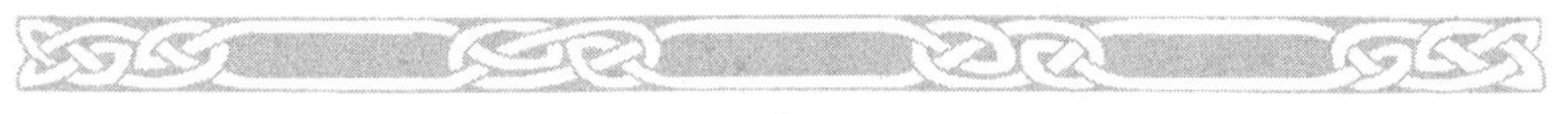

—jet fire, GO!

Erin teleported herself about 160 feet, almost straight up. In the very instant her weight left my back, most of it was replaced—by the lifelike dummy Erin that Tesla teleported into the backpack. That pack was empty for perhaps a quarter of a second or less . . . and nobody was looking in that direction. It was probably all over by the time my camera finished smashing and my shoulder muscles finished flinching.

I'm in! Erin reported triumphantly.

Thank God, Tesla and I both said. I was so keyed up I said it aloud instead of subvocalizing, but fortunately nobody around me seemed to hear the first syllable.

My companions converged cursing on the wrench, which was indeed the right size, kind, and type to belong there—was in fact an authentic NASA utensil, Transited from storage by Tesla. Then they took turns glancing up at God's Erector Set, the FSS towering above us, to try and determine what part of it the wrench had fallen from. There was nobody in the right position up there now, but eventually some poor soul was going to catch hell he didn't deserve for leaving tools unstowed, and I'd have felt sorry about that if I hadn't been distracted by overwhelming relief that my baby girl had not just killed herself (and incidentally destroyed history) Transiting into some solid object aboard the *Columbia.*

How's it look? I asked as the people I was with babbled at one another.

Like a coal cellar at midnight, she said. *Let me get this flashlight on . . . there.* Much *better. Now it looks like the inside of a black box.*

How was your placement? Tesla asked.

Perfect, Uncle Nikky. Absolutely nominal. I'm gonna get my stuff now.

Be careful, baby. Take your time. There's no—

It's done, Daddy. No sweat. I told you you were a worrywart. She had Transited her gear and provisions from Tesla's bus into two adjoining lockers . . . again, without causing an explosion.

Thank you for indulging my paranoia, Pumpkin. Ready to go now?

Yep.

We were done, now. Rehearsal successful. She'd confirmed her bearing on the target, established to my satisfaction that she could reach it safely and undetected. There was no further exploring she could do up there now: workers would be wandering unpredictably in and out of the orbiter all night long. Now we would go back to the bus and get some sleep, get ready to do it again tomorrow morning, just before liftoff.

The PR guy apologized, both for almost getting my skull caved in and for breaking my camera. I waved away both apologies. "Serves me right for standing under anything this big without a hard hat," I told him.

Okay, everything's cool, Erin said. *I just sent all the gear back to the bus, Daddy. Get ready, both of you: I'm coming back myself now, on zero this time . . . in . . .* five *Mississippi,* four *Mississippi—*

"Nice of you to take it that way," the flack said gratefully. "But I insist on replacing the camera."

—three *Mississippi,* two *Mississippi—*

"Very we—"

KLANG!

Another fucking wrench hit the deck, no more than three feet from the first impact site. Since I wasn't expecting this one, I jumped like everyone else—and felt horror flood through me.

—one *Mississippi, NOW!*

With a convulsive effort, I did my very best to return to precisely the position I'd been standing in—and felt Erin replace her doppel. She was off by no more than half an inch. The relief—as much as the lurching jolt—nearly stopped my heart.

Suddenly I had no sympathy at all for the poor bastard who was going to catch hell for sloppy tool discipline.

My host interrupted the PR guy's continued apologies, twinkling his eyes to alert me that a punchline was coming. "Well," he said, "try to think of these wrenches as, uh . . ." He paused for effect. ". . . hail: *Columbia.*"

I knew I would find the remark funny later, and pretended to now, but I was busy trying to keep *Nikky, tell the Lucky Duck I'm gonna kick his ass when I see him!* down to a subvocal level. "The hail you say," I riposted feebly.

What just happened, Daddy?

Fate decided to throw in a monkey wrench, honey. Not ours: a real *fuckup, this time. Are you okay?*

Yeah, fine—but I think that should have woken me up. She lifted her head, kicked her arms and legs, and began to wail. I found it even more unsettling than any other parent would have—for it was only the second time in her life that I'd ever heard Erin cry like a baby, the first being during her birth.

Misery inspired me. "He's from Barcelona, you know," I told my host.

He recognized the *Fawlty Towers* catchphrase, but was still puzzled. "Who is?"

I pointed upward. "The Spaniard in the works." There: honor was satisfied.

That does it, Erin subvocalized—no small trick while sobbing—*get me out of here, Daddy, or I'm Transiting out.*

You big lug, Tesla couldn't resist adding.

I made my excuses and got out of there as quickly and gracefully as I could. And that's the story of my wrenching experience on Pad 39-B.

The next morning, August 8, at 8:35 A.M., I was in Tesla's schoolbus, parked by the side of I-95 with hundreds of other vehicles. Also present were Zoey, Omar, Tesla, Doc Webster, Fast Eddie, the Lucky Duck for luck, and of course Erin. My hair was a different color and styled differently, and the ID I carried bore a false name. And I probably didn't resemble me a whole lot in temperament, either. I was as nervous as a man whose baby daughter is about to stow away on a spacecraft. One that exploded only four flights earlier. I wanted, very badly, to give her some sort of sage advice—but was hampered by the fact that I couldn't *think* of any advice that didn't sound insulting, even to me.

Zoey of course had the same problem. Maybe worse, for all I know or can know. In her case it had the effect of making her outwardly very quiet and calm-appearing. Me, I was working hard to suppress my sudden resemblance to a jumping bean. Part of a parent's job is to teach his kid how to deal with fear, right? Now if only someone would explain it to *me* . . .

Doc Webster, God bless his heart, sensed and understood the dynamic, and filled in the silence with a steady stream of harmless blather, designed to give us all something benign to think about. He was clever and witty and if you held a gun to my head now I could not tell you a single goddam thing that he said.

Finally, Omar lifted one headphone away from his ear and reported, "T minus two minutes thirty seconds. They just took the beanie off the carrot. All aboard."

The three of us exchanged one of those glances that seems to go on for a million years. Erin was the only one smiling.

Zoey swallowed, hard. "Have a nice time on the spaceship, honey," she said lightly.

"Break a law of physics," I agreed. But even I heard my voice quiver on the last word.

Erin was in her mother's embrace so quickly she almost seemed to Transit there, and a moment later she was hugging me too. I put everything I had into returning it. She gave me a wet smooch and backed away.

"I love you guys," she said. Then she took her place between her two piles of gear, placing her feet squarely on the X duct-taped on the floor. "Don't worry, okay?"

The luggage vanished with a barely audible popping sound.

"I'll be fine."

And Erin was gone too.

Two minutes later, they lit the candle over there, and 6.6 seconds later, Brewster Shaw, Richard Richards, James Adamson,

David Leestma, Mark Brown, and Erin Stonebender left town—and planet—together. The noise rocked the bus. We were much farther away than we'd been for the last launch, but it was still one helluva sight.

This time we had more riding on it.

I guess we were the first people in history who ever screamed "Go, baby, go!" during a space launch, and were punning.

Omar took off his headphones and put the sound on speakers so we could all follow the launch.

"Roll program initiated."

"*Columbia*, go at throttle up."

"Roger, go at throttle up."

"Houston, we have booster sep."

"Roger, *Columbia*, we show a clean sep down here."

WHEEEEEE, Erin sang, on a very different circuit.

"*Columbia*, Houston here, two engine Ben Guerrir." That meant the Shuttle now had enough altitude and speed to make it to Morocco even if one engine failed.

"*Columbia*, Houston. Negative return." It was no longer possible for Commander Shaw to turn around and head back for Kennedy if he took a notion to. Four more minutes to orbit.

God, you guys—this is so fun*!* Zoey and I looked at each other and smiled in spite of ourselves.

"*Columbia*, Houston, single-engine ATO." They were now high enough to make orbit even if two of the three engines were to fail. I began to breathe a little easier.

Time didn't pass; it tailgated. Finally:

"Houston, *Columbia*. We have MECO."

"Roger that, *Columbia*. We show a very slightly late cutoff. Eight minutes and forty seconds."

They were in orbit. And nobody had figured out why the computers had decided they needed to keep the engines on a few seconds longer than predicted to get them there. Erin's extra mass was buried away somewhere in a huge string of zeros and ones that nobody would examine closely for some time to come or, probably, believe when they did.

The bus rang with applause.

Nobody outside noticed, of course. They had all started their engines and driven away the moment the Shuttle was too high to see with the naked eye, just like the last time.

Oh, golly, Erin reported, *zero gravity is WAY cool . . .*

I could fill the next several pages with a lot of stuff I subsequently learned from my daughter. What five days in orbit is like, for one thing . . . but you can find that sort of thing in a lot of other places. What life as a stowaway is like . . . but that, too, has been amply recorded elsewhere. The crew rarely ventured down to the middeck, and never did so without announcing their intention to Houston first; Erin had no trouble at all remaining out of sight, and didn't have to spend *too* much time holed up in that damned locker. The biggest problem she had was that she couldn't use the zero-gee toilet facilities without being noticed. Things did get a little ugly in that department, but after reflection I don't think I'll be any more specific—except to note that, having completed toilet training only a short time earlier, Erin was much less squeamish about such matters than a grown-up in her undignified position might have been. And, of course, Transiting helped immensely: the problem was . . . uh . . . Transient.

I could also use up twenty pages with the details of exactly how Erin went about hacking her way into the Deathstar's computer without being caught at it, and what she did once she was in. I know because I have seen a written summary she wrote later, and it runs twenty pages. But I didn't understand a word in them, and will not inflict them on you here. Let it stand that she was essentially done by the third day—and stuck around only against the possibility that the crew might perform one more redundant systems check before launching the thing into space, and catch her changes.

Nor do I suppose you really need to be told the day-to-day details of how Zoey and I managed to get through those five days without quite going insane with fear, or with helpless boredom. If you ever find out *your* baby is going to go to orbit for that long, get hold of me and I'll tell you anything you want to know. The best general advice I can offer in the meantime is, get an Artificial Intelligence to teach the kid hacking, and lay in a supply of Irish whiskey for yourself. Oh yes—and try and arrange to have about a hundred of the finest, most decent human beings alive as your good friends. And be in Key West at the time.

Two small anecdotes from that week are perhaps worth telling.

During the second day, Erin allowed her attention to focus a little too closely on her work for a crucial moment—turned away from a panel, and saw an astronaut gaping at her.

She Transited at once—to a location where she could still see him, but he could not see her—and waited with bated breath to see how bad the disaster was.

It was nonexistent. The astronaut—we believe it was the pilot, Richard Richards—blinked, rubbed his eyes . . . and dismissed the hallucination. I don't think he said anything at all about it, to his shipmates or to Houston. Would you?

The second noteworthy incident came late in the fourth day of the mission, when Erin suddenly reported that Pixel had just showed up.

Fortunately, she was able to persuade him to go back home before anyone else up there noticed or heard him. A baby in orbit can be dismissed as an obvious phantom . . . but a cat is just barely possible enough to be taken seriously.

A couple of hours later, the Deathstar left the payload bay and took up its station in orbit. Both NASA and DoD remained sublimely unaware that it had been neutered.

The job was essentially done, then. But on the suspenders *and* belt principle, Erin remained there at her post until Commander Shaw actually began to deorbit the next day, against the faint remaining possibility of a final systems recalibration that would undo all her work.

By then Zoey and I had relaxed to the point of allowing her to come home the way she wanted to.

The original plan had been for Erin to ride the bird down. Zoey and I would take a commercial airliner out to the left-hand coast and wait somewhere near Edwards in a rented van. Once the orbiter came to a safe, smooth stop, Erin would Transit to the van, we'd all hug, and then fly home together.

Instead, we sat tight where we were.

At about 9 A.M. local time on the 13th, nearly all of us were gathered at The Place, staring up at the sky together. Zoey and I stood right in front of the bar with an arm around each other, and everyone had left a big cleared space before us.

Here I come, ready or not, Erin announced.

We all held our breath.

Whoa!

No sign of her. "Are you all right?" I screamed.

Fine—way off target, but fine. Hang on—

"Careful!"

Suddenly I seemed to see a baseball very high overhead, to the east and heading east. Mighty Casey had finally caught a piece of one.

That's a little better. Once more—

The baseball vanished; a stationary object appeared directly overhead, perhaps a hundred yards up, and began to fall. Then it vanished, reappeared at what looked like the exact spot where it had started, and fell again.

Okay: ready . . . set . . .

"Be careful!" Zoey and I both yelled.

The falling object separated into two components, and both

vanished. Erin's laptop suddenly appeared on the porch. Erin herself appeared before us in midair . . . grinned . . . folded over into a perfect swan dive . . . and dropped headfirst into the pool, cutting the water with scarcely a splash.

As we all gaped with surprise, she surfaced, grinned around at all of us, splashed water at Zoey and me, and cried, "God, I've been dreaming of that for *days*—I *stink*!"

They may have heard our triumphant whoop of laughter and applause down in Cuba, unless Fidel was talking at the time.

Erin swam to the side, pulled herself up and out, and Zoey and I found ourselves in a three-way hug with a wet kid. We held it, rocking back and forth together, while waves of cheering washed over us. I don't ever remember being happier.

As the applause died away, Erin broke away from the hug and went over to stand in front of Nikola Tesla. She looked up at him with those big eyes, and without a trace of parody whipped off an extremely snappy salute. "Mission accomplished, sir," she reported.

Oh! it was a treat to see that famous sad face light up like that. His smile took at least a hundred years off his age. For just a moment I saw, not the most screwed man of the twentieth century, but the optimistic young preacher's son from Smiljan he had been when the century began. He returned her salute with a flourish. "Well done, Erin Stonebender. And thank you from the bottom of my heart."

More applause. I felt proud enough to bust my buttons.

Tom Hauptman was already busy at The Machine, turning out Irish coffees as fast as they could pour, and Fast Eddie was serving anyone who wanted to drink something else. By the time *Columbia* touched down at Edwards, half an hour later—the only Shuttle ever to return to Earth with a passenger missing—the celebration was in high gear, and neighbors were starting to fall by to see what all the excitement was about.

An Irish coffee drunk that begins at nine o'clock Monday

morning, in Key West? Brother, that's a good day. Forget the saving-the-universe and only-child-not-dead parts . . .

It pretty much petered out by Wednesday. Some of us had jobs.

That was basically it. Our task was over . . . except for the tedious, boring, suspenders-*and*-belt detail of continuing to monitor DoD communications, on the slight off chance that those assholes might take it into their heads to flush and reload the Deathstar computer for some reason. But the chances of that comfortably approached zero. It was, for instance, electronically "hardened" against the imminent solar storm.

And, again mostly for form's sake, we kept track of the other converging events that, but for Erin, would have been components of the cosmic billiard shot that doomed the universe.

Five days later, for example, Tropical Storm Erin did indeed appear on schedule, way the hell out in the Atlantic, and by the 22nd it had been upgraded to Hurricane Erin. Many toasts were drunk to it at The Place. (We could afford to admire it. It would never come within a thousand miles of us—or of land, for that matter.)

And Nikola Tesla, by doing a very little bit of very careful Transiting to laboratory coat closets and washroom stalls in his old homeland—then still called Yugoslavia—was able to overhear enough scientist scuttlebutt to confirm that the Soviets had indeed made some sort of breakthrough in solar activity prediction, and believed they had found a way to use a transient magnetic lens to increase their chances of gathering extremely energetic cosmic-ray particles in the Kvant-1 trap on Mir.

The sun's acne flared up on schedule, too: the Aurora Borealis did indeed make another rare and historic appearance in the southern skies of America, scrambling phone calls and activating garage-door openers from San Francisco to Miami. And, we

learned from a new acquaintance at Boca Chica, toasting a couple of Navy satellites less well protected than the Deathstar.

Everything, in short, was going along in pretty close accordance with Tesla's original prophecy of doom. If my two-year-old hadn't taken out America's Deathstar, I'd have been pretty worried.

Excuse me. I just want to admire that last sentence a minute. I've had an interesting life.

It was an odd psychological position for all of us to be in, simultaneously exciting and frustrating. I mean, we were the only ones alive who knew the end of the universe wasn't going to happen . . . but then, we were the only ones who even suspected it had ever been going to in the first place, so there was nobody to amaze with our secret. The greatest news story of all time was unhappening before our eyes—and it did so with an unexpected element of anticlimax. The dog that didn't bark in the Big Night.

We responded characteristically. We pitched a ball.

On the evening of Friday the 25th, the day Tesla had tentatively predicted to be Der Tag, we all gathered at The Place. Zoey and Erin had made up a huge sign out of a sheet and hung it over the gate to the street, so that everyone had to pass under it on their way in. It read: "Today is the first day of the rest of your universe."

The Place has very nice lighting, thanks to Zoey and Margie Shorter, but we'd killed most of it that night, except for a few lava lamps and the soft red service lights at the bar. There was just no competing with the sheets of neon fire in the sky.

Green they were, mostly, but rimmed in scarlet, and shot through with tendrils of rich violet. The water in the pool made a shimmering mirror copy, as if the Northern Lights were trying to beam down but the transporter was malfunctioning. Faintly colored reflections danced everywhere, especially on perspiring drink glasses and on the faces of swimmers. The overall effect was magical.

In a spot that didn't really need any artificial help to be magical. It was another perfect summer night in Key West, just hot enough to encourage thirst and laziness. The air was redolent of sea salt and coral dust and lime and fine reefer and Cubano cooking from our neighbors to the west. There was plenty of booze and beer in stock, and The Machine was working well (now that Omar had adjusted it for tropical conditions). Fast Eddie was in rare form, doing particularly interesting Mind Melds, in which, for instance, his left hand summoned up Oscar Peterson while his right hand became Harry Connick, Jr., and showed no signs of tiring. Harry the parrot was banished indoors early on, when he showed a lamentable tendency to sing along. Obscenely, of course.

When a lull finally came in the traffic, I took a break, left the stick to Tom Hauptman, and came out from behind the bar to join a group of folks lying on their backs next to the pool, gazing up at the Aurora Borealis and lazily conversing. I stretched out beside the Lucky Duck and accepted the joint he passed me.

"You're just in time, Skinny," he said. "I was just proving that Jesus was Irish."

Pass me a joint, I'll play straight man. "How's that?"

"Just think about it. He never got married, he never held a steady job, and his last request was a drink. Case closed."

A few folks chuckled. Marty Pignatelli, the ex-trooper from New Jersey, said, "I think he was Italian. Talked with his hands a lot . . . seemed to have wine with every meal . . . worked in the building trades . . ." More chuckles.

"You're not looking at it right," Tanya Latimer said. "He called everybody 'brother,' had no fixed address, and got crucified for preaching without a permit—I figure the man had to be Soul Brother Number One."

"You're crazy," Noah Gonzalez told her. "Everybody knows he was Latino."

"How do you figure?"

"Hell, his first name was Jesus!"

That brought us from giggles to outright laughter. And with perfect timing, Acayib jumped in. "I'm sorry, but there can be no disputing this point: Jesus was a Jew."

He said it with a straight face, and Double Bill didn't yet know him well enough to realize his tongue was in his cheek; for a moment Bill thought maybe Acayib really was some sort of humor-deficient zealot. "Look," he said, "nobody meant to—"

"The evidence is clear," Acayib went on. "He went into his father's business. He lived at home until the age of thirty-three. And to his dying day, the man was convinced his mother was a virgin, and she believed he was God."

We all broke up, nobody louder than Double Bill. I had another hit, and passed the joint to Susie, and lay back and stared up at the fiery sky for a moment. It reminded me of an After Dark screensaver module Erin had found for our Mac, called "Psycho Deli," shimmering and psychedelic and hypnotic. And all of a sudden, it was as if some bug in After Dark had caused a second screensaver to superimpose itself over the first. The one called "Starry Night." One after another, three tiny pinpricks of white fire appeared in different parts of the night sky, left traçer tracks through the Aurora at high speed, and vanished. Then another—then another two.

Oh, right, I thought to myself, letting out smoke. *It's August. Meteorites. Leonids? No, they're in November. Perseids, that's it.*

Maybe two or three seconds later, the penny dropped. Did you ever just sense a disaster coming, without knowing quite how you knew? Suddenly I just *knew* . . .

Pick your own cliché for heartstopping horror. Blood into ice water—spine into Jell-O—toes into cupcakes, whatever. You know the ending to the Beatles' "A Day in the Life"? That's what happened with my voice. The "Oh . . ." started off at normal conversational level; the ". . . *holy* . . ." rose sharply in both pitch and volume; and by the time I reached *". . . SHIT!"* I was at the top of my lungs and perilously close to falsetto.

Everything chopped off. Conversations, laughter, party

sounds, Fast Eddie's piano, splashing in the pool, everything but the barely heard background *chuff-sssssh* of The Machine turning common ingredients into God's Blessing.

Nikola Tesla's voice was like a whipcrack. "What is it, Jacob¿"

I lay where I was, helpless to rise. With an effort, I managed to lift my arm and point at the sky. It's a safe bet just about everybody looked up.

When nobody said anything after a few seconds, I said, "Meteorites. Perseid group. August, every year. They peaked at least a week ago, but they'll still be coming for days."

"The Perseids run on a four-year cycle," Acayib said. "And this is a jackpot year."

I nodded. "Naturally. We never thought to factor *them* in. What'll you bet—¿"

Tesla was the first to get it. He flung his drink to the ground and said something in Croatian, as if he expected it to wither flowers within a forty-yard radius. "Erin, to me, quickly!"

"Yes, Uncle Nikky!"

Some equipment I didn't recognize and couldn't understand materialized out of thin air before him. He and Erin put earbeads in their ears and started doing things either with or to the equipment. Quickly, at first, and then progressively slower. The longer they worked, the unhappier they looked—and by the time they were done, they were both miserable.

"Aw, *shit,*" Erin said.

"Did I call it¿" I asked, knowing the answer from their faces.

Tesla nodded, frowning thunderously. "The Deathstar took a glancing blow from a meteorite late last night. No public announcement. Minor damage. Just enough to make them do a total software dump/reload . . ."

"The Deathstar is armed again," Erin said. "And there's nothing we can do about it."

In the horrid silence, the Lucky Duck's angry mutter was clearly audible. "Don't one of you sons of bitches so much as *look* at me."

I didn't. I knew perfectly well it wasn't his fault. Instead I looked to my two brightest hopes: the pair of heroes who'd saved us all the last time. Erin and Tesla. The brilliance of youth and the insight of age. One of the smartest and most intuitive men who ever lived, and the smartest girl ever born. Designated agents of Mike Callahan, time-traveling immortal and professional universe-saver.

And they both looked back at me, and at the same time they both said the same words, the last words on earth I wanted to hear just then. Worse: said them to *me*:

"What the hell do we do *now?*"

CHAPTER EIGHTEEN

Symphysis

"We are ready for any unforeseen event that may or may not occur."
—J. Danforth Quayle, September 22, 1990

SOME DAYS YOU'RE THE pigeon, some days you're the statue. I wished I had time to panic. Since I didn't, I thought of Mike Callahan. How would he have handled this? It helped. I felt some of his monolithic strength and calm enter me.

"Let me just run through the obvious and get it out of the way," I said. "You two can't do a remote dump-and-reload yourselves?"

Tesla shook his head. "Physical contact would be required."

"They just did it but you can't?"

He sighed. "I can explain why not," he said, "if you think we have half an hour to spare."

I nodded. "That's what I thought you'd say. Erin, can you Transit back up there with your laptop and 'twist again, like you did last summer'?"

For once she looked like a normal two-year-old. They find the world that dismaying a lot of the time. "You saw me on the way

down, Pop. My first hop, I missed the arrival point I wanted by more than a mile, and the vector I was trying for by almost a hundred miles an hour. It's not like hopping from a stationary bus to a stationary Space Shuttle."

"You got better with every jump."

"Sure—but they weren't three-hundred-mile hops. And even the others I never got perfect, even that last hop. I was planning to arrive standing on the water, like Peter Sellers. The swan dive was improv."

I bit my lip. She'd only been off by maybe six feet or so. But of course, an error of six feet in matching with the Deathstar could get her killed. And who knew how many hops it would take her to get even that close—breathing vacuum between each of them? What would she do for life support once she was aboard?

"Suppose," Omar said, "we steal a spacesuit—"

"I'm sorry," Tesla said, "but that is not a good idea. The Deathstar has antimeteorite defenses."

"Then how the fuck—"

"They were not good enough to stop a four-millimeter piece of rock," Tesla said, "but they would easily be good enough to hit a target the size of Erin, especially at a lower closing speed."

"I could hop *real fast*," Erin suggested.

"You know better," he told her. "Each time you arrive, you must look around, analyze your position and vector, and decide what to do next. You are very quick, Erin . . . but not as quick as the Deathstar. Or its weapons."

My head was starting to hurt. "No, honey, you may *not* play hide and seek with the nice laser beam. Okay, we can't influence the Deathstar any further. It's armed. What does that leave us?"

We all knew the answers. After a brief pained silence, Omar summed up, ticking off points on his fingers. "We could try and stop a hurricane . . . or douse the Northern Lights . . . or persuade the Soviet Union to abandon or deorbit Mir, for no reason we could explain . . . or talk a cosmic ray into changing course. Or, of course, we could ask the Defense Department to shut down its Deathstar—just for a few days."

There was another silence, then. A longish one.

"Which one ya wanna do foist?" Eddie said.

Well, of course we cracked up. Tension relief and all that. But the laughter didn't last long, and wasn't replaced by anything. We looked at each other and waited for somebody to come up with a Special Plan. After a while it became clear none of us was going to.

This was by no means the first, or even the fifth, time my friends and I had faced what looked like the End of Everything. We reacted the way we always had. One by one, we drifted toward the bar. I joined Tom behind the stick and began passing out medication with both hands.

And soon, inevitably, someone bravely tried to cheer us up. Long-Drink, it was this time. He nudged Doc Webster, and said in a voice loud enough to carry, "Well, one good thing, anyway: that new fascist law that lets the DEA rob anybody they can convict of everything he owns is finally finished."

The Doc knows his cue when he hears it—as Long-Drink had known he would. In a creditable imitation of Edward G. Robinson, he rose to the occasion. "Mother of God," he moaned, "is this the end of RICO?"

A rain of peanuts, crumpled napkins, and swizzle sticks descended on him from all sides, and groans split the night.

"Hey Eddie," Tommy called, "how about some music?"

Eddie nodded and headed for his piano. I found myself dizzily wondering what to request. Percy Mayfield's "Danger Zone"? "The End of the World"? "Goodnight Irene"? What was the proper soundtrack for Ragnarok?

He solved the problem by playing something I didn't know, either improv or a composition he'd never gotten around to sharing before. Whatever, it worked: upbeat, but not frantic, somehow cheerful and nostalgic at the same time. Some people started to dance.

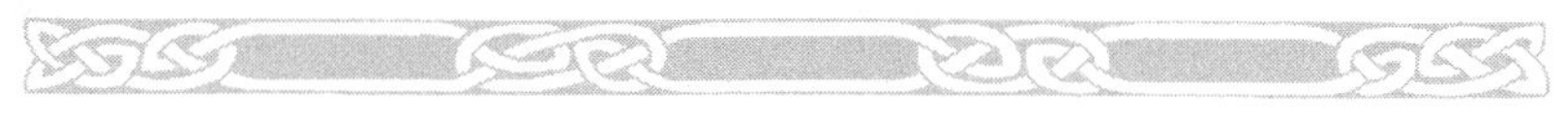

If this was the last party there was ever going to be, at least we had spent a lot of time practicing. Getting it right should be a cinch.

Finally I finished passing out drinks, and went down to the end of the bar where my wife sat. We joined hands over the countertop and looked into each other's eyes.

"Maybe I shouldn't ask," I heard Omar say, "but is there any way to know in advance just *when* the cosmic ray is going to arrive? Be nice to be able to pace my drinking."

Tesla sat bolt upright. I turned to look at him, and his face had gone blank. "What is it?" Omar said.

He came back after a moment, shook his head slightly. "I'm sorry, Jim. I believe the last piece of the puzzle may have fallen into place. Not that it answers your question."

"How do you mean?"

"In attempting to answer it, I had to consider what the *source* of the cosmic ray might be. Odd that I had not done so before." He shrugged. "It did not seem to matter, I suppose."

"I'll bite," the Lucky Duck said. "What is the source?"

Tesla didn't reply. After a moment, Acayib answered for him. "Well, Jim, nobody's positive what causes cosmic rays." He glanced at Tesla. "At least, in our time. But one of the leading candidates for the source for really high-energy cosmic rays is a supernova." Suddenly he stopped and slapped his thigh. "I see what you mean, Nikola!"

"I don't," the Duck said pointedly.

"Picture it, Ernie," Acayib said. "The Deathstar is keeping an eye on Mir. Solar flux begins to interfere with its communications, and is interpreted as an attempt at jamming. Hurricane Erin adds its gamma-ray fountain. I have always had some difficulty believing that even both those things together would be enough to trigger the firing of a secret superweapon. But suppose a supernova then occurs. Probably in this galaxy, but the important thing about its location is that, from the viewpoint of the Deathstar, *it is occulted by Mir at the time.*"

I began to see what he was driving at. "All of a sudden Mir is backlit like an aging actress," I said, "the brightest thing in the sky."

"And a moment after the photons," Acayib agreed, "the cosmic rays arrive, and meet the Tesla Beam."

"They wouldn't come simultaneously?" I asked.

"No," Acayib said. "Photons first."

"Huh." I nodded, and most of those within earshot also said "Huh" or "Mmm." The idea did seem to make sense, and satisfied the basic condition of being absurdly unlikely.

"This is terrific," the Lucky Duck said. "Armed only with the knowledge that the universe is gonna end, and with only about a brain and a half between us, we managed to dope out exactly how, just before it happens. I'm happy."

I felt an impulse to smack him. To divert myself, I turned to Tesla and asked, "So then, do we know enough about predicting supernovae to be able to answer Jim's question?"

"Oddly enough," Tesla said, "it should theoretically be possible to do so. But only theoretically."

"How so?" Omar asked.

"It's a matter of computational capacity, Uncle Omar," Erin said. "We talked about it. This kind of problem, if Uncle Nikky and I ransacked the Internet, used all the computer power we could possibly steal without getting caught at it, it would take us about a year to crunch enough numbers to get an answer."

I got interested enough to take my eyes briefly from Zoey's. "Maybe if you got a better computer from the future . . . no, that's no good. The future just became null and void, didn't it, Nikky?"

"I'm afraid it appears so," he agreed sadly. "And even if not, I may not borrow tools from it."

I returned my gaze to Zoey. "Maybe it's better if we don't know exactly when," she said softly.

I nodded.

"Maybe," Omar said. "But I can't help wondering."

"Would it help you any to know¿" the Lucky Duck asked sourly.

"Maybe," Omar insisted. "Taking out a Deathstar is a tough problem, granted . . . but if I only had to take it down for, say, a second . . . and I knew *which* second . . ."

"How would that help you¿" the Duck pressed.

"I don't know," Omar admitted. "But it might. It's something to think about. Something to *do*, besides kiss our asses goodbye."

Something rearranged itself inside my head. I let go of Zoey's hands and turned to face my daughter.

"Erin."

"Yes, Daddy¿"

"All you and Nikky need for an answer is enough computational capacity¿"

"Yeah, sure," she said. "But it doesn't exist yet." She frowned. "And now won't ever, it looks like."

"How about a big neural net¿ No, how about a bank of them¿"

She shook her head. "Neural nets are mostly theory. They haven't built any good ones, yet." She saw my expression. "Have they¿"

"Eddie!" I called. "Take a break." I came out from behind the bar. When Eddie had finished his verse and stopped playing, I called for everyone's attention, and got it.

"What's up, Jake¿" Doc Webster asked.

I explained Omar's question, and Tesla and Erin's computational needs. "All they really need," I finished, "is unrestricted access to a big interconnected bank of neural nets. We don't think there's one in the world, and if there is, nobody's gonna tell us about it in the next couple of hours."

"So what are you saying¿" Long-Drink called.

"Let's make our own."

ROOBA ROOBA ROOBA.

Double Bill was mystified. "What the hell is that supposed to mean¿"

I looked around at them all. All my friends. My loved ones. My companions. My family. I swallowed a lump in my throat and said, "I don't know about you guys, but—" I stopped. "No, that's silly: I *do* know about you guys—all but Bill and Mei-Ling, anyway, and you, Marty. What did we all originally come down here to do?"

"Have fun," Long-Drink said.

"To *get telepathic again*."

ROOBA ROOBA.

"Sure, we thought it might take ten years. And then we found out we didn't need to do it after all. So we stopped thinking about it. Stopped talking about it. Well, we'll not only never get a better chance, it looks like we'll never get *another* chance."

Doc Webster cleared his throat. "So you're suggesting—"

"I'm saying we try to hook up, and give Nik and Erin what they need. We got over a *hundred* neural nets, right here. Let's hook 'em up."

Omar looked down at Erin. "Can we do that?"

She looked helpless. "I . . . I'm not sure. Uncle Nikky?"

He frowned ferociously and thought about it. "Perhaps," he said finally.

Omar looked back to me. "Jake—can we *do* that?"

It sure was a good question.

"Well shit, Jim, how do I know?" I spread my hands. "One thing to think about, though: of the three times we've pulled it off in the past, every single one was a matter of life and death . . . and two of them were end-of-the-world situations. Maybe that helps, somehow. And how often does an end-of-the-world come along for us to run the experiment?"

"It would seem that this one will be the last," Tesla said.

"So let's not waste it," I said.

"This is nuts," the Lucky Duck said. "Even if we get our heads wired up right, even if Eyebrows and the midget there can hack an answer, what the hell good does it do us? I don't think I really want to *know* the exact second it's all gonna go to shit."

Omar sighed. "I know what you mean, Ernie. But somehow I can't shake the feeling it'd be good to know. Maybe I just feel like we ought to go out like a test pilot, still trying to solve the problem as he augurs in. Still reporting even the instrument readings he thinks are useless, in case they might turn out to be a vital clue for somebody . . ."

"Dat sounds right ta me," Fast Eddie said. A number of people expressed agreement.

"Me too," Long-Drink said. "Frog in a bucket of milk keeps kicking, he might just manage to churn his way out."

"Not if he's in a bucket of shit," the Lucky Duck said darkly.

"Come on, Duck, what have you got to lose?"

His features went blank for a moment while he thought it over. "Not much," he agreed. "A'right, let's do it."

A cheer went up. "Do it!" "Let's do it!"

I looked to Double Bill, Mei-Ling, and Marty Pignatelli, the only telepathic virgins present. "You all game?"

Mei-Ling took the Doc's arm and nodded without a word. Bill chewed on his pipe . . . then tossed it over his shoulder into the darkness and said, "What the hell: I'm in."

"Me too," said Marty. "Let's do it."

Then, of course, they all turned to me. And three or four of them said it at once.

"How do we do it?"

I took a deep breath and thought. Then I took another deep breath and thought some more. "Well," I said finally, "when in doubt, try what worked the last time." I held out my hands, and Zoey took one and Erin took the other. "Let's do an Om."

The Om is about as simple as a human group activity can possibly get. There's nothing to it; that's the beauty of it. Any fool, or rather any group of fools, can do it.

You gather round in a rough circle and join hands. Closing your eyes is optional. You pick a note out of the air—any note at all, as long as everyone present can reach it or an octave of it. You take a deep breath, and start singing that note, droning it from deep in your belly. Start with the syllable "AAAAAAAAA," and at your own chosen pace, gradually warp it into the syllable "OOOOOOOO," and when you feel your breath starting to go, bring it around to "MMMMMMMM." Then take a deep breath and start over. Repeat until time stops.

It's okay if your note wanders a little. It's okay if you can't carry a tune and miss it altogether, as long as there are enough people who can. Tonal and harmonic imperfections can lend a weird kind of resonance that actually helps things, somehow. So do the random variations that result from everybody running out of breath and starting over at different, overlapping times: the sound takes on a sort of slow unpredictable pulse.

I do *not* say that if you and your friends Om long enough, you will achieve telepathic symphysis. Thousands of people have Om'ed, sometimes for days, without that result. But just about any group of people who do Om will find that when they're done, they are at least more telepathic than they were when they started. It's just about impossible to do it for any length of time, and still remain *totally* locked inside your skull, chained to your personality.

And we had been trained by a master telepath, and tutored by two mutant human adepts. We had been telepathic before, more than once, and *knew* that it could be done. And we knew that once again, the stakes were much higher than anything as trivial as life or death . . .

One minute I was standing with my friends in a circle around the pool, watching the Northern Lights simultaneously dance on its surface and shimmer overhead, and concentrating on making my voice a pure strong thing—

—and then the next second, everything changed . . .

Again. It came on like déjà vu on steroids. Like taking acid again after a lapse of many years, feeling that odd mixture of

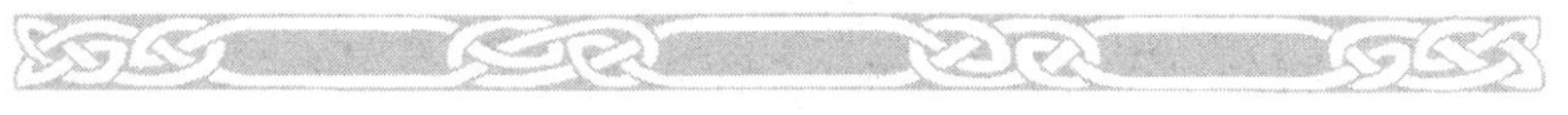

exhilaration and fear and thinking, *Oh, my God, I* remember, *now!*

I remembered again the thing that was so hard to remember in between, in those long intervals between my brief moments of symphysis: the utter certainty that this place (field/zone/plane/whatever you want to miscall it) I was now reentering was a place I had known before I was born, and would know again after I died. The first time I had ever gone there as Jake Stonebender, back in the old original Callahan's Place, part of me had recognized it at once.

I recognized it again now.

All of us were *touching.* Not just the feeble physical joining of our hands: we were as interconnected as cells in a hand, as neurons in a brain, as quarks in a particle. Our skulls became transparent and our minds touched. The persistent illusion of flesh was dispelled. We *knew* each other—of old, and anew. I felt my friends begin to flow into me, and I into them.

Vaguely, I wondered whether this place/zone/whatever would survive the destruction of the physical universe. Could my family and I simply remain here and be safe¿

The answer came from everywhere and nowhere. *NO.* If the universe ended, so did this. The answer seemed wrong, to me, but somehow I was certain. Mind and matter were different . . . but neither could exist without the other.

Then for the fourth time in my life, there stopped being a discrete I, and there was only I/we, using our individual voices to talk to itself with.

Okay, everybody, said the artist formerly known as Erin. *You all have to link up now, and surrender control to me and Uncle Nikky. Don't be scared, Bbiillll, Mei-Ling, Marty.*

Holy shit, said the part that had been Double Bill. But his fear lessened. The former Mei-Ling clung even more tightly to the once and future Doc Webster, and sent back, *I am ready.* And ex-state-trooper Marty said, *I've been dealing with fear a long time. Let's do it.*

Now! said the essence we had called Nikola Tesla.

And everything changed again.

This was different than any of the other times.

If transcendent experiences can be ranked, this fourth experience was somewhere between that first time and the other two. If you're an old-time head, say that the first time was smoking pot, the next two were massive overdoses of pure LSD, and this was a clinical dose of mescaline.

The second and third times, in the very instant of symphysis we had all become terribly busy, trying to build something urgently needed. Both times it had been the same thing: a kind of telepathic bullhorn—a virtual machine with which to communicate with another (and nonhuman) telepath, over vast distances. In each case we were expecting said alien telepath to literally come crashing through the ceiling and kill us all in some period measurable in seconds. Both times, a lot of what psychic attention we could spare from the design and construction of our "bullhorn" got devoted to trying to figure out just what the hell to *say* over the damn thing once we had it built.

And every bit of attention left over had been spent *exploring each other* . . . wandering around inside each other's heads and hearts . . . showing each other our secret places . . . reveling in openness and acceptance and compassion . . . laughing at shame and fear. Our very last telepathic experience had peaked with the birth of Erin and the death of Solace.

This time the experience was, without meaning to denigrate it, a "lesser" thing. Less intense, less profound, less transcendent. As telepathic experiences go, I mean.

It was more like the first time—when Jim MacDonald the mutant telepath had recruited us, had borrowed our mental energy to help him penetrate the catatonic fugue of his older brother Paul. We had not only had no idea what we were doing,

back then, we'd really had nothing much to actually *do*, except push. It was sort of like he showed us a hypothetical truck stuck in deep virtual mud, and we gathered round and put our imaginary shoulders against it and our conceptual backs into it and *heaved* until it popped free, then kept heaving until we got it up to speed and Jim could metaphorically jump-start it. There'd been no device to build, no strategy to invent: all we hadda do was aim the way he pointed and push. There'd been much less risk involved then, too: the stakes had been one man's life.

We were closer now than we'd been that first time—because twice since then we had, briefly, been as close as it's possible to get. But this time we built nothing, planned nothing, pushed nothing, and despite great temptation we did our level best *not* to interpenetrate and intimately explore each other.

What we tried to do, actually, was as little as possible. Not even to think, or even to feel, more than we could help, but just to *be*, together—to know without the experience of learning. Nikola Tesla and Erin required the use of as many collective neurons as we could possibly spare. Even wondering how they were doing was an unwarranted waste of processing power. Even hoping they succeeded might screw up an algorithm somewhere.

Perhaps I understood at the time, at least in part, the nature of the mental rewiring they did, the nature of the program they co-wrote, just what the hell it was they were computing and what factors went into it. If so, none of the knowledge came along with me when I eventually downloaded myself back into my own little individual skull. I think that I—that all of us—basically just trusted that they knew what they were doing, and tried to stay out of their metaphorical way, and cherished the precious moments we had to be all the kinds of naked and all the ways of touching there are together. The little fragment of volition that insisted on persisting, we put into singing "AAAOOOOOOOOOMMM" as cleanly as we could.

In that sense there was nothing "lesser" about it.

It also chanced to be our objectively *longest* experience to date. The others were over in minutes. This time, from external clues I noted afterward, I would say we probably spent somewhere between half an hour and an hour standing there around the pool together, holding hands and Oming.

Subjective duration is a different story. My memory firmly reports that the interval was *both* immeasurably long and indescribably short. It is perfectly aware of the contradiction, and apologizes for it, but stands stubbornly by its data. From my point of view, Nikola Tesla said *Now!*—

(and several trillion years passed)

—and at once Erin answered *Okay!* and the link dissolved and I was decanted back into my skull.

I barely had time to notice that my arms and legs were very tired and my neck hurt and I had to piss something awful, and then I didn't care about any of that because my eyes focused back from infinity to local features and I saw the broad smiles on the faces of both Erin and Nikola Tesla.

"Got the answer?" the Lucky Duck asked.

Tesla nodded.

"Better," Erin said. "We got the answer . . . and a plan."

A major cheer went up. The whooping, hooting, table-pounding sort, with outbreaks of the kind of dancing muddy men do in end zones.

"There's only one thing," she called over the tumult. "It's . . . uh . . . kind of outrageous. Even for us, I mean."

Another cheer, as loud as the first, and full of laughter. As it faded, Double Bill's piercing quarterdeck baritone rose over it. "Straighten me, darlin'—'cause I'm ready." And everybody quieted down and gave Erin the floor.

"Actually, I got it from your head, Bbiillll," she told him.

He glanced at me. "I love it when she says my name." He turned back to her. "You're shittin' me, Little Bit."

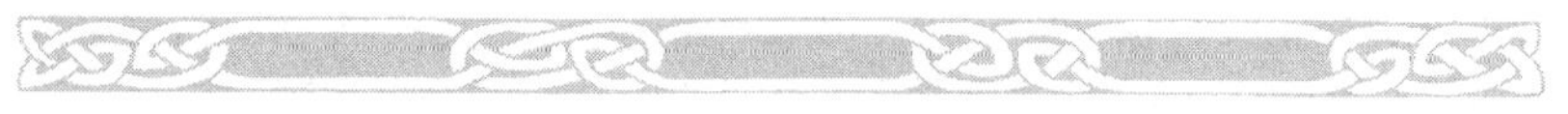

She giggled and shook her head. "While I was rummaging around looking for what neurons I could use, I got distracted by some of your memories. You've got some amazing stuff in there."

He grinned. "I've always thought so."

"Well, I found the one bit of useless information we needed."

"Cut ta da chase," Fast Eddie said. "We safe or not?"

Erin hesitated, and looked to Tesla.

"Let me put it this way, Eddie," Tesla said. "If the calculations Erin and I have just performed are accurate, and if together we can all do no more than two preposterous things . . . then, as you say today, we have a shot."

Erin winced. "No puns, okay, Uncle Nikky?"

He sighed. "As you wish, dear."

"Come on," Double Bill said. "There's something in my head that might save the universe, and I don't know what it is. Cough up, will you?"

She looked around at all of us. "You were all just in rapport with Bbiillll. You know he's lived here in Key West a long time, and had a lot of different occupations."

She was right. Most of the billion trillion things I had learned or relearned about myself and my friends just a few minutes ago were already fading away—for lack of brain room to store the information, I think—but I did retain a vague general impression of awe at how many different ways Double Bill had found to pass the hours in one lifetime.

"Well," Erin went on, "at one point he did a couple of years as a wino. Right, Bbiillll?"

He nodded. "Good years," he said. "Finally got some thinking done."

"And you found a great place to sleep rough."

"Sure." Suddenly his jaw dropped, and his pipe dropped into his sarong. "Jesus Christ." He began to laugh, then chopped it off. "How much time *do* we have?"

"A little over three hours."

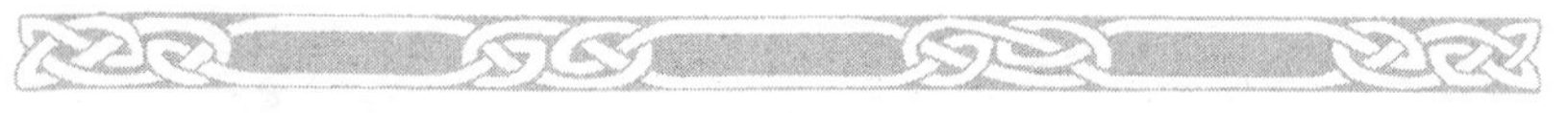

He started laughing again. "Son of a bitch, we might could just pull it off. Oh, that's funny! Their own petard . . ." He held his ribs and roared until his face turned bright red.

The rest of us were standing around looking at one another.

"Erin?" Zoey called. Her voice was soft, gentle; the mortal threat was all in the undertones.

"Sorry, Mom. You tell them, Bbiillll; I don't know if they'll believe me."

Bill wiped his eyes. "My pleasure," he said. "Folks, over by the airport, just past the end of the runway, is about the last sizable patch of real, undeveloped wilderness left in Key West. Nothing but mangroves and scrub and poison ivy and wheat grass and Christ knows what all, wild and overgrown. Pretty good drainage, mostly, so the bugs ain't too bad. Hop a fence and burrow your way in there, it's a terrific place to sleep off a drunk, or lay low till a warrant expires, or just get the hell away from everybody and everything and get a little peace." He laughed again. "That's the part I always found ironic."

"Keep cockteasin' us like this," the Lucky Duck said through clenched teeth, "and I swear to God a bolt of lightning is gonna come out of the clear sky and—"

"What's out there in the scrub?" I asked quickly.

Double Bill grinned like a pirate. "Half a dozen Nike-Hercules missiles."

CHAPTER NINETEEN

Great Balls of Fire

"It's time for the human race to enter the solar system."
—J. Danforth Quayle

ROOBA ROOBA ROOBA.

"Left over from the Cuban Missile Crisis days," Bill went on. "Abandoned for more than twenty years. They flang 'em up in a hurry, and forgot about 'em fast."

"I tried to look them up on the Internet," Erin confirmed, "and I couldn't find much information about them, not even how many there are. If information on those particular missiles still exists, it was never digitized. The government has forgotten they're here."

"Everybody has," Double Bill said. "I'm telling you, I used to sleep under one to keep the rain off."

"Hercs, you say?" Omar asked. "Not Ajaxes?"

"Said 'Hercules' on the side," Bill assured him.

Omar began to grin as big as Bill. "Solid fuel," he said. "If they were Nike-Ajaxes we'd be S.O.L.—they were fueled with red fuming nitric acid, which we are *not* equipped to handle. But the Hercs run on . . . well, basically on solidified nitroglyc-

erine." Tesla frowned, but let it pass. "Doesn't leak, doesn't boil off, doesn't go bad. Twenty years is nothing to that stuff. Light the candle today, that puppy's gonna go someplace." Suddenly his face fell. "Wait a minute. It's coming back, now. I was really into this stuff when I was a kid, and one figure stuck in my head because it was easy. A Nike-Herc has a max range of about a hundred miles." A good dozen of us said *shit* or some variation. "Even with a little payload like you, Erin, there's no way in hell we're gonna get one as high as even Low Earth Orbit—"

Erin started to answer, but Fast Eddie overrode her, waving his hand like the pupil who knows the answer. "How 'bout Erin just Transits more fuel up as she goes?"

There was a moment of silence as that sunk in. What a concept for space travel! Leave the fuel behind, and order it up as you need it—

But I was too busy being horrified to appreciate it.

Bad enough to send your baby daughter up on a Space Shuttle, which you have advance notice is not going to crash. A can of solidified nitroglycerine that's received no maintenance for two decades, has no ground support, and was never designed to carry anything more delicate than a bomb—or to land at all—is a whole different story.

"That's a really smart idea, Uncle Eddie," Erin said admiringly. "Except for one problem. I'm not going."

"You're not?" Zoey and I said together, both of us suddenly greatly relieved.

"A Nike-Hercules boosts at twenty-five gees, Daddy."

"Oh." A little more than six times what she'd experienced aboard *Columbia*. A home run leaves the bat at about twenty-five gees.

"For less than four seconds, and then it drops—but that's enough to kill a person, even with padding."

"So what *is* the payload?" Acayib asked. "And how do you get it high enough?"

Erin giggled and shook her head. "You're all missing the beauty of it. We don't need *any* payload."

I finally got what she was driving at—and my heart began to race. This might just work.

Say you're the Deathstar. You're scooting along in orbit, frazzled by sunspots, scanning the sky for threats. You're just about to mistake Mir for a threat and fire on it, just in time to hit a superenergetic cosmic ray coming in the opposite direction head-on and annihilate the cosmos.

Suddenly a column of fire unexpectedly rises, from a place on the map where your instruction set says there are no friendlies . . . that anybody remembers.

You will assume the thing has *either* a payload or orbital capacity or both—since anyone who lacked both would have no militarily rational reason to launch in the first place. And you won't wait around long enough to see it start to peter out about ninety miles up; long before that, you'll take it out.

And to do that, you'll have to take your attention off Mir.

"I get it," Doc Webster said. "A missile be as good as a mile."

Erin glared at him, and he pretended to look apologetic.

"Are you sure the Deathstar can't handle more than one target at a time?" Omar asked.

"With its Tesla Beam, no," Tesla said. He chewed his lip briefly and continued. "But it does have a very fast recovery time between shots. This will call for nice timing."

Rooba rooba rooba.

"This is nuts," the Lucky Duck said. "Sparky, you told us we had to stay out of the history books, right? Don't you think somebody's liable to notice if we *set off a fucking Nike*?"

Tesla shrugged. "It is a risk. Surely there will be visual sightings . . . but I do not expect they are likely to be believed without radar confirmation."

"So what about radar?"

There was not a hint of smugness or boasting in Erin's voice. "I can hack NORAD, NATO, the FAA, and the DEA. I've done it before. They're not going to record anything I don't want them to."

Does anyone ever really know his own child?

"How do we start?" I asked.

"We go out there and look over the Nikes," Omar said.

That sounded good to just about everybody.

"Okay, look," Tanya Latimer said, "the first thing we've got to do is pick a committee. No way we're going to sneak a hundred people onto the airport grounds, even at night. Erin, Nikola, who do you want?"

We weeded it down to me, Zoey, Omar, Acayib, Shorty, Isham, the Duck, and Tommy—and of course Double Bill, our colorful and canny native guide.

"Come as quickly as you can," Tesla said. "I will go on ahead, and wait for you there." He disappeared like a promise the morning after Election Day.

"I'll go on ahead too, Daddy," Erin said, and vanished too.

Not for the first time, I heard Mr. Zimmerman in my head, singing that my sons and my daughters were beyond my command—and had to grin at how the ideals of my youth had come back to bite me on the ass. Any "parental authority" I'd ever had, or ever would have, was just a politeness on Erin's part.

We all used the john, then caucused briefly and chose bicycles rather than cars, since both would be about equally fast in Key West, and it'd be easier to conceal a bunch of bikes outside the airport fence. With Harry the parrot shrieking obscene invective at us, Zoey and I and the others got our bikes, walked them through the gate, and pedaled like hell.

The journey should have passed in a blur. But it is oddly difficult to bicycle through Key West in a blur. I kept seeing things that tugged at my attention, or at my heart. Lovely old houses, some a hundred years old or more. Gorgeous blooms and blossoms, a riot of growth everywhere. Peaceful streets (once we got past the Duval corridor) full of palm trees and sleepy fat cats and a few slowly strolling people. People who nodded back as we passed, even the tourists.

I kept thinking that it sure would be a shame if we fucked this up. This was too nice a universe to lose.

Eventually we reached the Atlantic Ocean, and hung a left onto A1A just before the Reynolds Street Pier. Higgs Beach went by, then the road straightened out and widened into something as close to highway as Key West ever gets. Out of the residential area now, we put our heads down and our rumps in the air and rocketed east along A1A, Smathers Beach on our right now, all the way until we passed the East Martello Tower museum and could see the road ahead begin to curve north. At Double Bill's advice, we left our bikes at Houseboat Row, chained to the front gate of a friend of his, and went the rest of the way on foot.

Key West Airport isn't much: most of its scant traffic is small stuff. Security measures consisted of an unprepossessing appearance and a chain-link fence. We waited for a moment when no headlights were on us and slipped over the fence where Bill told us to. Almost at once we were in deep forest cover. We followed him through the woods on a path only he could see, collecting the expected amount of scratches, bruises, and bug bites.

It was dark in there, with enough canopy to hide the Northern Lights, and we had flashlights but didn't want to use them yet, and also I was preoccupied. So I cannot tell you exactly how those woods differed from the ones I'd known up north—but they were a lot closer to jungle. Bushes didn't behave the way I expected them to, roots went in weird directions, trunks and branches took strange turns, and the most unexpected things turned out to have thorns. Also it smelled kind of funky in there, a redolence of tropical rot and decay—with an oddly strong overlay of woodsmoke that got stronger as we went.

"How often do planes fly out of here?" I asked Double Bill.

"This time on a Friday night, maybe once an hour, maybe less. It ain't exactly O'Hare."

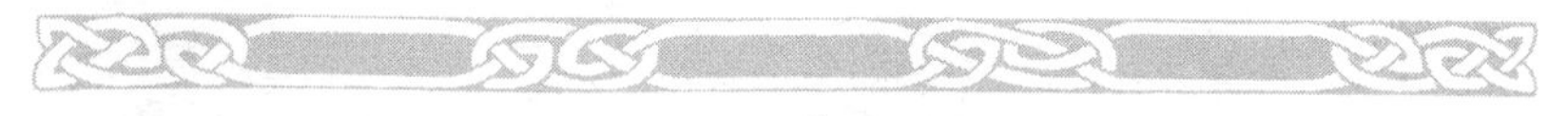

Eventually the tangle began to thin out, and then there were small clearings, and finally a largish, meadow-sized one—"clearing" meaning that nothing much grew much more than head high, and rough paths through it could be picked out by moonlight and Auroralight. In the approximate midst of it I could see Nikola Tesla from about the waist up, and all of Erin, though I couldn't make out what she was standing on.

Erin waved, and I squelched the impulse to call out to her and waved back.

As we wended our way closer through the undergrowth, I began to see that there really was an actual rectangular clearing around Tesla and Erin. A new clearing. It explained the woodsmoke smell. Apparently Tesla had made judicious use of his Death Ray at its lowest setting to clear away our work area for us.

A long narrow concrete platform lay perpendicular to us as we approached, roughly fifty yards long, five or ten yards wide, and a foot high. On top of the platform was a pair of steel trestles running its length like twin bridges to nowhere, their tops at about belly-button height. Erin was standing on one of them. Laid across the trestles, pointing toward us, were six launching racks.

And on each rack lay a Nike-Hercules missile.

I first thought it when I was a kid, but having seen them as an adult I have not changed my mind: a Nike-Hercules is a fucking beautiful thing. Even disfigured by a quarter of a century of malignant neglect and tropical tarnishing. They were about forty feet long, a little less than three feet in diameter at their widest point, and looked like God's darts, sleek and slender and elegant, the four raked fins on the upper body contrasting pleasingly with the cantilevered wings at the base.

"I don't believe it," Isham said as we tramped the last few dozen yards. "They're really there. The assholes actually went off and forgot 'em."

"They left Nikes scattered all to hell and gone around Florida," Double Bill said. "There's some on Fleming and Geiger Keys, some in Boca Chica, some up in Key Largo. A stew bum I used to know told me they still got some in Homestead, in the 'Glades—all kinds of places. That Cuban Missile Crisis was big business for Florida."

"Thank you, Fidel," Isham said.

"Not just Florida either," Omar told Isham. "Back on Long Island there's plenty of old Nike sites. Huntington, Oyster Bay, Amityville, Zahn's Airport in Farmingdale used to be one—hell, there's one pretty near where Callahan's used to be, in Rocky Point, that's still in halfway decent shape; I was there once."

"Kinda makes you wonder," the Lucky Duck said sourly.

"What's that?"

"Where the nukes they got *now* are gonna be in twenty-five years."

That shut us all up for a few steps. Finally Omar said, "Well, to be fair, Duck, I don't really suppose they actually left the warheads in those birds."

The Duck snorted. "Wait and see," he suggested.

We kept going, and shortly we were there, being greeted in low voices by Tesla and Erin.

"Yeah," Omar said, "this is a lot like the site I saw." He pointed east. "Over there in the scrub you can kind of make out the concrete bases that used to hold the acquisition and tracking radars. The alignment mast was over there." He pointed to a spot just west of us. "That's where the assembly and service shed was; you can see the foundation and some other crap. And right here where we're standing is probably where they had the launch control van. See, there's the blast berm."

"Fascinating," the Duck said, and Omar shut up.

"Nikky," I asked, "are there any warheads?"

"No," he said. "Erin and I have been researching, and we believe these used to carry thousand-pound W31 warheads, with a switchable yield of either two or forty kilotons—but they were salvaged long ago."

The Lucky Duck looked sour, and Omar grinned.

"Of course," Tesla went on, "just what was done with them I could not say," and Omar stopped grinning.

Before the Duck could comment, I jumped in. "So that's good, right? Without the half-ton payload, the bird goes higher, faster, looks more like a credible threat to the Deathstar."

Tesla nodded.

"The big question is," Omar said, "can we get one to fire?"

"That is the first big question," Tesla agreed. "I was just about to inspect them individually."

A small fireball materialized in his hand, and by its soft blue light he began studying the missile nearest him. Omar, Shorty, Tommy, and Acayib each picked a missile and began examining it by flashlight. I tossed Erin my own flashlight, and she scampered off to inspect the sixth Nike.

"Tools," Omar said almost at once. "I need tools."

"Behind you, Uncle Omar," Erin called.

Jim turned around, and there on the ground behind him was his own toolbox—the one he hadn't brought with him. "Thanks, honey," he called back, and selected a wrench. The others discovered their own tools suddenly close at hand, and called out thanks of their own.

"How about specs?" Tommy said jokingly.

"They're just ready now," Erin said. "Would you pass those around, Daddy?"

I looked down at my feet, and saw a stack of printouts. Zoey shone her penlight down at them, and I saw that the sheet on top was a schematic for the Nike-Hercules booster section. "How the hell did you get these?" I asked—but as I spoke I picked them up and began distributing them.

"A guy named Ed Thelen has put tons of general Nike information on the Net," Erin said.

"Yeah, but printouts?"

Two-year-olds can be very patient in explaining the bleeding obvious to grown-ups. "I scanned his site with my laptop over

there, downloaded what I wanted, put it on a floppy, Transited the floppy to Tommy's Mac back at The Place, and printed everything out on his laser printer while you guys were pedaling here. Then I Transited the printouts here."

I sighed. "Of course. Excuse me." Zoey and I exchanged a wry glance, found reasonably comfortable seats, and settled back to let the techies work.

A rare plane took off and passed over us, but the noise warned us in plenty of time to take cover. It seemed to be about Piper Cub size. The moment it was past, everybody went back to work.

A little while later Tommy called out, "This one's fucked. Crack in the booster nozzle."

"This one's no good either," Acayib reported. "Igniter looks shot."

"Some idiot managed to breach the liner on the upper stage here," Shorty said. "She might get a few miles up, but then she'd do a *Challenger.*"

"All the wiring looks lousy on mine," Omar said mournfully. "And the gyro's gone."

The Lucky Duck snickered. "The suspense mounts."

"Shut up, Duck," I said. "Nikky? Erin? Any joy?"

Tesla grunted and straightened up from what I could not help but think of as Nikky's Nike. "The gas generator in the upper stage sustainer appears inoperative."

We held our breath.

"I think maybe we're in good . . . oh rats," Erin said. "Sorry, I just noticed: one of the booster fins is about to fall off."

My heart sank. We all made little wordless sounds of disappointment and frustration.

"I think Acayib's is the one to work on," Erin went on, and disappeared, leaving us blinking at each other.

"Where's she going?" the Duck said. "Work on it *how?*"

After a moment's thought, I got it. "That guy up in

Titusville—what's his name, Gordon something? You know, the guy with God's own aerospace junkyard."

"Y-y-*yes*!" Omar said happily. "If there's a Nike-Hercules booster stage igniter assembly left anywhere in the world, Gordy'll have one."

"I will help her look," Tesla said, and vanished himself.

The rest of us stood around and looked at one another for a moment or two. "Damn," said Omar, "this is fun!"

"What do we do until they get back?" the Duck asked.

"Okay," I said, "assume we have at least one functional missile. What *else* do we need?"

Omar closed his eyes. "Let's see . . . heavy-duty batteries . . . a shitload of big cable . . . we can forget the radars, all four kinds, we're not trying to actually hit anything . . . so we don't need to throw up a radar alignment mast . . ."

Tommy Janssen suddenly said, "Oh hell."

"What?"

"The computer."

"What about it?"

"They didn't get PDP-8s until the Seventies."

Omar groaned.

"In English, Tommy!"

"I don't think Erin's going to be able to interface her laptop with the Nike. It's expecting to get its orders from an *analog* computer."

"What does that mean?" Zoey asked.

"It doesn't savvy digital bits," Omar explained. "It savvies voltage values—from a computer so ancient it has about five hundred vacuum tubes in it."

My roller-coaster heart began to sink again.

"Like that, you mean?" the Duck asked.

We followed his pointing arm. About ten feet away, just behind the blast berm, there now stood a silhouette not unlike the monolith from *2001: A Space Odyssey*, rising out of the mangrove scrub. I aimed my flashlight at it—

—and flashed back to my childhood, when a teacher had showed us a beast somewhat like that and proudly informed us that it was capable of storing sixty-four *thousand* bits of information . . . at one time! It was huge, about the size of the largest Ikea bookshelf unit, studded with a bewildering variety of dials and gauges and switches and display lights.

"Yeah," Tommy Janssen said gently. "Like that." He wandered over to examine it, whistling softly to himself.

As he was crowing over the manual he found in a drawer, another object appeared beside the computer, about the dimensions of a portable TV—followed by Tesla. "Give me a hand wiring this in?" he asked Tommy.

"What is it?"

Tesla hesitated. "A kind of battery."

"We're gonna need more than the one," Omar said.

"I designed it myself," Tesla told him.

"I stand corrected," Omar said.

Tesla and Tommy fiddled around behind there awhile, then Tesla said, "All right: try it." Tommy came around in front of the computer, slapped a few switches—and the damn thing lit up and started to hum!

I decided not to get elated again just yet. The mood swings were killing me.

But a few moments later, Erin arrived with a broad grin and a load of gear. Omar and Shorty fell on it with cries of glee, and went to work on the missile we'd selected. Apparently it was necessary, among other things, to disable a circuit that would cause the Nike to self-destruct if it didn't get targeting data every two seconds . . . from the tracking radars we didn't have.

As they tinkered, I decided to simply assume they would succeed, and looked for other things to worry about. "Erin, are you *sure* you can put blinders on NORAD and all the other sky-watching agencies at the right moment? What about private university facilities? The local Navy aviation people?"

"They're all on-line," she said. "No sweat. It'll take me about an hour to set it up."

I glanced at my watch. "Maybe you better get started."

Zoey nodded. "Whenever you're at the computer and you tell me you'll be done in an hour, that means next Thursday, honey. And we only have about two hours left."

"You're right," Erin agreed. She went to her laptop and began typing furiously.

An hour went by. Another plane took off. From the occasional murmurs the repair crew made, things seemed to be going reasonably well. For our part, Zoey and Isham and I killed quite a few mosquitoes. Without gunfire.

"I still say people are going to see this," the Duck said.

"Ernie," I said, "it's a Friday night, in summer, in Key West."

"Yeah? Well, what about those guys? They're professionals." He was pointing at the airport tower, visible in the distance.

I bit my lip. He had a point. "I guess we're gonna need a diversion." I thought about it, and had nearly settled on a plan when I heard Omar cursing.

"What is it, Jim?"

"We underestimated the Army. They weren't quite *complete and total* idiots, after all. Before they walked away and forgot these toys, they did exactly one responsible thing. They physically cut the hydraulic lines for the launch racks. See here? We were so busy looking at the birds, we never thought about the racks."

"What does that mean?"

"We've almost got this thing ready to fire . . . but we have no way to lift it up into launching position. For all I know we could skip it like a flat rock all the way to Cuba, but that won't make the nut. It's gotta go *up*."

Zoey turned to me and quoted a John Cleese movie we'd

both seen a couple of years before called *Clockwise*. "It's not the despair," she said. "I can take the despair."

I nodded and completed the quote. "It's the hope that's killing me." I turned back to Omar. "Can't you fix it? There must be hydraulic-whatever parts up there in Titusville."

"Sure," he said heavily. "But even with the parts, it's more than a one-hour repair job. And a welding torch out here is going to get us noticed."

"So what do we do?"

After some discussion, Tesla went back up to Titusville, and returned with a heavy-duty block and tackle tripod, the tallest we dared use, which he placed just in back of the Nike. The line was made fast to its nose, and everybody but Erin grabbed on and heaved. Then we planted our feet better and heaved again. And, with increasing dismay, again.

That rack had not moved an inch for at least twenty years of tropical weather; it was frozen solid. We tried greasing it, hammering on it (as loudly as we dared, and then louder), and cursing at it (likewise), without useful result.

"Can't you and Nikky Transit it upright?" I asked, already guessing the answer.

Both shook their heads. "Transiting doesn't work like that, Daddy," Erin said. "I can Transit a pair of scissors, but I can't make them open up by themselves."

"How about, screw the launch rack: just Transit the missile itself upright."

"It wouldn't stay standing," she and Tesla and Omar all said together. "We need that rack," Tesla finished.

Omar straightened up from where he was crouching, squared his shoulders, and took a couple of deep breaths. He walked round to the nose end of the Nike. "Nikky, Erin," he said, pointing to a spot beneath it, "Transit me something solid right here, about this high." He held a hand at about crotch level.

Erin stopped typing for a moment. She and Tesla exchanged a glance, and decided not to question the request. They closed their eyes together, and a concrete rectangle of the specified height appeared in the spot Omar had indicated. I believe I saw where they got it: one of the radar mounts Omar had pointed out in the underbrush earlier.

He climbed up onto it, squatted down, and squeezed himself in under the Nike. There was just room for his big frame. He settled his back against it, braced himself, and placed his hands carefully.

"Jesus Christ, Jim," I said, "you're nuts! That thing weighs a fucking ton."

"Closer to five, actually, with the rack," he said, took a deep breath, and then made a *HUNH!* sound and began trying to straighten up.

His arms and legs swelled up to about twice their normal size, splitting his pants and shirt. Sweat literally flew from him. We stood paralyzed with awe for a moment. Then Isham said, "Holy shit," clambered up on the concrete slab behind him, slithered under the Nike, and added his own mighty back. The rest of us ran back to the block and tackle, and heaved until we saw neon pollywogs. Ish and then Omar began to roar with effort.

For a long moment I thought it wasn't going to work. Then the rack let go with a sound like a brontosaur passing a kidney stone, and the nose of that damn missile rose about a foot.

Those of us on the tackle rope did a little dance, then regrouped and heaved again, and the Nike came up another foot and stopped.

"Belay!" Omar grunted.

Directly ahead of me was the foundation of the old assembly shed; I left the group (which made no perceptible difference), managed to warp the end of the tackle rope around it and tie it off. "Okay," I screamed.

"Ish, you roll right, I'll go left."

"On three," Isham managed. "One, two, go!" They both bailed out and dropped to the ground.

The Nike shuddered, the line hummed—and held.

Omar and Ish got up slowly, worked their shoulders, rotated

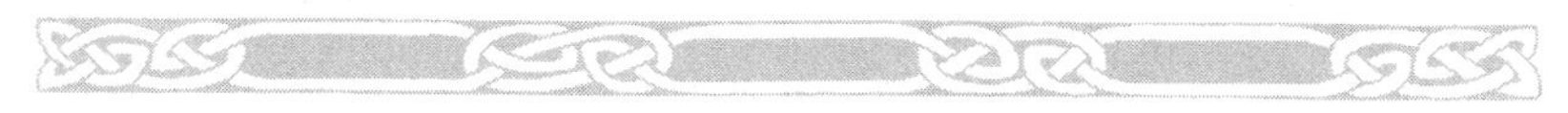

their necks in their sockets, shook hands, and came over to join the rest of us at the block and tackle. Maybe ten minutes later, we were all spent, panting and running with sweat . . . but that goddam missile was within about five degrees of vertical.

It was doing a lot better than I was. It seemed to take everything I had left to bring my watch up into view. Twenty minutes to go.

"Erin," I panted. "Need Nikky . . . help you fire . . . that thing now?"

"No, Daddy. Uncle Omar and I can do it."

"You ready . . . in time?"

"I'll have to be."

Somehow I lurched to my feet. "C'mon, Nikky. Ev'body. Follow me."

Twenty minutes later, the folks up in the tower, who had been lazily admiring the Aurora Borealis, were startled by a brilliant ball of blue fire that suddenly appeared at ground level, swelled, and began to rise skyward.

To the *west* of them.

Turning hastily away from the runway and looking in that direction, they saw a tall thin man with leonine hair and a ferocious mustache, dressed in an archaic black suit, standing out in the middle of the nearly empty parking lot, facing their way. The parking-lot lights all seemed to have just failed; they saw him only by the light of another fireball he held up in his left hand. This one was twice as bright as the first, and green instead of blue. He flung it skyward, and the tower crew tracked it with their eyes until it seemed to reach and blend into the Aurora.

They looked quickly back down to the tall man, and saw that now he had *two* more fireballs, brighter than the first two: one in each hand, one yellow and one red. This time he held them long enough for the tower crew to realize he was now surrounded by five other people.

They all appeared to be mooning the tower.

The tall man flung his fireballs into the sky, turned around, and dropped his own pants. The fireballs burst into noisy crackling showers of rainbow pyrotechnics, illuminating six pale asses, five rotating clockwise and one counterclockwise.

I venture to guess that everyone present at that airport was staring, transfixed, in that direction, when the Nike went up behind them.

It made less noise than I'd expected, easily mistaken for a trick echo of Tesla's fireballs, and was too high to see in only moments. There are very few photos of launching Nikes in existence; they tended to outrun the shutter.

I didn't see it go. I was too busy pulling up my pants and fleeing through the darkened parking lot with the others, and praying that Erin had timed things just right. I'm sorry I missed it; however brief, it must have been a sight to see. A Nike-Hercules, rising up into the Aurora Borealis, sent by a two-year-old to challenge its generational successor . . .

Star Wars, indeed.

Epilogue

"We don't want to go back to tomorrow;
we want to go forward."
—J. Danforth Quayle

I GUESS THAT'S PRETTY much the end of this tale. I mean, you *have* noticed that the universe is still here, right?

The Nike went up without being noticed . . . by anyone who was able to prove it afterward. Thirty seconds after it left the ground—at the top of its range, less than three seconds before it would have run out of fuel—the Deathstar took it out with ease, so totally that there was no flash visible from the ground. The light and then the cosmic ray from the supernova, and the gamma rays from Hurricane Erin below, had all hit Mir on schedule, just as Erin and Tesla had predicted. But the Nike had even more closely and urgently matched the Deathstar's parameters for a target—and by the time the Tesla Beam was pumped up to fire again, Mir no longer did. The Moment of Cosmic Danger passed—forever, one earnestly hopes—and the universe rolled on.

And I like to think that somewhere out there in the big dark vastness, Mike Callahan smiled.

The folks at DoD doubtless had shit-fits . . . but what with one thing and another they never got around to issuing a press release about shooting down a missile from Florida with a classified Death Ray. The tower crew at Key West Airport made, as I had expected, no incident report at all.

As for us, we made our way back from the airport to The Place without incident (except for a broken nose Double Bill incurred in trying to run with his sarong around his ankles), spread the good word, restarted the party, and basically all lived happily ever after. And peacefully—nothing else remotely that exciting happened to us all for another good ten years or so.

As Zoey and I were tucking Erin in that night, *way* past her bedtime, I stroked her hair and said, "Pumpkin, you did a real good day's work today."

She nodded. "It was okay," she said.

"Okay?" her mother said. "Honey, you saved the universe! You and Uncle Nikky."

"And Uncle Omar and Daddy and everybody else, sure."

"Well, what more do you want?"

Erin shrugged her little shoulders. "I don't know, exactly. But just preserving the universe, the way it is, doesn't seem like enough." She closed her eyes and rolled over. "I'm more ambitious than that," she said, and put her thumb in her mouth, and was asleep at once.

Zoey and I stood there together watching her sleep, and holding each other very tightly, for over half an hour before we tiptoed out together.

You could say the story ended there. But for me, at least, there was still one event needed to bring things full circle, to supply closure.

It was months in coming. I had almost forgotten I was waiting for it by the time it finally occurred.

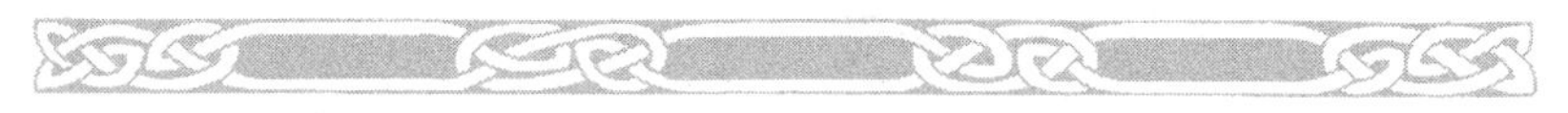

The only one of us missing that night was Nikola Tesla, off God knows where, doing God knows what, as usual. It was a hot Friday evening in March of 1990—the first anniversary of our arrival in Key West!—and a celebration was in full swing. Literally, in some cases: at Erin's insistence, we had hung swings from about half the trees in the compound. (One of her favorite hobbies, or perhaps charities, was reminding us dopey grownups how to have *fun*.) Those on their feet were doing some swinging of their own: Fast Eddie was in rare form, and the only earthbound toes not tapping were those of Chuck Samms, who'd had an unfortunate experience with frostbite in his youth. Not that everybody was actually dancing: we being us, there were several conversations going at once, in various locales.

One of them being the bar. I was as busy as Dan Quayle's spin doctors back there, but I'm never too busy to listen—especially when Doc Webster is perpetrating a pun. You can always spot it coming: his face gets very straight.

"Well, poor Artie's first job as a freelance hit man, some guy hires him to kill his wife—and Artie's so dumb, he only asks for a token dollar in advance. That night he waits in the parking lot outside the supermarket where she works, and she comes out alone . . . but just as he's strangling her, a witness comes along . . . and while he's strangling *that* guy, the cops show up. They were so impressed with his stupidity, the next day all the newspapers had the same headline . . ."

Unfortunately, the Doc paused for effect just a hair too long: Mei-Ling beat him to the punch line. *"'Artie chokes two for a dollar at Safeway.'"*

There was a roar of outrage, and both Websters nearly disappeared under a blizzard of peanuts. Harry the parrot felt moved to hop over to the top of the fireplace and flush his little commode.

Doc secretly *likes* being outpunned . . . if his wife does it. But he has his pride too. When the tumult had died down a bit, he called out to me, "Hey, Jake! What kind of computer did Erin use

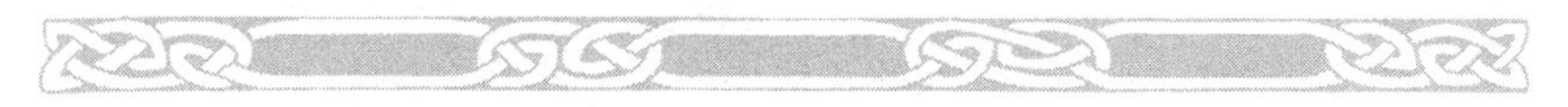

to fire off that missile last year¿" And his face was even straighter than ever.

I had to think a minute. "An analog computer, I believe Omar said it was. I didn't see a brand name. Why¿"

"You're sure she didn't use her Macintosh¿"

"No, the missile was too primitive to savvy zeros and ones. Again, why¿"

He shrugged elaborately. "No reason. It just would have been a nice twist, that's all."

He waited for Mei-Ling . . . but she said nothing this time, as puzzled as the rest of us.

"What's that¿" I asked finally.

"For Jobs to export Nike, for a change."

I follow Callahan's custom of keeping a seltzer bottle under the bar for moments like this, and I got it out and was just preparing to fire . . . when suddenly I was distracted by a vision. Hardly anyone else at the bar noticed it at first; a pun that rotten tends to wrinkle up your nose so bad that your eyes either close or squirt tears. But elsewhere in the compound, others saw the apparition at the same moment I did. Which reassured me that it wasn't just wishful thinking on my part. It was in midair, at poolside, about ten feet above the water, startling but unmistakable.

A naked man . . .

I dropped the seltzer bottle.

A *big* naked man, with thinning red hair. An instant after we saw him materialize, he dropped eight feet, landed on the diving board, rebounded back upward, executed a very impressive swan dive—deliberately spoiled it at the last moment—and belly-flopped hard enough to splash everyone near the pool, and soak my shirt behind the bar.

That got the attention of everybody but Fast Eddie; everything but his piano fell silent.

As we gawked, the naked man reached the side of the pool with three powerful strokes, and pulled himself out. He stood there implausibly bone dry, grinned past a smoking cigar that

hadn't been there a second ago, put his hands on his hips, and laughed out loud at our expressions.

The sound of that booming laugh silenced Eddie too. We heard his stool squeal as he whirled around. And then silence fell.

I broke it—and about a second later, just about everyone else present shouted the same thing, like the Raelettes.

"MIKE!"

Michael Callahan located me, took his cigar from his teeth, waved it at me, and said, "Howdy, stranger. Nice Place you got here."

A cheer went up that shook coconuts out of their trees.

"You got *that* right, darling," said another unmistakable voice.

Three more naked newcomers stood beside the pool, all three familiar and two of them beautiful. Lady Sally McGee, Mike's wife . . . Mary Callahan-Finn, their daughter . . . and Mary's husband Mickey Finn, the cyborged Filari warrior who'd once rendered us all bulletproof.

The cheer redoubled. And then the party *really* got started.

The next happy hour or two were full of general conversation. We introduced Erin to Lady Sally, who had never met her before. We introduced Pixel, and Harry the parrot, and Mei-Ling and Double Bill and Marty Pignatelli. (Marty did a lot of blinking, but maintained his aplomb; all the others seemed to take meeting legends in stride.) Doc and Mei-Ling's wedding was reported and raucously toasted.

And of course we all took turns showing the Callahans around the new joint, and filling them in on everything that had happened since the last time they'd seen us. I don't know whether any of it was news to Mike, but he acted as if it was, and appeared gratifyingly impressed with our achievements and our new home. I'm pretty sure everybody else wanted as much as I did to ask Mike and his family just what *they* had been doing lately, himself . . . but none of us was that indiscreet. It would have been a snoopy question. And we all knew that if he *could* have told us, he would have without prompting.

Anyway, what with six things and another, it was nearly midnight by the time I had a chance for a more or less private conversation with him. We sat on chaise lounges beside the pool and watched the moonlight dance on the water together for a few minutes in silent companionship. No Aurora that night. That thought sent my memory back to the events of a year earlier, to what had brought us all down here from the frozen north.

Did he read my mind? Or just seem to? What difference? "I'm sorry to have had to put you and the others to all this trouble, Jake," he suddenly said. "I hope it wasn't too much of a pain in the ass for you."

I thought about my reply. "Of the many Lord Buckley riffs I've memorized," I told him finally, "there is one I'd like to recite for you now."

He nodded. "Go for it."

"It's especially apt, because this one is supposed to have been written from Florida. It's Alvar Nunez Cabeza de Vaca—The Gasser!—writing home to King Ferdinand."

He raised an expectant eyebrow.

" 'Your most royal swingin' majesty,' " I quoted, " 'I been on a lot of sad tours . . . I been on a lot of mad beat bent-up down-gradin' excursions . . . I been on a lot of tilted picnics and a lot of double-unhung parties . . . I've suffered from pavement rash . . . I been bent, twisted, spent, de-gigged, flipped, trapped, and ba-bapped . . . but I never was so drug in my life as I was with this here last gig you put me on. . . .' You get The Gasser's drift, Mike?"

He nodded.

I smiled suddenly. "Well, that is the *backwards* of how I feel." I saw him relax slightly. "And the same goes for the crew. This was probably the best thing that ever happened to me—or any

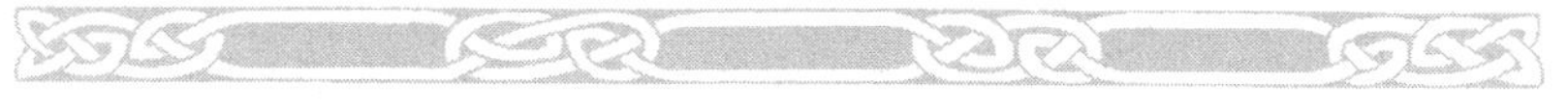

of us. If you hadn't laid this trip on Nik and us . . . well, regardless of how the universe made out, everything you spent forty years building here on Terra might have come apart, forever."

"I doubt it," he said. "But I'm glad I didn't make things any worse for yez, at least. I had no choice. Thanks for understanding."

I could see, over on my own front porch, Erin and Lady Sally deep in a private conversation of their own. So were Zoey and Mary, over near the parking area—and to my relief they were both laughing. "The only thing I don't understand," I said, "is why you didn't situate Callahan's Place down here in Key West in the first place. I mean, I'm glad you didn't . . . but . . . well, if it's not a snoopy question, why not?"

He took a puff on his cigar—God, the stench of it brought back years of happy memories!—and blew smoke to the winds. "Well, for one thing, they didn't need me down here."

"Yeah, I can't argue with that," I agreed.

"But that's not the main reason," he added. "I *had* to locate up on Long Island."

"How come?"

He turned and looked at me, a strange sort of smile playing at his lips. "You really don't know?"

I shook my head.

"Because you were there, Jacob," he said softly. "Because you were there." And he patted me on the shoulder and got up and wandered off somewhere.

A while later Zoey and Erin found me sitting there staring at the water, a cold Irish coffee on my lap, a big grin and a lot of tears on my face. Erin climbed up on my lap and hugged me, and Zoey knelt beside us, joined the hug, and kissed me for a long, long time.

The rest of that evening is a happy blur. Mike and his family were gone when I woke up, but I'm not sure just when they left.

• • •

Since this story is as much about our move as it is about the cancellation of Doomsday, I will report in passing, just for the sake of symmetry, that a little over *eight* years after all this happened, on a slow Tuesday in midsummer, sometime between 2:07 and 2:08 P.M., I found myself missing Long Island. I had a drink, and the feeling passed.

ABOUT THE AUTHOR

Since he began writing professionally in 1972, **Spider Robinson** has won three Hugos, a Nebula, and numerous other awards, and published twenty-eight books, eleven of which involve Mike Callahan and his family and friends.

Spider was born in New York City in 1948, and has been married for twenty-five years to Jeanne Robinson, a Boston-born writer, choreographer, former dancer, and Soto Zen Buddhist. The Robinsons collaborated on the Hugo-, Nebula-, and Locus-winning *Stardance* trilogy, which created the concept and basic principles of zero-gravity dance.

Spider's Op-Ed column "The Crazy Years" ran from 1996–99 in *The Globe and Mail*, Canada's national newspaper; his Technology column, "Past Imperfect, Future Tense," now appears there every third Thursday.

The Usenet newsgroup alt.callahans, inspired by the Callahan series, was rated the 151st largest newsgroup by bits posted, 172nd by messages posted (placing it in the top 1 percent of non-porn sites), and propagates to over 60 percent of all Usenet sites. Spider has never dared visit it, lest it swallow him whole. A website is maintained for him and Jeanne by volunteer friend Ted Powell at http://psg.com/~ted/spider/.

The Robinsons have lived for the last eleven years in British Columbia, where they raise and exhibit hopes. But they visit Key West every chance they get.